NIGHT OF LYONS

A Lyon's Den Connected World Anthology

Chasity Bowlin, Ruth A. Casie, Sandra Sookoo,
C.H. Admirand, Sara Adrien, Belle Ami,
Abigail Bridges, Jenna Jaxon, Jude Knight,
Rachel Ann Smith, Aurrora St. James

© Copyright 2023 by Chasity Bowlin, Ruth A. Casie, Sandra Sookoo, C.H. Admirand, Sara Adrien, Belle Ami, Abigail Bridges, Jenna Jaxon, Jude Knight, Rachel Ann Smith, Aurrora St. James

Text by Chasity Bowlin, Ruth A. Casie, Sandra Sookoo, C.H. Admirand, Sara Adrien, Belle Ami, Abigail Bridges, Jenna Jaxon, Jude Knight, Rachel Ann Smith, Aurrora St. James

Cover by Dar Albert

Dragonblade Publishing, Inc. is an imprint of Kathryn Le Veque Novels, Inc.
P.O. Box 23
Moreno Valley, CA 92556
ceo@dragonbladepublishing.com

Produced in the United States of America

First Edition August 2023
Print Edition

Reproduction of any kind except where it pertains to short quotes in relation to advertising or promotion is strictly prohibited.

All Rights Reserved.

The characters and events portrayed in this book are fictitious. Any similarity to real persons, living or dead, is purely coincidental and not intended by the author.

ARE YOU SIGNED UP FOR DRAGONBLADE'S BLOG?

You'll get the latest news and information on exclusive giveaways, exclusive excerpts, coming releases, sales, free books, cover reveals and more.

Check out our complete list of authors, too!

No spam, no junk. That's a promise!

Sign Up Here

www.dragonbladepublishing.com

Dearest Reader;

Thank you for your support of a small press. At Dragonblade Publishing, we strive to bring you the highest quality Historical Romance from some of the best authors in the business. Without your support, there is no 'us', so we sincerely hope you adore these stories and find some new favorite authors along the way.

Happy Reading!

CEO, Dragonblade Publishing

Other Lyon's Den Books

Into the Lyon's Den by Jade Lee
The Scandalous Lyon by Maggi Andersen
Fed to the Lyon by Mary Lancaster
The Lyon's Lady Love by Alexa Aston
The Lyon's Laird by Hildie McQueen
The Lyon Sleeps Tonight by Elizabeth Ellen Carter
A Lyon in Her Bed by Amanda Mariel
Fall of the Lyon by Chasity Bowlin
Lyon's Prey by Anna St. Claire
Loved by the Lyon by Collette Cameron
The Lyon's Den in Winter by Whitney Blake
Kiss of the Lyon by Meara Platt
Always the Lyon Tamer by Emily E K Murdoch
To Tame the Lyon by Sky Purington
How to Steal a Lyon's Fortune by Alanna Lucas
The Lyon's Surprise by Meara Platt
A Lyon's Pride by Emily Royal
Lyon Eyes by Lynne Connolly
Tamed by the Lyon by Chasity Bowlin
Lyon Hearted by Jade Lee
The Devilish Lyon by Charlotte Wren
Lyon in the Rough by Meara Platt
Lady Luck and the Lyon by Chasity Bowlin
Rescued by the Lyon by C.H. Admirand
Pretty Little Lyon by Katherine Bone
The Courage of a Lyon by Linda Rae Sande
Pride of Lyons by Jenna Jaxon
The Lyon's Share by Cerise DeLand
The Heart of a Lyon by Anna St. Claire

Into the Lyon of Fire by Abigail Bridges
Lyon of the Highlands by Emily Royal
The Lyon's Puzzle by Sandra Sookoo
Lyon at the Altar by Lily Harlem
Captivated by the Lyon by C.H. Admirand
The Lyon's Secret by Laura Trentham
The Talons of a Lyon by Jude Knight
The Lyon and the Lamb by Elizabeth Keysian
To Claim a Lyon's Heart by Sherry Ewing
A Lyon of Her Own by Anna St. Claire
Don't Wake a Sleeping Lyon by Sara Adrien
The Lyon and the Bluestocking by E.L. Johnson
The Lyon's Perfect Mate by Cerise DeLand
The Lyon Who Loved Me by Tracy Sumner

Anthology Contents

A Lyon With No Name by Chasity Bowlin	1
The Lady and the Lyon's Scandal by Ruth A. Casie	47
In Pursuit of a Lyon by Sandra Sookoo	101
A Lyon's Word of Honor by C.H. Admirand	145
Don't Tempt the Purring Lyon by Sara Adrien	213
Unmasked by the Lyon by Belle Ami	277
To Tilt at a Lyon by Abigail Bridges	335
The Lyon's Wager by Jenna Jaxon	381
Crossing the Lyon by Jude Knight	427
Mistaken for a Lyon by Rachel Ann Smith	473
The Lyon's Last Chance by Aurrora St. James	529

A Lyon With No Name

by Chasity Bowlin

Prologue

March 15

WILLIAM SAVAGE, THE very recently named Earl of Stamford, eyed the invitation before him with something he hadn't felt in a very long time. Was it excitement? Not exactly. But it wasn't boredom or disappointment, and that in and of itself was unique to his existence of late.

There was no question that the invitation had not been intended for him. It had been tucked into a drawer in the study, likely by his cousin Gerald. A terrible fever had claimed his uncle and his cousin, neither of whom had been what one might call robust. Now, he'd gone from scapegrace to heir in a matter of days. For that, he hadn't turned a hair. It wasn't all that surprising that it had occurred, but rather that it had occurred so quickly. The only shocking thing had been discovering just how impoverished his uncle and cousin truly were.

Whether it was ill health or simply a poor head for business, they'd essentially paupered themselves, and now he was left to clean up their mess. And as he had spent the entirety of his small inheritance on wine, women, and other wicked pursuits—well, he was in what might be considered dire straits.

Turning the heavy envelope over in his hands, he stared at the unmistakable seal of the Black Widow of White Hall, Miss Bessie Dove-Lyon. It was an *Invocation Mystère*. An invitation to her secret masked ball was highly sought after, thoroughly scandalous, and quite possibly worth the recipient's weight in gold. Gerald had been attempting to restore the family fortunes the old-fashioned way, it would seem.

Removing the gold-flecked paper from inside, he noted the date, the time, and felt his blood rise just a bit. It would be a challenge to have all in hand by then. Slowly, a smile began to spread across his face, his firm lips lifting at the corners. It didn't make him handsome. An accident of fate had done that. But it did give him a devilish appearance.

Reaching for the bell pull, he summoned his uncle's ancient butler. The only servants remaining in the house were those too old to get positions elsewhere. The others had fled like rats from a sinking ship.

"Yes, my lord?"

"Fowler, are there any servants in the house who are skilled with a needle? I know I can't afford a tailor, but I'll need to have some of my uncle's clothes fitted to me."

"My lord, I appreciate your desire to maintain appearances, but the truth of the matter is, we'd be better served to sell your uncle's things in a secondhand shop so we might pay the butcher."

William wasn't offended by the butler's harsh statement. He wasn't paying the man, after all. There was nothing left to pay him with. He was entitled to speak his mind. Still, he did lift the invitation and wave it about. "I'm to be the sacrificial lamb upon the marital altar, Fowler. I'll go throw myself upon the mercy of Mrs. Dove-Lyon, and she can leg shackle me to Medusa herself. So long as she has twenty thousand pounds, at minimum, it doesn't matter what she looks like."

The ancient butler might have wept with joy if he were capable of such displays of emotion. Instead, he responded, "Mrs. Felcher, the housekeeper, is quite handy with a needle and thread, my lord. I believe she's capable of taking in your uncle's clothes where necessary. It's the letting them out which might be an issue."

"We will make do, Fowler. Where needs must."

Chapter One

April 1

Miss Eleanor Craven—Ellie, as she liked to be called—took one last look in the mirror and smoothed the rather shockingly thin skirts of her gown. Between the diaphanous fabric and the slightly dampened petticoat (of which there was only one) beneath, she felt impossibly wicked. But then if she meant to marry any man other than the toad her stepfather was trying to foist upon her, she couldn't afford to be missish. Yes, she was an heiress, but not a great one. And her face was pretty. Not beautiful. Not stunning. Not unforgettable or even striking. Just ordinarily and passably pretty. She was the girl a gentleman smiled at as he asked the lady beside her to dance.

"You look a picture, Miss Eleanor," the maid said. "A very risqué one, but a picture nonetheless."

Ellie smiled. Lena had been her mother's maid before her mother had passed, and had stayed on as Ellie's maid to fulfill her promise to Ellie's mother that she would look after her. In fact, it had been Lena's aid that had allowed her mother to make these arrangements for Ellie before her passing several months earlier. "Pray that my courage holds and I do not spend the entirety of the evening hiding behind a column or a potted palm."

"You'll do fine, miss," Lena reassured her. "When you put on the domino, it'll help. A mask gives everyone a bit more courage."

The front door slammed below, and Ellie jumped. Her stepfather had left for the evening. It would be an endless night of drinking, carousing, and making wagers against funds to which he had no legal claim. That was the primary reason he wished to marry her off to Lord Fenthorpe. In exchange for securing the match, Fenthorpe, who had no need of the funds and simply wanted her, would return a significant portion of her marriage settlement to her stepfather. It was a plan they had cooked up only a month earlier, delaying execution only until an appropriate period of mourning for her mother had passed. It was that plan which had cemented her compliance with her mother's mad scheme to send her off to the Black Widow of Whitehall, Mrs. Bessie Dove-Lyon.

"He's gone. Is the carriage waiting out back?" Ellie asked.

Lena moved to the window and looked down. "Yes, miss. Amos is there with the carriage ready for you."

Ellie took another deep breath. She would come home with a future husband of her choice. He might be a bounder—an utter reprobate—but he would at least be one of her choosing and not someone who purchased her from her stepfather.

Pulling her cloak about her to hide her gown, Ellie took one last steadying breath. Then she reached for the gold filigree domino in Lena's outstretched hands. With it clutched against her chest beneath the heavy cloak, Ellie strode from the room and toward a very uncertain fate.

WILLIAM EYED THE crowd somewhat dispassionately. It wasn't very sporting of him, but he'd already identified a number of the other guests. A mask that shielded only two inches of one's face was hardly a disguise, after all. Miss Arabella Ballard was unmistakable as she laughed like a braying donkey. Unfortunate, really. She was lovely otherwise, until she opened her mouth and that particular noise escaped it. Lord Helton was there, as well. If he'd wanted to disguise his overly shiny and very balding pate, he should have donned a full hood rather than simply a mask.

He'd thought the golden invitation to this scandalous event would offer some reprieve from his ennui. And that it would help him to find a suitable candidate for a bride. Alas, it was failing. Perhaps no soiree, even one as scandalous as the one he presently attended, could compare to the debauched and hedonistic existence he'd enjoyed beforehand.

He'd just resigned himself to a stifling evening full of the same boring people saying the same boring things when he felt it. It was like a shifting current in swift waters. He could do nothing but turn toward the door and watch as she entered the room. Fate. Destiny. Love at first sight. They were concepts he would have laughed at before hand. But she stood there, her diaphanous gown clinging to shapely limbs. Her dark hair was piled high in a confection of curls that gave the illusion that plucking a single pin would send the mass of it tumbling over her nearly bared shoulders. And yet her face remained a mystery. In the shape of a butterfly, the golden domino concealed the entirety of her face but for dark eyes and cherry red lips. It was likely a calculated maneuver, but no less effective for it. He was seduced. Completely entranced by her in a matter of seconds.

Without conscious thought, he moved forward, closing the distance between them. He needed to know who she was. And he needed to stake a claim before anyone else could.

Chapter Two

It was all Ellie could do to step into that ballroom after relinquishing the comforting shield of her cloak. She felt naked and terribly vulnerable. The gown she wore was the most revealing thing she'd ever worn—period. Whether in public or private, she'd always been very modest. Now, in a costume that left very little to the imagination, she was to parade herself about in a room full of people, all in the name of finding a husband.

Nervously, she chewed her lower lip as she stepped deeper into the ballroom. In all honesty, as she looked around, her clothing was not as revealing as that worn by many others. It was just simply more revealing than she was comfortable with.

"You look very uncertain."

The voice was deep, sounding utterly masculine and very slightly amused. Turning to face the speaker, Ellie found herself confronted with a man who was more arresting than handsome. His features were rugged, his nose giving the impression that it had encountered another person's fist more than once. And yet she couldn't look away from him. She felt trapped—pinned by his gaze.

"I suppose I am," she replied. "Why are you not wearing your mask?"

He shrugged. "Because I'm already so scandalous, it doesn't matter if anyone knows I'm here."

"That was a rather alarmingly honest answer," Ellie replied without even thinking. She was so out of sorts with it all, she didn't have the ability to assess her own speech for social correctness and etiquette.

"I'm scandalous," he said with a shrug. "A rake, reprobate, rogue, fortune hunter... but I am, even with all my flaws, unfailingly honest. And I have every intention of marrying you."

"My fortune is respectable, but hardly the sort one would hunt. I think there are many ladies present here who are much more... affluent... than I," Ellie admitted.

"There are other considerations," he said. "You intrigue me. Your gaze says you are completely innocent, while your attire suggests something else altogether. I like the contradictions I see in you. You are something the other ladies present cannot claim to be: unique."

There were more people shuffling into the ballroom behind her. So when he offered his arm to escort her inside, she really had no other option but to take it. Not that she especially wanted another option. "I am hardly as interesting as you seem to think, sir. Also, despite your claim of infamy, I've no notion who you are."

He grinned. Wicked and mischievous, it transformed him. It was the devil's own smile, and she believed, in that moment, everything he'd said about himself.

"In the interest of keeping with the occasion's call for anonymity, you may call me William. And what, pray tell, my angel, may I call you?"

"Ellie," she replied. "It is a pleasure to meet you, William."

"Likewise," he agreed, plucking two glasses of champagne from a nearby footman's tray. "So, what sort of husband are you looking for? Young, handsome, and impoverished or old, ugly, and desperate?"

Ellie considered lying as she took a sip of the champagne, but in the end elected for the same sort of honesty he'd professed. "Any sort that isn't the one my stepfather has chosen for me. I can hardly make a worse choice. Younger would be nice, of course. Handsome is less important than kind."

For the longest time, he simply looked at her, that bemused smile curving his perfectly sculpted lips. Then he shook his head as a soft chuckle escaped him. "Be careful what you say, angel. This is a room full of predators. They will eat you alive."

"Are you? A predator, that is." She feared she already knew the answer to that.

"I'm the worst of them," he admitted as he led her to a small alcove with a black velvet and heavily gilded settee. There were numerous areas like that positioned about the room. While there was dancing and music to be sure, the purpose of that particular ball was to allow potential matches to steal private moments with one another. "But you have nothing to fear from me. I am not hunting rabbits. I prefer more sporting game."

"Did you just call me a rabbit?"

Another grin as he admitted, "I did, indeed. A wee and precious baby bunny... surrounded by a ballroom of foxes and hawks. But enough about that. Tell me about this wretched choice... no names. Just describe him. I wager that I will be able to identify him accurately. And if I do, you must grant me a boon."

"What sort of boon?" she demanded cautiously.

Another devastating grin lit his sharp features as he replied, "Nothing that will not be given willingly."

With no small degree of trepidation, Ellie nodded.

"Good. Now tell me about this unwanted betrothed of yours."

"He has terribly yellow teeth, and his breath... well, one never wishes to stand very close to him when he's speaking with any degree of enthusiasm. There's a tendency for spittle."

William nodded, as if he were taking in each detail. In truth, she could be describing half the aging men of the Ton. "And I presume he's older?"

"At least fifty," she agreed. "And he has jowls. Terrible jowls that practically obscure his neckcloth. And he's bald. Mostly bald, rather. He grows his hair very long in the back and combs it all forward as if it can camouflage the hair loss, but in truth, it only draws attention to it. And he has spots."

"Age spots?"

"No. More like sores or lesions. I can't bare to consider what might be their cause. But the whole of it is rather grotesque."

It was no longer fun and games for William. He had the sneaking suspicion that he already knew the identity of Ellie's would-be husband. For a man to allow a female under his protection to even be near Fenworth was unconscionable. He hadn't many scruples, but even the most depraved of men would prohibit that.

"Is he a large man?" William asked, needing confirmation of his suspicions.

"Yes... and no. His middle is quite large, but he has surprisingly spindly limbs. It's a wonder they can hold him up."

It was definitely Fenworth. "Listen to me, Ellie. Regardless of what happens here tonight, you cannot marry Fenworth. The man is an absolute monster. There are things about him that your stepfather—" And then he stopped, because he knew the identity of the woman before him. Reaching up, he plucked the strings that held her domino in place, watching it tumble to her lap.

Pale ivory skin, wide dark eyes with thick lashes, and those ruby red lips—and a shocking resemblance to the miniature of her mother that her father had carried with him into every battle. He barely managed to bite back the curse that sprang unbidden to his lips.

"You are Eleanor Craven. And your stepfather is Hilliard Amsdale. Please . . . tell me that I am wrong."

She shook her head, wide-eyed. "It would be very bad of me to lie to you when you have ferreted out the truth so handily!"

William sighed heavily. "Then, Miss Craven, will you do me the honor of being my wife?"

It was impossible to gauge which of them was more shocked by the proposal.

Chapter Three

Ellie simply blinked rapidly at him for some time. It wasn't even as if time were standing still. Things around them moved at a dizzying pace, but in that small alcove, everything had slowed to a crawl.

Finally, she managed to formulate a reply even as she kept shaking her head. "We've only just met."

"We may have just met, but you are not unknown to me. I knew your name very well, you see. Because your father spoke of you often and with great affection."

Ellie's heart stuttered in her chest, then took up a rapid-fire rhythm. "You knew my father?"

"I did. It was a long time ago, but he was my commander during my very brief tenure in the army. And he might possibly be the only man I have ever truly respected. Fair minded. Honest. He stuck to his scruples even when his lot in life would have been made much easier by being inclined toward a certain laxity in morality."

It was perhaps the most cohesive explanation of her father she'd ever heard. He'd stuck to his scruples, and those scruples had gotten him killed—not by the enemy, but by a traitor to the Crown. "Were you with him when . . . at the Battle of Rashid?"

"No. I had been injured prior and sent home, likely because they did not expect me to survive. My commission was discharged while I recuperated, and I remained in England devoting myself to purely hedonistic pursuits. But I was saddened to hear of his passing . . . and the circumstances which surrounded it."

"Thank you for that. Most people do not even acknowledge that he was lost to us through the treachery of one of his own. Most simply cluck their tongues and talk about the brutality of war. No one ever discusses the brutality of betrayal."

"If there is one thing I learned from your father, it is simply that the truth, even when unpleasant, must never be ignored. And the truth, Miss Eleanor Craven, is that I owe him many debts. I would not be here without his courage and bravery. And I cannot simply leave you to the awful fate your stepfather has planned for you."

"What other options do I have?"

"Me, Ellie. You have me. Do I have to ask the question when we both know there is only one acceptable answer?"

Ellie shook her head. "How can I be certain that you aren't as bad as Fenworth?"

"You cannot. I could give you my word, but if I am like Fenworth, then my word will not matter. There are other gentlemen here who might do, but none who will feel compelled to move so quickly and to go to whatever lengths are necessary to protect you from your stepfather and the toad to whom he means to sell you. I presume this *exchange* is to occur soon?"

"Within the next fortnight," Ellie admitted. She'd overheard her stepfather discussing it with his man of affairs, relaying his dastardly plan and discussing how best to use the funds that Fenworth would gift to him in exchange.

"Then let us go and speak with Mrs. Dove-Lyon. I have it on good authority that she can get a special license for us before the evening is through."

He rose, holding out his hand for her. Ellie took a deep breath, and then with only a shockingly small amount of trepidation, placed her hand in his. And just like that, she was betrothed.

HE'D INTENDED TO find a wealthy young woman with a tarnished reputation. Someone worldly enough that neither of them would have any romantic or sentimental expectations of one another. She'd restore his fortunes, and he'd restore her name, as much as a connection to him could. Instead, he'd found a young woman to whom he owed a debt of honor, little of it that he possessed, and whose fortune would likely only keep the wolves from the door temporarily. He'd proposed to perhaps the last truly innocent woman in all of London. That innocence poured off her in waves. And soon the vultures would pick her apart, unless he did something he was very unfamiliar with—the right thing.

But a glance at the young woman beside him was all he needed to reassure himself that it was the right thing to do. It was the only thing to do. Fenworth was a toad, just as she'd said. A depraved and pox-ridden toad, at that. He would destroy Ellie—with cruelty, disease, and perhaps worse. Fenworth had already buried two wives. And if her stepfather was foolish enough to think that Fenworth would keep their bargain and return the funds to him, then the man was clearly mad as a hatter.

"It will be all right."

Her head whipped toward his, and her eyebrows lifted. "Which of us are you trying to convince of that fact?"

"Both," he answered honestly. "Both of us. Ah, there's the indomitable Bessie. Let's go beard the lioness in her den, shall we?"

Chapter Four

Bessie Dove-Lyon watched the couple approaching her with a quizzical expression. She would not have put them together. When she'd issued an invitation to the previous heir to the late Earl of Stamford, she had done so on the basis of his suitability for a bride who could not afford to be discriminating. He was reasonably young, not terribly unattractive, and in need of a fortune. In short, he hadn't been someone who could afford to be a stickler about the propriety of his potential intended.

When he had passed, she had considered rescinding the invitation. But William Savage intrigued her. He always seemed to skate right along the edge of complete and utter ruin without ever tumbling headlong into the abyss—a rake with a shockingly dependable moral compass. What an enigma he was!

And now, he seemed to have formed some sort of attachment to Miss Eleanor Craven. It hadn't been Eleanor who had reached out to her, but the girl's late mother. Apparently, prior to her passing, she'd realized what a complete and utter bounder her husband was and wanted to take steps to ensure the girl's future since she wouldn't be present to do so.

Her first thought for Miss Craven had been someone sweet and not quite so worldly. After all, the girl hadn't even had a season yet. But now, seeing the very protective manner in which the present Earl of Stamford tended to her, Bessie was reconsidering. Perhaps the wolf really was the best choice to guard the lamb.

"My lord," Bessie acknowledged when they reached her. "Miss Eleanor. It is very good of both of you to come. I realize my ball might be a bit untraditional, but it certainly serves the function it was intended to."

"That it does, Mrs. Dove-Lyon," the earl agreed. "It serves it so well that we've come to request one of your *special* special licenses."

"Tonight?" Bessie asked, her head swiveling from one to another. In a low whisper, she asked, "You mean to marry tonight?"

"Circumstances dictate that we must. Miss Eleanor has a very limited amount of time before her stepfather forces her hand, quite literally. He intends to see her wed to Fenworth," the Earl explained.

Bessie could not hide her revulsion. The man was odious. "Surely—well, no. That is precisely why your late mother wrote to me, isn't it? She knew he would try to do something like this!"

"Yes, ma'am. I believe she had uncovered his plan but was too ill to intervene herself at that time," Miss Craven replied. "I realize this is very sudden and may seem unorthodox. But the prospect of being married off to Fenworth, with or without my consent, is hanging over my head like my very own Sword of Damocles. I've no idea when precisely my stepfather means for this *transaction* to be concluded, but I know it will be within the next fortnight. I do not have the luxury of waiting until we—Lord Stamford and I—know one another better."

Bessie looked from one to the other. Then she gestured to one of her trusted servants. "Escort the young lady to my private sitting room. I need to have a word with his lordship." To Eleanor, Bessie added, "Do not fret. I only mean to be certain that this course of action is the best one for all parties."

WHEN THEY WERE alone, or as alone as two people could be in a crowded ballroom, Bessie pinned the earl with a direct gaze. "She only has 25,000 pounds. It's a decent amount if one is capable of living modestly. That isn't something for which you are renowned."

William had expected to be questioned. After all, he was there on the pretext of finding a wealthy bride. While Ellie appealed to him instantly, her circumstances were not the most advantageous for him.

"I served with her father, who was a truly great man. My honor will not permit me to let his only child suffer such a fate. I may not be the first choice of husband you would have made for her, madame, but I assure you, I will see to her safety and comfort always. And there could be no worse prospect for her than Fenworth."

"And her heart? Will you see to that, as well? I make matches based on many things. Finances, certainly. Title and position? Absolutely. But I have never made a match where I didn't think love could bloom."

He didn't believe in the sort of thing she was talking about. Affection, certainly. Passion? Well, he certainly knew the power of that emotion. But love was just a pretty word for those things along with added responsibility. "I am not a romantic. But I do understand the fundamental requirements of being a good husband. Attentiveness. A lack of cruelty. Affection. Respect. I can offer her all of those things."

"And when her modest fortune fails to turn your circumstances around entirely?"

William sighed. "I will find a way to make it all work. The estates are in good condition but for the fact that there is no ready cash. Her marriage settlement will provide enough breathing room to make the estates truly profitable again without running them into the ground, as my late uncle had."

His answers seemed to sway her. After a moment, she waved her hand in another elegant gesture which had a servant rushing forward holding a black lacquered box heavily inlaid with gold. With care, Bessie lifted the lid and withdrew a rolled document, which she passed to him.

William did not unfold it to look at it. He knew what it was. There was a weight to it that indicated the total was much more than a mere sum of the parts. It was the license. He quite literally held his future, and Ellie's, in his hand.

"There's a rector waiting at St. James' Church. Give him that document, and he will know what to do. You may collect your bride on the way out. I have trusted drivers waiting with hacks by the side door," she explained.

William nodded. "Thank you, Mrs. Dove-Lyon."

"Do not thank me, my lord. But do not disappoint me either. I have a long memory and much longer reach."

It was an undeniable threat, and he acknowledged it with the sort of gravitas it demanded. Sketching a bow, he left their hostess and went in search of the woman who, before the dawn, would be his wife.

CHAPTER FIVE

*P*LEASE LET THIS *be the right thing to do.* Ellie had been silently imploring either the Lord himself or her departed mother to provide some guidance from the moment they'd climbed into the hack outside the Lyon's Den. Now, the vehicle was pulling to a slow and agonizing halt outside St. James' Church. She wasn't certain she'd be able to walk into the building under her own power. Her knees were shaking that badly.

I know I said that anyone would be better than Fenworth. And perhaps that's true. But simply better than Fenworth doesn't really offer much, now does it? Convicted and truly guilty murderers and brigands would likely be better than that lump of a man. Is he the one? Is William Savage, Earl of Stamford, the man I should marry, or is he simply the man I must marry?

Ellie's thoughts raced even as her newly betrothed climbed down from the vehicle and offered her his hand. With no small degree of reluctance, she reached out and placed her hand in his, allowing him to help her down from the hack. Behind him, the church loomed large and imposing, the stone facade dark and unforgiving in the night. A portent of things to come?

Stop being a silly goose. The building looks dark because it is night. It's not some omen for your future. It might be if you were still marrying

Fenworth, but you've been spared that fate. Do not be either a coward or an ingrate when such an opportunity lays before you.

Having lectured herself into some degree of compliance, Ellie went mutely into the church on his arm. There was a single rector present, and a pair of individuals likely employed by Mrs. Dove-Lyon sat in one of the pews. Paid witnesses. The matchmaker truly had thought of everything.

"One has to wonder how many couples wind up actually marrying on the night of the ball," he mused softly. "Surely there has been a precedent set for our actions, or even Mrs. Dove-Lyon could not have managed it all so efficiently."

His wryly relayed observation managed to penetrate the haze of panic which had engulfed her. It was true enough. Someone else had to have done it before, and others would likely do so after them.

Steeling her nerves, Ellie reminded herself of one very important fact. She knew, beyond question, that misery awaited her with Lord Fenworth. And perhaps she would be miserable with the man beside her, but at least with him there was a chance for something else. Hanging onto one slender thread of hope was surely better than resigning herself to a life of torment with a man so wretched few would even entertain him.

Those words of wisdom echoed in her mind, but she had the strangest feeling that they weren't really hers at all. That entire lengthy exposition on the matter had sounded so much like her mother that it simply took her aback.

"If you've changed your min—"

"No," she blurted out. From the startled glance of the rector, it appeared she had also been quite loud in her denial. In a more even tone, she continued. "No. I was evaluating my decision, and if anything, I am more certain now than I was before. It isn't simply the right choice. It is quite literally my only choice—and that sounds terribly unflattering to you, unfortunately."

A rueful grin curved one side of his mouth upward. "It would be unflattering if I were the only other choice and you still said no. As it is, I'll take what I can get."

"Then by all means, let us proceed."

For a life-altering event, it was surprisingly fast and efficient. With very little fanfare and no fuss at all, the rector pronounced them man and wife before ushering them quickly on their way. Within minutes, they were once more standing on the pavement outside the church.

Ellie looked at him bemusedly. "What now?"

That was certainly the question. "We go home . . . to my home. There are decisions to be made and strategies to plan."

There was a hack parked on the other side of the street, waiting for the patrons of a somewhat notorious gaming hall to stumble out, no doubt. Helping her inside, he climbed up after and rattled off the address. It wasn't far, not even a quarter mile, but the evening was chilly and she was not at all dressed for it.

Of course, that wasn't the only risk. There were several establishments nearby—brothels that catered to certain interests and clientele—where Lord Fenworth would likely be spending his evening. It was to their benefit for him to know that they had married, but not until such time as the marriage could not be contested.

As the hackney rumbled over the cobbled street, the interior of the vehicle was completely silent. William wanted to ask if she was well, if she had second thoughts. There were half a dozen questions, at the very least, that needed to be asked. Yet, he couldn't give voice to any of them. The need for discretion was paramount.

"My lord—"

"William. An hour ago, I was simply William. And you were simply Ellie. And I think we should cling to that," he replied.

"I really do not know what to do now. I don't know what is expected of me, William," she said softly.

"I expect you to be yourself . . . and to be honest with me about any doubts or questions you may have. Whatever complications arise from our actions, we will face them together," he answered gently. "But until we are someplace where we can discuss the matter in detail with some degree of privacy, I think we should keep our own counsel."

She glanced in the direction of the box where the driver was seated. "Of course. Discretion is vital."

Chapter Six

The elegant Mayfair home of the Earl of Stamford was not at all what Ellie had expected. Upon their arrival, a wizened little man, whom William had called Fowler, appeared to be the only servant about.

"The staff is a bit . . ." William trailed off.

"Gone, my lady," Fowler answered. "They've all gone to new positions, save for a scant few of us. Mrs. Hartleigh, the cook, is already retired for the evening, as her days tend to start much earlier than anyone else's. There is one footman, one maid, and Mrs. Felcher, the housekeeper. All of them have retired as well."

"Fowler, you may show the countess the rest of the house tomorrow, but that will be all for tonight," William instructed.

Countess. She'd known, of course, that he was the Earl of Stamford and that she was marrying him. But that was a very different thing than realizing that she was actually now the Countess of Stamford.

And then he was there, close to her side, one arm behind her back to keep her from collapsing to the floor. She hadn't swooned, but she'd definitely been on the verge of it.

"It has been a very . . . eventful evening. Goodnight, Fowler."

"Goodnight, my lord... my lady. If you need anything, you have but to ring for me," the ancient little man said. His concern was obvious.

"Thank you. I'm quite all right," Ellie offered. She wasn't entirely sure of that, but it would have been unkind to leave him so worried.

Carefully, she navigated the stairs that led to the upper floor. She noted that William remained behind her the whole way. Ready to catch her if she fell, one could only presume.

"I really am fine," she reassured once they'd reached the third floor. "I was simply . . . overwhelmed for a moment, I suppose."

"Understandably so," he concurred, taking the lead and guiding her down the corridor to what she thought would be her chamber. It was only when he opened the door that she realized how wrong she had been.

The room was large. Done in shades of deep blues and rich greens against dark wood, it was decidedly masculine. And based solely upon the scent of sandalwood, it was also his room.

With her heart pounding in her chest, Ellie stepped through that doorway. All the while, she was wondering what in heaven's name she had done.

"I'M NOT GOING to bite you. I've no intention of gobbling you up like some wicked villain in a children's story," William said with a smile. "But this is a house with limited staff. The other rooms have been closed up for months and are likely so dusty they are uninhabitable. More to the point, if your stepfather should come looking for you, I want to be close enough to protect you."

Her eyes widened, and then her lips parted to form a soft 'o' of surprise. "I hadn't thought . . . well, I don't know he would manage to find me."

"Because people love to gossip. At some point or another, it will get out—not how we met, perhaps. Mrs. Dove-Lyon is not a woman to cross in that regard. But the fact that we had a late night clandestine wedding by special license? That is the sort of information that the Ton thrives on."

"I'm afraid I don't know much about how the Ton does anything. I've never been in society. When I should have had my debut, my mother's illness had progressed to a point where leaving her to attend parties and balls would have been unconscionable. And then mourning—well, it wouldn't have been appropriate. Additionally, I had no chaperone to take me about. In retrospect, I think that oversight on my stepfather's part was intentional. A calculated maneuver."

William had already surmised as much. Everything he knew about the man indicated he was without even a shred of honor. "There are other topics that must be discussed, and I fear they will be . . . somewhat embarrassing for you. Namely, the consummation of our marriage."

He had made it a point to have that portion of the conversation while both of them remained fully dressed. Not because he didn't trust himself, but because he didn't want her to be utterly terrified.

"Oh, well . . . I'm not entirely sure what that entails. Only that until it occurs, our marriage might not be legally binding," she admitted cautiously.

It was his turn to simply blink in surprise. While he understood, in theory, that young ladies were kept very sheltered, that degree of innocence—and ignorance—was simply anathema to him. "Nothing at all?"

"No. Who would have told me?"

Who indeed. Her mother was gone and had likely been in no condition to undertake such a task during her illness. There was no one else to have done so. "No one, of course. Have you ever been kissed?" It would be a starting point at least. If she knew about kissing, then perhaps the rest of it wouldn't be quite so shocking.

She shook her head mutely. Twenty years old, based on the information she'd completed on the register at the church, and she might as well have been a babe in arms.

"We could change that . . . if you like," William offered.

"A kiss?"

"Yes."

She eyed him suspiciously. "Only a kiss?"

"If that is all you wish for, then yes. Only a kiss," he vowed.

And then, after a long and uncertain moment, she gave him the briefest of nods. *Consent for only a kiss.*

Chapter Seven

Ellie watched him walk toward her with her heart pounding and the blood rushing in her veins. Only when he was scant inches from her, close enough that her skirts brushed against his thighs, did he halt.

"I feel like a complete goose," she admitted. "I haven't the faintest notion what to do."

He smiled then, and it wasn't the devilishly teasing smile she'd seen earlier. There was something gentle in it, sweet even, if a man such as her new husband could ever be described in such a way.

"You don't have to do anything except close your eyes," he told her. "Close your eyes and savor the moment."

Ellie did as he suggested. Her lashes fluttered for a moment and then settled against her cheeks. On a shaky breath, her lips parted slightly and she waited. But it wasn't his lips she felt. One of his large hands cupped her cheek, the pad of his thumb dragging over her bottom lip in a delicious friction that made her shiver.

It might have been mere seconds, or it could have been an eternity that they simply stood there—her with her eyes closed as the sensation of that simple touch shifted her entire world. And then she felt him brush his lips against hers. Feather-light. So much so that she wondered if perhaps she had imagined it. But then he repeated it. Soft, teasing, achingly gentle. She felt herself leaning into that touch, seeking unconsciously to sustain it. Then his lips settled more firmly on hers.

She had never given much thought to what it would feel like to be kissed. Oh, in all the gothic novels she'd read, they'd described the emotion it could evoke within her. But nothing she had ever read could have prepared her for the very real, very sensually physical feeling of it.

His lips were firm yet tender as they moved over hers. She could taste something that was simply him—a mix of brandy and champagne. The rasp of his evening beard against her skin was surprisingly pleasant. And the longer he kissed her, the more she wanted that kiss to continue. Still, it felt as if it were leading somewhere, as if the kiss was not the destination but merely a step on the journey. She found herself eager to see what might be next.

When he traced the seam of her lips with his tongue, it was an instinctive response to part them for him. Even then, she was shocked at herself. More so, she was shocked at how much she liked what he was doing. Warmth was seeping through her body, from the top of her head to the very tips of her toes, she felt heat. With that came an awareness of her own body she'd never known before. She was supremely conscious of the way her clothing felt against her skin; of the nearness of his body to hers; of the way that, with the slightest movement, her breasts brushed against his chest. And each one of those sensations combined to only intensify the others.

Then abruptly, he drew back from her. His eyes were dark and fierce as he stared down at her, and she could see a muscle working in his jaw. Yet she knew he wasn't angry.

"I told you it would only be a kiss," he said, his voice strangely gruff. "If I'm to keep my word, I need to limit temptation."

"Am I tempting, then?" she asked, both bemused and emboldened by the notion.

"If only you knew how much," he murmured.

Ellie wanted to know. She certainly wanted more than just that kiss. But she was hampered by her own ignorance of the intimacies of marriage. "Are we really in danger from my stepfather if our marriage is not consummated immediately?"

"Only if he finds out. I suppose the good thing about having so very few servants is that there are less of them to spread rumors and gossip."

Ellie drew in a deep, steadying breath. "And if there was no rumor or gossip to spread?"

"You'd need to be very certain that is what you want."

Was she? How was it possible to be certain of something when she had no idea what *it* was? Ultimately, there was only one way to have those questions answered. So she met his questioning gaze and simply nodded.

HE MIGHT HAVE hoped. But he had not dared dream she would come so willingly to his bed. His instantaneous attraction to her at the ball had been a singular experience from him. No other woman had ever compelled him so. And now she was offering herself to him.

It was not a thing to be taken lightly. More to the point, how things went for them that night could well set the tone for everything that would come in their future. To say that responsibility weighed heavily on his mind was to put it mildly. While he had no question that he could please a woman of some experience, having the patience and gentleness to introduce a woman to passion when she had not notion of what it even meant—that was, he felt, a Herculean task.

"Under normal circumstances, I would leave now and give you time to prepare yourself for bed," he murmured. "Unfortunately, there is no maid to attend you, but my skills in that area are passable... and, I'm also afraid that if I leave you might change your mind."

"I'm afraid I would too, so it's just as well."

William stepped back, but only far enough to spin her around. Then he began carefully undoing each of the buttons down the back of her dress until the fabric parted and began to slip from her shoulders. Her stays followed, the laces of them loosening quickly. Within minutes she stood there, her legs still clad in stockings and her heeled slippers peeking beneath the hem of her bodiced petticoat.

Plucking the pins from her hair, he watched as the mass of dark curls tumbled down her back, falling over her shoulders. It looked like silk, shining in the room's dim light. Unable to resist, he lifted one heavy lock, testing the softness of it between his fingers. "Lovely... lovelier, I think, than you realize. You are a very beautiful woman, Ellie. And I am beginning to think that I am a very, very lucky man."

"I'm not very used to compliments or flattery," she admitted.

"We shall work on changing that, but for now, I think I'm done with talking."

Before she could say anything else, he swept her up into his arms and carried her to the velvet draped bed. After placing her in the middle of it, he removed his coat, then tugged his cravat free. He didn't stop until he wore only his breeches. She wasn't ready to see him without them, and he didn't trust himself enough to take them off just yet. He wanted it to be good for her, and that meant not racing to the finish.

Kneeling on the bed beside her, William drank in the sight of her, savoring it. And then he stretched out next to her, drawing her to him as he claimed the sweetness of her lips once more.

Chapter Eight

It was morning when Ellie awakened. The bed beside her was empty, but still warm. She could still see the indention of his head on the pillow. And the night's events came rushing back. Her face flamed as she recalled all the things that had transpired in that bed. Then, as if her mortification were not complete, the door opened and her husband appeared.

Husband.

The enormity of all that had occurred was simply too much to grasp. She'd gone to that ball hoping to find someone to marry. Never in her wildest dreams could she have imagined that she would marry them that very same night. She certainly could not have fathomed that consummating the marriage could have been—well, she lacked the words to adequately describe it. Wonderful, certainly. Transformative? Very likely. Regrettable? No. She had no regrets. Even if she should, even if he thought her a complete wanton and her behavior to be beyond shameful, she still couldn't regret it.

His gaze settled on her, and he smiled. Slightly wicked and very knowing, it was an expression that would have made the events of their wedding night rush to the front of her mind even if they were not already occupying her thoughts.

"Good morning. I sent Fowler to your house with a note for your maid, and he has returned with some of your clothes." He held up a valise that she recognized. "We'll need to confront your stepfather sooner rather than later, and I thought you might like to be more appropriately dressed for that particular engagement."

It was the last thing she wanted to do. Her stepfather would be furious. She couldn't even imagine all that he might say or do. "Must we do that now?"

"Either we do it now, or we run the risk of him raising the alarm about your absence. Then the circumstances of our marriage will become prime grist for the gossip mill," he explained. "For myself, I do not care. But I think you will not like being the object of lurid whispers."

Ellie sighed. "You are right, of course. But I dread it."

"It will not be pleasant, but you've nothing to fear from him." He placed the bag near the dressing table and then moved back toward the bed. There he sat down on the edge of it and looked into her eyes. "I'm likely not the husband you would have envisioned for yourself. Impoverished, scandalous, and barely respectable. But I can promise that I will not let him hurt you—not with heavy hands nor unkind words."

Ellie's heart fluttered in her chest. "You are very harsh. You will not let him speak unkindly to me . . . and I dislike hearing you speak so unkindly to yourself. I think you do not deserve it nearly so much as you think."

He leaned in then, capturing her lips in a kiss that was sweet and tender. It wasn't about the heat and passion of the night before, but about something else altogether. It spoke to a developing affection between them, and it soothed her jangled nerves.

"There are who would disagree with you, but so long as I have your good opinion, the rest may go to the devil . . . now, my skills as a lady's maid lend themselves much more to taking clothes off than to putting them on, but I'll do what I can. You are left to your own devices to tame your wild locks this morning."

AN HOUR LATER, after Ellie had brushed off his less-than-effective assistance in getting dressed, they had broken their fast and were en route to her stepfather's home.

Inside the hired hack, with the bright morning light filtering into the vehicle, he marveled at her. Lovely. Passionate. Sweet. A confounding mixture of innocence and sensuality, he found himself simply entranced by her. Infatuated even, which was a shock for him. It wasn't something he'd imagined that he would ever feel for anyone, much less that he should be felled by it so quickly.

It was more than simply the haze of post-coital bliss. He'd certainly bedded more than his share of women in the past, and none had ever made him feel the way Ellie did. Why was she so very different? Objectively, she was pretty. Beautiful even. But not extraordinarily so, not in a way that would make her stand out in a crowded ballroom. And yet that was precisely what she had done. From the moment she walked in, even before he'd looked at her, he'd felt drawn to her—compelled to turn and see her, almost as if he'd sensed her presence.

"Do you believe in fate?"

The question, once it emerged, surprised him.

She appeared to consider her answer carefully. "I'm not certain I've ever given it any thought, but I suppose it's possible. I think fate, if it exists, puts things in our path, and how we choose to act upon those things determines the outcome. So, yes and no, I suppose."

"So fate, to your mind, is simply the opportunity to make a choice?" he queried.

"I think so. What a strange question to ask!"

"Is it? I wasn't supposed to be at that ball, Ellie. The invitation had been issued to my cousin before his death. I just happened to find it in the drawer, buried beneath other things, two weeks before the event was to occur. And when I walked in, I was completely apathetic to the presence of every other person there. And then you walked in. The daughter of my former commander, a man I trusted and respected. Even having gone there for somewhat selfish reasons, I was presented with an opportunity—a fated choice, if you will—to save both of us with one swift action. It is one hell of a coincidence, you must admit."

All of his ramblings about fate and destiny had taken up the duration of their short journey to Amsdale's home. The hack rolled to a stop and he climbed out, helping her down. The door flew open before they'd even reached the top step. Amsdale stood there, a thunderous expression on his face, which was also purpled with rage.

"What is the meaning of this? Trollop!"

Chapter Nine

In one stride, William reached him. Wrapping his fist in the other man's cravat, he forced him back into the house. "You will not speak to her so."

"How dare you! She is my stepdaughter—"

"And she is my wife... the Countess of Stamford. She outranks you, sir. And do not think I will be above using our rank to your disadvantage. We will speak civilly, and you will not insult her again. Is that understood?"

When Amsdale hesitated, William tightened his grip, twisting the cravat until the other man coughed. Amsdale then gave a jerky nod.

Abruptly, William released him and Amsdale stumbled backwards. He barely caught himself by reaching out for an overly ornate console table, which groaned beneath his weight.

"You married him?" Amsdale demanded.

Ellie's words were softly spoken, but they were still confident and sure. "I did. We married by special license."

"I'll not give you a single pence!" Amsdale snapped.

"No, you will not. Nor will you steal one," Ellie replied, still calm and cool. "You do not control the fortune my father left for me. It is handled by trustees at the Bank of England, and I doubt very seriously that, despite the haste with which we wed, that they would object to my marrying an earl."

Amsdale simply crumbled. He sank to his knees. "I am ruined."

"You always were," William added. "You wasted your own fortunes—not that I am unsympathetic. But what you planned to do, gifting this sweet and innocent young woman to a reprobate like Fenworth—that, sir, will guarantee your place in hell. From this moment forward, you will not speak to her. You will not speak about her. If her name comes up in conversation or someone should dare to ask you how she fares, you will say she is well. You will smile and walk away."

"And if I do not?"

"Then I will take your neckcloth and I will choke the life out of you with it," William answered with incongruous good cheer. "And I'll enjoy it. Quite thoroughly."

Turning to Ellie, William added, "Get your things, angel. And your maid. I see no reason to leave her here in this sewer."

ELLIE WAS STILL floating as she came back down the stairs, despite carrying a valise. Lena followed behind her carrying her own things. William still stood in the entryway, and her stepfather was nowhere to be seen.

"Likely drinking away his worries. Bit early in the day, but if a man can't drink when he's hovering on the precipice of financial ruin, when can he?" William asked. "Do you have everything?"

"There's a trunk upstairs with some mementos and some of my

mother's things that I'd like to take with me."

"I'll have it sent over, my lady."

That toadying interruption had come from the butler, a man who'd never done more than sneer at her in the past. Ellie smiled at him, despite his past unkindness. "Thank you, Winchell. That will be most appreciated."

Afterward, they made their way to the Bank of England and met with the trustees. Once they'd provided the necessary documentation to prove their married state, they were assured everything was in order and that the transfer of the funds would go forward without impediment.

"We should hire more servants," Ellie suggested. "Poor Fowler will be quite beside himself with a full staff to direct."

William laughed in response. "By all means. Ensuring Fowler's happiness has always been the primary objective."

"Have we made the right choice?" Ellie asked.

His eyes narrowed speculatively. "Ask me in a year. By then we will both surely know the answer."

She grinned. "I will. I never forget anything, you know."

"I'm counting on it."

Epilogue

March 31, 11:59 p.m.

WILLIAM STARED DOWN at Ellie's sleeping form for a moment. A gentle smile curved his lips, but there was a bit of the devil in his eyes as he reached out and yanked the covers back.

Immediately, she sat up in bed. Her night rail had been discarded hours earlier and was likely lost beneath some bit of furniture or another. Poor Lena was always shaking her head as she struggled to track down her mistress' errant clothing.

"What are you doing?" Ellie demanded, reaching for the coverlet to pull over herself once more. It wasn't modesty. She'd long since given that up in favor of his hedonistic appreciation for nudity.

"Isn't there something you were supposed to ask me? It's been a year, after all. And you said you never forgot anything."

"To be pedantic about it, it's only been 364 days. We didn't have the conversation until the second of April," she pointed out primly. "But if you insist on having it asked early—"

"I do. I most certainly do."

Ellie leaned back against the pillows, her arms crossed over her chest and resting on the gentle rounding of her belly. "Very well. *Have we made the right choice?*"

It was the opportunity he had been waiting for. Reaching into his pocket, he withdrew a small leather box. "Since we didn't have the opportunity to get you a proper betrothal ring, I thought we should rectify that."

Placing the box in her hand, he watched as she opened the small latch. Nestled inside was the ring he'd commissioned for her—a gold band etched with butterflies and topped with a rosette setting of diamonds and pearls. "There is an inscription."

She lifted the ring from the box and held it up to the light, and then gasped. Her eyes shimmered with unshed tears as she turned her gaze on him once more.

He knew what it said, of course. He'd planned it to the last detail. *To my angel, with all my love.*

"To answer your question, I don't think we had a choice. Fate is a funny and wondrous thing."

Ellie threw herself into his arms then. "I love you. Oh, William, I love you so much. How on earth did we ever get so lucky?"

Another grin tugged at his lips. "Ask me in a year. Maybe you'll get a matching necklace."

The End

Additional Dragonblade books by Author Chasity Bowlin

The Hellion Club Series
A Rogue to Remember (Book 1)
Barefoot in Hyde Park (Book 2)
What Happens in Piccadilly (Book 3)
Sleepless in Southampton (Book 4)
When an Earl Loves a Governess (Book 5)
The Duke's Magnificent Obsession (Book 6)
The Governess Diaries (Book 7)
A Dangerous Passion (Book 8)
Making Spirits Bright (Novella)
All I Want for Christmas (Novella)
The Boys of Summer (Novella)

The Lost Lords Series
The Lost Lord of Castle Black (Book 1)
The Vanishing of Lord Vale (Book 2)
The Missing Marquess of Althorn (Book 3)
The Resurrection of Lady Ramsleigh (Book 4)
The Mystery of Miss Mason (Book 5)
The Awakening of Lord Ambrose (Book 6)
Hyacinth (Book 7)
A Midnight Clear (A Novella)

The Lyon's Den Series
Fall of the Lyon
Tamed by the Lyon
Lady Luck and the Lyon

Pirates of Britannia Series
The Pirate's Bluestocking

Also from Chasity Bowlin
Into the Night

About Chasity Bowlin

Chasity Bowlin lives in central Kentucky with her husband and their menagerie of animals. She loves writing, loves traveling and enjoys incorporating tidbits of her actual vacations into her books. She is an avid Anglophile, loving all things British, but specifically all things Regency.

Growing up in Tennessee, spending as much time as possible with her doting grandparents, soap operas were a part of her daily existence, followed by back to back episodes of Scooby Doo. Her path to becoming a romance novelist was set when, rather than simply have her Barbie dolls cruise around in a pink convertible, they time traveled, hosted lavish dinner parties and one even had an evil twin locked in the attic.

Website: www.chasitybowlin.com

The Lady and the Lyon's Scandal

by Ruth A. Casie

CHAPTER ONE

New Year's Eve 1815
London

"EVA, LADY ISLINGTON is ready," Madam Sybil Pembroke's voice echoed through the back room of La Femme à la Mode, an elite dress shop in London. Eva Barnard glanced up from her sewing table, rubbing her eyes. She inspected her work with a critical eye and came away pleased with her delicate lace and beadwork.

Madam wore one of the fashionable day gowns of her own creation that showcased her refined figure and impeccable taste. Her talent for motifs, along with Eva's exquisite lace and bead designs, made La Femme à la Mode the one shop elite women of the *ton* purchased their gowns.

The shop itself conveyed an air of sophistication and timeless grace. When you entered, you were transported to a world of sumptuous fabrics, delicate lace, intricate embroidery, and beadwork from the moment you entered. The interior was in soft hues, draped with fine silk curtains illuminated by delicate crystal chandeliers that cast a soft glow. Fittings were conducted in front of a long trifold mirror with a rostrum in the middle that was tucked into the back of the shop. Overstuffed chairs were available for admiring mothers and friends to rest with a cup of tea while they watched and commented on the exclusive fashions.

"Are you well?" Madam asked.

"I am fine. My eyes are tired." Eva smiled wearily. "Lady Roxanne and the Countess Fitzherbert's gowns are ready. I have one final adjustment to make on Lady Islington's gown."

"Lady Roxanne arrived a few minutes ago. She's with Lady Islington. Finish Lady Islington's, then see to her. I'll help Lady Roxanne with her gown."

Eva, a true artist with lace and beads, glanced at the stack of fabrics and patterns on her sewing table. It had been a busy week. She took up Lady Islington's gown.

"You have done remarkable work." Madam's praise made the hard work worthwhile. "Your talent with lace, beads, and gems has set La Femme à la Mode apart from other modistes. You've made our clients expect perfection, and you have never disappointed."

The final stitches were completed. The last bead was in place. Eva stood and held up Lady Islington's pale blue gown.

"The gown will look stunning with Lady Islington's black hair and blue eyes. Go to Lady Islington. I'll bring Lady Roxanne her gown." Madam took up the hunter-green gown. "I'm not certain which gown I like more—the pale blue will be beautiful on Lady Islington, but the beadwork on the bodice of the hunter-green gown is perfect. It will set off Lady Roxanne's auburn hair."

"The countess's gown is ready to be delivered." Eva motioned toward the dark purple gown, the black jet beads sparkling.

"I don't know how you convinced the countess that it was time to wear a color other than black. She was determined never to wear anything but black for the rest of her life. It's difficult to realize that it's been one year and one day since the earl's passing. This color is fitting. The purple is so deep, it almost looks black." Madam Pembroke took the gown, the last gown hanging on the rack.

"I didn't do a lot to convince her. I simply showed her the material, lace, and beads. I wonder if something has changed in her life. She isn't as dour as she has been. Perhaps it is the passage of time."

"It's good to see her in good spirits. I had Louise serve tea. I hope these fittings go quickly. We all want to close for the New Year." Madam Pembroke left the sewing room.

Eva went to the dressing room. "Good afternoon, Lady Islington."

"I can't wait to put the gown on."

Eva helped her client with her gown and buttoned it up. The seamstress arranged the folds and took note of the hem. She brought Lady Islington to the fitting area and helped her onto the rostrum.

Lady Roxanne Lawson came out of her dressing room and stood to the side, inspecting her friend.

Lady Islington stared into the mirror, tilting her head from one side to the other.

"Isabella, that pale blue is stunning with your black hair. You should wear your hair in long curls."

"If I may, my lady," Eva carefully interrupted. "Not down, but up with soft tendrils that appear to escape your chignon. It will create a soft look."

Still looking into the mirror, Lady Islington focused on Eva and smiled. "Yes. That would be perfect. I want tonight to be perfect. I'm wearing the slippers I intend to wear this evening. They're a bit lower than the same ones I wore at the last fitting."

Eva, her pin cushion on her wrist, kneeled and adjusted the hem.

"Isabella." Lady Roxanne stepped closer. Lady Islington glanced at her reflection in the mirror. "Yes?"

Lady Roxanne hesitated. "I don't know what I'm to do. Tonight's party is getting out of control."

"Roxanne, your brother gives the most extravagant parties, all to please you. That's why everyone wants to attend."

Lady Roxanne glanced around, not taking any mind to Eva working on the gown's hem. "I couldn't help but hear Reginald's argument with one of his partners, Templeton. He found a forged signature on a promissory note."

Eva had overheard the whispers of the Earl of Marswell's mounting financial troubles last week from another client. She could imagine the lengths he would go to in order to keep his creditors at bay.

"Templeton forged Reginald's signature?" Lady Islington asked, her voice filled with indignation.

"No." Lady Roxanne looked down. "It's the other way around. And there's more. I was with the countess. She told me there are rumors that Reginald had been moving money in an attempt to hide his debts and create an illusion of solvency."

The bell on the shop door rang. Moments later, Louise, the shop assistant, brought Countess Fitzherbert to the fitting area.

"Isabella. Roxanne. I thought you two might be here." The countess turned to Madam Pembroke. "I've come to pick up my gown rather than have you deliver it."

"I'll have it wrapped and ready for you in a few minutes." Madam Pembroke nodded at Louise. The girl quickly went into the sewing room.

"No need to rush. I can chat with Lady Islington and Lady Roxanne while I wait." She sat in one of the overstuffed chairs and made herself comfortable. "I've just come from tea with Lady Gladstone at The Tea Parlor. You may be interested in knowing that Andrew Montgomery, Duke of Amherst, stopped at our table and said hello. It must be at least five years since Drew left London. He is more handsome than I remember, with a mysterious, tantalizing roguish way about him. He was always a serious young man. That hasn't changed at all. His dark, brooding way adds to the allure. It's as if the weight of the world is on his shoulders.

"I do wish I was younger." Lady Fitzherbert let out a deep sigh. "There is this irresistible quality that surrounds him. I think he will be fighting off the debutantes, their mothers, *and* their grandmothers. I heard he has returned to find a new lover."

Eva fought back a laugh, finding the countess's enthusiasm amusing. She finished adjusting the hem on Lady Islington's gown and stepped back.

"Do you think he's come to London for a Golden Ticket for this April's birthday celebration? It would be the perfect place for Amherst to seek the object of his next affair."

"Shame on you, Lady Isabella." The countess shook her head. "Bessie Dove-Lyon and her Lyon's Den are shunned by the *ton*. Why would anyone—"

"Countess, you know everyone, and you know that e-v-e-r-y-o-n-e in the *ton* is eager for a Golden Ticket, and broods when they do not receive one. The guest list is the best-kept secret in all of England. It is a Mystère Masque with a night of dancing and romance."

"Ah, romance." The countess raised an eyebrow, a teasing smile playing on her lips.

"You are not so old that you have forgotten the feeling when you are desired by someone, and you return the affection." Isabella's voice was tinged with excitement.

"You're right, of course." The countess glanced at the others. "No one else has given of himself more than the earl has given for me. Without any demands or expectations, and not out of duty or responsibility. All out of love and devotion. It wasn't his title or wealth that I found attractive. It was him, the man." She paused for a moment. Her voice trembled with emotion. "I miss him. He enjoyed attending Bessie's birthday. And you're correct. Everyone in the *ton* wants a ticket, even though they look down their nose at her."

"Lady Islington. Please, step down. The hem is fine. I've tacked the lace at the bottom." Eva knew about the infamous gambling hell. Several of their finest clients swooped in each year for Madam to dress them for the event. "Will you take the gown, or would you prefer we deliver it?"

"Please have it delivered?" Lady Islington hesitated halfway to the dressing room. "Roxanne. We can talk later tonight."

Lady Roxanne nodded to her friend and then took her place on the rostrum, ready for her fitting.

"You look well, Countess." Lady Roxanne glanced at their reflections in the mirror.

Eva's first impression, when she saw Lady Fitzherbert, was that the countess appeared drawn, not at all herself, and she wondered if it had anything to do with the rumors she'd heard.

"You are kind. I know how I look. I suppose you've heard the nasty rumors." The countess poured her tea with a trembling hand.

Lady Roxanne took a breath and didn't answer.

"I was shocked when a young man arrived and asked to see me. I thought it was Ross who stood before me. I was devasted when he produced a letter from Fitzherbert. I thought he was daft, but it was the earl's handwriting. The letter instructed the young man to present himself to me within one year of his passing." The teacup trembled in her hand so that she put it down. "All these years, I thought he was dead."

Eva steeled herself not to react, but she was surprised as the countess confirmed the rumor. The countess's first son, born seven months after she married the earl, was stillborn, or so she was told. To have a gentleman of five and twenty arrive at her doorstep claiming to be her son could only be a shock.

"Many know that my son Ross and I have been at odds since his father's passing. Recently, he threatened a legal dispute over his father's will." The countess clasped Lady Roxanne's hand. "I must thank you, my dear, for your confidence and support. I was a headstrong young girl and thought I loved another. There was no way I could placate the earl and prove to him I carried his child. I never thought the sins of the past would come back to haunt me, but here they are. After our tea last Monday, I contacted my solicitor. He brought an accounting to my attention. I learned the earl provided for the boy and even settled a sum on him when he reached his majority."

"He appears to be a lovely young man, this Barclay Thomas." Lady Roxanne tried to offer some optimism.

"That remains to be seen." The countess sounded skeptical. "May God forgive me, but after I found out that Ross had sent Mr. Thomas a letter denouncing him and any claim, he intends to make on the family fortune, I hoped Mr. Thomas would take it all. And when Ross admonished me for seeing a bastard, I quickly reminded him that Mr. Thomas was *not a* bastard, and if he didn't like it, he could leave."

"I'm off." Lady Islington emerged from the dressing room, hastily adjusting her gloves. Without another word, she was out the door, the bell ringing in her wake.

"Where is Isabella going in such a hurry?" The countess stared at the door. "She's not going to see that captain, is she?"

"Isabella didn't tell me, but I would say yes from her smile and flush of her cheeks. I've warned her of the consequences should Lord Islington find out." Lady Roxanne was genuinely concerned. "There are illicit meetings with her dashing cavalry officer in secret places, far away from prying eyes."

For months, Eva had listened to the scandalous details as Lady

Islington and her cavalry officer's secret trysts unfolded.

"She hides his passionate letters from her husband. How much can this rogue care for her? Late-night carriage rides through dimly lit streets and secret encounters at society events. I wonder if she wants to be found out?"

Eva silently agreed with Lady Roxanne's doubt. *Did* the lady want to be found out?

"She won't speak of him to me." The countess's pained expression was evident. "I tried to share my own experience and what it took me to overcome. Isabella has other ideas. And Islington isn't blind, although he is about this. I've been with him when she goes off, and he tells her to enjoy her outing."

"She has no idea how her actions could have repercussions on her family or her fortune," Lady Roxanne said.

Madam Pembroke and Louise appeared with the boxed gowns. The conversation shifted to goodbyes.

"Have a wonderful time tonight." Madam showed the two women out, then turned to Louise. "It's time for you to go, too. Have a good holiday."

Louise turned to Madam Pembroke and Eva. "A good holiday to you both. See you on Monday."

The bell rang as Louise left.

The two women went into the back room when the bell rang again. Moments later, a gentleman poked his head into the room. Phillip Pembroke, Madam's brother.

"Sybil. I have the carriage out front." Phillip came into the room. He was a pleasant man. Eva was certain he didn't know how to frown.

Madam Pembroke turned to Eva. "Are you certain you won't come with me to Phillip's house?"

"Yes, Miss Barnard, please come. We are having a small gathering of friends." He helped his sister with her coat.

"That is kind of you, but not tonight. I want a hot bowl of soup, some crusty bread, a book to read, and then to bed. You go and enjoy your family."

Madam took her packed valise. Eva went to the door with Madam Pembroke and let her out.

"Lock up. I'll be back tomorrow afternoon."

Eva saw them out, locked the door, and pulled down the shade.

She went into the dressing room and fitting area and straightened them. Then she put the last few things away in the sewing room. Eva made her way through the shop toward the stairs that led to the apartment she shared with Madam and noticed an envelope on the floor. Someone must have slid it under the door.

She picked it up and went to put it on Madam's desk when she noticed the envelope was addressed to her. The lion stamp had her heart jump. This wasn't possible.

Eva took the paper-knife from the desk and carefully slit the envelope along the top, and removed a single folded sheet of paper. Eva held the message, not knowing what to expect. She unfolded the paper and gazed at an elegant seal—a family crest, depicting a delicate holly spring, and the intertwined initials BDL, for Bessie Dove-Lyon.

Her heart raced as she quickly glanced at the name on the envelope. Lady Eva Barnard. The truth hit her like a bolt of lightning, and she dropped the paper as if it were on fire. Only Madam Pembroke knew the truth, that she was the daughter of the Duke of Glenshire.

She picked up the paper and held it with trembling hands—the *Invocation Mystère*, the golden ticket.

Chapter Two

24 March 1815
Lyon's Gate Manor, London

Bessie Dove-Lyon, the Black Widow of Whitehall, sat comfortably in her private room at Lyon's Gate Manor. She glanced at the clock on the mantel and smiled, knowingly, at the knock on the door. Amherst was always punctual.

"Come in, Your Grace. I knew you would be on time."

"Mrs. Dove-Lyon. Thank you for seeing me."

"Before we delve into this matter, are you absolutely certain that you wish to pursue this issue? I've read your letter several times. It has been years." Bessie's stern gaze took in the lord in front of her.

"The issue must be resolved one way or another."

"Do you think the young lady in question will be willing to forgive you?"

"Bessie, you didn't know me then. I was a foolish young man. I took liberties that I shouldn't have. It cost my family and hers a great deal of pain. Instead of facing the truth, I threw myself into a different battle. I cared only for myself and took no thought of the consequences of my actions. I've learned my callousness caused family disputes that ruined one family financially and the other's reputation." He paused. "Even though I was my father's heir, he refused my presence and ceased providing for me. If not for the young girl's mother, he would have disowned me as a bastard and denied me my inheritance."

"I've done some research." Bessie lifted a paper on her desk. "All the parties of the incident have passed on, and there are no records."

"I, too, have done my research. There is a great deal of money involved. I have tried to have solicitors and bankers assist, and I have learned that others cannot do what I myself must do. I must make it right with the woman."

Bessie leaned back in her chair. "How did you learn this lesson? Or is it a fleeting whim?"

"I deserve your skepticism. I've earned it. But let me assure you, I understand the gravity of my actions and the unnecessary pain and suffering I have caused. It is for that reason that I must seek amends. My commanding officer, Lord Barrington, and I spent many hours discussing my predicament and how to resolve it."

"I hadn't realized you served under Lord Barrington. He is a man of unwavering loyalty and integrity. Tell me, do you plan to marry the woman?"

"Heavens, no. My mission is to make amends."

"Then, may I inquire if there is someone else you plan to marry?"

"Not at all." His Lordship was emphatic.

"I'm pleased you made that very clear. I've given this a great deal of thought, and I have reached my decision. You and several other young men will compete for the lady's affection. And if you are chosen—"

"When I am chosen," he interrupted.

"Yes," Bessie chuckled softly. "When you are chosen, you will have the opportunity to discuss the situation with her. She will decide what is to be done. All this will take place next week during Mystère Masque."

Amherst felt a sense of relief wash over him. He didn't know what to expect, but Bessie's proposal sounded fair.

"All that remains, Your Grace," Bessie added in a business-like tone, "is your payment."

MADAM PEMBROKE HAD spent a significant portion of the last four months designing and fashioning gowns for her clients attending the Mystère Masque. Each creation was breathtaking, but two, in particular, stood out: a ravishing red silk gown and an ethereal white one.

Madam and Eva poured their hearts and souls into every stitch, treating each gown as if it were their own. As March drew to a close, all the gowns were successfully delivered, yet Eva had not caught a glimpse of the gown Madam Pembroke had created for her.

On the evening of April first, Eva stood on the rostrum in front of the long mirror in the shop's fitting area. All she could do was stare at the woman who looked back at her, unable to reconcile that it was indeed herself.

"I knew this design would be perfect. The red silk bodice beautifully compliments your blonde hair, and the square neckline is truly flattering."

"Madam, is there a chemisette? You've cut the neckline very low. The material barely covers my bosom."

"Why spoil such a beautiful line? No, there is no chemisette. The long-tapered sleeves help balance the dress, making it appear less revealing. Please, turn around for me."

Eva turned around slowly. The white silk skirt fell softly around her, its bottom adorned with intricate embroidery and delicate beadwork in shades of gold and ruby, forming an elegant Greek pattern. Madam attached a flowing red train lined with white silk at the back of the dress. The elegant addition made a regal statement.

"I can't do this." Eva stepped off the rostrum. Madam's gentle touch stopped her.

Eva looked at her friend. "Everyone will know who I am—"

"No one will know who you are unless you want them to. You will be wearing your mask. Now, here is your reticule and the package for Bessie. Our carriage is outside."

Moments later, Eva found herself gazing out of the carriage windows at a grand blue building—Lyon's Gate Manor.

"When you go inside, carry yourself as the daughter of a lord, not as a seamstress. Take the place you were destined for."

"But Madam—"

"No, don't say a word. You possess greater knowledge, deeper emotions, and more substance than many women. Be true to yourself. You, Eva, are a beautiful, intelligent, and remarkable woman."

The driver handed her down from the carriage. She adjusted her gown and glanced at Madam Pembroke. The modiste leaned out the carriage window.

"Hermia and Helena will be at the door. They will tell you what is expected and what to do. Now go. Everyone in the *ton* would do anything for a ticket to this party. Few get their wish. Enjoy the evening."

Eva took a deep breath. What had Madam Pembroke gotten her into? She approached the door, clutching both her mask and invitation in her trembling hand. At the door, she handed the invitation to the women who stood at the entrance.

"Good evening, my lady. Please go with Helena. She will explain tonight's activities."

Eva followed Helena into the Ladies' Parlor. The women who were there sat in groups of two. Eva surmised that each guest was being told what to expect. Helena led her to the window seat.

"There aren't many rules this evening. Feel free to speak to anyone you wish. Formal introductions aren't necessary." Helena smiled at her. "It's a very liberating sensation. Regarding your mask, you must keep it on while in the main room. The anonymity that your mask provides is essential.

"Mrs. Dove-Lyon is extremely happy you are celebrating her birthday with her this year. To her, every guest is special and treated accordingly. For you, my lady, she has a special evening planned." Helena presented Eva with a small velvet pouch. "This is Mrs. Dove-Lyon's gift to you for her birthday."

Her eyes widened, mouth agape, as astonishment washed over her. Eva opened the pouch and pulled out a ruby hair comb in the shape of a rose. She quickly lifted her head and stared at Helena.

"I don't know what to say."

Helena took the comb from her and fixed it in Eva's hair. "It looks magnificent. It brings out the honey color in your blonde hair. As for what to say, you can thank Mrs. Dove-Lyon. She has asked to see you."

Eva turned to the window and looked at her reflection. The jeweled comb was indeed beautiful.

"After you speak with Mrs. Dove-Lyon, I will bring you to the main gambling floor, which is dark for this evening. Your game this evening is to locate the gentleman with a rose. He will not be obvious. The fun is in finding him. Several will offer you a rose, but only accept the rose from the gentleman with whom you want to spend the evening. Once you accept the flower, that part of the game is over. The rest of the evening is up to you and without any consequences. No later than 2:00 a.m., you and your gentleman will surrender the rose to Mrs. Dove-Lyon.

"There is one rule that I must tell you. Once you see Mrs. Dove-Lyon, the doors will be locked, and you will not be able to leave until 2:00 a.m. You may stay later, of course. Do you have any questions?"

An evening of no consequences. An evening of obscurity. Was that even possible? And no way out? "No. Not at all."

"Good. Then come with me. I'll take you to Mrs. Dove-Lyon."

The two women left the parlor and made their way to Mrs. Dove-Lyon's private room.

Eva's heart fluttered, unsure of what to expect. When Helena ushered her into her hostess's private room, Eva couldn't help but smile. The woman wore the white gown she and Madam Pembroke had made. This evening must have been Madam Pembroke's doing.

"Do come in, Lady Eva." Mrs. Dove-Lyon beckoned to the two chairs in the center of the room. The decor was elegant and tasteful, in shades of cream and tan with splashes of teal. The upholstery was cabbage roses in muted tones.

"Mrs. Dove-Lyon, thank you so much for your gracious invitation and your generous gift." Her hand gently touched the comb.

"You are most welcome. I must speak to your modiste." A subtle glint of amusement passed from her hostess, a silent acknowledgment of their shared secret. "Your gown is extraordinary."

"I will tell Madam Pembroke that you approve. I brought you a small token of my appreciation, a birthday present." Eva took a small package from her reticule and handed it to her hostess.

"Rosewater. It is my favorite fragrance. Thank you for your thoughtfulness." Mrs. Dove-Lyon opened the bottle and dabbed the stopper behind her ears. She took a deep breath and put the bottle down. "I wanted to meet you. Madam speaks very highly of you."

"Madam is a wonderful friend and, in many ways, a teacher. I don't know what I would do without her."

"I can see that she is. I have a special evening planned for you. You are under no obligation. Be prepared to be wined and dined. There are no restrictions or judgments here. It is a delicious freedom, one that men enjoy. It is my belief that women should experience freedom as well. Helena explained everything to you." Eva nodded. "Do you believe that you have a soulmate?"

Eva's eyes widened, caught off-guard by the unexpected question. "I'm not sure. However, I do know that I refuse to enter into a marriage simply for the sake of it. When I marry, it will be to a man who sees me as a partner, a man who respects and values me and treats me as an equal."

"That is a tall order." Mrs. Dove-Lyon gave her a knowing glance. "It is what I wanted as well. And it was what I found in my husband. When I met him, we had an instant connection. I knew he understood me. I wasn't mistaken. Now, put on your mask. Enjoy the evening. I will see you later."

Eva put on her mask and stood. "Thank you, again, for your invitation."

Helena ushered her to the busy main floor, where a sea of people mingled and conversed. They made their way toward the refreshments, but Helena soon turned her attention to another guest.

Eva's gaze swept across the room, curious if she could identify familiar faces, or possibly their gowns. Amongst the crowd, she noticed that only a handful of women stood alone, while the rest were engrossed in conversations.

As the chime of the mantel clock struck the hour, ten, Eva let out a deep breath, reminding herself she promised Madam Pembroke that she'd enjoy the evening. Her attention shifted to her right as if someone had asked for her attention. She gazed upon a captivating figure—a man with a commanding presence. Tall and self-assured, he possessed a refined elegance and an undeniable charm that set him apart.

To her surprise, his gaze was fixed on her, ignoring the rest of the room. His smile was an invitation. He graciously nodded in acknowledgment before glancing at the gentleman standing beside him.

In that moment, a chill and a sense of abandonment crept over her, leaving her feeling empty.

"May I pour you a cup?" Eva looked at a gentleman with warm brown eyes. Without waiting for a response, he positioned himself by her side as if staking his claim. However, his gaze lingered on her chest, making Eva uncomfortable. She should have insisted on a chemisette.

Her own gaze shifted downward, noticing a rose discreetly tucked into his shirt. It dawned on her that he must be one of the gentlemen vying for her attention. Though she attempted to establish eye contact, his focus remained fixed on her chest.

Eva felt a brief moment of panic but quickly regained her composure. "Thank you." She put on a polite smile to mask her unease. "But not at the moment." Desperate to get away, she scanned the room and spotted a sitting area. She gracefully made her way toward it, eager to be away from the man's unsettling gaze.

Eva glanced at the people in the room, none of whom paid her any attention, without caring about being noticed. Her interest shifted towards the women, finding their attire more captivating than the individuals wearing them. Several of the gowns had clearly been worn for more than a couple of seasons. She doubted the women who commissioned the gowns wore them tonight. The masks successfully concealed the identities of their wearers, adding to the evening's mystery.

"Well, well, look whom we have here?" An aristocratic gentleman remarked, his gaze sweeping over Eva's attire. "Another masked beauty attempting to masquerade as someone of significance."

Eva's eyes flickered with a touch of amusement. She had met arrogant men before, ones who thought highly of themselves. She responded with a calm yet assertive tone, playing along with the masked atmosphere of the party.

"Ah, it seems you have caught me." Her response was calm yet assertive. "But perhaps there is more to me than meets the eye. After all, the allure of a masquerade lies in the hidden identities and unexpected encounters."

The man's smug expression faltered. Eva supposed he was not used to anyone, especially a woman, with a quick-witted response.

He leaned closer. "An eloquent tongue alone cannot disguise the truth. A commoner like you could never truly fit in amongst the elite."

Eva's eyes sparkled with a glint of defiance, thankful for the mask. It gave her a freedom that she truly appreciated.

"Appearances can be deceiving." She added a hint of mystery to her tone. "For in this masquerade, identities are shrouded, and the boundaries of social status become blurred. It is a place where connections are forged beyond the limitations of birthright."

The man's expression wavered before he offered her a begrudging nod.

"I concede that you speak with conviction. Perhaps I should withhold my judgment until I have had the chance to know you better."

Eva rewarded him with a gracious smile, her eyes sparkling beneath her mask, as she inclined her head in acknowledgment.

"Wise words, sir."

The aristocrat removed a rose from inside his coat.

Eva relished the intrigue and freedom, but God's toes, did every man she encountered have a rose?

"Ah, my lady. There you are. Forgive me for being detained. I should have known better than to leave you unattended." Another gentleman approached with a determined step as if he knew her. She turned toward him. It was the gentleman she exchanged glances with earlier.

He swept his arm around her in a protective way, and they were off walking across the room.

"I've been waiting for you." He removed his arm and placed her arm on his. "Fear not. I will navigate you through this lion's den." He chuckled.

"That was a good pun, but do you always laugh at your own witticisms?" She began to turn back, but this gentleman didn't let her.

"He's an utter rake and an arrogant bastard."

"And you, sir, are you any better?"

"I am a lovable rake and never vulgar. He will insult you while I will tell you off, and you will ask me for more." He was trying not to smile, which made him all the more charming.

"And I see you are modest."

He glanced at her with an austere visage, looking down his nose at her.

Eva chortled a bit too loudly and clamped her hand over her mouth. A moment later, the two had their heads close together and were laughing.

"Amherst, good to see you." Eva and her new friend stopped as he glanced at the intruder. "Forgive me. The rule slipped my mind."

"Rule?" Eva asked. "You mean I'm not supposed to know that I am being accompanied by the most eligible wealthiest bachelor in London who cares not for rules or restraint? What a delicious notion." She turned to Amherst. "Am I correct, Drew?"

He leaned down and kissed her lips. They laughed as they

walked on, leaving a confused gentleman behind.

"Drew?" he asked, challenging her to explain.

She tried to hide her smile and nodded ever so slightly. "A lucky guess." Eva looked away. It was easy to place who he was. The moment she saw him approach her, she realized who he was. It was as if someone had whispered his name in her ear.

"Well done, my lady, but you have the advantage. You know who I am, but I do not know who you are."

She glanced at him, looking down her nose. "Precisely." Then kept on walking.

Chapter Three

Andrew Montgomery, Duke of Amherst, stared at Eva, his previous ease replaced with a tense and skeptical stare. "A lucky guess? I'll have to be careful, or you'll guess all my secrets, and I cannot have you do that."

Eva stood beside him, her hand resting lightly on his arm, but the woman's attention seemed to be elsewhere, anywhere but looking directly at him. "Do you have so many secrets to hide?"

"Not so many, but those I do have, I would rather keep to myself."

Eva faced him directly. He couldn't look elsewhere. His full attention was on her. "I promise your secrets are safe with me."

Amherst assessed the woman's words with a sharp and analytical gaze for any hint of deceit. To his surprise, he found an honesty that seemed genuine, a refreshing change from the world he lived in.

"Since you won't tell me your name, what would you have me call you?"

"I'll let you choose a name for me."

He gave her a thoughtful stare as he searched for an appropriate name. Dare he push her further, testing the limits of her willingness to continue this game? No. Not yet. He didn't want to give her a reason to walk away from him as she did with Olsen. The memory of the poor man still holding out his rose lingered in his mind.

"Angel." A wry smile touched his lips. "I'll call you Angel because you look so heavenly. Have you been to the den before?" He glanced at her and held up his hand. "Don't answer that. I can see you haven't. If you had, you would not need to come again. Now, if you see anyone of interest, let me know. I'll introduce you and release your hand. Otherwise, if you would be so kind as to let me be your companion."

"I think you mean your decoy. To keep others away." A shiver went down his back as she whispered. Her closeness provided a tantalizing view of her bodice.

His gaze traveled to the low neckline of her gown. A beautiful flush ran up her chest and neck, settling on her cheeks.

"If you don't want to meet anyone, why are you here?" she asked.

"Why do you believe I'm here?" He gave her a hint of his most enchanting smile.

"Rumors are circulating that you've come to seek out your next conquest, for your next love affair."

The musicians played the opening chords, and everyone cleared the center of the room.

"I'm sorry to disappoint the *ton*. It's Mrs. Dove-Lyon's birthday. I never miss an opportunity to wish her a good year." He gestured toward the center of the room. "Your flush is just the color needed with that exquisite gown. You will be the envy of every woman here. And I, the envy of every man for having you in my arms. Shall we?" He held out his hand to dance. He had this overwhelming need to hold her close to him.

Together, they stepped onto the dance floor.

THE LADIES HAD been correct in their description of Amherst. The man was mysterious and tantalizing, with a roguish charm that captivated her as they danced. Eva gazed at him, drawn to him by some invisible force. What was it about the man that intrigued her? Was it the knowledge that he was a known rogue? Or perhaps his playful nature? Whatever it was, there was a depth to him, a hidden secret that piqued her curiosity. Eva understood the art of hiding one's true self all too well. Perhaps it was this shared understanding that drew her to him.

Amherst gave her a sidelong glance, his lips pursing as he struggled to suppress a smile.

Eva couldn't help but chuckle. The man was a charming tease, with a hint of danger that dared anyone to explore his depths. For a moment, she wondered how many women had tried to capture him. It was apparent none had ever succeeded.

The music began. A waltz. A scandal. Eva wouldn't be surprised if every dance was a waltz, and at the moment, she couldn't have been more thrilled.

Amherst's left hand glided along her side, finding its place on her back, while he extended his other hand to her. She hesitated a moment, her hand hovering in the air as she mustered the courage to place it in his. As their palms touched, the shock of his warm hand sent a shiver down her spine. It was a pleasant surprise, very pleasant.

"Are you familiar with this dance?" The concern in his voice and eyes eased her discomfort.

"I'm familiar with the basic steps." Madam had made sure she was prepared.

His smile blossomed, and he expertly positioned her in his arms. "Perfect. Follow my lead. I won't let you lose your way."

He held her firmly, but she dared not be too close.

"It will be easier for you to follow if we weren't across the room from each other."

Eva took a small step toward him and welcomed the closeness.

"That is much better." Amherst led her through the dance, seamlessly transitioning from the basic steps to more intricate moves. With every twirl and spin, her excitement mirrored the excitement of the dance itself. His hand on her back guided her with gentle precision, and she surrendered willingly, enchanted by the rhythm they created together. Each rotation seemed to defy gravity, leaving her yearning for the dance to continue indefinitely.

Their graceful movements captured the attention of onlookers, stirring whispers and sparking curiosity as they glided by. As the dance drew to a close, they gracefully bowed to each other, their attraction evident.

He escorted her off the dance floor and deftly obtained two glasses of champagne from a passing footman and extended one to Eva. "To you, my angel. May we both find what we seek."

Eva raised her glass. What had she come for? She said nothing, just smiled and drank her champagne as she glanced around the room. Amherst was tempting. Very tempting. Too tempting. A part of her urged caution, but another part yearned for more. Taking a step forward, she hesitated, knowing her decision held the power to change everything.

"Are you leaving me so soon?" he asked.

She cast a gaze over her shoulder, raising her eyebrows in an unmistakable hint of flirtation. She handed Amherst her empty glass.

"You're welcome to come along if you can keep up." Eva turned away and took a confident step forward. However, to her surprise, Amherst was quick to catch up, his chuckle making her smile. In that moment, she remembered the joy of indulging in playful moments and embracing the thrill of the unknown.

He leaned closer, allowing his gaze to wander down her bodice before meeting her gaze once again. "As you wish, my angel. Come this way." His voice was a whisper as he intertwined his arm with hers.

"Amherst, is that you?"

Both Amherst and Eva halted mid-step and turned toward the source of the voice.

"Islington, you're the last person I'd expect to see here." Amherst didn't try to hide his surprise.

"It *is* you. I came to wish Bessie a happy birthday. My task is completed, and I'm ready to leave. These parties are for you, young rogues," Islington's gaze swept over Eva. "And for beautiful young women." His gaze returned to Amherst. "I'm glad you've returned. You've been away too long. We can talk more tomorrow when I see you. Until then." He gave Eva a slight bow and left the room.

Amherst guided her toward the garden door, the evening air mildly warm. As they stepped outside, they found they had the garden all to themselves. Together, they walked down the pathway through a maze of greenery and flowers providing a secret haven for them.

"I WAS SURPRISED to see Islington here." Amherst grappled with the puzzle. "I would think he would be home with his wife. If his wife is home."

Eva's attempt to conceal her sadness fell short, and Amherst caught a glimpse of the lingering sorrow on her face.

"Then the rumors have already spread." Amherst's comment surprised her.

"Lady Isabella has not been discreet, and the *ton* makes her indiscretions public knowledge. It doesn't take long for whispers to grow louder, spreading rumors of stolen glances, calculated touches, and discreet exchanges at social events to make their way through the *ton*." Eva let out her breath. "I had hoped she would come to her senses."

He plucked a rose from a nearby bush and carefully removed the thorns. He faced Eva, uncertain whether he should offer the flower to her or not. Her words hadn't been venomous. On the contrary, they carried a sense of sadness. He took a step closer, their bodies lightly brushing against each other. He delicately placed the stem down her bodice, allowing the rose to nestle between her breasts.

"May I see your face?"

His request was a small one, yet it held a larger meaning. She remained quiet.

"You can remove my mask, if you like." His invitation had a dizzying effect.

She reached for the ribbon on his mask and gave it a gentle tug. The mask fell away, the ribbon still in her hand. He was more handsome than she imagined. There was a softness about him that spoke of concern.

He reached for her ribbon. For a moment, she panicked. She should stop him. Instead, she did nothing and saw that her mask was in his hand.

"Beautiful. You should never hide behind a mask or anything else."

Eva lowered her eyes and stared at the rose bushes.

He lifted her chin with the crook of his finger, locking their gazes. "I should have warned you. No one will come to your rescue here."

Eva remained silent. He couldn't help but notice the delicate vein pulsating in her neck, and the flush that painted her cheeks. Her physical responses betrayed the intensity of her feelings. He was aware that her traitorous body was making its own demands and that her mind had seemed to cease functioning. If it was functioning, it would have told her to run. But, like Amherst, her heart had taken over.

Instead of speaking, Eva's tongue gently peeked out, moistening her lips, an unconscious gesture that spoke volumes, silently inviting him closer.

Amherst found the tenderness and sweetness of her unspoken invitation irresistible. He leaned in, their breaths intermingling, and enveloped her in his arms, drawing her nearer than when they had danced.

A deep sigh escaped Eva as their lips met. Her eyes fluttered closed, surrendering to his warmth. He deepened their kiss, each moment fueling a passionate fire between them. As she parted her lips, his tongue swooped in, claiming her completely as his own.

EVA'S MIND RACED with conflicting thoughts. Should she have objected to the rose, a symbol of their connection. Part of her reveled in the excitement it brought, the tangible mark of their intimacy. She stood rooted to the spot, paralyzed by the touch of his lips, and the unexplainable yearning that she couldn't quite explain. She dared not move for fear his enchantment would end.

He broke their kiss, and a small groan escaped her lips, betraying a desire for more.

"Hush, my angel," he whispered, his lips brushing against hers.

"I'll not go far. Your lips are too intoxicating." His forehead rested against hers.

He trailed small, tender kisses down her neck, continuing onto her chest. His fingers teased the edge of her bodice, sending shivers of anticipation along her skin.

Overwhelmed by the sensation rushing through her, Eva remained silent. With a gentle touch, she lifted his head, surprising him with her boldness.

"My God. You are…" She cut off his words and silenced him with a soft, gentle kiss.

"I can't get close enough to you," she whispered, her words filled with longing.

He wrapped his arms around her, cradling her head against his chest as if he wanted to hold her forever. They stood there, locked in an embrace, until her tumultuous emotions began to subside.

The sound of a distant bell echoed through the mansion, signaling that dinner was being served. Eva reluctantly lifted her head and stepped out of his embrace.

"We'll have to join the others." He looked toward the manor door and put on his mask.

"Here, let me help you with your mask." She took the mask from him and put it against her face while he tied the ribbon.

Eva adjusted her hair and dress. "Will I do?"

"You will do very well." He offered her his arm. They returned to the main room, where everyone was heading toward the dining room.

"We were discussing Islington and his wife before we wandered off. I know Lady Islington's, Captain Westcott. He's a dutiful soldier. Do you think she resents his lordship being so much older than she?"

Eva shook her head. "No. Lady Islington married his lordship because he loved and supported her, embracing her unconventional nature that others see as eccentricities."

"You have my interest piqued. What type of eccentricities?"

"It's not what you're thinking." She dismissed his misguided assumption. "Her ladyship is a spirited woman with a keen mind and strong opinions. Lord Islington encouraged her until, one day, he stopped. Her connection to Captain Westcott began innocently enough. I hear he is a longtime family friend." Eva paused. "Why your interest in Lady Islington?"

"Now it's your turn to wonder, but rest assured, it's not what you think. Lord Islington reached out to me regarding a business venture, which is quite unlike him. Financially, everything seems promising, but I can't help but wonder. He was very much enraptured with his wife, and her indiscretions could prove detrimental to him."

"Ah, so is she the cause of his decline or merely a pawn he can blame to protect his reputation?" Eva mused, her eyes narrowing with fresh insight.

Amherst gazed at her. "You have grasped the essence of the issue. Blame. Is Lady Isabella's romance merely a façade to protect her husband's honor and reputation? You have a sharp wit, and your astute observations of society's dynamics are captivating."

Chapter Four

Eva entered the dining room, her arm linked with Amherst's. They made their way to the buffet, where an array of delectable dishes was served. The centerpiece was the roasted capons that were arranged on a platter with sprigs of holly.

"The holly represents Mrs. Dove-Lyon's family crest." They filled their plates with roasted vegetables, small individual loaves of herb bread, and cranberry sauce with oranges. There was more to choose from, but despite the offering, Eva didn't have much of an appetite.

Amidst the chatter in the dining room, a gentleman at the neighboring table tossed his serviette onto the table and turned to face Lysander, an escort who stood behind him. "Have you located Titan? I don't see why the gambling tables are dark this evening. If the gambling floor is to remain dark, then a private room will do."

"My lord, you've enjoyed Mrs. Dove-Lyon's birthday celebration before. You know the gambling floor is kept dark and that gambling is not allowed in the private rooms this evening."

The gentleman swung back to the woman beside him. "Forgive my frustration, my dear. It appears the tables are unusually dark tonight. I had hoped to indulge in some gambling, but it seems the floor remains closed. Lysander informs me that even the private rooms are closed this evening for such activities. Perhaps a whisky will help ease my disappointment."

The woman with him remained calm and composed. "I understand your disappointment, my lord. It is unfortunate that the gambling floor is unavailable tonight. However, we can still have an enjoyable evening."

Lysander placed the glass of whisky in front of the gentleman. The woman glanced up at the escort, a clear declaration of thanks in her eyes.

Amherst put his hand over Eva's and leaned forward. "Would you prefer another table?"

There was something captivating about Amherst's eyes. At first, she had thought they were gray-blue, but at the moment, they seemed to shimmer with silver-gray, filled with compassion and longing. They held her as if she were a butterfly pinned to a board. She could feel his touch on her body, even though all he was doing was looking at her and holding her hand. *Control yourself. You may be in this rare atmosphere, but you are still Lady Eva Barnard.* She squeezed his hand.

"This table will do."

Amherst glanced sideways at the man, a question on his face. He nodded. She suspected he had recognized the man.

"Do you know Lord Marswell?" she asked.

"Upon my return to London after a five-year absence, I find that I have many friends, some who were not my friends when I left." He cut into his capon.

"The House of Amherst is a well-established, wealthy one. I would think you would have many acquaintances and friends." Eva placed her serviette on her lap.

"Precisely. Everyone wants to be in my pockets. Marswell wishes to discuss a partnership. I don't know why. He is well-financed."

Eva shifted her attention from Amherst to the food on her plate, attempting to compose herself. She picked up her knife and fork, slicing through her vegetables.

"Is he not?" Amherst asked.

She lifted her head to see Amherst staring at her. "Is he not, what?"

"Well-financed?"

A small gasp escaped her lips. What had Marswell's sister revealed? Reginald had forged his partner Templeton's signature. Reginald had been moving money in an attempt to hide his debts and create an illusion of solvency.

"He is well-financed, with markers."

"That cannot be." Amherst glanced to the side, then back at her. "He and Islington are scheduled to meet with me tomorrow. How do you know this?"

Amherst wasn't angry at her, but his mood had changed so swiftly that she was taken aback.

"I listen. It's not difficult to gather information. It seems that Lord Marswell lives lavishly and enjoys gambling."

"I was reckless, once. Marswell will find a way to right himself." Amherst returned to eating his dinner. "What have you heard?" He didn't raise his head.

"May I ask you a business question?"

"Yes, of course. What would you like to know?" He raised his head.

"Why would someone continuously move their money from one place to another? What do they gain from such transactions?"

Amherst put down his knife and fork and rested his elbows on the table as he interlaced his hands. Though it wasn't his hands that interested her at that moment, she observed him and waited for his response.

"There are various reasons why someone might frequently move their funds. One possibility is to conceal debts and create a façade of financial stability. However, such transactions require the accompanying paperwork and contracts."

"Thank you." Eva absorbed his description. "So, if someone required funds, they could potentially forge another person's signature."

AMHERST'S EXPRESSION TURNED grave as he nodded, understanding the implications of her statement.

"Are you suggesting," he lowered his voice and glanced at the surroundings, "that one of England's wealthiest landowners is involved in fraudulent financial practices?"

Eva shrugged her shoulders, causing the rose at her breast to sway gently.

"I believe Marswell is an opportunist who lives on his father's wealth. He has skillfully squandered his fortune and adeptly concealed his actions. He claims these extravagant parties are for his sister's benefit, but in reality, Marswell really wants a wealthy husband for Roxanne, someone he can exploit." Eva's eyes hardened. "The man has no moral compass. He has gotten himself into a precarious situation and would go to any lengths to free himself, even at the expense of his sister."

"Many a man has been enticed into situations that turned out to be less than rewarding. I'm sure you are aware of that."

Eva lifted her wine glass and took a sip. He felt her mind working, choosing her words, and was eager to hear what she would say.

"Marswell is only concerned about preserving his reputation and how the loss of funds affects him. His staff can and will find employment when he loses everything, but what about his sister? What of her well-being? Will she have the opportunity to marry? And if not, will she find employment? How will she fend for herself?" Eva paused for several heartbeats. "Some women possess the strength to face adversity head-on, but I fear Lady Roxanne would suffer greatly. Not everyone has family or a dear friend who will come to their aid. For that reason, I could never forgive her brother for putting her in this situation."

He stared at Eva as she searched his eyes. "And what about you? Could you be so callous as to disregard the well-being of those under your care?"

If she only knew how her words hit their mark. "Youth. We men often think we have all the answers when, in truth, there is much we still have to learn. Some of us learn more quickly than others. The real issue lies in finding a satisfactory resolution to the issue at hand."

"Do you mean confess, ask for forgiveness? Or simply walk away and allow the other party to shoulder the blame?" The woman was goading him.

"Are you suggesting that my gender is inherently cruel?" He waited for her to take his bait. He didn't have to wait long.

"Not at all. I believe that exceptional individuals, regardless of gender, do not perceive mistakes and misjudgments as weaknesses. They understand that a person grows by admitting their errors and making amends. I've said too much. Forgive me."

"But how else will I learn—" Eva's glare made him aware she didn't know if he was being sarcastic or teasing.

"Learn what you value in a man, as your friend," he asserted. "So, no, I will not forgive you but implore you to speak your mind, always to speak your mind."

His unwavering gaze held her captive as he tenderly turned her hand over, brought it to his lips, and gently placed a lingering kiss on her palm. When he was done, he replaced her hand back on the table and covered it with his own, a silent gesture of protection and understanding.

His mischievous grin played upon his lips, and the spark in his eyes held a tantalizing hint of untamed desires. In his confident charm, there was a touch of danger that drew her in, irresistibly like a moth to a flame. With a mere smile, he promised passionate encounters and exhilarating adventures, teasing and inviting her in a way that felt like his whispered secrets were meant only for her.

That captivating smile awakened a deep longing, igniting a desire to cast caution aside and surrender herself to him. She yearned to explore the hidden depths of passion that simmered just beneath the surface, waiting to be unleashed.

Chapter Five

Eva continued to eat her dinner, although she didn't taste the sumptuous food. Her mind was filled with Amherst.

"You have an uncanny way of understanding people and their actions. Have you always had this gift?" Amherst asked.

"It was a gift from my father." She smiled, remembering how her father explained the unspoken messages he heard when he spoke with people, from their choice of words to the signals their bodies sent. It had seen him well until, with one unsuspecting incident, everything came crashing down.

Chairs scraped the floor as the Earl of Fitzherbert stood. Even at a masked event, he wore his family's crest.

The whispers in the dining room ceased, and all eyes turned to the table in the middle of the room.

"Sir, you are not part of the House of Fitzherbert. Possibly the household, but definitely not the family." The earl stormed off. The other gentleman at the table ate as if nothing was amiss.

Amherst returned to his dinner while Eva couldn't help but join the collective gaze, even though she didn't intend to. The table in question was two tables in front of them.

"It seems the truth has finally come to light." Eva settled back in her seat. "It was inevitable that the truth would soon come out." She cut up the vegetables.

"Someone has already won that bet at White's." Amherst glanced at her. "This Barclay Thomas fellow does have counsel. If his papers are authentic, he may have a legitimate claim to the countess' family fortune."

"The only way that could be possible is if the countess was married to the earl when Thomas Barclay, the child, was born." Eva glanced over Amherst's shoulder. "Why did they willingly sit with each other?" She returned her attention to Amherst.

"I thought you were aware that Mrs. Dove-Lyon is a meticulous planner. She leaves nothing to chance. We are all seated according to her careful plan."

"It may be a calculated plan, but it feels rather callous."

"Do you really think so?" Amherst glanced over his shoulder. "Difficult, but not mean. How else will things get settled? Surely not by ignoring each other's invitations and rejecting all legal counsel requests. There is much at stake." He leaned close to her. "The countess had a suitor. From what I've been told, he was a wonderful gentleman, if reports are to be believed."

"I wish it were a kindness that Mr. Thomas waited until the earl passed away. But that is a foolish romantic notion."

"Why do you suppose he came to England?" Amherst asked her.

"Men and their egos." Eva shook her head. "It appears Mr. Thomas received a letter regarding the earl's passing. It was from his half-brother denouncing him and any attempt he may have to claim the family inheritance.

"It is said that Mr. Thomas went to the earl's estate to speak to the countess privately. When Ross, the oldest son, found out, he was furious. Furious that his mother would entertain a bastard.

"The countess not so calmly told Ross that Mr. Thomas was her son, and he, Ross, could leave."

Amherst's chuckle made Eva smile. He appreciated the countess as much as she did. "Why do you think she's parading Mr. Thomas in front of her son, and why would Mr. Thomas tolerate it?"

"I'm not sure," Eva pondered out loud. "But the countess has much to lose in this situation. I wonder if guilt plays a role in this drama?"

"Guilt?" Amherst raised his eyebrows.

"I have no evidence, but I find it difficult to believe that there was another man in the countess's life. From what I've heard, she was deeply in love with the earl. I suspect that her indiscretion was with him. It was widely believed at the time that the child died, and people thought it was for the best."

"You do not believe that story? What do you think was in the earl's letter that Barclay carried?"

"No, I do not believe that story. Not when you see the other evidence. The earl saw to the child's well-being and even settled an amount on him when he reached his majority. What would that suggest? As for what is in the letter, I believe the earl attested that although he is not Barclay's father, it is out of great love for his countess that he saw to the child's well-being and explained he had to ensure it was his bloodline that inherited. Furthermore, I do not think the countess knew that her baby survived. It's a tragic tale, and my heart aches for the countess and for Mr. Thomas."

"Not for the countess's other son, the one who thinks he is the rightful heir?"

"He rubbed his hands together, eager to get them on his father's wealth. It was Ross who firmly told his mother to vacate *his* estate. It was Ross who contested his father's will, not only to claim what was rightfully bequeathed to him, but also to seize what the earl had provided for his mother. No. I do not believe Ross deserves to enjoy what his father and mother built together. He has much to learn about duty, responsibility, and kindness." Eva gave Amherst a sad glance as she put her serviette on the table.

Amherst knew Eva's pain and wished he could erase it, but that was impossible. Would simply explaining what happened be enough? He understood that only the truth would suffice. There was one more scandal that needed to be unraveled.

Chapter Six

The clock on the mantel chimed one. Amherst rose from his seat and extended his hand to her. "Our time grows short before we need to present ourselves to Mrs. Dove-Lyon. Walk with me?"

She stood and accepted his hand. Their fingers intertwined, as they strolled together into the bustling hall, the music, and noise fading as they went deeper into the mansion.

"I had no idea what we would talk about this evening. It all seems to have revolved around gossip and truth." Amherst could only hope she would understand what he had to tell her.

A great deal depended on this conversation, on his confession. He couldn't be like the earl, withholding information from his countess for years, nor like Lord Islington, exploiting the information for his personal gain. And certainly not like Marswell, causing harm to his angel. He listened well to her lessons and thanked her for each one. He feared this might be their only night together. But he had to tell her the truth.

"Where are we going?" Eva asked.

"There is a private room nearby. I don't want to be disturbed. I have a great deal to share with you." He led her into a room, closed the door behind them, and ensured it was locked. "So no one interrupts us. You're free to leave whenever you like."

"Drew, what do you have to say that is so serious?"

He nearly gasped at the use of his given name. "Please, be seated. Would you like some sherry or port?"

"Sherry would be fine."

He poured two glasses and handed her one. He had prepared this speech ever since Mrs. Dove-Lyon had consented to arrange their meeting. Now none of what he prepared made sense.

"In about an hour, we will have to see Mrs. Dove-Lyon. I expect she will ask if I have told you the truth about myself. She will ask you what you plan to do with this new knowledge."

For the first time all evening, he saw a flicker of recognition in his eyes. She found his vulnerability.

"I plan to tell her that I found the correct gentleman." She gave him a coy smile.

He laughed that short playful laugh that she had grown to adore in a matter of hours.

This was not going to get any easier. Amherst decided to say what he had to, speak to Mrs. Dove-Lyon, and be prepared to leave alone.

"Six years ago, I thought I was an intelligent man. Smarter than my father. Smarter than your father, Griffith, Duke of Glenshire." He heard her gasp and knew there was no going back.

"I engaged in a business transaction that I knew carried risks. The people involved, who trusted me, advised against my proposition. But I arrogantly believed I knew best. I proceeded with the deal, aiming to prove to them that I was right."

He paused, haunted by the memories of his father's and his father's partner's pain. Their faces still lingered in his mind, etched with disappointment at his betrayal.

"The investment failed. I had no way to make it right. My determination to prove myself had led to their trust being shattered, and their funds entangled in a losing venture." He paced in front of her, his voice growing louder with each word, as he relived the events.

"I worked hard to make amends, eventually succeeding. But it was for my family. The other family." He stopped in front of her. "Your family would have nothing to do with me."

"You!" She got to her feet. Her voice filled with anger. "You were the one who took away my father's dignity. No one would engage in business with him. We lost our home and property. My parents died as paupers.

"What was all this about? Did you expect me to forgive you? Fall at your feet? What you did was unforgivable. You destroyed my family, and for what? To satisfy your own ego? To prove that you were smarter than them?"

She turned, went to the door, and pulled on the latch. He stood behind her. His hand snaked past her and undid the lock.

As she felt the warmth radiating from him, she closed her eyes, grappling with conflicting emotions. How could she still long to touch him, to kiss him? He was driving her to the edge of madness.

Eva yanked open the door and fled. She ran straight to Mrs. Dove-Lyon, seeking guidance in the midst of chaos.

"Come," Mrs. Dove-Lyon called out, calm and composed.

Eva rushed into her room, out of breath and distraught.

Bessie glanced past her at the open door and waited patiently.

"Will your gentleman friend be joining us?"

"Never. You knew who he was. How could you play such a cruel game? I am certain Madam Pembroke told you about my family. Yet, you played this game and forced me to face the very man who stripped everything away from me and my family."

Eva reached into her bodice, yanked out the rose he had given her, and threw it at Bessie's feet.

"Are you finished? I must admit, I find tantrums rather tiresome. I will wait, but not much longer." Bessie's firm tone drained Eva of her temper and left her feeling empty and lost. She sat in one of Bessie's overstuffed chairs.

Magically, a glass of whisky appeared next to her.

"Drink up. Whose rose did you accept?"

"The Duke of Amherst's." She spat out his name and then drank the whisky.

"I see. From what I observed, you and Drew were getting along quite well. What seems to be the problem?"

Eva looked up at her, confused and frustrated. "Surely you already know. He revealed his role in my family's downfall."

"Ah, I see. Then you didn't let him finish his story."

"What else is there for him to say?"

Bessie took a seat next to her. She reached out and held Eva's hand.

"I saw the expression on your face throughout the evening. He may be playful, but there was something beyond his masculinity that attracted you. Can you tell me what that was?"

"There was nothing else." She gazed at Bessie. The woman knew she was lying. "He is a rogue and a seducer, and I allowed myself to be taken in by his charms."

"Yet, when you walked away, in your case ran, were you truly disappointed? Did you still desire him?"

Eva's chin trembled as she struggled with her emotions. "I'm confused. I need to…"

"What you truly need is the complete truth, not the half-truths, or illusions you create in your mind to hold onto something that isn't real."

Bessie reached behind her and retrieved a ledger sheet. She handed it to Eva. The name was concealed.

"Do you have any idea what that is?"

Eva glanced at her. "It's the ledger sheet of a very wealthy person. You've covered the name."

"Every month for the last six years, funds have been deposited into an account as reparation for a failed investment." Bessie removed the paper hiding the name.

Eva gasped. "My father... but I don't understand," she murmured, as she studied the intricate details of the activity. "Some of these dates were before his passing."

"Drew worked tirelessly and repaid your father every penny within six months. But your father wouldn't accept his apology or the money. Drew continued to deposit funds into the account, known only to your father's solicitor. Drew's father never dissolved the partnership. However, your father instructed his solicitor never to tell anyone and never to use the money. Your father said it could lie there and rot.

"What you and your mother went through was not Drew's doing at all. It was your father's stubbornness. I've known Drew and the Amherst family for more than two decades. I witnessed the hardships he faced when that investment went bad. My investments were tied up as well.

"Not only did Drew bring those who defrauded them to justice, but he was determined to repay every penny. And he did, and more."

"Your father was a proud man, and he was rightfully angry. However, his refusal to provide for you and your mother with shelter, food, and the knowledge of the reparation that had been made is inexcusable."

Eva stood, glanced toward the door, and contemplated what to do next. She turned back to Bessie. "He'll never forgive me. What if he's not there?"

"He can't go anywhere. The doors don't open for another five minutes." Bessie retrieved the discarded rose from the floor and handed it to Eva. "Now, it's your turn to present a rose. Who will you choose?"

Eva hugged the woman tightly and rushed out of the room. She sprinted back to the private room, praying that Drew hadn't gone.

As she came down the corridor, she saw that the door remained open, and her heart skipped a beat. She stood at the threshold. "Drew?" she called out, scanning the dimly lit room. Eventually, her eyes fell upon a silhouette by the window. He turned to face her.

Moonlight filtered through the window, casting a soft glow upon them before it was hidden behind a cloud. Eva stepped into the room and closed the door behind her. She turned the lock. Her hand found support on the bookcase, as she struggled to find her way in the shadows.

"Why did you come back?" His voice thundered from behind her. She turned to face him.

"I came back to hear the rest of your story. You didn't bring me here," Eva gestured at the room, "only to tell me you ruined my family."

A tense silence hung in the air as their gazes clashed. Drew pressed his hand against the bookcase, his body leaning closer to hers until their breaths mingled, his words lingering against her skin. "Why do you care what I have to say?"

"Because tonight's discussion revolved around understanding and forgiveness." Her voice was so low he could hardly hear her.

"Why should I concern myself with your forgiveness?" His voice trembled.

Her gaze shifted between his face and the floor, but she mustered her courage. Lifting her chin to meet his gaze, she found it void of the earlier fervor, longing, and passion they shared.

"I cannot control your forgiveness. I can only control my own. I want to know the rest of the story so that I can forgive myself for being foolish."

"What do you want to know, Lady Eva?" The use of her title was a bolt that hit its mark.

She took a deep breath and steeled herself for the answer. "Everything."

"I'll give you the abridged version so we both can be done with this. I worked tirelessly to repay all the funds. I sought out the scoundrel who deceived me and made him face the consequences. However, your father rejected my attempts at restitution. He turned a deaf ear to me and my father's pleas. Instead, he allowed his house and estate to be seized through foreclosure. He dismissed his loyal staff, and let his wife and daughter suffer."

No. Eva couldn't bring herself to believe such a claim. Not her father. Without a second thought, she raised her hand and delivered a resounding slap across his face.

"Now, that wasn't what a fine lady would do." His eyes blazed with a new intensity. She attempted to push him away, but he held his ground, his hand cupping the back of her head. He drew her close. The force pressed her against the bookcase, causing the books to tumble to the floor.

Her heart pounded in her chest as she witnessed the silver-gray hue return to his eyes. Her breath quickened with the rekindling of their earlier passion.

He lowered his head, closing the distance between them, and in that heated moment, Eva gently took his head and pulled him closer, their mouths meeting in an eager and possessive kiss. She broke the kiss and gazed into his eyes, uncertain if this would be their final embrace.

Eva, filled with determination, slipped her hands under his jacket, relishing the sensation of his firm muscles. Her touch didn't cease. Her hands trailed up to his shoulders, urgently removing his coat.

He deepened their kiss, his lips seeking hers. Swiftly, he unlaced the back of her gown, the fabric slipping from Eva's shoulders and cascading to the floor, leaving her standing before him.

He drew in a breath, captivated by her beauty, his gaze intense as he whispered in her ear, "Do you forgive yourself?"

Her heart pounded so loudly she was sure he could hear it. Swallowing the knot of emotion in her throat, Eva mustered the strength to respond, tears welling up in her eyes. She didn't want to show her vulnerability, not to him. "I was foolish to come here tonight, thinking I could control anything. I was foolish to believe that nobody cared about my family. Madam Pembroke certainly did, and now I see that you did too. I was foolish to think...."

He interrupted her, tenderly kissing her before he pulled away slightly. "To think what?"

"I was foolish to think you would fall in love with me. You were here to tell me the truth, and for that, I am grateful."

"Why were you here?" he asked.

She closed her eyes as tears welled up. A hot knot in her throat got bigger and made speaking more difficult. "I thought I was here to find the true Eva and not the seamstress—"

Before she could finish her sentence, he pressed his lips against hers, silencing her. His hands ran up her torso and stroked her bosom. He wouldn't let her pull away.

His hand found the hem of her chemise as he stroked her thigh. Her body quivered beneath his touch. The intensity of their connection ignited a whirlwind of emotions, leaving her breathless. He pulled away gently. The warmth and taste of his kiss lingered.

Without a word, he lifted her into his arms and gently laid her down on the chaise. She gazed up at him with anticipation and longing.

"You did find the true Eva, Lady Eva Barnard, daughter of Lord and Lady Glenshire," he whispered. "The angel who stole my heart."

At that moment, as their lips touched, the world outside Lyon's Gate Manor faded away. Time seemed to stand still, and with every breath and every touch, they surrendered to the overwhelming power of forgiveness, redemption, and a love that would endure forever.

The End

Additional Dragonblade books by Author Ruth A. Casie

The Ladies of Sommer-by-the-Sea Series
The Lady and Her Quill (Book 1)
The Lady and the Spy (Book 2)
The Lady and Her Duke (Book 3)

Pirates of Britannia Series
Donald
Hugh
Graham
The Pirate's Jewel
The Pirate's Redemption

About Ruth A. Casie

There was never a time when *USA Today* Bestseller, RUTH A. CASIE hasn't had a story in her head. When she was little, she and her older sister would dress up and act out the ones Ruth creative. Today, Ruth writes exciting and beautifully told legendary historical romances that are both rich and engaging. Her stories feature strong women and the men who deserve them, endearing flaws and all. Her stories are full of, 'edge of your seat' suspense, mind-boggling drama, and a forever-after romance.

She lives in New Jersey with her hero, three empty bedrooms and a growing number of incomplete counted cross-stitch projects. Before she found her voice, she was a speech therapist (pun intended), client liaison for a corrugated manufacturer, and vice president at an international bank where she was a product/marketing manager, but her favorite job is the one she's doing now—writing romance. Ruth hopes her stories become your favorite adventure.

Fun facts about Ruth:

1. She filled her passport up in one year.
2. She has three series. The Druid Knight is a time travel romance. The Stelton Legacy is a historical fantasy about the seven sons of a seventh son. Havenport Romances are contemporary romantic suspense stories. She also writes for the Pirates of Britannia connected world.

3. She did a rap with her son to "How Many Trucks Can a Tow Truck Tow If a Tow Truck Could Tow Trucks."
4. When she cooks she dances around the kitchen.
5. Her sudoku books is in the bathroom and that's all she'll say about that!

Social Media Links:

Website:

ruthacasie.com

Instagram:

instagram.com/ruthacasie

Facebook private reader's page, Casie Café:

facebook.com/groups/963711677128537

Facebook Author Page:

facebook.com/RuthACasie

Twitter:

twitter.com/RuthACasie

BookBub:

bookbub.com/authors/ruth-a-casie

Amazon:

amazon.com/author/ruthacasie

Goodreads:

goodreads.com/author/show/4792909.Ruth_A_Casie

YouTube:

bit.ly/3hI5eQr

In Pursuit of a Lyon

by Sandra Sookoo

Chapter One

January 1, 1817
Littlefield House
Marylebone

"The post has arrived, my lady."

The sound of her butler's voice pulled Astrid Basinger—Viscountess of Littlefield—from her current task of writing a letter. "Thank you, Benton."

"There is another missive, but it didn't arrive in the post. Neither did I admit a courier."

"I'm sure it was merely overlooked." She collected the three envelopes from a silver salver. "If I have an inquiry, I'll ring for you."

"Of course, my lady."

A breeze came into the morning room despite it being January. She lifted her head while the butler departed, for she would always choose fresh air. The faint aroma of bread from her favorite bakery a few streets over reached her nose, and she smiled.

Though behind on her correspondence, she always looked forward to the daily post, for it had been a trifle lonely since her husband had died three years before.

But then, her life had often felt that way. She hadn't come from the *ton*, and neither had she been born or bred with that lifestyle in mind, yet somehow—a simple twist of fate perhaps—her whole life had changed with one little act of kindness.

It had become the cornerstone of her existence, and one she strove to repay and push forward at every opportunity.

With a sigh, she turned her attention to the few envelopes in her hand. An invitation to a rout next month, a letter she already knew would be breezy and full of happy news from a friend tucked away in the Hampsteadshire countryside, and oh! The third envelope was quite different. Her heartbeat accelerated and her hand shook. Her name and title had been written with a bold yet feminine style. The back featured the seal of a lion pressed into green wax.

After tossing the other envelopes to her desk, Astrid gingerly opened the envelope and unfolded the single piece of paper that had a thick feel and gold flecks woven into the fiber. Then she frowned, for there was nothing on the paper except for the initials "BDL" in a flowery script with a sprig of holly beneath. But she knew, oh goodness she knew, what this was! Everyone within the *beau monde* did. It was an Invocation Mystère, or essentially a golden ticket to the year's most sought-after and forbidden event, the Mystère Masque, held at the infamous Lyon's Den gaming hell, to celebrate Mrs. Dove-Lyon's birthday. She was the proprietor of the establishment, and though very few people in the *ton* had ever met her directly—and if they did, she was always veiled and unseen in the shadows—she was never anyone's close contemporary. And guests could never randomly attend this ball, for it was invitation only.

The trouble was, no one knew who would receive one of the golden tickets, nor did they know why or even how they arrived to the addresses chosen.

"Why was *I* given one this year?" Ever year since she'd married her husband, she'd heard hushed rumors regarding this masked ball, but no one she'd ever known in her circle had received an invitation.

Yet one *had* arrived for *her*. Quickly, she glanced into a small, gilt-framed mirror that rested on her desktop. Over the years, she'd come into her looks. Strawberries and cream complexion. Dark brown hair the color of French chocolate. A few wrinkles on her brow, but then life had been difficult for many years, which had added a touch of grief and experience deep in the backs of her hazel eyes.

Not bad. Time had been kind.

Slowly, Astrid stood as she stared at the blank piece of stationery. Beyond being among the favored guests invited to attend such a scandalous masquerade—all the proper denizens of the *beau monde* shunned the event as well as the people who indulged—she would be afforded an opportunity to finally meet Sutton Waincroft, the Marquess of Rockwood, and that was the real reason for the sudden acceleration of her pulse.

For years the man had been largely unattainable, but she had long fancied him. Not for his title, money, position, or looks but because he worked tirelessly in the House of Lords for reform and change. More often than not, he spent time with London's poor and less fortunate. He orchestrated feeding the hungry every Sunday afternoon without praise, without fanfare, and oftentimes he did so while in disguise.

The only reason Astrid knew about his charitable efforts was because she had lived in the rundown and derelict neighborhoods of the Dials. As a young woman of sixteen, she'd come to London with her mother after her father had died of a disease of the lungs. Though Astrid and her mother were down on their luck, she was adamant that Town would offer a better life for them both. Yet determination didn't always get one that far. She and her mother worked as seamstresses for a couple of years, but then her dear mother had succumbed to a bout of influenza that had swept through the area.

Her death had hit Astrid hard, but when one struggled every day merely to survive, there was very little time for grieving.

That was when she'd met the marquess. His benevolence and charitable visits to the Dials had kept her alive. Not that she'd been ready to succumb to death, but she hadn't thought the meager income she'd made as a seamstress would continue to pay for rent and food. During his weekly visits to her location, he would pick a few young women, send them to his townhouse, and had his staff give them baths and toilettes as well as a fresh set of clothing. Then he would send the chosen few to a woman in Town who would offer domestic training for household work.

It was an invaluable service, and one every girl and young woman hoped would happen to her. Each Sunday without fail Lord Rockwood would visit. Not only was he handsome, he was patient and kind. One day, when she wasn't toiling at the shop, he'd picked her for said training, and she thought she'd died and gone to heaven.

Finally, her fate had changed!

A month later, she saw him again. He spoke kindly to her and asked of her progress, and she'd fallen in love with his sapphire blue eyes and the way his smile was slightly lopsided and the way the delicate skin at the corners of his eyes crinkled when something delighted him. Probably ten years her senior, he was easily the most attractive man she'd ever known, and she had passed many nights with him in her dreams. There were worse things she could have visit her in the night. The marquess was inordinately pleased when she landed her first position, even wished her well. Then he'd told her he was due to be married, and her heart had broken, even though she legitimately had no chance of ever having a life with the man.

Faithfully, she'd read about his nuptials in the paper she'd gotten thirdhand in the house where she'd found employment as a maid. Unfortunately, the lord's son was a womanizer and had cornered her one day in the butler's pantry. He'd taken what she hadn't wished to give, and because of that, she'd lost that all-important position and therefore her only connection—however fleeting—to the marquess.

At twenty and with no prospects, she'd become a courtesan for a brief time. That living had kept her busy enough and had allowed her to mingle and meet with various members of the demimonde as well as the *ton*, but she never moved in the same circles as Lord Ravenwood, and eventually she'd stopped looking for him at the opera or other places where her protectors had taken her.

At the age of three and twenty, fate had interfered once more. She'd become the mistress to a viscount, and unexpectedly they had fallen in love. The dear man had more coin than brains, but he was adorable and slightly absentminded, and what was more, he genuinely loved her. Marrying him had brought her into society, and not a day had gone by where she didn't thank God as well as the marquess for removing her from that horrid start in the Dials.

However, marrying the viscount had also put her in the same circles—at times—as the marquess. Every so often she attended a society event and caught a glimpse of him and his pretty wife, and they seemed happy together, which was wonderful, for she felt the same about her husband. Life was so much more than she could have ever imagined, and never did she forget the kindness and compassion Lord Rockwood had shown her, and the nudge he'd given to remove her from her old life.

She'd had three remarkable years with her viscount, and during that time, he'd been quite attentive to her in the bedroom. It was through his guidance she'd been introduced to toys that enhanced bed sport, and she had taken to such unorthodox play with aplomb.

Unfortunately, a riding accident had stolen him away from her. Though they hadn't been blessed with children, the life she'd led had been amazing. Now, at the age of nine and twenty, all she had ever wished to do was thank the marquess for saving her life with his grace and compassion. Because of him, she worked with a couple of her own charities—one of which involved helping young women who'd fallen from grace—and wanted to show others the same mercy as he had given her once upon a time. It had merely been one way for her to honor him.

A call from the street yanked Astrid from her musings.

Once more she glanced at the paper clutched tightly in her hand. She didn't know how or even why the invitation had found its way to her, but she supposed it didn't matter, for fate had again interfered in her life. The Lyon's Den was usually out of reach for many of the *ton's* elite—Mrs. Dove-Lyon was quite mysterious had a very specific design for her clientele, or so the gossip went—yet for one night she would see the inside of the scandalous gaming hell and perhaps, if she were fortunate, she might come into contact with the Marquess of Rockwood, for it was rumored he frequented the club and had done so with regularity after his wife had died a couple of years back.

Finally, she could thank him in person. If she were honest with herself, she'd never quite forgotten the *tendre* she'd carried for him over the years. She fanned her suddenly heated face with the envelope and sheet of paper. There was nothing in societal rules that said she couldn't thank the man while indulging in a dance with him. If there happened to be an opportunity to lead him into a shadowy corner and kiss him, who could blame her? He was an attractive widower who might perhaps enjoy spending a scandalous night with a woman whose life had turned around because of him. And perhaps, if fate were with her one last time, she might even pleasure him with some of her favorite toys in the bargain.

"Oh, dear." Astrid looked at the invitation again and allowed herself a small smile. The masquerade would be held in four months' time. "I need to have a gown made up as well as a mask, perhaps remove some of Littlefield's jewelry from the safe for cleaning." She needed an outfit that would be sure to catch the marquess's eye as well as show her charms to advantage. After all, she had waited the whole of her life to meet this man.

Now that she had coin and connections at her disposal, there wasn't anything she couldn't do.

Chapter Two

January 1, 1817
Rockwood House
St. James's Place
London, England

I'LL BE DAMNED.

Sutton Waincroft—Marquess of Rockwood—stared at the blank piece of stationery he held in his hand. Flecks of gold were imbedded into the thick paper, and the only clue as to the sender was a seal bearing the scrolled initials "BDL" with a sprig of holly beneath.

It was an Invocation Mystère, or essentially an invitation to the year's most sought-after and forbidden event, the Mystère Masque, which was put on at the Lyon's Den gaming hell, to celebrate Mrs. Dove-Lyon's birthday. Every year she held a masquerade ball, and it was as daring, scandalous, and risqué as anything a dedicated rogue could envision. This particular ball would be held on April 1st, but even at this early date, excitement buzzed at the base of his spine.

Yes, he was a regular attendee to the Lyon's Den, for he needed that release to forget what he toiled with on a weekly basis, to forget the disparate gulf separating the classes in London. Sometimes he lost huge amounts of coin; sometimes he amassed a fortune or two in a night, but always there were drinking, gambling, and courtesans if a man wished to seek a different sort of release.

Since his wife had died a little over two years before, he wasn't too proud to admit that he'd utilized the women at the Lyon's Den a few times. After all, he had needs and he wasn't in the market to take a mistress. Though he'd adored having a wife, his marriage had been arranged by their parents while they'd both been in leading strings. The union had experienced its ups and downs, but eventually they had learned to appreciate and even love each other. Though they had discovered they'd been increasing several times over the course of the marriage, none of those pregnancies had resulted in full-term or live births.

Disappointment had followed, of course, and more than a couple of midwives as well as a doctor had told them his wife would never be able to bear a child, but none of them could tell them what exactly ailed her. Such was the minimal knowledge of the female body.

They'd continued on the best they could, but there was always a pall of depression hanging over them. He'd never wavered in his commitment and charities, one of which had been visiting the Seven Dials neighborhoods and distributing food, blankets, and even nominal medicines and tinctures when needed. The young men he thought would do well with a life removed from the area, he sent to a gentleman he knew who had retired as a butler but now owned a school of sorts. They were cleaned up, given a medical examination, and then were taught how to be footmen. Once the training was complete, they were given their first positions within households throughout Mayfair. Whether they wished to work hard and dedicate their lives to service was up to them, but at least Sutton had given them a chance and the tools to better themselves.

The same could be said for young women he'd hand-picked during his numerous visits. They were sent to a woman in London who looked after them, gave them the same treatment as the men, but then they were trained into domestic staff positions such as maids, housekeepers, or even cooks depending on where their skills lay. Once the woman in charge was satisfied at their progress, she placed them into homes throughout London.

It was the least he could do with his time and coin. Most of the people who lived in poverty and struggle didn't deserve to be there, but the horrid way London—and even England—was divided and structured made certain to keep the downtrodden in the gutters while the titled and rich gained even more fortune and property. Such disparity needed to change, and he worked tirelessly in the House of Lords for just that, but many men opposed progressive views and wished to keep that divide out of fear they might lose their stations or privilege.

Still, he persisted, and he wouldn't stop until there were laws that made daily living better for everyone. At the age of nine and thirty, it felt imperative that he work tirelessly for that change, because he desperately hoped the future would be made brighter for those who needed help the most.

Or all his efforts might be for naught, and then what would he have left?

The sound of footsteps at the door to the drawing room jogged him from his musings. He glanced up in time to see his best friend enter the room. "Ah, Crispin. I wasn't expecting you."

"That is quite the fun of a pop-in call, hmm?" He held the title of Viscount of Wynnefield, and he recently had come into it, for his father had been violently murdered while in his mistress's bed.

The man was Sutton's opposite in every way. Where he had blond hair, his friend's was as dark as a raven's wing and prone to curl at inopportune moments. Sutton's blue eyes were a touch more kind than Crispin's gray ones, and where he stood at six feet, the viscount was several inches shorter but more robust in form. And to top it off, the viscount wore a pair of spectacles set in round, silver-wired frames. For as long as Sutton had known him, he could never see past the end of his nose. Literally, not figuratively.

"What can I do for you, my friend?" Once more he glanced at the blank piece of stationery as the flecks of gold glinted in the afternoon sunlight.

"I came by to see if you might have received a very puzzling blank sheet of paper dotted with gold." He removed said stationery from an interior pocket of his jacket of blue superfine. Then he cocked an eyebrow over the spectacles' frame. "I am not a regular at the gaming hell, but I make my presence known with risky wagers enough that she must remember my name. Does this mean I have finally been invited to Mrs. Dove-Lyon's birthday extravaganza?"

"That is indeed what it means." He grinned. "So have I, as a matter of fact. Second time for me."

"Oh?" Wynnefield's other eyebrow soared. "When was the first time?"

"A few years before I married." Then he frowned, for it suddenly made sense as to why. "I suppose during the years of my marriage, I was considered off-limits by the proprietor. Not much she could do with a happily married man." It was no secret Mrs. Dove-Lyon arranged matches for many of the men who came to her club, and the women she arranged for them to marry didn't exactly have the best of reputations. And the harder a rich man fell, the better.

"So why did you receive one now?"

"I have no idea." Sutton shook his head and glanced over Wynnesfield's paper. It was as blank as his own, only containing the initials and seals. "Do you plan to attend?"

"Of course! Every year I have heard rumors surrounding this

birthday masquerade and how risqué it is." Excitement gleamed in his eyes. "Now I have the opportunity to witness everything firsthand."

"It does have potential to be quite the scandalous affair." As Sutton moved across the room, he tucked his own letter away. Once he reached the sideboard, he lifted a cut-crystal decanter. "Brandy?"

"Have I ever turned down a glass of your finest?" The viscount sauntered over to his location. When Sutton handed him a glass then poured a measure of the liquor into it, Wynnesfield nodded his thanks. "The question of the hour is, are you going to attend? You rarely go out in society anymore, and visiting your clubs isn't the same. There are no women there."

"Well, there are but—"

The viscount huffed. "You know what I mean. No women of breeding or character. No heiresses or vapid beauties who are willing to trade fortunes for a chance at being married."

"Perhaps, but the masquerade isn't about courting or asking Mrs. Dove-Lyon to indulge in matchmaking." It was well known that the widow enjoyed tricking men into marrying women who were all wrong for them. "The Mystère Masque is to put the attention on dear old Bessie as well as to provide a night of debauchery with dinner following at midnight." He shrugged. "Which means I need to decide if that is something I'm interested in."

The viscount snorted. "Heaven forbid you have a mask made and then go share a suggestive dance or two with a beautiful, anonymous woman." He grinned as he sipped his brandy. "And I suppose you are much too noble to take said woman to bed for nothing more than mutual pleasure, physical release, and the joy of a good fuck without it meaning anything."

Heat crept up the back of Sutton's neck. "I never modeled myself into such a person."

"No, you haven't, but you do have a bit of a reputation. An

honorable man. A man who puts his charitable pursuits ahead of all else." Wynnesfield lowered his voice. "A man who is more or less hiding from life, so he won't suffer any further disappointments."

For long moments, he stared at his friend. Slowly, he nodded and finished his brandy in one gulp. The burn of the liquor in this throat was a welcome distraction. "What you say is true. I haven't exactly been myself since Charlotte died." Hell, since the last few years of their marriage after the last babe was born far-too premature to survive.

"Then attend the masquerade." Compassion shadowed Wynnesfield's eyes. He set his glass on the polished sideboard. "See where the night—and a mysterious woman—might lead."

"Perhaps you are right. It's time to start living again beyond my charities and politics."

Unbidden, an image of a heart-shaped face swam into his mind's eye. Hazel eyes filled with gratitude and embarrassment, a sprinkling of freckles across her upper cheeks and the bridge of her nose, a gentle smile with red lips that still had the power to arouse him, all belonging to a young woman he'd rescued years ago. As soon as he'd seen her, he knew she didn't belong in the Dials. Hell, she was a treasure in the midst of the muck, and if he could turn anyone's life around, he'd hoped it would be hers. In fact, eventually, according to his sources, she'd done quite well for herself when she'd married into the *ton*.

Was it possible she might have received a golden invitation to the masquerade as well? The thought of that sent a shiver of pure need down his spine, and that was something he hadn't felt for far too long.

Whatever happened to her after she married?

"Good." The viscount clapped a hand to Sutton's shoulder and gave it a hearty shake. "You are not a Lyon for nothing, my friend. Let yourself go during the masquerade and enjoy everything to the hilt. There is plenty of time to return to your world of crusading for justice and equality after the fact."

Sutton's lips twitched. "Can I help it that I adore what I do? Helping others is much like an obsession after a while."

"So can a night of indulging in filthy, hot, uninhibited depravity with a masked stranger whom you will never see again." The viscount winked. "Or perhaps you might, which will make that addiction even more powerful, but now that I know you are committed to attending, I wouldn't miss it."

"Such gammon you speak." But he couldn't help his grin, for it was past time for him to do something wholly reckless and completely irresponsible merely for the enjoyment of it. "Don't come crying to me if you make a cake of yourself and land headfirst into scandal. I shan't pull you out of it."

"Who says I'll want out?" Wynnesfield chuckled. "That is the glory of flying too close to the flame that is the Lyon's Den. Sooner or later, we all know we'll be burned, but oh, how wicked that inferno will be before we are singed too much and have to reap the consequences."

"Ah, how I can refuse with such an incentive as that?" Anticipation danced over his skin. "I think a visit to my tailor is in order."

"Quite." A wicked gleam came into the viscount's eyes. "Now, walk me through the layout of the upper stories. I have only been accustomed to the gaming floor itself…"

Chapter Three

April 1, 1817
The Lyon's Den
London, England
Night of the Mystère Masque

Finally, the premier social event of the year had arrived, and while all of London's movers and shakers longed to attend, because of the highly selective nature of the party, many had been excluded, so they hid their disappointment beneath ire and vitriol. However, none of that mattered to Astrid, for she *had* received a golden invitation, and she wouldn't hesitate to make use of it.

The gown she'd commissioned fit like a dream. Due to the risqué nature of the event, she wanted a dress to match. Hers was made of a red silk and satin blend that featured a low bodice. The material had been shot through with golden silk. Tiny red glass beads and red spangles had been meticulously sewn all over the skirting. Small red feathers bordered the neckline and even still, it was anyone's guess if her nipples would remain covered while dancing, but she wanted the daring bodice to match the attitude of the event. The same feathers decorated the bottom hem of the gown. The slippers were also of red silk and gold thread, and the domino mask was of red satin, decorated and covered with the same beads, spangles, and even smaller red feathers. Around her neck she wore a black velvet choker complete with a round ruby broach pinned to the ribbon. Tiny diamonds glittered around that central stone—the last gift she'd received from her husband. Somehow, it seemed fitting to wear it now.

It was a costume designed to make certain she was noticed…by the marquess.

Already, she was late, for the ball had been slated to begin at nine o'clock, but there was an inordinate amount of traffic ahead. Many carriages wished to attain the same destination as she did, and she was forced to wait as each vehicle had a turn in unloading its occupants.

As her carriage pulled up to the building, the blue-painted façade caught her eye and sent shivers of anticipation down her spine. So many rumors had flown through the *ton* regarding this gaming establishment that it had the hush of anything could happen, and she hoped it did. After alighting, she told her driver that if she needed his services later, she would send for him, then with a deep breath and her golden ticket tucked into her reticule, she went up to the unassuming front door of the club.

The panel swung open as soon as she approached. She nodded to the burly attendant—who would no doubt toss out anyone who wasn't invited—and went past him. Through the eye holes of her mask, she could already discern a crush of people, but just after the man who'd opened the door, a woman dressed in a black gown that shimmered with jet beads asked to see her invitation.

With an air of smug excitement, Astrid gleefully produced the somewhat crinkled piece of gold-flecked stationery. The woman nodded, and the paper was securely tucked back into the reticule.

"Thank you."

"Please proceed to the main gaming room. Dancing is already underway. Fireworks to celebrate Mrs. Dove-Lyon's birthday will go off at eleven; supper will be served at midnight."

"Fireworks? How exciting!" Though she hadn't wished to come off as a star-struck schoolgirl, Astrid couldn't help but be caught up in amazement. She'd only ever seen fireworks once before in her life, and that was well after she'd come to London.

"Yes, well, the whole evening is sure to be like nothing else you have ever experienced." The woman shooed her along. "Enjoy."

The low buzz of conversation blended with the lively notes of a country reel played by a string quartet with a violin accompaniment, punctuated here and there by laughter. A large crystal chandelier in the center of the ceiling glittered from the light of many candles. Other candles were set in holders and sconces throughout the open space. Round tables and their matching wooden chairs had been shoved to one side of the room; obviously, the gaming tables were not in use for the evening, for the bulk of the high-polished floor had been reserved for dancing and mingling.

Interestingly enough, there were no chairs set up on the other side of the room where potted ferns and hothouse flowers brought needed splashes of color. There would be no unwanted wallflowers here, for everyone had been specifically invited. It was quite heady knowledge, indeed.

Everywhere she looked, jewels flashed in the dim light, gowns of rich and luxurious fabrics swayed, couples danced or talked, crystal clinked as copious champagne was poured, and the dark evening clothes of the gentlemen added a needed contrast to the jewel-toned dresses. Men and women alike had donned elaborately decorated masks, so it was difficult to discern anyone's true identity. As she continued on her tour around the perimeter, she caught sight of a woman in a lovely golden gown that shimmered and winked with her every footstep. A wonderfully embellished golden mask obscured a good portion of her face, but her lips were a ruby red obtained by the use of cosmetics. She gave off the air of confidence and poise, so she must be someone of importance to the gaming hell. When their gazes accidentally met, a tiny smile curved those lips in welcome. *Was* she Mrs. Dove-Lyon? There was no way of knowing for certain, and the next time Astrid glanced in that direction, the woman had disappeared.

Odd, to be sure, but the woman in gold was quickly forgotten when her notice landed on a gentleman who stood at average height. Yes, he was dressed in the same tailcoat and black trousers as every other man, but the black satin waistcoat embroidered with silver swirls drew her in. His blond hair gleamed like a golden Adonis beneath the light of so many candles, but she would recognize those sapphire eyes beneath his black mask that glimmered with jet beads and thin silver metal scrollwork anywhere.

He's here!

Immediately, her heartbeat accelerated. Heat went through her cheeks, for she hadn't seen the marquess unless in passing ever since she'd married Littlefield. As the last notes for the country reel ended and the couples on the makeshift dance floor broke away, Astrid hastened her steps toward Rockwood. The last thing she wanted was for another woman to turn his head, steal him away from her before she had her chance.

And he was popular indeed, for a few other ladies—all masked and clearly on the prowl—had descended upon him, straining to be the one he chose to dance the next set with, because, of course, it was a waltz, and a Continental or American-style, at that, which meant dancers had more freedom to be close to each other's bodies than they would in the traditional yet still controversial Viennese-style waltz. While the masks were supposed to render the attendees unrecognizable, there was something about the man that couldn't remain hidden.

If she arrived before him slightly breathless, she tried not to show it, and had to elbow her way through the crowd. Daring much, Astrid threw a look of victory to the other women as she put a gloved hand on his sleeve. "Since it appears you haven't been taken yet, I choose you as my partner for this set."

"Ah!" His eyebrows rose. Surprise reflected in the depths of his eyes. "Far be it for me to disappoint a lady." The grin he gave the others sent flutters into her lower belly, especially as he roved his gaze up and down her form. "I haven't danced a waltz in an age, but I am very much looking forward to doing so again."

No sooner had he led her to an open spot on the floor, slipped a gloved hand to the small of her back and held her hand with his other one than the opening notes of the song burst into the air. Before she could properly acclimate to being in his arms, the marquess had set them into motion.

"That is quite a provocative gown." While he said it, his regard dropped to her décolletage that was clearly on display. "You seem vaguely familiar to me. Have we met before?"

"Yes, we have, but it was some years ago." In the process of trying not to answer in such a breathless voice, her tones were rather more husky than usual. Would he remember? And if he didn't, would she tell him?

"Mmm, then I look forward to solving the mystery." The deep rumble of his voice never failed to send gooseflesh rushing over her skin. Over the years, the sound of that voice had woken her in the dead of night, and she would fantasize that he was in bed with her.

For several heartbeats, they went through the steps in silence, but with every turn, he managed to pull her closer and closer until her breasts rubbed against his chest. By the time they reached the next corner, their hips brushed, and the hand at the small of her back had slipped to the curve of her rear.

"Do you have plans for the remainder of the evening?" Though she could hardly get the words out, for his scent of the earth before the snow flew was quite intoxicating, Astrid tried not to let her insecurity destroy her chance.

"That largely depends on what happens between now and the next half hour." The marquess tugged her a bit closer and put his lips to the shell of her ear. "However, I can tell you I wouldn't mind seeing you in nothing except that choker and perhaps your stockings." With every word, those two pieces of flesh brushed her skin and set off an avalanche of shivers down her spine.

Heat enveloped her, and when she stumbled a step, he took it as an opportunity to haul her tighter against his body. "That could be arranged, as long as you are equally undressed." If she didn't dare now, she'd never capture his curiosity. She moved the hand resting on his shoulder to his nape and furrowed her fingers through the hair there. "Perhaps with your wrists restrained and you utterly and *completely* at my mercy."

"Ah." His eyes rounded with shock but darkened with desire behind his mask. "How intriguing. Is that a promise?"

"It could be. To start. Why don't you procure a glass of champagne, and we shall discover that together." The words came out of their own accord; the daring made her reckless. What would his hands, his lips, feel like on her body, between her thighs?

"Your wish is my command." Once the waltz drew to a close, his hand was once more on the small of her back as he ushered her across the room where a footman waited with flutes of champagne on a silver tray. With a small grin playing over his mouth, the marquess plucked up one of the glasses. "To risqué delights in the offing tonight." He raised it to his lips and took a sip before offering it to her.

"May it prove a night to remember." Watching him the whole time, Astrid fit her lips to the exact place on the flute from where he'd drunk. She took her own sip. "Imagine how lovely it would be to lap the remainder of this from your chest, your abdomen..." In a softer tone, she finished, "Or perhaps sucking it from your hard, straining member." And she ran her gaze down the length of his body to pause at his crotch before finding his gaze once more. "Are you game?"

"You tell me." The man took the glass from her then proceeded to dribble some of the bubbly wine directly onto the swells of her breasts above the feathers lining her bodice. "Just a little taste, hmm?" No matter they were in full view of everyone in the makeshift ballroom, he dipped his head, licked at the moisture on her skin. When she gave into a shiver, he hooked a forefinger into her bodice. It didn't take much effort to tug the fabric down to reveal an already pebbled nipple, and when she gasped, he sucked that bud into the warm cavern of his mouth, then gave it a light, fleeting nip that had hot need rushing between her thighs.

There was no turning back. She pulled away, and as she put her bodice back into place, she started toward the door. "Upstairs. Now."

Chapter Four

Amused that she wished to take the lead in what was sure to be an unforgettable tumble between the sheets, Sutton guided her through the corridors and to a narrow set of wooden stairs. Though she seemed all too familiar to him, he would only know more when she removed the mask, but right now, the delicious mystery enhanced his awareness of her and the raw desire coursing through his veins.

That tiny taste of her when he'd dared take a nipple into his mouth in the makeshift ballroom had fired his lust, and he hadn't realized how much he needed a night like this for the release and the forbidden excitement. He halted her on the stairs just past the second landing, trapped her between the wall and his body, and then claimed her lips in a hard kiss designed to keep that arousal front and center. To his surprise and delight, she layered herself against him as she returned the kiss, and all too soon their tongues were mating, dancing, warring for dominance as they frantically drank from each other.

She wrenched away, her breathing slightly ragged. "I want you." The woman wasn't shy, he'd give her that, and as she stared up at him, the need in those hazel eyes tightened his length. He'd seen those eyes before.

Could it be? "Then, by all means, have at me." Curious and all too aroused, Sutton tugged on her hand, half-pulling, half-leading her up to the third floor. Midway along the corridor, he pressed on the brass door handle, assured that at this early hour, all rooms would be available. When the wooden panel swung inward, he ushered her inside. As soon as it snicked closed, he threw the lock, for he didn't wish to be disturbed this evening.

Across the small room, a decorative oil lamp burned at the lowest setting to flood the space with anemic golden light, but it was enough to illuminate the bed and would allow him to see every bit of her body. The rooms available for trysting at the Lyon's Den, though small, were luxuriously appointed and well-maintained and often cleaned. He was not certain which one of them moved first, but one second, they stood there staring at each other and the next they were intwined in an embrace, kissing as frantically as they had in the stairwell.

Never had he an immediate or heated reaction to a woman before, but he wasn't about to question it. Beneath this roof, anything could happen, and since every risqué thing was encouraged by attending the ball, he would take whatever was offered.

"Remove your clothes, if you please, Rockwood." That touch of desperation in her whispered command worked to further send the blood rushing into his shaft. With some impatience flitting across her face, she removed her gloves and threw them in the direction of the bed.

Ah, so then she knew who he was. Interesting. "As soon as I render you naked."

It was all too easy to tug at the laces at the back of her gown while she worked to shove the tailcoat from his frame. The garment slid from her body to puddle at her feet with naught but a sigh and a glimmer of beadwork.

"I adore unwrapping a woman who willingly offers herself up as a feast." Her stays fell away, and for the space of a few heartbeats, he paused to admire the dusky shadows of her hardened nipples as they thrust beneath the thin lawn of her chemise. Oh, yes, he would taste his fill of her, and soon. Then he removed that garment while she toed off her red satin slippers. "Now the mask." It took seconds to shed his own gloves and drop them to the floor.

"Not until you're nude." She stood there, unashamed, and completely confident in nothing but the choker, her stockings, and red-ribboned garters, which further worked to stoke the flames of his arousal.

"So demanding." Sutton tsked his tongue and toed off his shoes. He followed her command as quickly as he could. Cuffs, collar, and cravat were tossed indiscriminately to the floor. She undid the laces of his waistcoat and helped him to remove it. All the while, the faint scent of apple blossoms wafted to his nose from her close proximity.

The touch of her fingers as she assisted in removing his shirt had the power to sear his skin and tighten his shaft. When he attempted to claim her lips, she danced away, but the heat in her eyes was all too evident. She retrieved his cravat from the floor, and he gawked at the lines her body made as she moved. With nothing for it, he shucked out of his trousers and then removed the hosiery with more haste than finesse. Finally, he met her gaze.

"Masks, if you please. I want to see your face when I do unspeakable things to you." And the mask would be quite in the way once he pleasured her orally as he planned.

"I never knew you were so commanding, Your Lordship." She lifted her hands, and the second the glittering red mask came away from her face, he recognized her. How could he not? The sprinkling of freckles over the top of her cheeks and the bridge of her nose combined by those familiar hazel eyes made her unmistakable.

"Lady Littlefield." Knowing he'd soon bed the woman he'd long-ago helped into a better life worked to further tighten his shaft to the point of pain.

Surprise mixed with pleasure in her eyes, but she nodded. When he let his mask drop, she smiled, and the gesture tugged at his heart. "Lord Rockwood." She held up the cravat. "On the bed. As promised, I'm going to tie your wrists to the headboard, then show you how much I appreciated what you did for me years ago."

Damn and blast. Sutton nearly came prematurely, for her announcement and his imaginings of the same were far too arousing, but he complied, watched her while she busied herself with the task. "Please, call me Sutton." Once she'd finished, he tested his temporary bonds and grunted when they held not too loose and not too tight.

"Very well. I am Astrid."

What a lovely name. "Have you prior experience in such things?" Suddenly, he wanted to know everything about her, but perhaps not while pleasure was in the offing.

"My husband enjoyed adding spice and excitement to our play, especially after we had difficulties conceiving." She joined him on the bed, settled to one side of his legs. "It helped fill the void."

"I understand that all too well." He sucked in a breath as she leaned over him and pressed her lips to his abdomen.

"Then perhaps this session will help us both forget that even when life is better than where we began, it still has disappointments." As she talked, she danced her fingertips over his chest, swirled those digits through the mat of hair there.

As she explored, he looked his fill over her body. A very light sprinkling of freckles decorated her arms and torso; how had he never noticed before? When she flicked the flat disc of his nipple with her fingertip, pleasure streaked through his chest, and as she worried that sensitive nub, he strained at his bonds. Oh, to have her at his mercy and retaliate!

"Uncomfortable, Sutton?" Then she drew her hands downward, caressing them lightly over his skin, encouraged his legs apart, and once he did so, she used feather-weight touches along the inside of his thighs.

The sound of his name in her voice was heaven. Every touch was like fire and ice, each stroke a current of charged energy. Sutton tugged on his restraints, but they held fast, and still she continued to tease him with a slight smile curving her lips. "I like a man who doesn't take much effort to become hard and rampant." She changed positions and settled between his splayed legs. With a wink, Astrid caressed her fingers along his shaft.

"Ah!" He nearly vaulted off the bed. Wild sensation zipped through his body to concentrate in his member. His pulse pounded in his temples, an ever-present drumbeat as she fondled his stones, squeezed first one and then the other. "Gentle, else I'll embarrass myself and satisfy neither of us."

"I know what you'll like. All men do." Then she dipped her head down, licked the tip of his arousal, and while she held his stones firmly in her hand, she slowly, so damn slowly, took the length of him into the hot cavern of her mouth.

"Damn." The difference in temperature was astounding. The ambient coolness of the room contrasted with the heat surrounding his shaft, and a shiver racked his body. Up and down, she bobbed her head, taking him in deep, then easing off where she swirled her tongue beneath the head before going back down on him fully.

All the while, Astrid fondled and squeezed his stones until she found a particular rhythm she enjoyed. It wasn't long before he rocked his hips in time to her ministrations, and the closer he went to the edge of bliss, the more forceful his thrusts became. Once, when his tip found the back of her throat, she swallowed, and the light massage of those muscles nearly became his undoing.

"Astrid, hold." Already, the need to spend pulsed through his member.

She came off his prick with a *pop*. "Spoilsport, but I'm not nearly done with you."

That's what I'm afraid of. Shivers of anticipation moved over his body, but when she continued to caress and fondle, his breathing came all too fast. How was it possible this woman whom he'd only spoken to in passing years ago could have him hovering at pleasure's edge so quickly? Of course, he'd often dreamed of her, had taken himself in hand more than a few times after his wife had died to the image of those eyes alone.

Frenzied need lanced through him, yanking him from the thoughts when she stroked a fingertip along the thin, highly sensitive skin between his stones and anus. "Oh, God!" Sutton's hips bucked off the bed. He pulled at his bonds as exquisite pleasure cycled through his body. "Astrid, stop. I cannot survive much more." Already, his shaft ached and throbbed with immediate need.

And when he came, he damn well wanted it to be in her body, not all over her. At least, not this time. Perhaps if he had his way, there would be time enough to claim her like that later.

"Oh, I could torture you in many different carnal ways tonight if you let me." Her voice was a purr and would spell his doom if he wasn't careful. "I do so love drawing out the torture, for the payoff at the end is unbelievable."

"I have no doubt, and I'll even encourage it, but first untie me so that I might give you the same pleasure you've already given me." Above everything, he wanted to explore her, taste her, make her writhe with the same frantic, helpless agony, and if he were fortunate, send her through it all over again. There was something so stimulating about watching a woman come to completion.

One of her brown eyebrows rose. "Then this won't be the only coupling tonight?" That tiny gleam of hope in her hazel eyes fired his own curiosity.

"It will not be. You have my promise." He wasn't about to let her slip from his life so quickly. A woman didn't haunt a man's thoughts for years without him wanting to know why.

The smile that curved her slightly full lips almost had his control slipping. One of her hands drifted to a tightened nipple and she gave it a light pinch. It strained the limits of his sanity, but finally, she nodded. "I shall hold you to it, for I have long dreamed of being in your bed, of having your length fill me."

"You have?" Now it was his turn for breathlessness. He tugged at his restraints. How interesting.

"Oh, yes." Mischief danced in her eyes as she moved to straddle his chest then she leaned over him in a blatant attempt at teasing while she untied the cravat from his wrists. A delighted laugh escaped when he managed to graze one of her pert nipples.

As soon as he was free, Sutton immediately caught her into his arms and pushed her onto the mattress so that she reclined on her back with her legs on either side of him.

"Turnabout is fair play, my dear." But first, he took one breast in his hand and suckled hard at the other one, grinning when she loosed a moan of pleasure.

CHAPTER FIVE

Astrid wasn't prepared—physically and emotionally—for being this close to the marquess or of sharing carnal pleasures with him.

Already, she shook with reaction, and all he'd done was tease her breasts and nipples. But oh, she wanted so much more! "Sutton..." She gripped his shoulders, peppered the underside of his jaw with nips and kisses. "Touch me. Make me fly." Long ago, she'd learned to enjoy intercourse and foreplay from her husband, and there was no shame in that. "Restrain me if you'd like. It enhances pleasure."

"Oh, I definitely will indulge in that." He slipped from the bed then pulled her to the edge until her legs dangled over the side then he kneeled before her. "But just now, I am going to taste you, feast upon you until you come." So saying, he put his large hands on her knees and urged them apart.

"And then?" The inquiry was a breathless whisper, and she shook from anticipation.

His grin sent flutters dancing through her lower belly. "I'll send you over again before I finally claim you." He winked and urged her knees over his shoulders. "Lean back and enjoy."

"Yet I was supposed to be the one doing naughty things to you to show my gratitude." As she reclined onto her elbows, her thighs quivered, and anticipation played her spine.

"I quite like this." Seconds later, he spread open her folds, buried his head between her legs, and licked her quim.

"Mmm." One of her favorite parts of bed sport was being pleasured by a partner orally, and the marquess was more than skilled. Each swipe of his tongue to her folds provoked shivery sensation, but when he brought the tiny, swollen bud at her center out of hiding and suckled it, she uttered another moan and moved her hips to give him greater access.

Being penetrated by his tongue was an exquisite sensation that made her breathless, but when he conducted a cycle of sucking coupled with flicking the tiny bundle of nerves, she stirred, restless, urged him closer with a heel to his back. The man followed instruction splendidly. He had a certain way of using his lips and teeth that nearly had her vaulting off the mattress. Needing more direct stimulation, Astrid struggled to sit up. She wrapped a hand around his nape, guided him to where she needed him to be. "Just here. Harder and with more friction."

"I admire a woman who knows exactly what she wants." The vibrations from his chuckle added another layer to the sensations he invoked.

A few more determined thrusts from his tongue offset with concentrated suckling and soothing turned her blood to molten pleasure. "Yes. Oh, yes." Her pulse quickened; pressure built and stacked in her lower belly, and when she put a hand to her nipple, rolled it between her thumb and forefinger, gave it a tweak, it was enough to send her over the edge into a moderate release. With a tiny squeal, Astrid fell into bliss. She clamped her thighs together, holding him in place as mild contractions rocked her core. "Not a bad showing the first time out," she said, from around panting breaths.

Sutton snorted. "I can do much better." As soon as he disentangled her legs from his shoulders, he stood while she crawled back to the center of the bed. "But that was quite the aphrodisiac."

Heat went into her cheeks. "Keep that up and I might find it too difficult to leave your company tonight."

"That is quite the point of the evening, hmm?" When he reclined at her side, he encouraged Astrid to rest her head in the cradle of his arm. She didn't mind, for his naked form was quite delicious, and she wouldn't mind having the whole of the night to explore him. "Now, let's see where else you like to be touched."

"Start here." Already, her body craved his attention, so she took his free hand and laid it on one of her breasts. "I adore when men play with my nipples. There are times when I almost fly just from that."

"Then by all means, let us hope for the best." Each time he moved, the fresh, clean scent of him wafted to her nose and sent flutters of need into her belly, but when he slowly stroked her breast using only his fingertips, that need became more pronounced.

Circling, always circling, he went round and round the mound of flesh but never touched the straining tip. What was more, he held her gaze the whole time, which somehow made the whole act more stimulating.

"Sutton, please." Arching her back didn't help, for he wouldn't be rushed. She both respected him for it and was annoyed by his teasing.

"So needy." That grin he flashed was like an exquisite work of art. Finally, he touched her nipple, circled that bud with a tip and then strummed all of his fingers over the straining nipple until she squirmed and gasped with reaction. "Do you like that, or should I do this instead?" He pinched the tip at the root then slowly rolled it.

Waves of sensation crashed through her body. With a moan, Astrid nodded. "Yes, yes, do more of that." While he continued on, she moved the hand that rested between their bodies to wrap her fingers around the hot, silk-over-satin length of him.

The marquess's eyelids fluttered, and for the space of a heartbeat, he paused with his fingers on her nipple. "Is that how it's going to be, then?"

"Why can we not both play?"

"Minx." A swift pinch followed. He chuckled when she squealed then moaned as she stroked her curved fingers up and down his shaft. "Or perhaps a siren."

"I rather like that."

"Ah, good." Then he left off with the breast altogether in favor of lightly dancing those fingertips along her ribcage to her hip then down to her thigh. "Now, if I remember correctly, you enjoyed it last time when I played here."

"Tease." But she spread her legs to provide him better access.

"Mmm, I can think of a few better terms." The heel of his hand rubbed her mons while his fingers when through her folds. "For now, I will settle for lover." He penetrated her first with one finger then added another as she moaned. "Or perhaps you could say a god." In and out, he stroked, and when he paused to crook those fingers along the front wall of her core, a tiny scream issued from her throat. Wild sensations pinged throughout her body.

"Do hush, Rockwood, and make me fly." There was a time and a place for teasing banter, but not when she hovered at the edge of bliss again.

"Quite a managing baggage, aren't you?" But he applied himself to her pleasure with more vigor and attention.

While he continued to stroke his fingers into her passage, he worried the swollen bud at her center with his thumb. She put a hand atop his, moved his moisture-covered fingers to her button.

"Fast friction and don't let up. It won't take long."

"Thank you for the tips, but fair warning." As soon as he played with the bundle of nerves, he chuckled as her hips bucked. "The next time we come together, *I* will be in full command, and there will be punishment for any interruption." Faster he worked those fingers, and as an incentive, he took one of her nipples into his mouth.

Truly, the man was a surprise on many levels, but she would think about that later. Right now, with the pressure bearing down on her and need circling through her belly like a voracious beast, pleasure streaking from her breasts to her core, Astrid tightened her hold on his shaft, moved her hand as quickly as he did his. When the release roared over her this time, she still wasn't ready, and as she fell over the edge into bliss, a surprised scream left her throat, for the sensations were more powerful than the last he'd given her.

"Damn, but you're a much-needed distraction." Sutton rolled her over onto her back while contractions continued to rack her core. "Enough of the preliminaries."

She looped her arms about the wide breadth of his shoulders, as he came over her and settled between her bent knees with the tip of his member kissing her opening. "Give me all of you." Emotion graveled her voice, for she'd waited for this moment for far too long.

"Gladly." In one swift motion, he flexed his hips and penetrated her body. And he didn't stop until he was fully seated.

"Oh, yes." It was one of her other favorite moments during intercourse, that first moment a man speared into her, and he filled her with his length. The marquess was large enough that she swore he could touch her soul.

"Like that, do you?" His chuckle released another host of butterflies in her lower belly. "Good. We'll pursue that again later." When he withdrew, she softly whimpered at the loss of that connection, but he quickly joined with her again, and it was as sweet and intense as the first.

"Don't stop." When she wrapped her legs about his waist and locked her ankles, he grunted his approval.

The man went deep, so incredibly deep, that she cried out from the sheer loveliness of it. She wriggled her hips into a more comfortable position, slipped a hand down the length of his back, and at his buttocks, she squeezed a cheek, much to his amusement.

He kissed her, made love to her mouth in a mirror of what he did to her body, and Astrid hung onto him as if he'd dissolve into the air. The sensations were overwhelming. After so many years of dreaming about just this thing, it had finally come true. Tears filled her eyes, leaked onto her cheeks as they moved together in a dance as old as time.

Deeper and deeper he drove. Their bodies crashed together in the frantic need to claim each other. The heat of him was addicting; the way he claimed her again and again sent her closer to the edge of reality. The sound of flesh slapping against flesh filled the air. He was strong and powerful. It reflected in the way he moved, how he stroked into her, the feel of his hand at her hip, holding it in a tight grip, while the other cradled the back of her head as if he would protect her.

Her heart trembled from the imagery and the sensation pinwheeling through her body. The more frantically he thrust the more she lost her hold on control. Then her limbs stiffened and seemingly every muscle failed. A keening cry left her throat. "Sutton!" She wasn't just hurtled over the edge into shimmering bliss; she was thrown, launched, sent flying into the void, a place where she'd not been able to reach in a very long time indeed.

The marquess thrust twice more before he, too, joined her in that release. When he collapsed on top of her, Astrid wrapped her arms about him and held him as close as she could. This night was the pinnacle of everything she'd ever wished since she'd first seen him.

Eventually, the weight of him grew to be too much. She stirred beneath him. Immediately he rolled to his side and took her with him. Though her intimate connection broke, he held her close, with her backside nestled into his front and his arms around her.

"Stay with me for a moment," he whispered against the shell of her ear as he tugged the edges of the bedclothes around them.

"All right." With a sigh of contentment, she let her eyes shutter closed and she laid an arm over his.

THE CHIMING OF a longcase clock from somewhere nearby proclaimed half past the eleventh hour, and the soft nuzzling at the crook of her shoulder woke Astrid from her doze.

"Oh, goodness. I hadn't realized it had grown so late." When she stirred, would have struggled into a seated position, Sutton's arms around her kept her reclining in his embrace. The warm, lean length of his body spooning hers sent a shiver of renewed need down her spine, but there was a gentleness there as well that left her yearning for so much more.

"There is no rush to return downstairs yet." He followed the statement with a tiny nip to her earlobe while he splayed a hand over her torso just beneath her breasts.

Outside, a loud explosion echoed into the room and the sky erupted into silver and pink fireworks. Apparently, the birthday celebration had begun.

She relaxed into him, for it was all too lovely to be held again. "Thank you for tonight. When I received that golden invitation, I knew it my last chance to get close enough to you."

"Why? You could have sent 'round a note."

A snort escaped her. "That wouldn't have been the same. For years I'd thought of what I would say to you if I had the opportunity. Then I thought it might be better to thank you by offering up myself." It sounded crass and empty when spoken aloud. "For no matter where I ended up, in many ways, I am still that frightened young woman you met in the Dials." She let her fingers drift lazily up and down his arm. How much did she adore the strength, the hardness of those limbs? "Because of your compassion, I was given the chance to change my fate."

"That is always my intention when I make those weekly visits." The deep rumble of his voice tickled her ear and trembled through her chest, awakening her awareness of him. "I still remember that day. I like to think I saw you, the *real* you, through the grime, hunger, and desperation. I glimpsed your beauty and your soul, and I hoped you would find a better life. It is why I do what I do for some of the young people I see."

The man's capacity for giving never ceased to amaze her. "Why?"

"Oh, many reasons, I suppose, but when I was a young man, I'd befriended a boy from the streets, learned about his life and how it differed from mine. Eventually, we lost touch, and I never knew what became of him. I missed our friendship." He paused to once more nuzzle the crook of her shoulder. "I vowed when I had the title I would use that privilege to help others. My father used to tell me to leave such people to their fate, for there were many layers of society and that we all couldn't be fortunate."

"What a terrible thing to say to a child." Another firework burst punctuated the statement. No doubt partygoers had moved outside to the gardens in an effort to watch the display in the skies.

"Indeed. Those words stuck in my brain and shaped the man I

would eventually become." He licked at the spot beneath her ear that had flutters of anticipation filling her belly and her nipples tightening with need.

"Well, that man is a beacon."

He held her a bit closer. "I couldn't turn my back on that portion of my world, especially after knowing, after seeing, after acknowledging people needed help. It wasn't right, and I still cannot stomach the gap between classes." Determination rang in his voice. Another firework burst outside and temporarily lit the room with its colorful flash. "Everyone deserves a chance."

"Yes, they do." Tears welled in her eyes and spilled onto her cheeks. There was no shame in the release of that emotion. "You rescued me, Sutton. All those years ago, when I had no hope, no chance, you came into the Dials and plucked me out. Because of that, I worked hard to make it into London society, to have a place where I might be listened to, so that I might enact some of the same changes that you had." She brushed at the moisture on her cheeks while the dear man pressed a fleeting kiss to her nape. Another firework burst outside, glowing green. "In fact, I urged my husband to do the same things that you had, because the more voices that shine light into the darkness, the more it will shrink."

His breath caught and his hands stilled on her person. "Viscount Littlefield."

"Yes. He was such a lovely man."

"I worked with him a handful of times on laws and various causes in the House of Lords. Some of those things went through; some did not."

"He talked about you often. Said he looked up to men like you. I encouraged him to keep at the fight, in the hopes men like you both could effect change, make laws, help the people who need it most." There were times when it appeared that sentiment would win, but more times when it was obvious that it would not.

Another couple of fireworks echoed in the night. "It is a process." Sutton buried his nose into her hair. "And one where a man must be patient. Hearts don't change overnight."

Astrid lifted his hand and brought it to her lips. "You *are* making a difference. Please continue to follow that calling."

"I will, but that is lovely to know." He nudged Astrid onto her back and then peered into her face. A firework burst illuminated the caring in his expression. "Incidentally, it was my influence that guided Littlefield in your direction. I'd hoped you two would make a match of it."

"What?" She gasped and felt her eyes widen. The couple of fireworks reverberated in her chest. "That is twice you pulled my life into better things."

He shrugged, but it was his grin that squeezed her heart. "I wanted your future settled. From the moment I saw you, I knew you didn't deserve a lifetime of struggle."

A handful of fireworks erupted into the silence of the night. Colorful sparks shot across the darkened skies. They watched out the window, and still his hand rested on her hip while he held his head in his other with the elbow propped on the pillow.

Then, as the finale lit the sky with a multitude of colors and booms, she let loose a shuddering sigh. "We should dress and go downstairs. Dinner will be served soon. I will leave directly following." When she maneuvered into a sitting position and tried to leave the bed, he caught her hand and held her back.

"Astrid, please stay with me, beyond dinner."

"Why?" Her heartbeat accelerated.

"You are exactly the type of woman I need."

"For a mistress or to work with your charities?"

"No." In the dim illumination from the candles, there was no mistaking the love-light in the depths of his sapphire eyes. "For my marchioness. I have long had a *tendre* for you. This brings us full circle, and perhaps will give us more than we have ever dreamed."

"I see." Stunned and more than a bit pleased, she slowly nodded. "I have carried the same feelings for you." She'd come here tonight in pursuit of a lion for no other purpose than to live out a fantasy and show her gratitude. What a quirk of fate it was to learn their lives had been intertwined years ago, and would cross here at a gaming hell with love and romance in the offing. Feeling all too daring and not willing for the night to end yet, she said, "That depends."

"On?" He was darling in the vulnerability that he might be rejected.

Astrid grinned. She leaned over, snagged her reticule, and then pulled an object from its depths. "On how you perform for me in a second round of bed sport." She held up a polished wooden diletto. "Who needs dinner when you will satisfy my hunger after all this time?"

"I see." He bounced his gaze between the toy and her face, but there was an eagerness there that set fire to her blood all over again. "I never back down from a challenge." And he took the phallus from her. "Shall we begin?"

The End

Additional Dragonblade books by Author Sandra Sookoo

Willful Winterbournes Series
Romancing Miss Quill (Book 1)
Pursuing Mr. Mattingly (Book 2)
Courting Lady Yeardly (Book 3)
Guarding the Widow Pellingham (Book 4)
Bedeviling Major Kenton (Book 5)
Teasing Miss Atherby (Novella)

The Storme Brother Series
The Soul of a Storme (Book 1)
The Heart of a Storme (Book 2)
The Look of a Storme (Book 3)
A Storme's Christmas Legacy
A Storme's First Noelle
The Sting of a Storme (Book 4)
The Touch of a Storme (Book 5)
The Fury of a Storme (Book 6)
Much Ado About a Storme (in the *A Duke in Winter* anthology)

The Lyon's Den Series
The Lyon's Puzzle

About Sandra Sookoo

Sign up for Sandra's bi-monthly newsletter and you'll be given exclusive excerpts, cover reveals before the general public as well as opportunities to enter contests you won't find anywhere else.

Just send an email to sandrasookoo@yahoo.com with SUBSCRIBE in the subject line.

Or follow/friend her on social media:
Facebook: facebook.com/sandra.sookoo
Facebook Author Page: facebook.com/sandrasookooauthor
Pinterest: pinterest.com/sandrasookoo
Instagram: instagram.com/sandrasookoo
BookBub Page: bookbub.com/authors/sandra-sookoo

A Lyon's Word of Honor

(Connected to The Duke's Guard Series)

by C.H. Admirand

Dedication

For DJ ~ my Heavenly permanent date

Acknowledgement

A special thank you to Arran McNicol, my wonderful editor, for his attention to detail, and ability to get to the heart of what I'm trying to say!

Author's Note

When Alasdair Cameron showed up on the pages of *The Duke's Hammer*, I knew he would demand his own story. I didn't realize he would be too impatient to wait until I'd finished writing the Duke's Guard series. Thank goodness my publisher decided to publish Night of Lyons—it is the perfect place for Alasdair's story!

Happy Reading!

Chapter One

ALASDAIR CAMERON DELIVERED a lethal right cross to his opponent's jaw and swore. "*Bollocks*, Tremayne! Ye're supposed to fall at my feet unconscious!"

Tremayne grinned. "Face it, Cameron, you've gone soft since leaving the dragoons."

Cameron stared at his friend, a man who carried an identical scar to the one he bore on the right side of his face—forehead to chin. Each man had attained the rank of lieutenant in the King's Dragoons, having fought bravely and with honor, before their last battle and the slashing blow that nearly ended their lives. Both men stood over six feet tall, and were evenly matched in muscle and strength in a bare-knuckle bout.

Cameron delivered an uppercut that had the other man's head snapping back, dazing him for a moment. The Scotsman taunted him, "Soft, is it, and a fine Welshman such as yerself isn't? I'm not the one at the Duke of Wyndmere's beck and call."

Gryffyn Tremayne rallied, aiming a jab to Cameron's throat. Cameron blocked it, irritating Tremayne. "I answer to Captain Coventry, which you know, as he's been trying to recruit you."

"I've found my calling," Cameron reminded him.

"As a healer to the less fortunate?" Tremayne asked as the men circled each other.

"Miss Michaela needs my skill—and my protection." Cameron got a solid punch in beneath Tremayne's guard, pleased when the other man winced. "I don't have time to back up the duke's illustrious private guard."

Tremayne's eyes narrowed, and Cameron slowly smiled. "Take yer best shot, then I'll deliver the final blow!"

To his surprise, Tremayne dropped his guard and stepped back. "Colonel Lord Merriweather is dying."

Eglantine!

Cameron never thought the day would come when he'd be called upon to honor the vow he'd made a six years ago. He raked a hand through his hair. "How much time do I have?"

"Not long, though Coventry was not certain. He was hoping I could knock some sense into you, and convince you to join our ranks, before you present yourself on the colonel's doorstep."

The memory of dark lashes, dreamy green eyes, and silky hair, a warm, rich brown, entrenched Miss Eglantine Merriweather firmly in his mind. "What of her betrothed, Lord Pottshire?"

"Cried off a sennight ago after Miss Merriweather demanded he give up his vices." Tremayne walked over to the stall door, grabbed two linen cloths, and tossed one to his friend. "Decided he'd rather dedicate his life to gambling and his trio of mistresses than marry her."

Cameron caught the cloth, bracing himself as the memory of the lassie demanding he leave the King's Dragoons sliced through him. Serving king and country was not a vice, but a duty and an honor.

After wiping his face and chest, he donned his shirt. "Did she ask for me?"

Tremayne wiped the sweat off himself before answering, "She's has her hands full, caring for her father and younger sisters."

"His lordship cannot believe she'd change her mind. Look at me! I'm not the man I used to be."

Tremayne laid a hand on Cameron's shoulder. "If anyone understands that sentiment, it's me. But we're both decorated former members of the elite King's Dragoons. We have beaten the odds and survived a near-killing blow. And, from what you've said, you've put away a sizeable amount of blunt, though you'd never know it looking at your worn frockcoat and tattered trousers."

Cameron met his friend's direct gaze. "Ye know I cannot wear a finely tailored frockcoat, or my prized dragoon's coat, when I'm working with Miss Michaela. I'd end up fighting off those who'd challenge me for my coat instead of helping heal the poor lassies who need us."

"Aye," Tremayne agreed. "I've dressed similarly when I'm in the bowels of London."

Cameron slipped into his coarse linen shirt and donned his frockcoat. "What if the lassie refuses me again?"

"With two younger sisters just out of the schoolroom, begging for their first season?" Tremayne snorted. "She'll need a strong man to bring a sense of balance to their lives—and to protect them."

"What makes you think I'd marry her and take on the burden of her hellion sisters?"

Tremayne grinned. "As to that, Coventry and the colonel came up with a plan. You've heard of the Lyon's Den?"

"I cannot believe the colonel would allow Miss Merriweather to set one foot inside of that establishment! They'd circle the lassie like wolves before they go in for the kill—her innocence...and her inheritance!"

"She would be incognito."

Cameron scoffed. "Wearing a veil like the Black Widow of Whitehall?"

Tremayne shrugged. "Captain Coventry mentioned Captain Broadbank and his brother met their perfect matches there."

"Didn't Broadbank inherit a title recently?"

"Aye. On the death of their eldest brother. He's the new Viscount Moreland, though titles don't matter as much in the Lyon's Den as they do to the *ton*."

"I still cannot believe the colonel would even consider it," Cameron muttered.

"There is another consideration," Tremayne said, capturing Cameron's attention. "I understand invitations will be going out soon to a very select few to attend Mrs. Dove-Lyon's birthday *Mystère Masque*. Guest cannot enter unless they wear a mask. These invitations are coveted, and feted as the golden ticket—akin to receiving a voucher to Almack's, if you were one of the *ton*'s matchmaking mammas."

Cameron digested that last bit of information, all the time wondering how in the bloody hell he'd fulfill his vow to his former superior officer: to protect his eldest daughter and her sisters with his life, should anything ever happen to him. "Ye don't think she'll receive an invitation because of her father, do ye?"

"Colonel Merriweather's request added to Captain Coventry's will pique Mrs. Dove-Lyon's interest. She's partial to men who have served in the military—her husband Colonel Sandstrom T. Lyon served king and country."

Cameron's heart clenched, and his gut roiled at the thought of anyone laying a hand on *his* Eglantine. "Dinna think I'll allow her to attend a masked ball in that den of iniquity! She could be ravished behind a potted plant and no one would be the wiser. Worse, the bastards attending will be foxed on brandy and champagne and more likely to place wagers on whether or not she truly *is* an innocent before they roll the dice to see who goes first!"

Would she accept him now that he was no longer a member of

the King's Dragoons—her reason for refusing his offer for her hand? His gut roiled at the realization. While he no longer served the Crown, he'd forever carry the reminder of his time in the dragoons—the ugly raised scar that marred the entire right side of his face.

"A word of advice, Alasdair."

He scrubbed a hand over his face. "Aye?"

"Merriweather's daughters are as honorable and stubborn as he is. Though she hated his dedication to king and country that kept him away from home for years, Miss Merriweather would never dishonor what could be his last request."

Cameron held out his hand to Tremayne, who shook it. "Oh, and Cameron?"

"What now?"

"I have a decent coat and trousers you can borrow."

Cameron snorted. "Bugger off!"

Chapter Two

Two hours later, Cameron was standing outside the Merriweather town house on the fringes of Mayfair. He wore his pristine dragoon's coat—a gift from the colonel when he'd been injured and had to retire. A reminder of how he'd received the badge of honor marring his face. He raised his hand to knock, and hoped the lassie wouldn't refuse to see him.

His knock was answered by Hendricks, the colonel's dour-faced butler and former batman. "Lieutenant Cameron. It's good that you've come." He opened the door wide.

Cameron stepped across the threshold into what used to be a rather boisterous household. The silence shocked him. "Has the physician been to see his lordship today?"

Hendricks's brow furrowed. "Miss Eglantine booted him out last night."

Cameron's eyes widened. "How did she manage that?"

The butler grinned. "She stood guard outside the colonel's bedchamber—his saber drawn and at the ready."

Cameron grinned. "The lassie always had a way of getting a man's attention." He scanned the entryway and massive staircase.

"Where is everyone?"

Sorrow flashed in Hendricks's eyes. "Miss Eglantine and her sisters have camped out in his lordship's bedchamber since he fell ill."

"He must be very ill if his gregarious daughters are this quiet. How long ago was that?"

"A sennight."

"Have ye sent for another physician?"

"Nay."

Deciding action was needed, Cameron said, "I'd like see if I can ease some of his lordship's suffering."

The gratitude in the butler's eyes assured him that Hendricks approved and Cameron had not overstepped his bounds. The man's question confirmed it: "How do you feel about crossing the petticoat guard?"

Cameron sensed Hendricks was deeply worried about Merriweather and sought to distract him. "No quarter. No prisoners."

Hendricks coughed to cover his snort of laughter. "Cook has plenty of salt in the kitchen, should you need it."

Cameron chuckled. "Once I win the battle, I'll come back for it. Care to watch while I salt the proverbial fields after I've won?"

Hendricks's lips twitched. "I believe I shall wait here—you may need my assistance clearing his lordship's bedchamber of his well-intentioned daughters so you can examine him."

Cameron took the stairs two at a time. He paused outside of Merriweather's bedchamber, knocked, and waited. The door swung open, and the dark-haired, green-eyed goddess he'd dreamt about for the past six years stood before him.

She glared at him. "What in the bloody hell do *you* want?"

"To see your father." When she didn't move, he added, "You know he'll want to see me, Eglantine."

At the sound of her name, she blinked. "You have five minutes. I sent his former physician packing."

Her worry was a tangible thing, but the Miss Merriweather he knew had a backbone of steel. Ignoring the time limit she set, he asked, "Did ye now? Do ye mind telling me why?"

She gripped the fabric of her gown, then smoothed her skirts as if that had been her intention all along. "The fever won't break. Father is weak from all of the bloodletting."

"Where are yer sisters?"

"I sent them off to their bedchambers—they were trying to cheer Father, but their chattering was too much for him. Though he hasn't said as much, his head pains him."

"Do ye mind if I speak to yer father alone?"

She didn't answer, but stepped aside to let him enter the bedchamber. She walked over to where her father lay, pressed a kiss to his forehead, and said, "Lieutenant Cameron is here to see you, Father."

Lord Merriweather slowly opened his eyes, and Cameron saw that his former commander still had plenty of fight left in him. "I was hoping Coventry would get word to you." Without glancing her way, her father said, "Close the door on your way out, Eglantine."

Used to her father giving orders, she did as he bade her, shooting one last look Cameron's way before closing the door.

He acknowledged and understood her silent warning not to upset her father. "Now then, colonel, tell me what's led ye to lying abed when ye should be issuing commands to the trio of females who have been running yer household."

The relief in Merriweather's eyes was evident. "It all started the night that blackguard Pottshire was here. I heard the door to the sitting room close and Eglantine's demand that he give up gambling and his three mistresses."

"Needs the practice to please a woman, does he?"

Merriweather's lips twitched. "By God, it's good to see you!"

"Then what happened?" Cameron asked.

"I had my hand on the door when he refused at full volume, and opened it in time to see my darling eldest fling her mother's favorite vase at the lout's head."

"I take it her aim was true."

"Aye, but at the last moment, he ducked, and the missile caught him on the shoulder."

Adjusting the pillows behind Merriweather, Cameron helped him to sit up. "Do you remember what you had to eat or drink that night? Anything out of the ordinary?"

"I wasn't particularly hungry—Pottshire was due to call, and that excuse for a man always put off my appetite. I sent word for Cook brew a pot of tea and send it along with some of her tea-cakes."

"And afterward?"

"My usual."

Cameron smiled. "Ah, good Scots whisky."

"Aye," Merriweather agreed.

"Tell me what pains ye, besides yer head."

"How do you know my head aches?" Irritation colored Merriweather's words.

"The determined lassie who guards yer bedchamber mentioned it."

The older man frowned. "She notices everything. Why, then, didn't she notice what Pottshire was about before accepting his offer of marriage?"

"Ye're asking the wrong man. I haven't spoken to, or heard from, Eglantine since the day she refused *my* offer of marriage."

"Six years is a long time to hang on to anger, Alasdair."

Cameron shrugged and returned to questioning the colonel. "Any vomiting or diarrhea?"

"Aye, later that night."

"Was it after yer daughter tried to crease Pottshire's brainbox?"

Merriweather's frown was fierce. "I wanted to refuse his suit outright, but, knowing my headstrong daughter, thought to give *her* the opportunity to do so."

"But she didn't refuse."

The frustration in the colonel's gaze surprised Cameron. "If I had any inkling that she would accept his suit, I would have refused out of hand and sent him packing."

Cameron shook his head. "She would have something pithy to say to ye if ye had."

"Aye. She gets her determination from me... Thank heavens not my looks."

Cameron nodded. "Let me have a look at yer hands?"

"What are you looking for?"

"At this point, anything unusual." He noted a few mottled patches of skin and searched for other signs of what could be wrong. Looking deep into eyes the same bright green as the colonel's daughter, his gut clenched. They were dilated.

Sharp as ever, Merriweather asked, "What aren't you telling me?"

"I need to check yer arms and legs, then yer chest and back."

"What is it?"

"Still gathering information. Let me help remove yer shirt." When he had, Cameron's aching gut tied itself into knots. The man's chest had larger patches of discolored skin. "Any abdominal pain, dizziness, or difficulty breathing?"

"At first."

"Thirsty, restless?"

"Aye. Eglantine was right."

"To send yer former physician packing?" Cameron asked.

Merriweather grumbled. "Aye. You're asking questions he had

not. He couldn't find anything wrong, but kept bleeding me. I'm lucky to have any left."

Normally Cameron would have found the humor in the older man's words, but the worry that something was very wrong overshadowed everything.

Merriweather locked gazes with him. "Give it to me straight, lieutenant."

"This may sound odd to you, but I've come across similar symptoms since I began working with my associate in London."

The colonel harrumphed. "Hah! In the bowels of London, if my sources are right."

"Sources?"

Merriweather shrugged. "Just keeping an eye out for one of my favorite underlings."

Warmth slid over the ice in Cameron's gut at his former superior's words. "Thank ye, colonel."

"Do you think you can cure me, or shall I do as my physician suggested and get my affairs in order?"

Cameron raked a hand through his hair as he studied his mentor. "There is a chance—a slim one—but yer physician bleeding ye may have actually done ye a favor, as yer body has already replaced the blood he took from ye. If it's the type of poison I fear, purging is important, but best done immediately."

"My body has already spent the last few days purging itself," Merriweather reminded him.

Cameron nodded. "I'll have to consult with my associate."

"Is Miss Michaela more than an associate to you?"

Irritation mixed with frustration and fear, creating a noxious brew in Cameron's belly. Anonymity was essential to keep his friend—and her crusade—safe. "How do ye know her name?"

"I have an equal number of contacts in and around London and up into the Highlands. Do you have feelings for her?"

"Aye, and ye'd best have a good reason for asking such." Merriweather held out his hand, and Cameron immediately grasped it. "Are ye in pain?"

"No more than before you arrived."

"What is it, then?" the Scotsman asked.

"Eglantine."

He knew Merriweather had every intention of calling in the favor...while he was still alive.

"You gave your word," the colonel reminded him.

"Aye."

"And you will not go back on it."

Frustration and temper roared through Cameron as he shot to his feet. "I thought ye knew me better than that!"

A satisfied look settled on the colonel's face. "I do. Be a good man and ask her to come back inside."

"I thought she returned to her bedchamber."

"Under the circumstances, would you have?"

"Nay."

Merriweather waved his hand at the door, and Cameron had no choice but to open it. The woman who'd occupied far too many of his thoughts tumbled into his arms. Staring at her plump lips—the very same that had been featured in his dream just last night—he wished her to perdition. Needing to prick her temper as she'd pricked his, he asked, "Didn't yer father teach ye not to listen at keyholes?"

She pushed out of his arms. "Didn't yours?"

CHAPTER THREE

Eglantine tilted her head back and frowned at the auburn-haired giant who had tortured her in dreams. She never would have considered Pottshire's offer if Alasdair had followed along with what she wanted him to do—resign from the dragoons. She tried not to let her gaze shift to his scar—proof that she had been right. It was too dangerous!

Deep down, she knew it was not just a matter of pride. The man bled honor and duty, but in her heart she had feverishly hoped he loved her more.

"Are ye listening to me?"

For a moment, she stared into eyes the color of midnight. "My mind was elsewhere."

He placed a hand to her shoulder, and the warmth and the weight of it seared through to her bones. Lifting her eyes, she was surprised by the flash of desire that evaporated into worry. "He's dying, isn't he?"

"I won't give ye false hope, lassie, but there's still a chance that he won't. A very slim one."

"He...he cannot die." She knew saying the words did not make it so. Hadn't her father told her everyone had a set amount of time on this earth and to make the best use of it?

Alasdair's hand slid from her shoulder to the middle of her back, and the warmth of his touch soothed her. He bent and whispered in her ear, "Don't lose yer backbone now, lassie. Whatever yer father asks of ye…don't deny him."

They approached the bed, and the colonel smiled. "Ah, Eglantine, there you are."

Her answering smiled wobbled. "Alasdair said you wanted to speak to me."

"I do, my darling girl. Whatever is wrong with me, know that I will fight it to my last breath."

Tears pricked behind her eyes, and she fought to hold them back. She would not be weak in front of her father. He needed her to be strong for her sisters. "I will not let you die!"

He held out his hand, and she rushed into the shelter of his arms. "Would that you had that power, I would not have had to send for Cameron."

She eased out of his hold and swiped at the tears that fell despite her fight to control them. Warily, she asked, "Why did you send for him?"

"I would see you and your sisters well cared for."

"Father, I—"

"Will listen and do as I bid you."

She did not like the finality in his tone. "I will listen, and form my own opinion before deciding what to do."

"Eglantine!" His sharpness was a warning.

She acquiesced. "I'm listening."

"After I'm gone—"

She shot to her feet and backed away from the bed. "You will get better. I've sent for a physician who comes highly recommended by your friend over on Bow Street, Gavin King."

She bumped into an immoveable wall—Alasdair. "Ye will not disrespect yer father! Find yer courage and go back and listen to him. Ye owe him that...as ye owe him for yer life and that of yer sisters. It will be on yer shoulders if the Lord decides to call him home and ye ignored his last request."

Tears slipped past her guard at Alasdair's words. "You are right." She slowly approached the bed. "I cannot imagine life without you."

The strong arm that slipped around her waist gave her the strength to do what had to be done. Leaning against the man she never thought she'd see again, she borrowed a bit of his strength. "I'm sorry to have turned my back on you. Never once in my life have you ever turned your back on me. Forgive me, Father, please?"

"Of course, my dear. I know this is difficult and how hard it will be to face the future as the sole guardian of your sisters." A ghost of a smile appeared and just as quickly vanished. "They will be a trial to you, but remember, they are younger and have always had you as the buffer between themselves and whatever trials they faced." He slowly smiled. "Even if it was my wrath for whatever they'd done to deserve it."

"You were going to tell me something," she prompted him.

"I amended my will recently and have tasked Alasdair with the guardianship of you and your sisters."

She must have misheard him. "I beg your pardon?"

"After I am gone, Lieutenant Cameron will see to your protection and well-being. As your guardian, he will be responsible for accepting or denying any offers for your hand, and that of your sisters."

Fury rushed up from her toes. "Over my dead body!"

"Nay, Eglantine...over mine."

Alasdair's grip on her shoulders was the only thing keeping her from storming out of the room. She pinched his arm, but he did not let go. "Hush, lassie. I have a feeling yer father has more to say to us."

She never thought the great and honorable Alasdair Cameron would let anyone dictate to him. Hadn't he disappeared from her life after her demand he leave the dragoons…after she refused to marry him because of it? "You cannot let my father tell you what to do!"

"I pledged a vow, and am honor-bound to listen. Ye are, too. Now be quiet."

It wasn't the volume at which he spoke, but the words themselves. Never in all the years she'd known Alasdair had he told her to be quiet. It was not to be borne!

"I won't be quiet."

He spun her around and demanded, "Ye will unless ye want me to gag ye."

"You wouldn't dare."

His eyes, normally a beautiful midnight blue, flashed to black. Mystified by the change, she hesitated.

CAMERON USED HER hesitation to his advantage, whipped the handkerchief out of his waistcoat pocket, and wrapped it around her mouth. She wasn't still for long and fought against him. He was faster and tied the knot. "It was yer mistake to dare me, lassie."

Merriweather's gaze turned speculative as it slid from his daughter, who glared at Cameron, and back to the man he knew would protect his darling girls with his life. The colonel did not demand that he remove the gag. "Now then. I have already informed Hendricks of my wishes, so he and the rest of the staff will ensure that Alasdair will not be barred from our home. Is that understood, Eglantine?"

When the stubborn lassie standing beside Cameron remained

still as a stone, he gave her a gentle shake. She turned and glared at him, before turning back to her father to nod.

"Excellent. Alasdair, ring for Hendricks. Oh, and I think my daughter understands what is expected. You can remove the gag now." As Cameron loosened the knot, Merriweather said, "You will comport yourself like the lady your mother and I raised you to be. You will thank Alasdair for what will surely become as distasteful a duty for him to perform, as it will be for you to endure."

Cameron could not have said it better.

"Yes, Father." It sounded as if it pained her to speak when she added, "Thank you, Alasdair."

Hendricks arrived a few moments later. "Eglantine is weary from tending to me, Hendricks. Kindly show her to her room."

"I don't need—"

Cameron waved the handkerchief in front of her face, and her face flushed. She closed her mouth and followed the butler from the room.

Watching her walk away, Cameron squelched the perverse need to crush her to him and plunder her lips. A need that had not waned since the last time he'd done so. It burned brighter. Hotter.

He hoped to God he would be able to find an herbal cure to for whatever poison Merriweather ingested, because he would not be able to be in the same room with the feisty lassie without slowly going mad. "I'll take my leave of ye, but will return shortly with something to ease yer suffering."

"Not necessary. If I'm meant to suffer, then so be it."

"If I am meant to find the antidote for the poison," Cameron countered, "then so be it."

"Are you convinced that's what is wrong with me?"

"Without a doubt. Give me a few hours, and I will know more." He paused on the threshold and looked over his shoulder. "Where is the whisky decanter?"

"Which one? I have a few."

"The one ye drank from the night Pottshire was here."

Their gazes met and held, and understanding flowed between them. Pottshire had had the opportunity and reason to poison him. "My private study."

Cameron inclined his head. "I shall return. Dinna fret about the lassie. She's afraid. Ye know she will do whatever ye ask of her."

"Will *you*?" Merriweather countered.

"Ye have me word on it."

"That is all I ask. Thank you."

Cameron quietly closed the door behind him and went in search of the decanter.

Chapter Four

Eglantine stayed in her bedchamber long enough for Hendricks to see her inside. With her ear to the door, she waited until she heard his footsteps retreating, then opened it a crack. The hallway was empty! Slipping out of her room, she dashed along the corridor to the servants' staircase. Pleased no one was about, she made her escape. She did not stop until she reached the stables.

Young Mick had delivered messages for her before. She needed him to do so again.

"Trouble, miss?"

She rushed toward him, grabbed his coat sleeve on her way past, and dragged him into the tack room. "I need you to deliver a message."

Mick sighed. "Will it get me in hot water again?"

She wished she had the time to reassure him. "I don't know, but I'm desperate. I need you to deliver a verbal message to Lady Catherine."

"I will," Mick promised. "Just like before."

She nodded and blew out the breath she'd been holding. "Tell her I'm ready."

"Is that all?"

"Yes."

He straightened to his full height, just a few inches shorter than herself, and doffed his cap. "You can count on me, miss!"

Eglantine watched Mick sneak out of the stables and disappear around the corner. Now all she had to do was wait and hope her good friend Lady Kit...er...Catherine would send the prearranged missive to Mrs. Dove-Lyon.

She had feared a day like this would be coming after the fiasco with Lord Pottshire. She never anticipated her father would fall gravely ill. And God help her, she never anticipated her father would give the man who had broken her heart the right to have a say in her future...a future that did not include him!

Frantic with worry, she prayed, "Lord, please let Mrs. Dove-Lyon help me."

A SHORT WHILE later, her prayers were answered.

"A missive for you, Miss Eglantine."

She put down the book she was pretending to read. "Who is it from, Hendricks?"

His dour expression softened. "Lady Catherine."

"Thank you, Hendricks. I do hope her mother is feeling better."

"You are a good friend to bolster her through her mother's illness." He took his leave and returned to his duties.

Eglantine broke the wax seal. Her heart began to pound with anticipation. She and Kit had been planning for this very night for weeks, ever since her friend had relayed what she had learned about

Lord Pottshire. Between them, they came up with a plan: Eglantine would insist he give up gaming and his lightskirts…or she would give him her *congé*. It was far less than the dastard deserved, especially after he refused to give up gaming or his three mistresses! *Three!* It boggled the mind.

She read the reply and sighed with relief. Kit had sent the missive to Mrs. Dove-Lyon requesting a meeting. As Kit's aunt was currently using Mrs. Dove-Lyon's services to find a husband for her niece, they hoped the widow would meet with them so Eglantine could plead her case.

Everything was ready—the gown she would wear to their meeting and their transportation from her friend's home, a hired hack instead of using either of their families' carriages. They were still perfecting the tale they would tell their families, afraid the truth would have them bundled off to distant relatives in the borderlands until they were old and gray!

Mrs. Dove-Lyon was her only hope. Eglantine had to find someone to marry before disaster struck—when Alasdair Cameron was in charge of her life!

She folded the note and returned the book to the shelf. It was time to take control. She gathered her reticule and shawl from her bedchamber and went in search of Hendricks.

"There you are, Hendricks. Lady Catherine needs me. Father seems to be feeling a bit better after speaking with Alasdair. Mayhap that will enable him to rest. I promise not to be gone too long."

"I'll have the carriage brought around."

She hated subterfuge, but it was essential if she were to get out from beneath Alasdair's thumb. "Thank you, Hendricks. Please send for me immediately if Father needs me."

"Of course, Miss Eglantine."

While she waited, her mind kept coming back to the same thought—Alasdair Cameron would marry her off to some weak lord who would do everything the Scotsman told him to do. A sickening thought popped into her mind: had Father set aside a monthly stipend as payment for Alasdair's guardianship?

Her heart ached. She could not countenance that the man she'd loved for the longest time would want her to marry someone else, let alone accept coin in exchange for looking after the interests of herself and her sisters. The flash of heat in his eyes earlier had given her hope. Had she only seen what she wanted to see—or expected to? The man she pined for still had that heart-stopping smile, dark blue eyes, and auburn hair that glowed in the sunlight. His shoulders looked as if they could still carry the weight of the world on them, but appeared even broader. A glance at the breadth of his heavily muscled chest had scattered her thoughts. But she'd misjudged him when he called her bluff and tied a gag around her mouth. The dastard!

The thick scar that slashed from his forehead to his chin had her heart clench… The pain he had to have suffered from the blow—and the agony of having his battered flesh sewn back together—nearly shattered her heart. It had saved his life, but at what cost to the proud man he'd been? He had not contacted her when he'd been injured. Had he sent word to her father? Those two were as close as father and son, so of course he had. In that moment she knew she had killed his love for her when she demanded he forsake his duty. It cut deeply, but the searing notion that he had never loved her as deeply and truly as she loved him slashed far deeper.

Was love only for those who believed it could last a lifetime? Father still loved her mother, though she'd been gone for a dozen years. Alasdair had professed to love her, but not enough to give up his duty. Botheration! She knew it had more to do with the code her childhood friend had lived by than his lack of love for her. His ardent kisses had convinced her that all she had to do was ask and he would comply. She could not have been more wrong.

Hendricks opened the front door with a flourish and accompanied her to the carriage. She reminded him, "Remember to send word immediately if Father needs me."

"You have my word." He closed the door and signaled to the coachman.

Once the carriage started moving, her mind was crowded with questions. What if Mrs. Dove-Lyon could not be convinced to find her a husband? What if Kit's assurances that she knew the guards at the ladies' entrance to the Lyon's Den were wrong? What if they refused them entrance without an invitation?

"A MISSIVE ARRIVED for you, Mrs. Dove-Lyon."

"Thank you, Titan. Is the messenger waiting?"

"Aye."

She smiled. She trusted her head wolf to keep a tight rein on her employees—and those admitted to her establishment. Titan and his wolf pack ensured the Lyon's Den ran smoothly. It was expected that situations would arise when tempers raged out of control and gentlemen were escorted off the premises. "I shall let you know when my response is ready."

He nodded and returned to his post outside her private office.

She read the note and smiled, deciding at once to meet with Lady Catherine's friend, Miss Eglantine Merriweather, and find out more of her situation. While the young miss may feel she was in dire straits, it did not sound as if she were on the brink of ruin. Bessie had been remembering how she foolishly thought she and Sandstrom would have had more time together, but her beloved Colonel Lyon had died just a few years after they were wed.

She drew in a fortifying breath and set the past where it belonged. Her time would be better served concentrating on those currently making use of her connections and talent for matchmaking. There were a few men that would never be the first choice for a young Society miss…who just might suit the daughter of a highly decorated, retired member of the King's Dragoons.

Smiling as she penned her response, she assured Lady Catherine that she would be delighted to meet Miss Merriweather. The prospect of including the yet-to-be-seen Miss Merriweather among those who would receive the coveted *golden ticket* to her *mystère masque* was in the back of her mind as she sanded the missive, folded it, and affixed the wax seal.

She rose and walked to the door. Titan must have heard her approach, because he opened it as she was reaching for the handle. She handed him the note. "Thank you, Titan. This year's *mystère masque* should prove to be quite entertaining."

He raised an eyebrow, but she merely smiled at him before retreating back inside. She had some additional thinking and planning to do.

In her response to Lady Catherine, she had not mentioned her annual ball. Being masked oftentimes encouraged behavior normally frowned upon in ballrooms of the *ton*. She scoffed at the *ton* and their rules. She encouraged dalliances behind the potted plants or in her private rooms. Seduction was permitted and applauded. Bold suggestions that would lead to seduction were also acceptable—after all, she wanted her guests to have a good time.

While she frowned upon blood being shed, it was permissible, depending on the situation. Violating a woman was never to be tolerated! The man—or men—responsible would be ejected immediately and banned forever. Come to think of it, she had only had to eject a handful of guests over the years—and twice they were female!

She smiled thinking of the mix of guests she had already selected to receive the special invitation.

A short while later, Titan knocked a second time. She bade him enter and was momentarily surprised to note Hermia was standing next to him. "Is there a problem, Hermia?"

"Lady Catherine arrived with a guest. She said she'd sent a missive ahead of time. As no missives arrived through the ladies' entrance, I told her I had to check with you before she and her guest would be permitted entrance."

"I intended to let you know to expect them, but time got away from me while I was arranging meetings for my next few clients. Please do show Lady Catherine and Miss Merriweather in."

While she waited, she wondered—had the young woman been compromised? Was there a gentleman who would demand Bessie force Miss Merriweather's hand in marriage? Always interested in the tales of doom and gloom—as well as the those of daring and adventure—she wondered what type of trouble this latest miss was in. Was she beyond the pale, or terribly plain? A few well-placed questions would satisfy her curiosity and help her decide which trio of gentlemen would suit.

Realizing this would meeting could go on a bit longer than normal, she opened the door and signaled to one of her wolves and requested a tea tray.

She hoped the young woman was up for a challenge. Bessie decided Miss Merriweather would need to wear a Roman costume to her *mystère masque*. They were quite revealing, which would be the entire point, and a favorite of the prospective gentlemen she had in mind.

She frowned, hoping the young woman would not balk at the prospect of donning the gown or mingling with gentlemen who would most likely be deep into their cups before arriving. Virginal misses were apt to put up a fuss about all sorts of things. Bessie preferred working with hellions and hoydens. It was much more interesting finding their perfect match.

The knock had her turning her thoughts to more important matters. Her choice for the colonel's horse-faced daughter would have to wait until she observed the miss in question.

Hermia opened the door and stepped back to allow the young women to enter the room.

"Lady Catherine, so good to see you again. I have three more gentlemen in mind who will be competing for the right to offer for you, as the first three ended up in a brawl—against my warning not to. Tedious of them." Bessie turned to greet Miss Merriweather and was surprised to note she was quite attractive, with an acceptable figure, dark brown hair, and bright green eyes. "Miss Merriweather, a pleasure to meet you. I understand you have an unusual request."

Another knock interrupted her. "Come in." She nodded to the servant carrying a large tea tray. "Just set it on the table by the settee. Thank you.

"Won't you ladies have a seat? While I pour, Miss Merriweather, why don't you tell me about yourself and your reasons for seeking my help finding a husband?"

"My father is dying, and the man he plans to name as guardian to myself and my sisters gagged me to keep me from speaking my mind!"

Bessie's decision to continue to wear a dark veil to preserve her anonymity came in handy—the young miss could not see her smiling. She nodded and handed a cup and saucer to Lady Catherine and Miss Merriweather. Adopting a soothing tone, she replied, "That seems a bit extreme. Who is the man who would dare to gag you?"

"Lieutenant Alasdair Cameron."

"He is currently serving His Majesty?"

"Uh...no...not since he was gravely injured in battle," Miss

Merriweather replied. "He was in the King's Dragoons, but"—she paused and blinked back tears—"he received a life-threatening slash to his face."

"It sounds as if he is a fortunate man. I admire a man who does not shirk from his duty and keeps his vow of honor." Mrs. Dove-Lyon paused to carefully lift the edge of her veil a smidgeon in order to sip from her teacup, then let the veil fall back in place. "I wonder if you would indulge me by answering a question."

Miss Merriweather was quick to reply, "Of course."

"What prompted Lieutenant Cameron to gag you?"

She frowned. "He told me to be quiet or he would gag me!"

This was too diverting! Bessie would have to meet this Lieutenant Cameron. "And what did you do?"

Miss Merriweather placed her cup and saucer on the table in front of them and gripped her hands together before answering, "I may have said, 'You would not dare'..." She paused, then nodded. "Yes, I do believe I told him he wouldn't dare."

Mrs. Dove-Lyon swallowed her snort of laughter. Oh yes, she was definitely going to enjoy the fireworks when these two met at her ball. "And he accepted your dare?"

"Aye, the bloody *arse*." Miss Merriweather's hand flew to her mouth the moment the words escaped. "Forgive me. I normally do not curse."

Lady Catherine's laughter had Miss Merriweather frowning at her friend. "You know you do."

"Not often," Miss Merriweather retorted. "And never in public!"

Delighted with the idea forming in her head, Mrs. Dove-Lyon made her decision. She raised a hand, and the two women fell silent. "I will agree to take you on, Miss Merriweather—for a fee. I do believe I am going to enjoy finding just the right man for you."

While they finished their tea, Bessie was already making an adjustment to the guest list for her birthday ball in her mind, making room for another late addition—one Lieutenant Alasdair Cameron.

"Every year, I throw a birthday bash," she told the women. "A masked ball—they are such fun. Being incognito grants a bit of courage to those who are reticent when meeting new people." She stared at Miss Merriweather. "Have you ever been to a *mystère masque*?"

CHAPTER FIVE

ALASDAIR ENLISTED THE aid of physician and friend Lieutenant Sampson, formerly with the dragoons. When you fought and bled with a man…you trusted him. Though Sampson was older, they'd become friends and trusted one another during their time serving together. Sampson was connected to a mutual acquaintance, Gavin King of the Bow Street Runners. It came in handy in his line of work.

Cameron stood off to the side, not interfering while Sampson examined the colonel.

The physician straightened. "You have the constitution of a warhorse, colonel. It most likely will have had a hand in saving your life."

Merriweather tossed the covers aside and had one leg off the bed before Sampson stopped him. "You are confined to quarters and that bed!"

"You cannot order me around. I outrank you!"

"And the both of ye are retired…the same as me," Cameron reminded them.

Sampson chuckled. "He has us there, colonel. Now then, let me clarify that while you have improved—as in you are not dead yet—I must caution that even the slightest hint of a fever or congestion in your chest could finish you off."

"I am tired of being tired! I want a chance to even the score with that bloody, buggering, snot-nosed simpleton, Pottshire!"

Cameron reassured the colonel, "The proper authorities have the evidence and are looking into the situation."

"Hmph." Merriweather pointed a finger at Cameron. "Have you spoken to Captain Coventry or Gavin King of Bow Street?"

Before Cameron could answer, Lieutenant Sampson said, "King is a friend of mine. I would be happy to tell him my findings and diagnosis, to add weight to your case."

"Thank ye. We may need it," Cameron replied before turning to ask the colonel, "Do you intend to send a missive to the brigadier?"

Merriweather exhaled audibly. "If we were still in the dragoons—and Pottshire was one of my men—it would be up to you to notify the brigadier. He would strip Pottshire of his rank and have him facing the firing squad for murdering a superior officer!"

Sampson cleared his throat to get their attention. "I have a gut feeling that you may have the opportunity to have King and his men closely interrogate Pottshire. I am quite sure, though, that he won't be a firing squad of dragoons for attempted murder if—"

"He will pay," the colonel interrupted.

"If," Sampson continued, "you follow my instructions to the letter…or the charges may not be *attempted* murder."

Merriweather's frown intensified. "Depends on your instructions."

"Ye'll be following them," Cameron barked. "Do ye think I want to be saddled with yer addlepated eldest and her younger sisters for life?"

The sharply indrawn breath from behind him had Cameron's gut icing over. *Eglantine!* He spun around in time to see her face drain of color and hurt flash in the depths of her grass-green eyes. "Wait!"

She yanked the door open and ran.

"Go after her!" Merriweather ordered him. "I can't die until you mend fences with my daughter. She'll never go along with the changes to my will otherwise."

Cameron caught up with her at the top of the stairs, and pulled her back flush against him. He slipped his arms around her slim waist and held on tight. If he let go, she'd never give him the chance to explain that he spoke in frustration, hoping to get her father to agree to follow the physician's orders.

"Lassie, let me explain. Oomph!" The pointy elbow to his gut should have been anticipated. Proof that whenever he was near this woman he lost his ability to think, to reason, to react properly. She stamped on his foot and kicked back with her heel, connecting with his shin before he manacled her wrists with one hand and raked the other through his hair. "Bloody hell, that's enough!" She opened her mouth and leaned toward his forearm, but he managed to evade the bite. "Will you stop acting like a termagant and start acting like the lady you always professed to be?"

"You are a brute and a bully!"

Her words cut him to the bone. He slowly turned her around so they were face to face. "Do ye truly think so?"

"What else am I to think when you call me names and then use your superior strength to hold me captive?"

"I was trying to stop ye from running away from me."

"You called me addlepated!"

He snorted. "Well, now that's not a lie if I think ye are."

"How dare—"

He frowned at her. "Ye don't want to use that word again, do ye?"

She closed her mouth and glared at him. "Say whatever you will so I can leave. I have an appointment."

"Don't ye want to know what yer father and I were arguing about?"

She yanked against his hold, and he let her go. Hands to her well-rounded hips, she shouted, "I already know. You have not, nor will you ever, forgive me and have no wish to be saddled with my sisters and me!"

"Bugger it! I was trying to get yer stubborn father to stay in bed and listen to the physician's orders. God help me, ye're as hardheaded as the colonel!"

"Do not bring him into this. He's old and frail. I intend to make his last days comfortable—not difficult."

"Do ye not realize that storming around the house like a whirlwind, shouting at me, and leaving the house for long stretches of time worries yer father?"

"How do you know what I have or have not been doing? Has Father asked Hendricks to spy on me?" He opened his mouth to answer, but she cut him off. "I will not stand for it. Do you hear me?"

"Oh aye, and no doubt, they heard ye all the way over on Bow Street! Calm down, lassie, or I'll ask yer father to have ye confined to yer bedchamber."

Brilliant green eyes flashed. "You wouldn't—"

"I would." He held her gaze. "When ye're ready to be reasonable and put someone else's interests above yer own, Dr. Sampson would like to speak to ye."

It was her turn to ask, "Do you think so little of me?"

"Actions speak as loud as words, lassie."

When they were right outside the bedchamber door, she whispered, "I don't want him to die."

He hugged her to his side. "I don't want him to, either." He knocked and, when bade to enter, ushered her into the room.

It wasn't Merriweather who spoke to them—it was the lieutenant. "I trust the two of you have your tempers under control?"

"Aye," Cameron answered.

"Er…yes," she said.

"Need I remind you how fragile your father's health is, Miss Merriweather?"

"Forgive me, Lieutenant Sampson. I do not know what came over me."

Her father snorted, then frowned at her and Cameron. "I do! Are the two of you ready to listen? Apparently I'm not going to be allowed to do anything for a sennight, and then only if I start to regain my health."

Eglantine rushed to her father's side and threw her arms around his neck. "You're not leaving us? You're going to get better?"

"Only if I follow Lieutenant Sampson's orders. Now then, darling girl, I have something to say to you."

Cameron stepped up to guide her over to the empty chair beside the bed. "Why don't ye sit down and speak with yer father? I need to have a word with the lieutenant."

She did not even bother to thank him or turn around—all of her concentration was on her father. As it should be, he told himself. He wasn't going to matter to her anymore, now that there was the slimmest of chances her father would recover.

Then just how in the bloody hell would he ever be able to apologize to the lassie if he never saw her again?

Chapter Six

Cameron frowned at Tremayne and the sealed missive in his hand. "What in the bloody hell are ye doing delivering messages like an errand boy?"

"A favor." The man he'd fought and bled beside cursed and shoved the note into Cameron's hand. "Here!"

It was Cameron's turn to grumble. "Are you going to wait for a reply?"

Tremayne snorted. "Hell no. I'm on my way to meet with Coventry."

"Then what am I supposed to do with this?"

Cameron held up the sealed note, and Tremayne chuckled. "Read the bloody thing!"

He watched Tremayne disappear down the hallway leading to the staircase. "As if I wouldn't." He closed the door to the small room that had become his home since he'd been forced to retire from the military due to injuries. Truth be told, his superiors had not expected him to survive the saber wound that flayed open the right side of his face. Neither had he.

He broke the wax seal and scanned the note. "Must be a mistake." He turned it over and read his name and direction on the other side. Curiosity overrode his need to follow after Tremayne and demand to know how he happened to be delivering an invitation to the Black Widow of Whitehall's notorious *mystère masque*.

Staring down at the highly coveted invitation, he was about to toss it on the fire when he realized it just might be the answer to his tenuous situation. If the colonel recovered, then his former superior would no longer require his services interviewing potential husbands for addlepated Eglantine and her sisters. In that case, he should attend the ball and mayhap find the perfect woman for him... Hopefully one who would not shrink back in horror at the sight of his scarred face. Eglantine hadn't.

If the colonel took a turn for the worse, as Sampson indicated was still a strong possibility, then Cameron would be called upon to perform the duty of guardian, which he could still very well do when married. In fact, it would be to his benefit to be married. That way, the colonel's eldest—and decidedly most difficult—daughter would be more inclined to believe that those he interviewed as prospective husbands would have nothing to do with the feelings he still harbored for the lassie. He would hold those to his heart until the day he died.

As THE NIGHT of the *mystère masque* approached, Eglantine was torn between elation and fear—elation that her father seemed to be improving every day, and fear that she would make a complete cake of herself arriving at Mrs. Dove-Lyon's ball wearing a gown that was, in her opinion, beyond daring and quite *risqué*. Though soft as a dream and of the palest blue, the design was *à la Grecian*—completely baring one shoulder—before falling into an elegant drape that showed off her curves and left nothing to the imagination. Glancing at her reflection in the looking glass, she shuddered.

"I feel half-naked!" Kit's fit of giggles had Eglantine sighing. "Well, at least I'm not the only female wearing an indecent gown. Tell me again whatever possessed Madame Beaudoine to create gowns of this particular style for us?"

Lady Catherine lifted her bare shoulder in an elegant shrug. "Apparently at the request of Mrs. Dove-Lyon."

Eglantine walked over to the fainting couch in Kit's bedchamber and lifted one of the dominos that had been delivered along with the gowns. "At least she added a touch of color with our cloaks. This midnight-blue velvet is exquisite." She held up one of the masks, admiring the way firelight glittered off the crystals outlining the curves of the mask. Not for the first time, her uneasy stomach felt nauseated. Tamping it down with a will of iron, she walked over to the washstand, where Kit's maid was trying to tame her friend's dark chestnut waves into a fashionable updo.

"Are you quite certain that Mrs. Dove-Lyon knows what she is about?" Eglantine asked. "After all, the gentlemen who were supposed to pit their skills—and talent in heaven only knows what—to win your hand were all escorted from the Lyon's Den."

Kit frowned, but did not move her head, lest she ruin the beautiful coiffure her maid was fashioning. "Would you mind not bringing that sorry situation up again? I'm haven't given up hope that I will find the man of my dreams tonight!"

Kit's maid let her hands drop to her sides, then leaned one way and then the other, studying her mistress's hair. "All finished, your ladyship."

"You look beautiful, Kit." Eglantine was more than aware of her own shortcomings, standing beside her very best friend's willowy beauty. She wished, and not for the first time, that she too had strands of red scattered in her dark hair. But hers was an odd combination of varying shades of brown—light to dark. Where Kit had the warmest brown eyes, hers were changeable green. She would have to remember to maintain an even temperament tonight, else her green eyes would fade to pale green if someone upset her...yellow if she was angry.

"What is that look for?" Lady Catherine demanded. "You cannot go to the ball with such a fierce frown on your face."

"Just an unsettling thought."

"See that you only think happy thoughts. Your green eyes change to emerald and positively glimmer when you're happy."

Unease slithered along her spine. "I shall try."

"Do more than try, Eglantine. For my sake. Mrs. Dove-Lyon does not do favors at the drop of a hat. You are beyond fortunate that she agreed to take you on—and that she bestowed upon us invitations to the most coveted ball of the Season!"

"What of the Andrews' ball?"

"I have nothing to say about the *ton*—they gave my mama the cut direct when Father died."

Eglantine slipped an arm around Kit. "I know, and I'm so sorry. Will all of the gentlemen attending be on their best behavior, or will we have to be on our guard the entire time?"

"A bit of both," Kit replied, "if it is like my last visit to the Lyon's Den."

"Care to share a bit of that adventure with me?"

The knock on the door and the announcement that the carriage awaited ended their conversation. "We'd best be on our way," Kit said.

Eglantine watched Kit's maid settle the domino around her friend's shoulders, secure the clasp, and then hand her mistress her reticule and mask. Holding the mask in front of her face, Kit asked,

"Well, do I pass muster?"

Eglantine was amazed at the transformation from simply donning the domino and holding the mask in front of her face. "You are lovely, which of course you already knew. I daresay you will have to fight off suitors."

Her friend beamed. "Now it's your turn. Stand still."

Eglantine did so while the maid helped her on with her domino, then handed the mask and reticule to her.

Kit waited until she dismissed her maid to ask, "Have you remembered to bring one of your father's small folding blades with you?"

Eglantine lifted her reticule and shook it. "If you ask me, that is the only sensible thing about this entire evening."

"What about the prospect of meeting the man who will offer for your hand, and sweep all thoughts of that clammy-handed, three-mistress dastard Pottshire?"

Eglantine paused to think about it. "You always know just the right things to say to me. I have to admit, I am quite anxious about the entire affair."

Kit slipped her arm through her friend's and leaned close to confide, "I am too."

They descended the staircase, and for once, Kit's aunt did not frown at them. "Although I would rather interview another half-dozen gentlemen than have you attending Mrs. Dove-Lyon's ball at her establishment," she said, "at least we have her assurances that she will make an excellent match with either a titled gentleman or someone with deep enough pockets to keep you in style for the rest of your life."

"I wish I had more time," Kit said.

"We've been over this before, Kit darling. In order to inherit, you must marry by the age one and twenty."

"What about the codicil to Father's will?"

Her aunt walked over and gave Kit a brief hug. "I would give anything to have my brother back. But some things are beyond our wishes...and our grasp. I am trying to do the best for you and your ailing mother, Kit."

"I know you are, Aunt. Thank you."

Her aunt waved them off. "Have a wonderful time, ladies."

The butler had just opened the door for them when her aunt rushed over and whispered, "Did you remember to bring a deterrent with you?"

Eglantine snorted, then covered her face with her gloved hand. "I beg your pardon?"

Kit laughed. "Yes, Aunt. We both do."

Her aunt frowned. "I wish I didn't feel it necessary."

Eglantine and Kit shared a glance, and Kit told her aunt, "We promise to be on guard. Don't worry so."

"I shall trust that the two of you have listened to my advice, and will be careful."

"Yes, Aunt."

"You will only drink lemonade."

"We promise."

"The gentlemen do tend to get a bit foxed at events of this sort." Her aunt's eyes danced with merriment. "Dancing can be quite comical."

Armed, and lighter of heart, Eglantine and Kit relaxed once they were in the coach and rode off into the night.

The *mystère masque* awaited!

Chapter Seven

Cameron drew in a calming breath and approached the entrance to the Lyon's Den. He'd debated wearing evening garb, but at the last moment changed his mind and wore his clan's hunting tartan, a plaid of muted blue and gray. He *was* hunting, after all…for a wife! He would rather forgo the cravat, but knew it might come in handy if he were called upon to defend a young woman's honor, tying up a rogue who thought to take advantage. He'd also tossed a length of plaid over his left shoulder. It had been too long since he'd worn it. The weight of it covering his heart reminded him of promises kept, though drenched in blood. It too would come in handy if he were called upon to subdue any malcontents.

He donned the new black waistcoat and frockcoat of the finest wool. It had set him back, but the coin spent had been worth it. The fit molded to his broad frame and didn't constrict his movement. At his side was the saber he'd worn defending the king. The plain black mask was a bloody pain in the *arse*, but he knew it would be essential. It wouldn't do to be recognized the moment he walked in the door. Mayhap conforming to standard dress for the evening would've ensured anonymity.

Nay, he decided for the third time that evening—the kilt had been essential, and his choice for tonight. He'd had to leave his clan behind in order to keep his promise to his grandfather to serve the English king—and he had for a decade. His grandfather's last words to him were to *never* forget he was a Scot in heart, in bone, in blood!

Grumbling beneath his breath, he entered the Lyon's Den. Passing through the lounge, he nodded to a few of the guests. He entered the smoking room, and then the main gambling floor just beyond. The room was crowded—and loud. The deep, rumbling laughter of the men gathered was oddly in harmony with the higher-pitched voices of the ladies present.

He scanned the different gaming tables, and the groups gathered in and about them, and continued on past them. That was not the reason he'd accepted the invitation. He was here on a fact-finding mission. He needed to find a bride: a woman with a pleasant disposition, who wasn't hard on the eyes, had a decent figure...and all of her teeth! How hard could that be?

As he wound his way through the room, one of Mrs. Dove-Lyon's wolves was staring at him. Recognizing the posture and stance as that of a man who'd served in the military, Cameron strode toward him and held out his hand. When he noticed the man's injured hand, he immediately offered the other one.

The other man gave a brief nod, and they grasped hands. "Army?"

"Dragoons." From the intense look on the other man's face, Cameron wondered if a bit of his scar showed beneath the edge of his mask.

"Infantry." The man lifted his maimed hand. "Name's Titan."

Cameron nodded and lifted the bottom of his mask to show his scar, then let it fall. "Cameron."

Some would shun them for their injuries, but there were those who understood their vow of honor and call to serve.

"Looking for a wife, Cameron, or just here to enjoy the ball?"

"A bit of both."

Titan nodded. "You'll need to keep your head clear and your eyes and ears open tonight."

"Just tonight?"

"Aye. Normally things are not quite as volatile as they will be in another hour or so."

Scanning the room, Cameron realized he was not sure what was normal in the Lyon's Den, but what he was witnessing wasn't run of the mill for him. "I haven't attended a ball in years," he admitted, "and it was a military ball at that."

Titan's eyes narrowed as he scanned the room for trouble. "Neither have I." He glanced at Cameron again and said, "I've heard of a woman who rescues injured or abused young women off the streets of London. She has a scarred Scotsman who protects her and those she rescues."

Cameron met Titan's inquiring stare, but chose not to reply.

"We need more people like her…and you."

Cameron shrugged. "It was a struggle to find my place after—" He nearly raised his hand and touched his scar, then thought better of it. "I thought I'd found mine, but things have changed. I find myself called to honor one last request from my former superior."

"Colonel Merriweather."

"How did ye know?"

Titan shrugged. "Heard a former colonel in the dragoon's had been poisoned to gain an inheritance…and a bride. If you need my help, you have it. Only a bloody, buggering coward would poison a man who valiantly served king and country to steal the man's daughter and her inheritance."

Cameron held his temper in check to reply, "Colonel Merriweather's daughters are in the middle of this. If ye have information, I'll do whatever ye need in exchange for it."

Titan's jaw clenched. "You have feelings for one of the colonel's daughters?"

Cameron decided not to deny it. "Aye, his eldest daughter Eglantine."

Surprise showed on the other man's face before his neutral expression returned. "Pottshire is in attendance tonight, as is Miss Merriweather. If anyone asks how you found out, I'll deny that I told you."

Cameron's blood ran cold. "Eglantine is here?"

"Aye. She and Lady Catherine are dressed alike. Midnight-blue dominos, masks outlined with crystals. They've caused quite a stir tonight—especially when they removed their cloaks. Would you like me to point them out, or—"

A high-pitched scream of terror had Cameron's instincts kicking in. He shoved people out of his way to reach the doors to the gardens. His heart nearly stopped at the second scream, and he saw a woman being accosted.

"Ye bloody bugger!" He grabbed hold of the man's shoulder and yanked him away from the vision in ice blue. Terror-filled emerald eyes stared out at him from behind her crystal-lined mask. *Eglantine?* Incensed at the red marks marring her bare shoulder and chin, he spun the maggot around and planted his fist in his face. The man's mask flew off as blood spurted from his nose.

Bloody hell! "Pottshire?"

"You broke my nose!" the lord wailed.

"I'll break more than that for laying yer hands on her!"

"You can't! I received a ticket to the ball, and everyone knows anything goes at the *mystère masque*."

The lustful look on the man's face turned Cameron's stomach. Pottshire never even saw him curl his hand into a fist before he delivered an uppercut that lifted the other man off his feet and into the air.

Titan and two of his wolves arrived as Pottshire landed in a heap on the walkway.

"Trouble?" he asked.

Cameron swept the still-masked Eglantine into his arms. "Not any longer. Do ye have somewhere quiet I can take the lassie until she regains her composure?"

Titan handed him the key to one of the private rooms. "Lock it from the inside and stay as long as you need to. When you're ready to leave, just step outside the room and stand in front of the door. I'll summon a carriage for you."

Cameron nodded. He couldn't speak past the lump of anguish in his throat. His poor lassie! Why would the man attack her so viciously?

As he cradled her close to his pounding heart, he heard Titan give the order: "Escort Pottshire out the back entrance, and let Snug know he is not to return."

"Dinna weep, lassie," Cameron told her. "I'll take ye somewhere quiet…safe."

Her sharp intake of breath had him wondering if she was afraid of him. Did she know who he was, or did the mask hide his scar and the shape of his face from her?

"Easy now," he soothed. "Almost there." Fitting the key into the lock, he opened the door, stepped inside, and locked it behind them.

The sconces hanging on the walls were lit, giving the room a soft glow. Relief speared through him as he noted the pair of settees facing one another—and a fainting couch.

"I'm going to set ye on the fainting couch, lassie."

She didn't answer. Was she in shock from being treated like a common trollop? Was there any truth to the rumor Titan had heard about Pottshire? Speculation must be rife, though no one mentioned her refusing to marry him.

Shaking his head, Cameron concentrated on the trembling

woman in his arms. "Ye have to let go, lassie, so I can fetch ye a glass of whatever is in that decanter on the sideboard."

EGLANTINE KNEW THE scent and feel of the man who held her, and had missed him to the point of pain. She may never have this chance alone with him again, and had no intention of moving until she'd tested her theory—that he was only angry because he still cared. In spite of all that had happened between them and *to* them since he'd refused her offer, she hoped that he would not turn his back on her and walk away a second time.

She had been terrified when Alasdair told her he was joining the dragoons! Her father had been injured while serving His Majesty. She could not bear for anything like that to happen to the young man she loved! In hindsight, she wondered why she had given up all they had shared because of some bacon-brained idea that he would be safe if he resigned from the dragoons. People died from many causes other than serving in the military. What's to say that he wouldn't have been in a carriage accident, or contracted a fever, had he stayed and married her?

He'd refused her demand, and she never should have asked it of him. She knew that now. He would never give up his vow of honor, no matter how badly he wanted something... At one point in their lives, he had wanted her, and she him. How had her question tossed all those years of friendship, and the mind-numbing kisses that had stolen her heart?

He kissed her for the first time that fateful day he'd found her dangling from a tree branch. She'd landed in his arms, and he'd kissed the breath out of her. From that moment on, his name had been etched upon her heart. When he asked for her hand, she'd been elated—

"Lassie, are ye listening? Do ye need me to send for a physician?"

"I... Er... What?"

"Ah, ye can speak. Can ye tell me what happened?"

"I never should have left Kit's side."

"Who's Kit?"

"Lady Catherine," she told him. "We arrived together, but when that beast grabbed hold of my arm, we got separated in the crowd."

"I heard ye scream."

"He threatened to take me against my will." She'd been so shocked by the change in Pottshire's personality that she'd forgotten the weapon in her reticule. "He told me everyone would believe him when he claimed I was with child by another man, and that he was marrying me to save my reputation."

"I should have hit him harder."

His threat of violence soothed her almost as much as his appearing out of nowhere to rescue her. She slid her arms around his neck and pulled him close. "Kiss me?"

CHAPTER EIGHT

GOD IN HEAVEN, he wanted to…needed to. He'd missed kissing her. The sweetness of her mouth had always been a sharp contrast to the tartness of her words. Her lips were a breath away from his when it hit him—and he wouldn't be satisfied with one kiss.

It took a herculean effort, but he untangled himself from her grasp and eased back from her—and the temptation of her tender red lips. "Ye're only grateful I stopped Pottshire in time."

"I am, but that isn't why I want to kiss you."

He narrowed his eyes at her.

"You could never hide from me, Alasdair. I know the depth of your voice, the shape of your broad shoulders. Your scent and how it feels when you hold me in your arms." She boldly traced his lips with the tip of her finger. "The taste of you."

Her touch sent shock waves from his lips to his loins. "Then why didn't ye wait for me to come back to ye?"

She punched him in the shoulder. "After what you said to me, why would I?"

"I told ye I—"

"'And if that be your choice, then may you live to regret it.'"

He'd forgotten he'd said those words to her in anger. "Eglantine—"

"I have regretted my decision every day since you turned and walked away from me, Alasdair. I spent all of my time waiting to receive word that you'd been killed. I retreated into a dark place, where the only light was the memory of what we had been to one another." She met his burning gaze and asked the question that haunted her. "Why didn't you tell me you'd been injured?"

He ripped off his mask. "Take a good look, lassie! I'll never be that man again!" When she didn't react, he confessed, "I couldn't bear to have ye turn from me in fear or disgust because of my scar."

The tips of her fingers swept along the ridge of scar tissue bisecting the right side of his face with a featherlight touch. Pulling him closer, she pressed whisper-soft kisses along the same path—from his forehead to his chin. "How could you think I would ever turn from you in fear or disgust?"

Her touch gave him hope. Sliding the mask from her face, he felt the punch of love in his heart. "How could I know ye would not come to revile my hideous scar over time?"

She pressed a swift kiss to the widest part of his scar. "It's a badge of valor. You decided what you thought was best for the both of us…and you were wrong."

"Did ye not do the same when ye gave me the ultimatum? In order to marry ye, I would have to resign from my regiment!"

When she fell silent and dropped her hand from his face, he felt the keen loss of her touch.

"We were both too hardheaded to compromise," he rasped. "If we had, we would not be here having this conversation." He was desperate to press his lips beneath her ear and watch her melt the way she used to, but he held back. "We'd be wed and in bed right now, lassie. I was a fool to walk away from ye."

"I was the bigger fool. You're right; we were hardheaded, but I was afraid, too. I never should have made a demand that I knew you would never be able to honor."

"Mayhap we could begin anew. Right here, right now. What if I said I wanted to court ye—would ye allow it or spit in my face?"

She gasped. "I never in my life spat at you."

He slowly smiled. "Then ye don't remember the time ye'd swallowed a bug that had been swimming in yer lemonade?"

Her lips lifted in a half-smile. "That does not count, and you know it!"

She'd been through a harrowing experience at the hands of her former fiancé tonight, and he should be comforting he. If he gave in and kissed her as he wanted to, deeply, lingering over the taste of her, the scent of her, the feel of her in his arms...he wouldn't be able to stop from wanting more. Asking for—

Her lips were warm, pliable, and quietly demanding as she kissed him with a fervor that had not been there before. He groaned and kissed her back with equal passion. Resting his forehead to hers, he whispered, "Ah, lassie, I wasn't going to kiss ye yet."

She snuggled close and pressed a line of kisses along his jaw, stopping to nibble at the cleft in his chin.

The fire banked inside of him flared to life, threatening to consume him. "Eglantine, stop."

"Nay."

"Nay?"

"You heard me. I've waited long enough. I'm asking you to forgive me...to give me a second chance. I love you, Alasdair. I always have, but I let my stubbornness and pride get in the way."

Her words burned through to his last line of defense, and he felt his control slipping.

She reached up and pulled the pins from her hair. Lilac-scented waves of the softest brown flowed over her shoulders and down to her waist. Unable to stop himself, he reached out, twined a lock around his forefinger, and brought it to his lips.

Entrancing emerald-green eyes locked on his as she slipped her hands inside his frockcoat and shoved it off his shoulders.

He held himself still, fearing his last strand of control would snap. God, he wanted to make love to her. He felt the tug on his waistcoat and heard buttons pinging as they were torn free. His mouth dropped open at the sight of the woman in his arms—a woman he'd known most of his life—as she tried to tear the garment off him. But he stayed her hands. "Lassie, I will not take yer innocence until and unless we are wed."

"Yes," she said in between covering his face with kisses. "Yes, I'll marry you."

"I didn't ask—" He swallowed his words when she untied his cravat and tossed it aside.

"Yes, you did—you said 'unless we are wed.'"

He snorted. "Aye, not 'will ye marry me'!"

She looked deep into his eyes. "I will marry you, Alasdair. I've said it aloud twice now. I'll marry you. And a third time for good measure. I've proclaimed aloud my love for you and my promise to you. By Scottish law, you have to marry me."

"Ye aren't Scottish."

"I will be when you marry me."

"There are no witnesses to yer claim."

She shoved at him. "Then go find some."

He groaned. "Lassie, ye aren't listening."

"I will when you make sense. I have loved you forever, Alasdair Cameron. Make me your wife—right here, right now. I do not want to wonder for the rest of my life what it would be like between us. If you hadn't been here tonight, Pottshire would have taken me against my will. I would die before letting another man take what I have saved for you and you alone."

"Yer mind's made up?"

"It is."

He reached for her hand, tugged the plaid that had slipped off his shoulder, and wrapped it around their joined hands. "I pledge my life to ye, lassie, and vow to have ye as my wife from this day forward until I breathe my last. Will ye welcome me into yer body as ye've welcome me into yer heart?"

Her eyes locked on his. "I vow to have you as my husband from this day forward until I breathe my last." She paused and slipped the dress off her shoulder, never taking her eyes off his as it caught for a moment on her full breasts and then slid to her waist. "I will welcome you into my body as I have welcomed you into my heart."

She pressed a sumptuous kiss to his mouth, lifted his shirt over his head, and let her hands roam across the breadth of his chest and the width of his massive shoulders.

The tip of her tongue tasted the hollow at the base of his throat before licking a path along his collarbone then dipping to circle his nipple. He wrapped his arms around her and crushed her to him. "Lassie, ye'll be the death of me."

Her soft laughter was music to his ears.

"It's my turn to sample ye, lassie." His mouth commanded, then soothed, as he pressed open-mouthed kisses and tiny nips with his teeth along the underside of her jaw and beneath her ear.

She breathed his name as he eased her back onto the fainting couch and looked his fill. "Ye're more beautiful than the dawn breaking over the loch near my home." He trailed the tips of his fingers along her collarbones to the hollow between them and then bent to follow the same path with his lips and tongue as he kissed and licked his way toward her breasts. His mouth poised above her left breast—where her heart beat frantically. His eyes met hers as he bent and circled her nipple with his tongue before drawing it into his mouth.

He switched to her other breast, savoring, tasting, until she moaned out his name. He paused only long enough to ease her gown the rest of the way off. Without taking his eyes from the banquet of her body, he removed his boots, sword, and belt, letting his kilt pool at his feet. Stepping out of it, he watched her eyes widen in shock, and then anticipation, as he levered himself over her and settled between her legs.

Instead of doing as she expected, he licked and nibbled his way up one thigh and then then other until he reached the very heart of her, then drove her to the edge of madness with lavish licks, delving deeply into her core until he wrung every last ounce of pleasure from her.

She was dazed and well loved with just his lips and his tongue, and he knew she was ready to receive him. He waited for her to meet his gaze once more. "Now and forever, lassie."

"Now and forever, Alasdair."

He thrust into her and slowly eased out, over and over, taking them higher and higher, closer to the edge. When she begged him for more, he let go of his control, drove into her one last time, and filled her with his seed.

Gathering her to his heart, he held her there, whispering a silent prayer of thanks that the woman in his arms loved him enough to forgive him for walking away.

Chapter Nine

Eglantine slowly opened her eyes. She had never thought to experience anything like Alasdair's lovemaking. Had she truly let him make love to her with his mouth?

She buried her face in his shoulder and squeezed her eyes shut. How would she ever face him again after what she'd let him do? But they were married in the eyes of God. Had pledged themselves—handfasted. In Scotland, it was equal to having a priest witness their vows.

"Are ye ready to stop hiding from me, lassie?"

She sighed and slowly lifted her head. "I am."

Lying on his side, he brushed the tip of his finger along the curve of her cheek and pressed a soft kiss to her forehead, one cheek, and then the other—the tip of her nose and, finally, *finally*, her lips. His own lips were insistent, his mouth commanding. She sighed and opened her heart to her husband.

Instead of giving in to his overpowering desire to make love to her again, he eased his hold on her. "It's time I take ye home, lassie. We've news to share with the colonel. He'll be wanting to post an announcement in the papers."

Eglantine laughed. "He may want us to marry a second time."

He shrugged. "As long as you and I both know that this first time is the one that counts. We said our vows to one another with God as our witness...and the entire Clan Cameron. 'Tis their hunting plaid I wrapped around our joined hands."

"Hunting plaid?"

"Aye, lass. I didn't just come tonight to attend a ball."

"You didn't?"

"Nay, I came hunting for a bride."

Before she could think to smack him in the head, he wrapped her in his arms and rolled over until she was on top. "I found what I was looking for. But I must warn ye, now that we're wed, if ye smack me, I'm allowed by law to smack ye back."

"You wouldn't—" She bit the inside of her cheek to keep from saying the word that had prompted him to gag her.

"Well now, since ye've learned the one word ye should never say to me, and heeded me, I'm thinking I'd let ye smack me without retaliation a few times."

His smile had her insides melting. How could she resist him when he looked at her like that?

"Kiss me, lassie."

"If I must." Her giggles turned to moans as he swept his hand from her nape to bottom and back.

"One more time, Alasdair?"

He filled her with one stroke. "If I must, lassie."

Epilogue

Two weeks later...

"GAVIN KING AND Captain Coventry to see you, colonel." Merriweather nodded to his butler. "Show them in and ask my daughter and her husband—" He paused and shook his head before confiding in his former batman, "Never thought to see the day they would marry. Did you?"

Hendricks smiled. "It was inevitable."

"Was it?" Merriweather was not sure he agreed. "How so?"

"The gag."

The colonel snorted with laughter. "By God, I thought she was going to tear a strip off his hide for that."

His butler, who seldom smiled, grinned. "She's partial to the lieutenant."

"Her pride got in the way of his honor. I never thought I'd say this, but I'm almost thankful that bastard Pottshire tried to poison me."

Hendricks paused with his hand on the door. "Don't let your daughter hear you say that. Oh, and by the way, Lieutenant

Tremayne arrived a short while ago."

"Have him join us, too."

A few moments later, King and Coventry were shown into his study. "Gentlemen, I trust you have good news?"

"I've had my Runners investigating the situation since Cameron asked for my help," King replied.

Cameron, Eglantine, and Tremayne arrived. "Ye wanted to see us, colonel?" Cameron asked.

"I wanted the three of you to join our conversation. King and Coventry just arrived with news."

Cameron frowned at the men. "I trust Pottshire will be shot, or at the very least hang for his crimes."

Merriweather watched his daughter place a hand to her husband's forearm, instantly calming him. "Forgive me for speaking out of turn, but that bloody bugger—"

"Deserves whatever punishment is meted out to him," Merriweather interrupted. "You were saying, King?"

"While we have the proof obtained from your whisky decanter, Pottshire was not observed tampering with it."

"Bloody hell," Cameron growled. "What about accosting my wife?"

"You were there to stop him," Coventry said. He glanced at the couple and locked eyes with Eglantine. "I'm afraid as no one saw him manhandling you, Mrs. Cameron, there is little that can be done to detain him further."

"Are you forgetting what the Duchess of Wyndmere, Viscountess Chattsworth, and Countess Lippincott were able to do when faced with an equally untenable situation?" Tremayne asked. "They bravely facing the possibility of receiving the cut direct from their peers by standing their ground—with their husbands supporting them—as they spoke the truth."

Coventry nodded. "I was thinking only of the legalities. I agree with you, Tremayne. It turned the tide."

Cameron frowned. "Then social condemnation of the bastard is possible, even though neither my wife nor I bear titles?"

Tremayne, Coventry, and King agreed, and King answered, "Without a doubt."

"Well then," Merriweather said. "I believe I shall send off urgent missives to His Grace, Earl Lippincott, and Viscount Chattsworth, asking for their assistance in spreading the truth."

Coventry nodded. "I will ask my wife to do the same, sending missives to the duchess, the countess, and viscountess."

Cameron put his arm around his wife and hugged her closer to his side. "And the truth will set you free, my love."

She frowned. "I'd rather nail his *bollocks* to the wall."

Cameron's mouth hung open before his booming laughter filled the room. "By God, ye're bloodthirsty! Is it any wonder why I love ye, lassie?"

Tremayne looked at Coventry and then King before meeting the speculative look in Merriweather's eyes. "I know someone who would be willing to see to the task."

"I'll do it!" Cameron volunteered.

"You will not—think of our babe," Eglantine protested.

Cameron stared for a moment before her words sank in. "Are ye carrying our babe?"

"I might be, and refuse to let you take any chances that could take you away from us."

"Lassie, ye're going to be the death of me."

She lifted on her toes and pressed a kiss to his scarred cheek. "Ah, but you'll never be bored."

He was laughing when he pressed his lips to hers.

The End

Additional Dragonblade books by Author C.H. Admirand

The Duke's Guard Series
The Duke's Sword
The Duke's Protector
The Duke's Shield
The Duke's Dragoon
The Duke's Hammer

The Lords of Vice Series
Mending the Duke's Pride
Avoiding the Earl's Lust
Tempering the Viscount's Envy
Redirecting the Baron's Greed
His Vow to Keep (Novella)

The Lyon's Den Series
Rescued by the Lyon
Captivated by the Lyon

About C.H. Admirand

Historical & Contemporary Romance "Warm...Charming...Fun..."

C.H. was born in Aiken, South Carolina, but her parents moved back to northern New Jersey where she grew up.

She believes in fate, destiny, and love at first sight. C.H. fell in love at first sight when she was seventeen. She was married for 41 wonderful years until her husband lost his battle with cancer. Soul mates, their hearts will be joined forever.

They have three grown children—one son-in-law, two grandsons, two rescue dogs, and two rescue grand-cats.

Her characters rarely follow the synopsis she outlines for them...but C.H. has learned to listen to her characters! Her heroes always have a few of her husband's best qualities: his honesty, his integrity, his compassion for those in need, and his killer broad shoulders. C.H. writes about the things she loves most: Family, her Irish and English Ancestry, Baking and Gardening.

Sláinte!
CH

C.H.'s Social Media Links:
Website: www.chadmirand.com
Amazon: amazon.com/stores/C.-H.-Admirand/author/B001JPBUMC
BookBub: bookbub.com/authors/c-h-admirand
Facebook Author Page: facebook.com/CHAdmirandAuthor
Facebook Private Reader's Page ~ C.H. Reader's Nook: facebook.com/groups/714796299746980
GoodReads: goodreads.com/author/show/212657.C_H_Admirand
Instagram: c.h.admirand
Twitter: @AdmirandH
Youtube: youtube.com/channel/UCRSXBeqEY52VV3mHdtg5fXw

Don't Tempt the Purring Lyon

by Sara Adrien

Chapter One

"SHE CANNOT PLAY if she has no skin in the game!" a man called from the room of wagers. Seth cringed at the gambler's domineering voice shouting from behind a line of at least a dozen tiny empty glasses that clinked as he threw his fist on the table. A drinking game. It was Seth's first time at the *Mystère Masque* in honor of Bessie Dove-Lyon's birthday, a risqué night of high stakes that his brother, Alfred, was more apt to enjoy than him. He didn't know which one of these rooms was Alfred's favorite but if he was going to pretend to be his brother, Seth better behave as Alfred would. Hopefully, nobody would call him out under the mask, so he mustn't forget to refer to himself in third person as *Dr. Alfred Stein*, a tic his brother had when he was nervous in the presence of men with inherited titles. Alfred always made a point of showing his title was one he'd earned.

He poked into the room of wagers where men and women sat around tables with lavish dessert plates. All were masked, the women's of embroidered silk that covered the tops of their faces, men in black velvet ones with gold rims. Seth's eye caught a young woman with a delicate figure. She wore a jewel-green dress and had a pile of curls on her head that promised a seductive mane. Her décolletage was smooth, adorned with a ruby and gold brooch at the bodice of her gown. But her collarbone was exquisitely exposed and looked warm and inviting in the dim light. She looked out of place, like a delicate rose growing among weeds. The curves of her neck made his mouth dry, and he licked his lips as he imagined kissing her at the nape of her neck.

Seth shook his head. Bollocks. He'd never thought of kissing a complete stranger before—nor should he ask given the sinful place where he was this evening. After all, Seth hadn't planned on enjoying himself tonight. He was only here on behalf of his brother, Albert, who frequented the Lyon's Den for the thrill of winning and whatnot, but Seth had never stepped foot inside a gambling den.

It was all elegant enough, but Seth felt uneasy knowing the highstakes games that went on here, especially the one his brother had been entangled in. The atmosphere was charged with excitement and anticipation as fortunes were won and lost on the turn of a card or the spin of a roulette wheel. Ladies in their flowing silk gowns and gentlemen in their tailored waistcoats mingled effortlessly, their conversations punctuated by the clink of champagne glasses. As if the surroundings had dressed up like the guests, the walls were adorned with sumptuous damask curtains, their rich fabric cascading gracefully to frame the large windows. Their deep hue and intricate patterns provided an air of exclusivity. Seth couldn't help but feel flattered to be there, even though he wasn't fooled by the seeming sophistication.

With a deep sigh, Seth reminded himself that he couldn't let Albert down. He'd somehow irked Mrs. Dove-Lyon and was avoiding the Lyon's Den. An Invocation Mystère, if unanswered however, would mean that Albert would be forever shunned from the Ton, and lose all the business opportunities he and Seth had forged over the past few years. That's why he'd agreed to pretend to be Albert, donned his brother's black silk waistcoat that he wore when he frequented this place in case the sharp eyes of the staff doubted his identity.

Seth's hair was similar enough to his brother's and Alfred's black evening attire fit him well. He was only about half an inch shorter and two years younger than Alfred. Unless they stood right next to each other, most people thought they were twins. For the time being, he hoped the mask hopefully hid any of Seth's distinguishing features.

Another round of wagers forced Seth to feign interest and he moved closer. When he was just a few steps away from the young woman, he smelled an alluring combination of sweet pear and rose, a combination that reminded him of sunlit clouds glowing pink and orange at dawn. If she was as innocent as his instincts told him, she didn't belong here, and he somehow didn't want to see her ruined in just one night at the masquerade ball. This time the bet was made on how fast someone could solve a mathematical equation, which was also a riddle.

"What is the difference between 90 + 7, 7 + 90, and (4 x 20) +10+7?" a guest asked while one of Mrs. Dove-Lyon's wolves collected bets. Silence in the room. One man even retrieved a piece of paper and started scribbling some mathematical equations on it. Another shuffled papers.

"'Tis the same," Seth mumbled to himself, secretly judging those who wagered on such a trivial riddle.

"It's not really," she whispered. The gorgeous woman was younger than he'd expected and even more alluring now that she stood by his side. Her elegant perfume enveloped his senses, and he was suddenly painfully aware of how tightly Alfred's evening breeches fit him. Seth couldn't take his eyes off the delicate flyaways that brushed over her smooth neck. Seth suddenly found it hard to breathe. His collar and cravat were also too tight. Although, he decided, it was the proximity of the gorgeous brunette beside him that seeming stole the air from the room. He wished to take her away from this place. Save her from danger.

"What did you say, Miss? The lady in the green dress?" the wolf at the table said.

"Nothing, I'm sure it was of no significance." The girl waved him off.

She didn't look like the other women here, who could be categorized as rich and wanton with either bad reputations themselves or as daughters from wealthy families who had fallen from the Ton's grace. Her features were truly refined, not merely groomed like those of the other women. There was more to her beauty than looks. Spirit. From her posture, he could tell that she was studious, and she blinked into the round with intelligent eyes that captivated him despite her mask as if she were calculating ten steps ahead of everyone else in the room.

"It's like in chess, milady. Touch and go. You spoke, thus you ventured a guess." The wolf waved grandly. "Share it with us, please!"

"I was just thinking that the mathematics works out the same, but the difference lies in how you might say or write the numbers in English, German, and French. Ninety-seven, *siebenundneunzig, quatre-vingt-dix-sept*." The room grew silent, and Seth blinked at her, astonished that she was so smart.

"Explain your reasoning!" the wolf asked.

"Well, ninety-seven in German is seven-and-ninety, but in French it's four-twenties-ten-seven. The same, but also not." She winced at her explanation, seemingly aware of the bets that others placed on a riddle she'd solved.

"This round goes to you!"

"I dare her to get this one!" the gurgling voice of a rather plump man shouted from the corner. He had a lilt to his voice and was clearly well into his cups. Some long greasy strands of hair were combed over his shiny, naked head drawing more attention to his baldness. Like hiding something in a bulging fist—it didn't hide anything.

The girl nodded and wrung her hands.

"I'm full of sugar without being sweet." Heavy like the liquor in the musky air, the riddle floated aimlessly in the room.

Seth's eyes darted to her. Her lips twitched in a suppressed smile.

"A sugar bowl?" Her voice was clear, and she enunciated every vowel as if English wasn't her first language. Seth listened more closely for an accent but couldn't detect any.

The man banged his fist on the table. "Unbelievable!"

"Ten pounds!"

"Fifty on the next one!" another voice chimed in.

"One hundred pounds!" Bets were made from all directions of the room. The girl blushed.

"What cannot talk but will always reply when spoken to?" The man asked.

"An echo?"

"Unbelievable!" The small crowd cheered.

"One hundred pounds!" A woman exhaled sharply at her loss.

"I can be sun, I can be sand, and I can be a bird. What am I?"

"A clock?"

"Nonsense, a clock cannot be a bird," someone shouted from the back.

"A cuckoo clock?" She corrected herself and crinkled her nose. Her dark green and midnight blue feathered mask rose, and he could make her delicate features out, sweet and elegant. And very, very young. Probably no more than twenty.

"Two hundred pounds!" came a woman's voice. "Or her brooch!" A general murmur went through the room. "She hasn't wagered anything herself! I won't play if she has no stake!" The woman's voice rose above all others. "I dare her!"

The young girl crossed her arms but placed a protective hand on the brooch. "I take it." Swept up in the excitement of solving riddles, Seth feared she'd lost control of the bets that the other guests shouted into the room. She'd wagered too much considering how she clutched the jewel on her dress. It must have meant a lot to her.

Seth grew increasingly uncomfortable. He could guess where this was going, had seen his brother gamble in an attempt to secure the down payment for his medical practice. Always in vain.

He broke a sweat seeing her enjoy herself like a wallflower who found sudden popularity with the children at the park, seemingly oblivious to the risks of the unconventional wagers at the Lyon's Den—and Seth hoped he'd be right about her innocence. That's what it was all about, the extravagant bets and mysterious matches made by its proprietor, Mrs. Dove-Lyon. This was not child's play.

"Fine!" the man said. "What is stronger than steel but can't handle the sun?"

Seth watched her rub her hands together. It was her tell, he realized. She knew the answer and just pretended to need some time to think about it. This girl was obviously so much smarter than everyone else in the room, that she'd grown used to feigning ignorance. But she was naïve to think that she could get away unscathed. Visibly enjoying the attention, she still didn't fit in here.

"Ice," she said with a smile.

A rumbling applause went through the room and Seth overheard various suggestions for dares that he didn't like. Not at all. She seemed naïve and smiled back politely at one of the gamblers who cast her a threatening once-over. The young beauty was clearly out of her place unlike the others, who were frequent guests here.

"What is there one of in every corner and two of in every room?"

"The letter *o*."

Seth was astonished. She must have a wit sharper than any man he'd ever met. Yet, he didn't like seeing her in the context of the other guests, she stood out as a pearl far too precious among various paste beads. "All or nothing on this one. If you lose, I get a dare," a man with crooked yellow teeth and a mustache said. He had a look when his eyes skimmed her silhouette which made Seth angry. He had to get her out of here; she didn't know what could be at stake, but he had a bad feeling about it.

"What is it that given one, you'll have either two or none?" Moments of silence washed over the room. The chatter stopped. Seth held his breath and stared at the girl. Oh no, what had she done? Had she gambled herself away? At The Lyon's Den, a bet made would be enforced, or else their hostess would take matters into her own hands.

Seth found himself granted a reprieve as the girl hesitated, biting her lip—her unmistakable tell. He slumped and couldn't stifle a triumphant smile. She had wagered her brooch and he was glad for her, she hadn't lost it. Not yet.

"A choice!" she called out. Another guest, a man near the curtain at the far end of the room had a dangerous gleam in his eyes. Seth took her hand. He had a choice right now, and he was taking it.

"Come with me." He didn't wait for an answer, eager to remove her from this room of wagers.

He pulled down a dimly lit corridor and along a jewel-toned wallpapered hall. They rushed past a couple fumbling with each other in a dark corner, moans escaping them as their heads were close. She turned to look as if she'd never seen two people in heat. She probably hadn't ever... Seth pulled her along. He had to save her from this place, a gallery of vice.

Where was the ballroom anyway? He came to a sudden halt and wanted to orient himself, but at this moment, her lithe body bumped into him with a blunt whop. He'd stepped on her hem, and she stumbled and nearly fell. With a swift motion, he lifted her hand that he'd been holding and turned to catch her with his other arm around her waist. *Swish!* She knocked him off balance, and they toppled over.

Chapter Two

A FEW MINUTES earlier, at the entrance to the Lyon's Den, Lucy had handed in her invitation and had been ushered to the grand entrance hall where all newly arrived guests were offered a glass of champagne. She gracefully accepted the effervescent treat. It was sweet and tingled her lips deliciously. She downed it hoping for courage for the night and handed the empty crystal glass back to the server.

Her eyes trailed along the dimly lit halls and reflected images of the sparkling chandeliers in the mirrors lining the walls. It didn't look like a gambling hell as she'd pictured it but like a palatial foyer to a predatory cave. A former home, the ground level was furnished for entertaining, gambling, and drinking.

"You know, the more you touch it, the more you make me look." A tall man with broad shoulders appeared from just behind her. He'd probably also just handed in his invitation at the gentleman's entrance and stepped to her side. His voice was fresh and friendly. "Always a pleasure to meet another *Invocation Mystère*, milady." He bowed and Lucy noticed the piercing blue eyes under the simple black mask sparkling like alpine snow in the sun. As he straightened, his back his mask slid down his perfectly straight nose. His chin and jaw had an edge that made Lucy's insides flutter.

He pushed his mask up as he straightened, and Lucy noticed a slightly cross-eyed look down her cleavage. "And you are?" His low voice was manly and oozing youth just like the dark blond strands falling over his forehead. The shiny golden curls were a contrast to the matte velvet mask. Gleaming from behind the black fabric that hid half his features, his eyes sparkled as if they were rough gems from the depths of a cave.

Lucy bit her lip and his eyes fell to her mouth immediately.

"You can tell me your first name. It's not an entirely anonymous affair tonight."

"Lucy."

"Lucy as in Lucile, Lucina, Luciana?"

She shrugged over her shoulder, feigning a worldly dismissal of his question. In truth, she wasn't sure if he was flirting with her and how she should react. She wanted to flirt back but she was afraid. The notorious matchmaker might be watching her, and she didn't want to be coerced into marriage. Lucy always thought she'd marry for love, even if her parents dismissed the idea as a dream that Jewish girls in Switzerland should forget about. They were not free as citizens, much less as women. Choice in matrimony was a luxury few girls had. That's why Lucy secretly hoped she could extend her stay in London. A sense of freedom and excitement lingered around her like the inevitable scent of snow back home in the Alps.

"Call me Cavalier," the elegant and handsome man said.

Lucy took in the dazzling atmosphere and felt the tension in the air as fortunes were won and lost on the turn of a card or the spin of a roulette wheel.

The night felt like the guilty side of a celebration as if everyone had already consumed too much liquor, and yet they seemed awake and agile.

It was later than the usual balls and there was more of everything—more chatter, more music, and more on the buffet. Uncertain how to navigate the rooms filled with strangers without Mrs. Grimshaw to guide her, Lucy rubbed her hands together and stood at the door, watching. Like a hot summer rain, she felt his eyes all over her skin.

"May I have this dance?" Mr. Cavalier bowed and extended his hand.

Lucy's heart pounded heavily, and she grew even more nervous. Then his eyes met hers. Despite his mask, he rattled her. It would be rude not to oblige though, so she placed her hand in his and followed him onto the parquet. She knew how to dance, had taken lessons, and practiced in the parlor with Mr. Grimshaw. But she'd never danced with a gentleman before, much less a handsome British one like the one whose hand came to the low of her back. Burning heat emanated from his gentle touch and she longed for more. Perhaps this was entirely improper, but wasn't that her prerogative to explore while masked? And if it was so bad, how could it feel so good?

Considering his refined attire and elegant demeanor, he was probably an aristocrat. And the Ton, Lucy knew, was off-limits for a girl like her. Lucy shivered when her hand rested in his. Maybe her mask hid enough of her that she could enjoy the evening as if she were a debutante of the Ton.

His strong arm wrapped around her waist, and he gave a friendly nod as if he were grateful she'd accepted his invitation to dance.

As the music soared, her feet took flight and she let him swirl her around the dance floor. A forbidden hunger threatened to erupt within her as he exhaled and the warmth of his breath caressed her skin, sending a strange shiver down her spine. She felt herself drawn even closer to him as if her feet knew the way better than her mind. Gliding effortlessly across the polished dance floor, she surrendered to the rhythmic sway and gentle guidance of his hand. Instinctively, she nestled against him. The figures around them, the lights of the chandeliers, and the levied servants blurred into stripes of colors. All she could focus on were the icy blue eyes of the man who had her firmly in his grip.

He extended his soft and youthful right hand gentlemanly to receive hers and his fingers enveloped hers completely. As if he wanted to hold her tighter, he grasped her back, but kept the rest of his body stiff and at a polite distance. It was a heady feeling, and she felt a rush of excitement when she realized that his eyes were only on her.

And then it was over, and he let go of her. With a bow, he took his retreat and thanked her for the dance. Lucy shivered at the loss of his touch and felt desolate among the masked strangers.

Her mind drifted to earlier that day.

"Miss Lucy," the butler had called. "This arrived for you." He handed her an envelope with gold-embossed swirls. She'd arrived a few weeks ago to tutor the Grimshaws' daughters in French. In return, Mrs. Grimshaw was supposed to introduce Lucy to London's high society so that Lucy would "get some polish," as her parents had requested.

"Oh dear," Mrs. Grimshaw set her cup down on the saucer. "An *Invocation Mystère.*"

"*Qu'est-ce que c'est?*" What is this? Lucy asked, convinced that her ladyship had switched to their habitual French when they were alone. Lucy had left their native Switzerland only a few weeks ago.

"What is the invocation for?" Lucy asked as she tore the envelope open with her fingernail and retrieved the invitation. Mrs. Grimshaw scooted up to her and read over her shoulder.

"It's the masquerade. Oh, dear." Mrs. Grimshaw put her hand on Lucy's arm and whispered, "It's the most shunned event of the season." She spoke with gravitas, "But everybody wants a ticket."

"And do you have one?"

"Oh no, of course not!" The middle-aged lady laughed. "I'm married, I'd never expect to receive one." Lucy inhaled sharply as realization dawned on her what the event entailed. She put the invitation on the table and rubbed her hands over her thighs. She was most uncomfortable. "But you must go," Mrs. Grimshaw added.

"Without you?" Lucy couldn't hide the protest in her voice.

"I've heard all about this event, Lucy. It's in honor of Mrs. Bessie Dove-Lyon's birthday."

Lucy swallowed uncomfortably and hoped Mrs. Grimshaw would explain the meaning of this ball that had her all in a tizzy.

"Did I hear you say the name?" Mr. Grimshaw walked in. His wife gave a sideways smile and handed him the gilded invitation. "Oh, boy," he said as he skimmed it.

"We're staying home with the children this time; it was addressed to Lucy only."

Mr. Grimshaw froze and wrinkled his forehead. "Lucy is going to the masquerade alone?"

"I'd be happy for you to take my place instead. I can stay home with the girls," Lucy suggested so they didn't worry about who would watch their daughters.

"Go on behalf of all of us!" Mrs. Grimshaw said to her husband instead of Lucy. "I heard the rumors, and this is a chance like no other."

"I don't understand." Lucy felt panic rising. At Mrs. Grimshaw's side, she had managed to hold her nerves together at both balls that Mrs. Grimshaw had taken her to this season, but she didn't want to go alone.

"What my wife meant is ..." Mr. Grimshaw spoke with gravitas, "None of us, ever! None of us have been to one of these before!"

"A *Mystère Masque*—," Mrs. Grimshaw beamed at her husband, "—but the rumors must be true. Someone challenged Mrs. Bessie Dove-Lyon, London's most notorious matchmaker, to unbiased matches."

"What does that have to do with me?" Lucy asked as Mr. Grimshaw crossed his arms over his chest.

"Rumors say that Mrs. Dove-Lyon was challenged to make matches outside the aristocracy. I think she's inviting Jews to make favorable matches. She's playing *shadchan*," Mrs. Grimshaw said.

It dawned on Lucy why she was supposed to attend alone, as an unmarried candidate for the matchmaker's pleasure. There weren't many assimilated Jews, and she'd been to some balls already. She was an ideal candidate indeed.

"This is surely not what her parents intended when they wanted us to give her some polish," Mr. Grimshaw mumbled. "If you go into the Lyon's Den, you might not make it out the same as you went in," he warned.

"Oh please, darling. As long as she behaves, she has nothing to fear." Mrs. Grimshaw patted Lucy's hand. "Just don't gamble away your future," she warned.

Lucy gasped in alarm that losing her favorable prospects could even be a risk of this ball she apparently couldn't refuse to attend.

"It's a… how shall I say it… risqué night," Mr. Grimshaw seemed unconvinced of the harmlessness of the night ahead. "Much gambling, drinking, and dancing, and—"

"Romance," Mrs. Grimshaw interrupted. She pinched her lips as she gave him a meaningful smile.

"They do it every year and while the Ton shuns the ball, it's secretly the hottest ticket in town," Mr. Grimshaw explained. "It's an exclusive invitation-only event. Everyone wants to be there. And all the matches that Mrs. Dove-Lyon orchestrate are comprised of happily besotted couples."

"None of us has ever been!" Mrs. Grimshaw added as if it were a revelation. "The Ton count on Bessie's services, but no Jews ever ventured near her."

"You were selected for a reason, I'm sure of it," Mr. Grimshaw said in a foreboding tone. "But don't invoke Mrs. Dove-Lyon's ire. You know what they say about tempting a purring lion…"

"Just don't do it!" Mrs. Grimshaw clapped and rose with a sense of enterprise. "We must ready you for the ball of the season."

THE NIGHT OF the ball had arrived quickly, Lucy thought as she eyed herself in the mirror.

"I look plain," Lucy frowned at herself in the resplendent gown. She felt like a mouse in a cat's extravagant fur coat. She did not recognize herself in the mirror.

"The most memorable gowns, my dear, unite elegance with simplicity," Mrs. Grimshaw said as she gathered Lucy's hair and looked over her shoulder at their mirror images. The gown was of rich Italian emerald sarsenet, soft and shimmering in the light. Over the white satin petticoat, it draped over Lucy's body like liquid. The back, cut low and square, and the cool April air sent a shiver down her shoulders.

"Here is a little something to complement the deep green." Mrs. Grimshaw pinned a rather large brooch on the center of her neckline, just where the ribbons crossed at her cleavage.

"Oh, this is too much!" Lucy's hand flew to the precious jewel.

"Not at all, it's necessary." Mrs. Grimshaw smiled. "This is for a special occasion. It's an olive branch wrapped around rubies, a special piece commissioned from the crown jewelers," she explained as she set the brooch slightly askew. "It's a symbol of peace and victory. One of us finally made it to not only the Ton's most coveted balls but also the most exclusive."

Lucy's stomach twisted. In only a few weeks she'd somehow slipped into the role of a Jewish debutante. "They noticed your beauty and more. You get to go on our behalf, darling, I'm so happy for you."

Fearing to disappoint Mrs. Grimshaw, Lucy decided that she'd do her best in her new role as guest of the mysterious ball. Against the dark green silk of the dress, the ruby was bursting with fiery hues that reflected the sparkles of the gold vines encircling it.

"It's a treasure that I am afraid to lose," Lucy said.

"The stakes at the masquerade ball are much higher, my dear. You just make sure not to lose yourself in the games and excitement."

Little did Lucy know she wouldn't lose herself—but she would lose her balance and definitely fall, albeit with less grace than she'd wished.

Chapter Three

"Ouch," Lucy said, sitting on the slippery oak floor and holding her foot. Seth disentangled himself from her and crouched beside her.

"Are you all right?" He reached both hands out to help her up, but she pulled at his arms and couldn't stand.

"I can't—" She jerked in pain.

Seth realized that her injury was serious and felt his heart thump erratically. *Not again, not this time.* He wouldn't let such a sweet innocent suffer. That time his brother had been hurt, it was his fault, and he could never forgive himself even though it was an accident.

Seth lifted her up to face him, gently supporting her lower back. She was trusting and light.

"I can't put weight on it." A tear built in her eye. Had she been hurt just because of his clumsy disguise? If his brother had just shown up himself instead of being entangled in his own drama, Seth wouldn't have needed to be here and none of this would have happened. But then he wouldn't have met her either…

"Whatever is the matter?" An elderly lady in a gown the color of coagulated blood appeared from the direction of the ballroom. Seth swallowed acid, hoping he could fool the woman who had a reputation that she could never be fooled. In an instant, he knew this woman in the burgundy satin with gold embroidery was Mrs. Dove-Lyon, the hostess and queen of the matchmaking underworld. Her hair was grey but intricately curled, barely peeking out from behind the black veil that shrouded her in a mystery greater than the other guests and their masks. She moved energetically and her voice was strong. Did she know that he was not Alfred?

"I saw them taking a tumble and rushed for help," a servant said, probably another of her wolves.

"Thank you, Puck," Mrs. Dove-Lyon said. "Can you stand?" She asked Lucy, paying little attention to Seth at first.

Fragile as she looked, the elderly lady offered to support Lucy, intent on the injury that Seth's clumsy extraction from the room of dares had caused. When Lucy shook her head and cringed in pain, Mrs. Dove-Lyon sent a poisonous glare to Seth. Oh, *now* she saw him!

As if he were in her line of fire, he had the urge to run as far away and as fast as he could. His brother would know what to do, he was a doctor. But as a financier, Seth was clueless. And yet, he had to keep appearances up.

As he scooped Lucy into his arms like a groom carrying a bride over the threshold, she gasped in surprise. He preferred not to look back over his shoulder at Mrs. Dove-Lyon. Overcome with the trust she emitted as he held her, Seth realized that his entire body reacted to the contact. It was much different from their waltz, he wasn't ready to let go of her again.

"I'll take her to André's practice, the orthopedist," Seth said. "You know, just to make sure I don't miss anything worse than a sprain." Was *sprain* the right word? Could a foot be sprained? Or should he pretend to examine her ankle right here? What would Alfred do?

"At this time? You won't find anyone!" Mrs. Dove-Lyon protested. "Bring her to one of the bedrooms upstairs, I'll make arrangements—"

"I know them, of course, they'll see her," Seth declared in a matter-of-fact diagnostic voice imitating his older brother. Then he nodded his goodbye and he made for the exit. He wouldn't let Lucy stay the night. He knew what happened here and that she'd be betrothed to an indebted titled gambler by sunrise. Whoever this girl was, she was too pretty and too smart for such a fate. He wouldn't allow it, especially not because of his clumsy fall.

EAGER TO GET away from the Lyon's Den, Seth held her tight in his arms and cherished her firm grip around his shoulders. He sent for a carriage, but none came.

She shivered in his arms and pulled her mask off. When she blinked at him as a few stray hairs clung to the pins that had held her mask in place. Seth's breath hitched as she batted her beautiful eyes at him, and he nearly dropped her. Fiercely intelligent eyes with long dark lashes reflected the light from the Lyon's Den windows. With the noise from the masquerade drifting into the hollowness of the empty streets, Seth expected to calm down. But his pulse raced as he took in her gorgeous features. Her brows arched elegantly, and her eyes sparkled as she blinked. She bit her cheek and flashed teeth as white and delicate as snowdrops. He forced himself to look away, lest he stare at her mouth forever. He raised his eyebrows and felt his mask budge, but he had to keep it on. For his brother's sake.

No carriages. It usually took a while and most hired hacks wouldn't gather near the Lyon's Den unless there were several guests leaving. The drivers of the hired hacks had to find rides in the meantime to earn their wages while their patrons gambled the night away. Private carriages wouldn't take strangers.

The rush of feeling her in his arms gave him herculean strength, and he set off walking. The streetlights were going out ahead, but he knew the way. Devoid of people, the streets resembled bare pages in a book. Somehow Seth couldn't shake the feeling that he was writing his own story with every step he took through the night, with the beauty in his arms and her injury that he felt responsible for.

Her gaze was on him as if she were studying his features. Could she recognize him under the mask? Tonight, he had to be the Cavalier, but he had started to regret the lie. To her, he'd rather just be Seth. When a branch rustled over his head, he ducked, nearly losing his mask. She cowered against his chest, and he instinctively placed a comforting kiss on the silky hair on top of her head. *Why had he done that?*

He halted for a moment and clenched his eyes shut. His body ached because he'd carried her along Piccadilly and down Regent Street for about a mile, or more. Lucy tightened her grip on his neck, and he took heart. When Seth adjusted his arm to support her backside, desperately trying not to let his hand explore her delicate body, she exhaled deeply, and he cherished her closeness.

"We are almost there," he whispered as he saw her tense frown. She was in pain, it was dark, and he'd taken it upon himself to bring her to Marylebone. In front of a white building with black wrought iron railings, he stopped.

"Can I set you down for a moment?"

She slid down him to a standing position and even though his muscles relaxed, he felt a pang at the loss of her warm body on his.

HE'D CARRIED HER.

Carried.

Her.

All the way!

Lucy had felt his deep breaths and the quickening of his heart. With every step along the dark paved streets, her side had rubbed against his. And with every step, she felt a heat building within her. Unfortunately, her foot also throbbed with a dull ache. And yet, the excitement of being carried like a princess by a knight in shining armor—no, in a black velvet mask—took precedence over the pain.

At the white stone building, Mr. Cavalier set her down. Lucy stood on her left leg, unable to put weight on her right, and held on to the railing for support. She read the understated brass sign next to the door.

87 Harley Street

Mr. Cavalier knocked. Then again, harder. The house was dark but within moments she heard shuffled steps inside. The fanlight over the door lit up from within.

Just as the door opened, he stepped in and called, "André?" He pushed the door but held it askew. Lucy waited outside and heard him speaking in a muffled voice to a woman. "Oh Wendy, good evening."

"Why did you—" a woman said but he shushed her and closed the door, keeping one hand on the handle. Lucy couldn't make out the words, but the woman suddenly said "Oh" and walked away.

Her curiosity peaked, but with as much nonchalance as she could muster, Lucy leaned against the cold iron railing when he came back out.

"The orthopedist will be with us shortly."

Us? He'd stay with her?

He reached his hand out and helped her into the foyer. Lucy could only stare at this odd house, which had merely seemed like someone's residence from the outside. She didn't quite know what she'd expected but it wasn't such an elegant waiting room. Against the walls on either side of the doors were several simple chairs arranged in a neat line. There was a medicinal smell mixed with pungent herbs. Nobody seemed to be downstairs at the time and Lucy noticed the wall clock in the foyer. It was past midnight. They were at the doctor's office. One of the doors on the right had a big glass panel with writing on it. *Apothecary.*

A young man came down the stairs, in beige breeches and a plain white shirt. His hair was dark and short. He had a slightly scruffy look about him. It was probably too early in the morning hours to have shaven. But his eyes were bright and awake.

"What happened, S—"

Mr. Cavalier's eyes widened as he shook his head and interrupted him. "S-slipped and fell. She hurt her foot."

With an arched brow, the young man who must have known Mr. Cavalier pointed at the mask. It was odd that he'd kept it on, but Lucy's foot hurt so badly that she dismissed the question immediately. As though Mr. Cavalier's friend wanted to say something, he opened his mouth. At that exact moment, Lucy tried to put weight on her foot and winced in pain.

The dark-haired man reached out to support Lucy before she lost her balance. From the corner of her eye, she noticed that he made a face at Mr. Cavalier but then shrugged and said, "Good evening, I *mean*, morning, Ms...."

"Lucy, just Lucy."

"Hm," he said and crossed his arms, taking in the situation. "I'm

André," he said as he opened the door to another room off of the foyer.

"This is Dr. André Fernando, one of the best orthopedists in town," Mr. Cavalier explained.

Together, the two men helped her into the examination room. It was a clean and neat space; the walls were lined with oak and the parquet shone. Suddenly, Lucy shuddered and jerked her head back. A full-length skeleton hung in a corner of the room. She couldn't take her eyes off it.

"Is that a real human?" She managed.

"It used to be, yes. They're human bones."

The doctor had just washed his hands in a sink on the side of the patient's cot on which she had taken a seat. Wiping his hands on a white linen towel, André sat down on a nearby stool and turned to face her. He gently reached for her foot, and she pulled the layers of her gown and underclothes up to reveal the full extent of her injury.

CHAPTER FOUR

SETH COULDN'T EXPLAIN his reaction. By now, he'd caught his breath from carrying the girl through London and he was relieved that his friends had opened the doors for him. Well, they probably were used to patients coming at night, but still. Wendy, the nurse, quickly understood his need to see André, which was directly connected with the reason for impersonating his brother, and why he was not the one who could look after Lucy's injury. To cut a long story short, it felt good to have friends one could rely on, even in the wee hours of the night.

But when Lucy exposed her smooth skin, Seth was more affected than he'd expected. He hadn't slept since… oh, it had been over a day without sleep but there was no excuse for his reaction. It was just her foot and the lower part of her leg. He couldn't even *see* her knee.

Then, *swish*, she exposed her leg, and he could see up to her thigh. André expertly grabbed her shin and maneuvered her knee. It was the drawer test to see whether the tendons around her knee were all right; he knew about it from his brother, but he had no idea what the doctors were feeling for exactly.

Her legs were long but not too much so, and her silky white skin with an even tone almost made his vision blur. How could he lose his mind over mere legs?

And yet, he'd never seen any as pretty as hers. Even though she'd exposed a part of her body for André to examine, Seth was fascinated by the promise of more. How would it feel to trail his hand along her shapely calves? Or to hook his hands into the hollows of her knees and kiss his way up her thighs?

"Ah!" She gave a faint cry that woke him from his stupor. He had to walk around the room to adjust his breeches, or else his reaction to her would be too obvious. Especially to André's watchful eye.

"It's not a broken bone, Miss... Lucy."

"Will she heal completely?" Seth asked, immediately chastising himself for the panic in his voice. He didn't manage to sound like a convincing doctor, especially not like his brother Alfred.

"Of course, she will." André gave him a skeptical look that told him to back off. "It's only a sprained ankle."

"What does it mean, doctor?" She sounded worried, but Seth was secretly grateful that she'd asked.

"A sprained ankle occurs here," he reached behind him and pulled the suspended skeleton's foot. Pointing at the outer side of the foot, where screws held the bones together but allowed them an oddly human range of motion that gave Seth chills. "The ligaments that hold the ankle in place can be stretched too far if an injury occurs. You said you slipped?" Lucy nodded, apparently transfixed by the bones in André's hand. "In a few weeks, you'll be as good as new. I'll get some ice for you to put on it. Once the swelling goes down, you can put weight on it again." André left and Seth followed him to the kitchen at the back of the house.

"You really pulled a number tonight," André said once they were behind closed doors in the kitchen. He took some clean linens from a cabinet and spoke without facing Seth.

"Thank you for not saying anything."

"Why the mask? Why can't she know who you are?"

Seth pulled the mask up and rubbed his eyes. "Because Alfred is in trouble and sent me to the Lyon's Den in his place. He did something to get on the wrong side of the owner... long story."

"That's why she calls you Mr. Cavalier?"

Seth plopped on the chair by the window. André had knocked some ice off a large block in a wooden box and packaged it in a clean towel. "If you like her, you should tell her your name."

"I don't think I'll ever see her again after tonight," Seth explained as he scratched his neck. The cravat was tight, and he was growing uncomfortable in the evening wear.

"Bring her the ice for the ankle. I'll get a camphor tincture for the bruise and send her home with our driver."

BACK IN THE exam room, Seth found Lucy seated with her injured foot straight on the patient bed and her other leg dangling from the side. She seemed like a child, careless and free. And yet her curves were those of a femme fatale, quite literally the beauty for whom men would lay down their lives.

"It'll heal in a few weeks." She feigned cheerfulness. Her lips were pinched into a thin line that signaled her pain even as she kept her tone light.

"I'm sorry I made you fall. I'm so sorry." Seth took the stool that André had sat on and reached for her ankle. If he was impersonating a doctor, at least he could enjoy the privilege of touching her beautiful legs. No more, of course, it would be improper. Although he wished to caress her soft skin more, he didn't dare and merely tapped his fingers on her ankle as if he were examining the injury.

His breeches grew uncomfortably tight again and he felt terrible for pretending to be his brother. Still feeling responsible for her injury, he couldn't forgive himself if she had to suffer for his clumsiness.

"It's not your fault," she said. "Thank you, though, for bringing me here."

"The least I could do—"

"You carried me through London in the darkness of night." She gave him an adorable smirk. "Why?"

For the first time, Seth could take a good look at her without the mask. It had been too dark on the way here and he'd been distracted when André examined her earlier. Her hair was coming undone, and it lay softly on her shoulders in large waves that curled on the bottom. She was flushed but there was a rosy tint to her cheeks that Seth imagined was part of her fiery personality. If only he could get to know her better. He wanted to tell her the truth about who he was and how his brother had once hurt his foot because of Seth's clumsiness but couldn't speak the words. He'd never told anyone that the day Alfred fell down the stairs and broke his leg. Seth had tripped him with a toy lion. He was only three at the time, and Alfred six, but still. Seeing his big brother crying at the bottom of the steps with his leg twisted at an unnatural angle had given him nightmares. The enormous bruises that followed, the screams behind closed doors when Alfred's bone had been reset... no, Seth couldn't speak of it. It was a common injury in childhood but that didn't mean that the accident hadn't left scars in his mind as well as in his brother's.

"I detect a slight accent, where are you from, Lucy?" he asked.

"*Aarmühle*," she said as if everybody ought to know exactly where that was—or know how to pronounce the vowels she uttered effortlessly. "The Canton of Bern?" Her eyes met his and he didn't manage to hide his ignorance. "Switzerland."

"That's why you speak German and French?"

She blinked at him acknowledging friendliness but then looked down at her leg. She pulled her hem up higher and rubbed her ankle. Was she in pain?

"The ice will help with the swelling." Seth dared to set the towel-wrapped ice on her ankle. *"Es vet filn beser."* It'll feel better, he said in what he hoped would come across as German.

She winced when he put the cold package on her skin but then relaxed visibly once the numbing effect had set in, and the pain had receded.

Then she tensed again and looked at him. "What did you say?" An entirely different expression washed over her face as if she were regarding him with renewed interest. Or was this an effect of her injury, and she sought assurance? Alfred usually spoke of healing and recovery, rest, and … was she worried her injury would leave her limping? He should try to soothe her just as Alfred did with his patients.

"Du first hobn a ganze refuah." You will have a full recovery, Seth said in Yiddish, hoping it sounded just like German. In times of pain, he knew, homesickness could be unbearable. He eyed her intently and noticed that she bit her lip. Her tell. Then her cheeks stretched into a girly grin as if she'd discovered a rare flower.

"You are Jewish?" Her eyes were wide, and Seth's heart dropped. He understood German by virtue of speaking Yiddish, but the reverse was—as his parents used to warn him—merely a way to expose oneself. And yet, he'd risked it with this girl. He couldn't condemn himself, however. She seemed so vulnerable, and he just wanted to console her.

"I am." His admission stood in the room like a skunk and Seth feared it would poison her view of him. His people were not well-liked among the Swiss, nor the Germans or Prussians. Yet, they were on English soil, and he refused to hide his religion.

His identity was another matter since he still pretended to be Alfred behind the mask. Let her turn her back to him after this night. At least the Swiss beauty couldn't accuse him of not seeing after her injury. He wasn't an aristocratic gentleman, but he'd been taught the chivalry of one, nonetheless.

To his surprise, she didn't turn away. Instead, she smiled and blushed. Then she pulled her gown up and laid her hand on his, pressing the ice package onto her ankle. She sighed in relief and patted her ankle.

Was she exposing her leg on purpose?

Seth laid the hand that was not holding the ice pack on her lower leg. She watched his hand trail down to her ankle and then again up toward her knee. When she didn't withdraw, he knew his advances were welcome.

"You are so beautiful," he marveled. "You could make me fall."

"*Ikh finish tu menst far mir.*" I wish you were meant for me. She responded in Yiddish. Seth couldn't believe his ears. This wasn't German, nor some Swiss dialect. It sounded just like what his parents and grandparents spoke at home.

He frowned as he processed what this meant. Whoever this mysterious girl was she wasn't off limits anymore. Yet, his good sense was muddled by sleeplessness, desire, and something deep he couldn't quite name yet. Could she feel as he did? It had been only hours since they met, but Seth had never felt an attraction of this magnitude. Ever.

He took a deep breath and shut his eyes which were burning from a lack of sleep. He squinted from behind the mask. Hoping that a moment to think would help him gather his senses, but her closeness made his mind go blank. It must have been well past five in the morning now. The birds had started to chirp outside, and the sky assumed the foreboding purple of the day to come. Unfortunately, Seth realized as he opened his eyes, Lucy's bruised ankle had become nearly the same shade.

It had all been his fault, his clumsy fault just like the time he made Alfred fall. How could he ever make it up to this girl? She was a fellow Jew. Why had she been at the masquerade? And how was it possible that anyone was *this* beautiful?

His insides clenched but he ignored the feeling because she stretched her neck toward him, leaning in as if she expected a kiss, and that he'd comply.

He cupped her face with his hands and closed the distance between them.

"Lucy, *di klige sheynkeyt*, the smart beauty." He spoke onto her face. She was so close now.

She beamed at him flashing her perfectly pearly teeth. When she licked her cupid's bow and locked her gaze on his mouth, all of his restraint dissolved. Seth leaned in. He felt her tenderness as he pressed his mouth onto hers, but she puckered her lips. Oh, she had never been kissed before. He was going to make this count.

He opened his mouth gently and trailed his lips along her until she relaxed. With one hand behind her head, he supported her, but then she surprised him. She tilted her face sideways and granted him access to deepen the kiss. Seth's entire body hardened when their tongues touched. The kiss reached the guarded corners of his heart and even with the mask, he knew he was exposed. Overwhelmed with the force of their attraction, he felt his guard splinter. Her soft kiss crushed his resolve to protect his heart. She was so sweet and so perfect. He wished he could hold her forever.

CHAPTER FIVE

THEY'D BEEN CAUGHT when André interrupted their kiss, and his driver brought her home. In light of her injuries, Mrs. Grimshaw hadn't commented on her long night out nor her flushed face. And Lucy was glad not to have to explain herself, for she hadn't made sense of the events of the night before herself. The next morning, Lucy pretended to sleep late. Like a dream, the events of the previous night were a blur of excitement, from the waltz with Mr. Cavalier to his heroic act of carrying her to the doctor. Lucy pulled her covers up to her chin as the tingling memories of his gentle embrace washed over her. He'd kissed her passionately and lifted her onto the carriage in the early hours. And in the carriage, just when she felt the goodbye wring her heart, he'd hopped into the cabin to kiss her again. He never took his mask off but—silly her—she knew that he'd given him her heart. At that moment, his kiss communicated and promised a sense of completeness that was only ever possible if they were together. She'd felt his hunger for her at that moment in the carriage—and then it was gone. He'd hopped off, shut the door, and left her wondering. How did one go on living after such an earth-shattering kiss? Would she ever feel complete again without him?

And Lucy didn't quite know what to do today. She pulled her leg up, still sore. Sometimes the most childish impulse seemed the wisest, so she curled up under her covers and closed her eyes, hoping to dream of the handsome stranger who'd given her her first kiss and stolen her heart. Unfortunately, her comfort was short-lived.

"Lucy?" Mrs. Grimshaw knocked before she carried a tray into her room. "There's someone here to see you."

Lucy squared her shoulders and felt a pang in her lower leg. She sat up, instinctively wrapping her hand around her ankle. Instead of setting the tray down for her to enjoy alone, Mrs. Grimshaw left the room and another figure appeared in the door.

"Lucille?" A stern voice came and an elegant lady with a black veiled hat and satin gloves entered. "Don't get up on my behalf, girl," she said and took a seat on the chair next to the little table with the tray.

"Mrs. Dove-Lyon?" Lucy said as she combed her fingers through her hair in an effort to make herself more presentable. This time, instead of the burgundy gown, the elderly woman wore black, but her coiffure was still neatly tucked away under the black veil. As if calling into a lion's cave, Lucy didn't expect an emotional echo from her face.

"Darling girl, you got yourself into quite some trouble last night, and I've come to right it," she said matter-of-factly as if all decisions had been made.

"Whatever do you mean?" Lucy dared to ask as she spotted Mrs. Grimshaw standing in the corridor beside the door left ajar.

"My dear, don't feign ignorance. It doesn't suit you. I know all about how you cleared the wagering room by solving Mr. Tate's most difficult riddles. My wolves tell me everything." Mrs. Dove-Lyon looked over her shoulder. Mrs. Grimshaw ducked out of sight. "You fell head over heels into the arms of Dr. Alfred Stein and then let him carry you into the night. You don't think your reputation remains unscathed after you disappear for several hours and turn up with a broken leg the next morning, do you?"

"I slipped." Lucy rubbed her leg under the covers. "I only sprained my ankle."

"Oh good, then you can walk down the aisle in a matter of weeks."

"The what?" The room seemed to spin, and Lucy's heart began to pound. Had she heard the woman correctly? The aisle? What did she mean?

"I'LL MAKE ALL the necessary arrangements, dear. Don't worry and focus on your recovery. You'll need all your strength with a man like Alfred."

"Who is Alfred, and why do I—"

"You don't know his name? The man who carried you... Did he take you to his home?"

"No!" Lucy nearly shouted at the widow's insinuation. "He took me to 87 Harley Street. His friend is an orthopedist and he—"

"Oh yes, I know the doctors there. They're the best. Be it as it may. When are you going back?"

"Where?"

"Well to the orthopedist, of course! Don't you need to get this swollen ankle looked at again?" Without blinking, Mrs. Dove-Lyon pulled the covers off Lucy and pointed at her leg. It looked quite swollen and displayed various hues of purple.

"Mr. Cavalier—"

"Just *the* Cavalier, darling. He's Dr. Stein when not at my *rouge et noir* tables."

"Oh!" Lucy felt the heat rising to her cheeks. Considering how she'd kissed him, she should really know his full name.

"He's a gambler, and he's quite good. Nerves of a doctor, I suppose," the widow said. Lucy considered how out of breath Mr.

Cavalier—the Cavalier—had been. Nervous, even when he touched her ankle. He didn't sound at all like the man Mrs. Dove-Lyon described. "I have had a terrible time since the rumors were started that I don't match anyone besides aristocrats, and then he won against the house. Biased, they called me. Me! Can you imagine?" Absorbed in her own trouble, she reached for the cup of tea and took a tiny sip, quietly slurping it through her teeth. "I will not stand to be called a bigot. Time to take on some Jewish clients."

Lucy's head throbbed as she realized what her visitors meant. Mr. Grimshaw had warned her.

"So you have a match for Mr. Cavalier?" A sense of loss overcame her, but she felt stupid. How could she bemoan a man whose name she'd just learned? He'd kissed her like a prince in a fairy tale last night, but that didn't mean he had any obligations toward her.

Her mind flooded with the memories of his touch. Alfred, the Cavalier.

LATER THAT DAY, as she'd promised, Mrs. Dove-Lyon's carriage arrived to take her back to the doctor. André, the orthopedist, dutifully examined her ankle and dismissed her with a pungent camphor ointment from the apothecary before she hopped back into the black-upholstered carriage with the ornamental D and L, Mrs. Dove-Lyon's personal carriage. But instead of taking her home, the carriage retraced the steps that Mr. Cavalier—the Cavalier, a nickname Lucy had to get used to—had taken her the night prior.

And when they arrived, Lucy deflated. She'd been summoned by the notorious matchmaker of Whitehall. This would not be a casual visit.

Chapter Six

Meanwhile, Seth walked down Piccadilly and back to Marylebone. He'd been up all night and couldn't stop thinking about Lucy. Thus, he resolved to seize this newfound feeling, whatever it may be because it felt like a once-in-a-lifetime chance. Except that he didn't even know where to find Lucy again. It had been difficult enough to part with her when she left in André's carriage. He'd forgotten to ask for her address. And without knowing where she lived, he couldn't call on her.

"André!" He searched for his friend as soon as he walked into the practice at 87 Harley Street.

"Back so soon?" André emerged from his exam room, wiping his hands on a white towel, as usual. "Is there another girl you'd like to deflower in my office?"

"I didn't—" Seth took affront at the comment and pinched his lips.

"You might as well have, I suppose. But it's not in my hands anyway. I didn't say a word."

"To whom?"

"Who do you think, if you met her at the *Mystère Masque?*"

Seth's heart plummeted to his knees, almost knocking the floor out from under him. "She came in Mrs. Dove-Lyon's carriage and then she left in it a few minutes ago."

"Where to?" Seth started to run as soon as André told him where his driver had taken Lucy. He ran as fast as he could, almost being hit by several carriages. The streets that had been so wonderfully empty the night before were annoyingly crowded, and he had to maneuver around peddlers with wares, women carrying baskets, and even a newspaper boy screaming from the top of his lungs. Seth also felt like screaming.

How could he have been so blind? A girl like her at the Lyon's Den wasn't just an *Invocation Mystère*, she was there to be matched by the matchmaker—for Seth knew that the widow always got her will.

OUT OF BREATH, he arrived at the light gray townhouse and walked up the stairs to the front door. A large oleander tree was in bloom as few trees were, with early springtime petals. The magnificent light purple blossoms provided an embrace of natural elegance to the bustling city backdrop of the townhouse. So this is where Lucy lived? Seth knocked and waited.

Seth knocked again and heard voices inside. His heart soared with a peculiar feeling of joy at the idea of seeing Lucy again.

Someone pulled the curtains of a nearby window aside and looked out at him. Then the door opened, and an older man stood there, staring out at him. A servant, perhaps? Or maybe her father, or another, older male relative? His thinning hair, tinged with silver, was neatly combed back, and he wore a plain shirt and neatly tied cravat. If this was Lucy's home, it seemed most respectable at first glance.

"Good day, Sir, my name is Seth Stein. I'd like to call on Lucy." He'd never openly courted a woman, but he had no choice but to make his intentions clear. If Mrs. Dove-Lyon had set her eyes on her, time was of the essence.

"Luc-... oh, Lucille?" An older woman with upswept curls piled atop her head joined the man who had now opened the door wide. So that was her real name, Lucille. *French. Hm.*

"She's not here, ma' boy." The man said in a friendly voice but with a concerned frown, but not concerned enough. Seth thought that it was odd that Lucy lived here but these people were not her parents, but he didn't have time to ask. A rush of fear bubbled up in his throat. He had to find her now or else he feared it might be too late to confess his feelings.

"Was she expecting you?" the lady, in a frilly white blouse and black floor-length skirt, asked. Seth shook his head and raked his hand through his hair. "Aren't you supposed to be with them?"

"I beg your pardon?" Seth's heart began beating fast, faster than it already was from his mad dash to this house. Something was underway and he had to stop it, but he wasn't even sure what was wrong or where to go.

"Mrs. Dove-Lyon sent for her, so I thought Lucy was with her." As the lady spoke, Seth's arms grew cold, and his chest throbbed with hot panic. If she was with the matchmaker already, he had even less time than he thought.

"W-where are they?"

"I supposed she was meeting you at the Lyon's Den," the man said. As the older man's piercing gaze met Seth's, a sudden surge of emotions welled up within him—a potent mix of fear, anxiety, and an overwhelming urge to protect the newfound love he had discovered with Lucy. His heart raced in his chest, and his breaths grew shallow as he struggled to maintain his composure under the weight of the man's scrutiny. Seth darted off. "Go get her!" he called after Seth and chuckled as he shut the door.

Seth's instincts took over as he broke into a sprint, desperate to find Lucy. The wind whipped through his hair as he raced down the cobblestone streets, his heart pounding in his ears while his thoughts raced with equal fervor.

SETH RAN DOWN the street and turned the corner to Cleveland Row just a few minutes later, stopping at the gentleman's entrance to the light blue building. It was rather inconspicuous, considering what was inside. A lion's den indeed, and it should have been infernal red, throwing flames from the roof. Instead, all looked quiet, and he was ushered in rather calmly. On the inside, Seth was all but calm. Desperation clawed at his chest, making it difficult to catch a breath. The cool spring air around him seemed to thicken, suffocating him with every gasping inhalation. A horrible, overwhelming sensation threatened to burst out of him from within as if he were on the verge of popping from his own skin.

The streets swished by, but he knew exactly where he was, and how much farther he had to run to the Lyon's Den. His senses heightened, and the world around him became a cacophony of noise and color. The clatter of horses' hooves, the murmur of voices, and the rustle of leaves all seemed to amplify in volume, drowning out his own thoughts.

Yet, in the midst of the chaotic traffic, one thought echoed repeatedly in his mind: *Lucy! My Lucy!* She should be his. He'd just found her and experienced a connection deeper than he could have ever imagined, and now, he feared losing her forever. Panic set in as he weaved through narrow alleys and past street vendors, desperately scanning the streets and estimating how much farther he had to run.

What if she wasn't there anymore?

"Lucy!" he cried out, his voice straining with urgency. "Wait!" His pleas filled the air, echoing off the walls of the surrounding buildings. As his desperation grew, so did his determination to find her, for he knew that without Lucy by his side, his newfound happiness would be but a fleeting memory, forever lost to the anonymity of the masquerade ball.

He didn't stop but raced up the stairs and pounded on the door. But when the guard opened it, he could barely catch his breath to ask for Mrs. Dove-Lyon. It didn't matter. He couldn't wait. Instead, he pushed his way past the door guard and into the foyer, almost colliding with a woman carrying a tray of drinks.

He stopped himself just in time. "Where's she?" he demanded, hoarse from the lack of air.

"She's with someone, sir, you'll have to w—" But he didn't stay to hear the rest of what she said.

Seth burst into the opulent gambling hall, his heart hammering in his chest. He paid no heed to the guards chasing after him, or the players huddled around various tables, their eyes locked on cards and dice, their fates hanging in the balance. With a fierce determination, he charged towards the grand staircase, each thunderous step announcing his presence as the sound reverberated through the cavernous space and ricocheted off the walls.

Upon reaching the top, Seth didn't pause for even a moment. A row of elegantly dressed women stood on a balcony at the top of the stairs. He knew they were awaiting their matches; this was the Lyon's Den after all. The Black Widow of Whitehall was at work. *Oh no, oh no! Was Lucy one of her candidates? Had he missed his chance to confess his love before she was promised to another man?*

Driven by an unrelenting urgency that propelled him forward, he sprinted down the dimly lit hallway. His breath came in ragged gasps. He could feel the weight of the world bearing down upon him, fueling his desperation to find Lucy.

As he approached Mrs. Dove-Lyon's private chamber, a menacing figure loomed before him—a burly man with eyes like a predatory wolf, standing guard at the door. Undeterred, Seth brushed past the imposing sentinel, who lunged in an attempt to apprehend him. With a swift, deft maneuver, Seth evaded the man's grasp, pushing the heavy door open and slipping through the narrow gap just as it threatened to close.

The intensity of the moment hung heavy in the air, time seemingly slowing to a crawl as Seth crossed the threshold, fueled by a relentless determination to reunite with his beloved Lucy, but what he saw gave him a shock.

Chapter Seven

Meanwhile, upstairs at the Lyon's Den, Lucy had apparently been expected.

"Why am I here?" The man named Titan helped Lucy from the carriage, but he didn't answer. Instead, he led her to Mrs. Dove-Lyon's private room. Each agonizing step sent a jolt of pain shooting through Lucy's body, causing her to wince as she carefully lifted her injured ankle to meet her other foot, step by step. The torment was unbearable, yet it was nothing compared to the gnawing dread that consumed her thoughts. She couldn't shake the suffocating fear of what the matchmaker might have done, and how it could affect her future with the handsome stranger who had so unexpectedly stolen her heart.

Lucy's mind swirled with vivid memories of their passionate encounter—the intensity of his piercing blue eyes, the electrifying sensation of their first kiss, and the tender Yiddish words he had whispered in her ear. Each recollection was like a bittersweet melody, filling her with both longing and despair as she hobbled towards the door.

The wolf was behind her and even though she wanted to run

away, she couldn't. Though her physical movements were slow, her heart raced at a breakneck pace, as if trying to bridge the distance between her and her newfound love. As she neared the threshold, an overwhelming mixture of hope and trepidation washed over her—she wanted nothing more than to be reunited with the man who had awakened a love within her more profound than she had ever imagined possible.

Once the wolf opened the door, Lucy knew she found herself in the den of the lion indeed. A luxurious set of curtains dressed the window and muted the bright afternoon sunlight. Lucy blinked a few times until her eyes adjusted. She looked for a place to lean to ease the pain shooting through her ankle.

"I asked my driver to bring you here." Mrs. Dove-Lyon had the tone of a strict headmistress at the most prestigious finishing schools, but she was the Black Widow of Whitehall, and this was not just a lesson. It was Lucy's life, and she couldn't quite explain how she'd gotten herself into this mess.

"But why?"

"So that you can accept your soon-to-be husband, why else?"

Lucy gulped. The woman was insane. Far be it for Lucy to marry someone only because the town's most notorious matchmaker commanded the match. One reason why Lucy had come to London—no, *the* reason why Lucy had come to London—was to find the freedom that she couldn't have back in Switzerland, where Jews were *vershatchet*, matched. How could she have traveled so far and yet so little had changed?

"I am not interested," Lucy said.

"Of course, you are, my dear. You have no choice." Mrs. Dove-Lyon gestured to the settee across from her high-backed chair that looked like a throne and Lucy sat down. Yet the momentary relief was fleeting when the elderly woman lifted the veil and shot Lucy a stern look from her nearly transparent-grey eyes. With slow and deliberate motions, Mrs. Dove-Lyon removed the veil that had been pinned to the pile of grey curls on her head. Her face was wrinkled but her cheeks were painted a shimmering rose that gave her an air of ethereal beauty. She was intimidating and probably very wise.

"You spent the night alone with a man who frequents my establishment, you were unchaperoned and even injured."

"But I slipped here, you saw me leaving *with* the injury. Mr. Cavalier took me to the doctor." What seemed an entirely logical protest to Lucy didn't impress Mrs. Dove-Lyon, for her expression remained stern.

"The Ton doesn't care about the sequence of events, only that they occurred. And if the word spreads to the Jewish community, you have no prospects."

There came a knock on the door. "Ah, here he comes."

Titan opened the door and announced a gentleman. "Dr. Alfred Stein. *The Cavalier*. He compromised you and is now your groom."

Lucy's heart skipped a beat at the cold stare that the man's blue eyes sent her way. As if he had never seen her, he approached and inclined his head.

"Good day, Mrs. Dove-Lyon, and you are…?"

Lucy gasped and clasped her chest. After all that they had shared last night, how could he pretend not to know her? Was he so desperate to avoid the forced match?

"Mr. Cavalier?" she croaked, swallowing bile.

"Alfred, this is the girl you will marry," Mrs. Dove-Lyon said without much ado.

He blinked at Lucy, and she felt herself blush. It was the most embarrassing moment in her life. What had she expected after her wanton behavior the previous night? She'd practically melted into his embrace and now he was the sifter that prevented her from trickling between the cracks to the fallen girls. With just one escapade, she'd ruined her own prospects.

"Mrs. Dove-Lyon, I'm afraid to disappoint you, but I am not marrying her." The man she wanted to marry was supposed to be Mr. Cavalier—but it was too awful to be true for this was not him. "I'm sorry," he said to Lucy with a slight tremble in his voice. "As lovely as she is, I refuse."

Mrs. Dove-Lyon stood up and banged on the table, so that the teacups set there on a tray clanked on their saucers.

"Dr. Stein. Alfred. You must be jesting. First, you allege that my matches are biased toward the Ton, then you storm out of here in the middle of my *Mystère Masque*, and now you refuse to accept the match I deem fit for you? Have you any inkling what you are doing to your life?"

He raked his hair with both hands. Was it longer than last night? He seemed strange altogether. Different. "Have you gone mad, boy?"

Lucy horrified and embarrassed, almost cried out. This was the moment, of her fall from grace. She was losing all respectability and couldn't even explain how she'd gotten herself into this mess. The sweet gentleman who'd whispered Yiddish niceties into her ears had vanished, replaced by this cocky blonde with icy blue eyes who barely looked at her.

"I'm quite aware of what my last name implies. We are of Jewish descent and proud to carry the name on," Mr. Cavalier said.

"*Humpf!*" Mrs. Dove-Lyon seemed most unimpressed.

"I have maintained all propriety by gambling under a nickname at your establishment; my behavior has been beyond reproach." He seemed convinced by the finality of his justification.

"It doesn't matter now. Kiss," the elderly lady ordered.

"No!" Lucy protested. "I don't want to!" She darted up from the settee and nearly stumbled when her ankle gave way from the pain.

"Kiss him now. Seal the deal. You weren't this squeamish last night." Mrs. Dove-Lyon's tone sobered. Lucy inhaled sharply. She'd spoken to Mrs. Dove-Lyon in her bedroom, in confidence, as she would speak with a grandmotherly figure. And the woman had betrayed her. "My dear girl, only because society thwarts sexual gratification, it doesn't prevent erotic longing." She stood and came to Lucy's side. "And what's more, if you ask me, is that the expression of passion is the only way to satisfy desire if met by the right person. That is where I see cause to interfere because it is hard for most men to distinguish erotic pursuits from passion for the right woman."

"I harbor no such feelings for this girl," Alfred said, jerking his head back until his throat lay in wrinkles under his chin.

"I cannot kiss him!" Lucy protested again, trying to pull her arm back from Mrs. Dove-Lyon's grasp.

"It's not your first kiss, girl. At least women at my establishment don't feign sexual ignorance and pretend that their utmost virtues are chastity and elegance. Believe me, darling girl, I have lived many more decades than you, and I know that women's interest in sex neither makes them unmanageable nor are they devoid of libido."

Lucy's blood boiled with rage and embarrassment.

The elderly woman continued, "Here, we can at least admit that the pleasures of the flesh are mutual for men and women and that the act in marriage goes beyond the purpose of procreation—if you have the right partner, that is."

Alfred took another step back.

"Which brings me back to my first point and why we are here. Is this the right partner for you?"

"How do you intend to prove it one way or the other?" Alfred asked, his arms crossed and his legs in a wide, defensive stance, ignoring the Black Widow's tirade about passion altogether. Maybe a doctor was just too used to hearing of the natural states of the body, but Lucy's head was spinning.

"Simple," Mrs. Dove-Lyon said as she sat down and poured

herself a cup of tea. "Kiss her!"

She took Lucy's hand and gestured toward the tall, blond man. Then she shoved her toward him. Lucy fixed her gaze on the medallions of the silk carpet. If she counted the flowers and followed the paths of the swirls, maybe …

"Go on, don't act coy now!" She pushed Lucy, who lost her balance given that she wasn't able to put much weight on her sprained ankle yet and Lucy tumbled inelegantly into Mr. Cavalier's arms. He caught her mechanically, as if he'd instinctively stopped her from falling. He felt different than he did last night. There were no sparks, and she saw a green tint in his blue eyes. Although he looked down at her, his eyes were a different shade of blue. How had he faked that the night before?

Chapter Eight

"Alfred! Stop!" Seth shouted as he stormed through the door. He was out of breath and had run up the stairs as fast as he could before the tree of the guard or whatever Mrs. Dove-Lyon called her bouncers, could stop him.

He couldn't believe his eyes. There was his brother, his arms wrapped around Lucy. Mrs. Dove-Lyon's hand on her back, shoving her at him. Lucy's hair flew wildly out of her coiffure as if she'd been caught *in flagrante delicto*.

"Seth?" Alfred said, seemingly puzzled that he'd been found.

"Get your hands off her!" Seth tore his brother's arms from Lucy and wrapped his around her waist, supporting her as he'd done the night before. She tumbled against him. Was that an expression of relief washing over her face?

"M-Mr. Cavalier?" Lucy asked, wide-eyed and blotchy as if she'd been crying. "Alfred?" Lucy's eyes darted from him to his brother and back. "There are two of you?"

"Oh dear," Mrs. Dove-Lyon stepped back and surveyed the trio. "This is Seth, Dr. Stein's younger brother."

And how could that possibly matter? "Alfred, what was this all about?" Seth growled and held Lucy who buried her face into his neck and held on to him tightly.

"I have no idea. She summoned me here and wanted me to kiss the girl. Someone compromised her and apparently, I am expected to take the fall." Alfred looked at Lucy with a disgusted expression.

Seth boxed Alfred in the stomach before he could even think about it; his brother bucked with a sharp exhale. Lucy wasn't compromised, and she certainly wasn't worthy of his brother's disdain. She was the woman he loved!

"What was that for?" Alfred grunted bent over in pain.

"That someone was *me*. And she's not 'some girl' that has fallen from grace. How dare you!"

Lucy gasped and hugged him. He could feel her shaking. A warm rush flooded him just as it had last night. She lifted her face to his; he met her gaze. Soft and full of the same sharpness that he'd admired only yesterday, but now hurt dulled the sparkle. His heart blistered when he thought of Lucy in pain. It cut his breath off.

"If he's the masked man who carried out through the night, prove it," Mrs. Dove-Lion said.

Lucy's mouth twitched in a weak smile and Seth lowered his mouth onto hers. She responded immediately, and he shivered with desire. Their lips touched and blazing flames erupted deep in his gut. She felt so right in his arms, as if she'd been made to complement him. Made him feel whole.

"I love you." He faced her. "*Ikh hub mike farlibt in dir.* I am in love with you."

Lucy blinked at him dewy-eyed as a smile brightened her features.

"Is this the Mr. Cavalier who took you to the doctor at 87 Harley Street?" Mrs. Dove-Lyon asked more softly.

Lucy nodded, tears pricking her eyes.

"But this is Alfred, *the* Cavalier." A deadly and cruel look flickered in Mrs. Dove-Lyon's eyes. "Unless, they fooled us both."

Lucy's heart cramped with the pain of realization. She'd been betrayed. Yet, somehow, she didn't care. The right man had kissed her after all, no matter who he pretended to be.

"My brother, Seth, took my place here. We deceived you—" Alfred tried to explain but Mrs. Dove-Lyon paled and suddenly looked her age.

"You ... you..." she growled and wagged her index finger menacingly. Danger flickered in her eyes and her posture changed like a purring lion who'd pounce at her prey...

Chapter Nine

Mrs. Dove-Lyon had stayed true to her reputation and preyed on the Stein brothers, Alfred and Seth. But none of it mattered, because he was her Seth now. Even though the Black Widow of Whitehall had terrifyingly unconventional ways and Lucy had been *vershadchet*, matched, after all, she couldn't have been happier.

In a hasty but dignified ceremony, Mr. and Mrs. Grimshaw had stood in lieu of her parents and led her to the *chuppah*, wedding canopy, in the lavishly decorated garden of the Lyon's Den. She'd been made an example of, put on display, and used to repair the dent in Mrs. Dove-Lyon's reputation as a matchmaker. And that was all right for, in the end, Seth had made a vow to her that still made her heart sing with joy.

In a double wedding, standing next to Seth's brother Alfred and his bride Ada, Lucy had taken her place as the wife of the sweetest, kindest, and most handsome groom she could have ever imagined.

"Welcome to the family and *Mazal tov*," Alfred said with a proud smile after she and Seth had exchanged rings.

"You woke the sleeping lion and now look at us," Seth said to his brother, with mock rapprochement. He beamed at Lucy, and his gorgeous smile made her shiver with glee.

"Maybe I did," Alfred responded as he wrapped his arm around his bride, Ada. "But you shouldn't have tempted the purring lion either."

LATER THAT EVENING, Lucy withdrew to rest her ankle. She moved it in a circle without pain, but the strain of standing up and accepting the congratulations had been tiring. Although it was hasty and different than she'd imagined, especially because her parents weren't there, Lucy's wedding day couldn't have been further from perfection. As long as Seth was there, she felt whole.

But where was he now?

Waiting for him was hard. Lucy stepped to the window facing Green Park. Seth and Alfred's rented townhouse on the corner of Berkeley Street and Piccadilly was built on three stories, the newly furnished master suite on top. She'd met her new maid and gotten ready for the wedding night.

It was as if the world was in anticipation. Even the sun hung low, wrapping the buildings outside in a golden glow, and even the floor-length mirror in the corner reflected the light. Lucy felt naked in the thin layers of sheer cream-colored silk even though she had long sleeves.

She pulled the heavy blue drapes shut and the atmosphere in what would be her new bedroom as of tonight changed. The bustling of the busy town was outside, peeking in only through the glow surrounding the thick fabric.

Hm, where should I stand?

Lucy walked to the bed but then dismissed the idea of crawling under the covers. She didn't want Seth to think that she was hiding in a burrow like a field mouse. So she sat at the desk next to the window and crossed her legs one way, then another... no, sitting wouldn't do. As she got up and pushed the chair back to the desk, it screeched on the floor.

A knock sounded at the door.

"It's me," Seth sang in a friendly voice.

Her stomach fluttered and her heart began to race. "Enter please!" Lucy tried to match his tone, in spite of her nerves and excitement.

The handle pushed down inside as Seth opened the door. "Have you been tidying up?" he asked as he surveyed the room.

"No." Lucy wrung her hands. His gaze caught on her like a fish on a hook. "I didn't know where to sit or stand or what to—"

He was close already and reached to wrap his arms around her. "I didn't know either. I took two baths and…" His eyes trailed along the lace on her cinched bodice, then lifted to meet hers. He cupped her face with his right hand. "You are so beautiful."

"I'm nervous," she admitted.

"Me too." Seth smiled.

"I have never—"

"I would hope not!" Seth laughed. She laid both hands on his chest. He only wore a crisp, white linen shirt and black breeches. "What can I do to make you comfortable?" He laid his other hand atop hers on his chest. "I'll do anything for the rest of my life to keep this gorgeous smile on your lips."

She looked up at him and into his clear blue eyes.

"Do you know that your eyes are the same exact color as the sparkling snow on Lake Thun?"

He beamed at her, and his cheeks stretched into a boyish smile. "I didn't know." He caressed her cheek. "Will you show me?"

"Oh yes, when you come to meet my family."

"I'd love to. I'm sorry they missed your wedding."

She shrugged and gave a wistful smile. "I wrote to them earlier today and told them all about you."

"Everything?" Feigned alarm pierced his voice.

"Not everything."

"So not what we did at André's office?"

She shook her head.

"And what about what we did this morning?"

She pinched her lips in alarm and shook her head more vigorously.

"So you won't tell them about this, either?" He sounded amused.

"That depends."

"On what?"

"On how scandalous it is."

"Oh, what I have in mind is quite scandalous." And just like that, she was at ease. He had a way of making her heart soar but her mind calm.

His lips found hers and he pressed them against hers slowly. She knew how to return his kiss and moved her lips now. But when she opened her mouth, he changed his demeanor altogether. He grew almost possessive, and his hands trailed along her arms, then to her back and...

"Oh!" she squeaked.

He froze.

"You surprised me," she said, but he didn't move his hands from her bottom.

"I have many surprises for you tonight." He pulled her close and she felt the hardness in his middle.

"I want to see."

"I beg your pardon?" He let go of her and stepped back, inclining his head as if he hadn't heard her correctly.

She took a deep breath. The mystery was about to be revealed. And to think this all had happened as the result of a *Mystère Masque*. Lucy bit back a nervous giggle. "I want to see you in the nude."

For a second, Seth's eyes darted from one of her eyes to the other as if he were calculating something in his mind. Then he wriggled his toes and she noticed that he'd come in without shoes. His feet were bigger than hers, and a slight tuft of hair dusted each toe.

"Explore as you wish." He flapped his hands on his sides as if he was surrendering to her and invited her touch.

Lucy began where she'd known she had touched him before, with her hands on his chest. But now it was not enough, and she pulled up the hem of his shirt. He lifted both arms and she pulled the garment up and over his head, before dropping it on the floor.

His shoulders were broad and smooth, his chest defined by muscles like the marble statues in the British Museum that Mrs. Grimshaw had taken her to when she'd arrived in London. Lucy walked around him, her fingertips never leaving his taut skin. His back was just as muscular as his front, and she saw his scapula twitch. He cleared his throat.

Then he twisted his upper body to grasp her hand and lead it down to the waistband of his breeches.

"Go ahead. I have nothing to hide and will never keep anything from you." He turned then to face her and led both of her hands to his middle. She gasped at his bold command, then opened the buttons of his trousers. He shimmied until they began to slide down his legs and his member sprang free. Seth stepped out of the pool of fabric on the floor.

Chapter Ten

Seth's cock twitched in her hand. Her touch was gentle but curious. He let her explore as long as he could but then she stood with her side to the dim light that flooded the room with the orange hues of the setting sun. The world, even just out the window, in the street, seemed so far away. It was just the two of them. Seth couldn't quite believe his luck. Because right there within his reach was the siren whom he had married.

She bit her tongue and was about to go down on her knees to take a close look when he noticed her nipples had hardened under the fabric.

"My turn, all right?" He supported her with his hands under her arms and took her mouth more vigorously than he'd ever allowed himself before. She responded in kind and moaned into his embrace. When Seth fumbled with the sash that held her robe together, there was altogether too much fabric. He stepped forward, she backed up, and so they made it to the wall next to the door in an instant.

Panting with her sweet breath, she rested her head against the wall as if she were relieved to have something to lean on. Then she arched her back.

She dropped her coat and was only slightly veiled in a transparent lace chemise, tied with red ribbons on her shoulders. As she drove her hands through his hair, he plunged into the delicious mounds of her perky breasts. They were tight but lush, perfect in his hands, and erotically delicious.

"Seth!" She called as she seemed to melt down the wall.

His mouth still on her nipples, first one then the other, he caught her as she slid down the wall. She was ready, but he didn't want to overwhelm her too quickly. So he propped his knee against the wall and let her rest on his thigh. Their kisses turned into a hot mess, seeking closeness and touch—not just with their hands but with every part of their bodies.

Driven by a deep urge to feel more of him, she rubbed her wet center against his leg, seeking friction, and that was when he grabbed her behind again, shifted his center, and stood in a wide stance pressing his cock against her.

She surprised him by lifting her arms to hold his shoulders. She really was ready.

He parted her folds with one hand and gently came to her secret place. And it felt good.

She shut her eyes and pressed her head against the wall. "Deeper."

Seth shivered. Then he adjusted his position. "Ready?" he whispered.

She clasped his shoulders and wrapped her legs around him.

"I've wanted to do this since I saw your gorgeous legs at the doctor's." He plunged in to the hilt and groaned with pleasure as he hooked his hands into the hollows of her knees. Her shift was pushed up all the way. It should have been scandalous but was letting him in, so he could be enveloped in her warmth. She felt perfect and right.

"I have one last riddle for you," Seth said as he leaned his forehead against hers. His voice was hoarse with need and desire. "What is all mine but only you can have?"

Lucy smiled and put her arms around his neck. "Your heart?"

"Absolutely right, my love." And it would be, forever. "You've won my heart. It's all yours."

The End

Author's Note

Lucy is from a village called Aarmühle, which is now known as Interlaken. Caught between the cities Basel and Bern, there were only a few transient efforts noted to establish Jewish settlements, mainly baths to attract tourists. In the time that our story takes place, Jews in Switzerland were usually francophones and their children attended public school or were tutored by members of the community.

Even though their rights were relatively equal on paper, they were *de facto* second-rate citizens and had to work extra hard to "earn the approval of the agencies," as some historic documents suggest. In other words, Jews were under extraordinary scrutiny and were not afforded the same opportunities as other citizens.

It is during this time that an educated girl like Lucy would be sent away from her loving family with the hope to find a husband in a place with more freedom. Her parents took an enormous risk because she might have forsaken their religion in favor of the lavish lifestyles of wealthy aristocrats. Thus, finding a husband in England was no easy feat for Lucy and she should have considered herself lucky to get Mrs. Dove-Lyon's help. As any young girl of twenty, however, Lucy didn't see the meddlesome matchmaker as more than a threat to her plans.

Jews have been employing matchmakers called "shadchan" as marriage brokers for centuries—many still do.

I hope you enjoyed Mrs. Dove-Lyon's matchmaking in Sara Adrien's signature romances with a Jewish twist, that take on distinctive flavors that pick up little-known aspects of history.

Now that you read Seth's story, find out how Mrs. Dove-Lyon's matchmaking brings romance to his brother, Alfred, in **Don't Wake A Sleeping Lyon** and **The Lyon's First Choice**. Stay tuned for more Regency Romance with a Jewish twist from Sara Adrien's pen.

Read the love story of André, the Italian orthopedist from 87 Harley Street in **A Touch of Charm**.

Also by Sara Adrien

Miracles on Harley Street Series (forthcoming with Dragonblade):
A Sight to Behold
The Scent of Intuition
A Taste of Gold
The Sound of Seduction
A Touch of Charm

Infiltrating the Ton Series:
Margins of Love
The Pearl of All Brides
A Kiss After Tea

Diamond Dynasty Series:
Instead of Harmony
In Eternal Love
In Tune with His Heart
In Just a Year
In A Precious Vow
In a Perfect Moment

Check Mates Series:
Captured at the Ball
Baron in Check
Love Is a Draw
Brilliance and Glory

About Sara Adrien

Bestselling author Sara Adrien writes hot and heart-melting regency romance with a Jewish twist. As a law professor-turned-author, she writes about clandestine identities, whims of fate, and sizzling seduction. If you like unique and intelligent characters, deliciously sexy scenes, and the nostalgia of afternoon tea, then you'll adore Sara Adrien's tender tear-jerkers.

Sign up for her VIP newsletter to be the first to hear about new releases, audiobooks, sales, and bonus content at https://SaraAdrien.com.

Catch up with Sara Adrien here:
linktr.ee/jewishregencyromance
saraadrien.com
instagram.com/jewishregencyromance
facebook.com/AuthorSaraAdrien
bookbub.com/authors/sara-adrien
goodreads.com/author/show/22249825.Sara_Adrien
youtube.com/channel/UCK9OLp1wN6IaGkXe7OugfHg

Unmasked by the Lyon

by Belle Ami

Prologue

London, England
November 7, 1795

"Don't move, Lizzie sweetheart—Mama needs to open the brolly."

"Mama, the kitty is lost."

"Yes, yes, there are lots of kittens that lose their way in London, darling. Drat!" Her mother continued to battle with the brolly. "This bumbershoot is not cooperating. We will surely be soaked to the skin and catch our death of cold."

"I get kitty," Lizzie whispered, toddling into the road. She bent to pick up the cat, but before she could get her hands around it, the cat dashed away.

"Lizzie!" her mother screamed.

Lizzie froze and looked back in confusion. She'd never heard her mother scream like that before.

Her mother ran toward her, arms wide. "Dear God, Lizzie!"

The next thing Lizzie felt was her mother's hands pushing her so hard she went flying, and then there was only blackness. When she opened her eyes there was a crowd of faces looking down at her. Fear gripped her and she cried, "Mama!"

Speaking all at once, dozens of voices accosted her. She didn't understand what they were saying. Who were these people, and where was her mama? She raised her head and looked back to where she last saw her mother running to her, and her eyes widened. A hackney coach lay on its side, and beneath one of the wheels, she could see a body. "Mama?"

She sat up and slipped from the hands that tried to hold her back.

"Stop her."

"She mustn't see, poor dear."

"Mama!" Lizzie ran to the woman trapped beneath the wheel and let out an ear-piercing scream. She dropped to her knees sobbing, took her mother's lifeless hand, and pressed a kiss on the palm before being dragged off. "No! No! No! Mama needs me! I need to help Mama!" she wailed as the constable carried her away.

She wouldn't stop crying for her mother. Not even when Papa held her tight in his arms and told her everything would be all right as tears streamed down his face. Not even when her older sisters slept on either side of her night after night and cuddled her after a nightmare. Only after the doctor came to see her, and gave her a medicine that Nanny Sparrow stirred into a cup of warm milk and honey, did she finally stop crying. As her eyelids grew heavy, she prayed to the angels that she would see Mama again…

Chapter One

Buckinghamshire, England
December 1, 1815

"Potsy, my darling, would you not agree that the joys of love and marriage are highly exaggerated?" Lizzie swept through a row of potted white orchids, snipping off dead leaves and tossing them on the floor. "Don't look at me with that censorious gaze—of course I'll sweep the floor when I'm done." She sighed and pushed back a few unruly blonde curls that had escaped her bun and tumbled over her eyes. "Truth is, I'm afraid my chances aren't promising. Twenty-four years is a bit long on the shelf."

"Don't you find it interesting that when I speak with you, I don't stutter in the slightest bit? If only the same were true when I'm in the company of other males." For as long as Lizzie could remember, the thought of interacting with men outside her family caused her such palpitations that she could barely speak a coherent sentence, let alone engage in witty and flirtatious banter. It was a horrifying affliction that prohibited her from speaking with strangers, except for a brief hello.

Her beloved late father Alfred Villiers, Duke of Buckingham, had been a kind and devoted parent and had raised Lizzie and her two sisters Agnes and Patience with much love and good humor. *I miss you, Papa.* Lizzie wiped her eyes that had gotten misty from her sadness. "Potsy, when does the pain stop? It's a year since Papa left us, but I find no relief. I wish I had told him how sorry I was to have caused him such embarrassment over the years."

Her debut six years ago had been a disaster. At Queen Charlotte's end-of-the-season ball when she was introduced to the Prince of Wales, affectionately known as Prinny, Lizzie had stumbled over her words so badly that he'd been struck dumb and made a hasty departure. The snide laughter that erupted around her had made her want to turn and run out of the ballroom and never look back. And, of course, the gossip rags had seized on the debacle and dubbed her the *Dreadful Debutante*. Lizzie had left London soon after and retreated to her father's estate in Buckinghamshire. She hadn't been out in Society since.

She'd made her peace with it, sort of, and had let go of all the pain and sorrow—well, almost all of it. Instead, she'd filled her days with productive activity, and had cultivated her passion for gardening. Nurturing seedlings and helping them grow and flourish brought her immense satisfaction, and spending her days surrounded by the beauty of flowers and plants filled her with a sense of serenity.

She inhaled the sweet scent of citrus and flowers that perfumed the air in the greenhouse and breathed out a sigh of contentment. *In the greenhouse, my hard work bears fruit.* She chuckled as she realized she'd created a pun by chance.

Potsy regarded her with a curious look in his velvety-brown eyes. "Oh, I could just kiss you, dear Potsy!" She bent and picked up the King Charles Cocker Spaniel and cuddled him close, burying her face in his soft fur. Potsy licked her cheek, making her giggle.

She gazed about her, and still marveled at the magnificent glasshouse her father had built for her on her sixteenth birthday. He had always encouraged her love of nature and built her the largest and most modern greenhouse in all of England, rivaled only by the one at Buckingham Palace. Lizzie knew it had cost a fortune, but the duke had done everything he could to make his youngest child happy. After the horror of her witnessing her mother's tragic death, he'd understood how gardening was a balm to her grief.

The glass structure featured a heating system where hot, dry air from a cockle stove flowed over water that charged the air with moisture, which made for a perfect environment for Lizzie to grow plants, flowers, and fruit. Her "green thumb" was praised by family and close friends, and the tropical fruit and flowers of her labors overflowed vases and bowls throughout the manor. In all of England, no more beautiful flowers ever bloomed.

She turned to the iris bulbs she'd planted last week and watered the delicate stalks of green that had begun to shoot out of the soil. She looked over the final row of bulbs. Satisfied with her efforts, she clapped her hands together, shaking off the damp dirt that clung to her fingers. Without thinking, she wiped the excess off on her muslin gown. "Oh, drat, Sarah will have my guts for garters if I ruin another gown." Lizzie was always forgetting to put on a garden apron when working in the greenhouse. "I do hope Vera can sponge out the stains."

Potsy stood up on his hind legs and danced around, making Lizzie laugh. "Oh, are you agreeing with me about the stain, or do you want a treat?

Potsy barked in reply.

Lizzie fished in her basket and took out a biscuit. "Sit, Potsy." The dog obediently sat. "Good boy!" Lizzie tossed the biscuit, and Potsy caught it in his mouth. "And it's quite all right to like Phillip. He's a kind man, and I'm glad he inherited Papa's title. He's going to be a great duke. I think."

Potsy barked and thumped his tail in clear agreement.

After her father's death, it had taken the solicitors nearly a year to find Phillip Villiers, Papa's nephew, who was next in line to inherit the title and estate. The new duke had been injured in the calvary while serving at Waterloo under Arthur Wellesley, the first Duke of Wellington, and, having retired from his service to His Majesty George III, had returned to England with a modest pension. Estranged from his family, he had no idea of his uncle's death.

She grabbed the broom and swept the dirt-packed floor. Another errant curl slipped from her bun. The bun itself had all but collapsed, and when Lizzie glanced down, she noticed there were pins everywhere. She heaved a sigh, imagining what she must look like.

Lizzie glanced at the spaniel who was sitting patiently watching her. "Potsy, it is no wonder that I love you when you look at me with those adoring, deep brown eyes."

The spaniel wagged his tail in reply.

Lizzie found it rather amusing that the only other person who claimed the dog's utter devotion was the new duke. When Phillip returned home, whether it was from an hour spent at White's or a day spent visiting his tenant farmers with Sarah, the spaniel greeted him with the same exuberance. Lizzie suspected there might be something more to Potsy's extraordinary devotion. She had the sneaking suspicion that the duke was giving Potsy forbidden treats on the sly.

"Confess, Potsy—does he stuff his pockets with bacon?" Potsy's eyes gleamed with excitement at the mention bacon. Lizzie scratched the dog's neck. "That's it, isn't it?"

Potsy barked in answer.

"Sarah was right, Potsy—Phillip can now join the small and exclusive club of men that I don't stutter around. Oh, and of course you, my darling pet, as you too are of the male persuasion."

Sarah had been barely twenty when she married Lizzie's father. It was not unheard of, but it had been a shock to the family. That was until they knew the reason why Father had married her. But it didn't take long for Lizzie and her sisters to adore Sarah. Their stepmother was all that was kind and good.

Lizzie, being the youngest, and haunted by the death of her mother, absorbed Sarah's care and devotion like it were a soothing balm. She'd only been three years old when her mother was mowed down and crushed beneath the wheels of a hackney carriage. And beyond the memory of holding her mother's hand and kissing her palm as she lay dying, Lizzie remembered nothing of that tragic day.

Lizzie didn't speak for a year after her mother's death, and when she finally did begin to speak again, her words had come out in a terrible tangle. Over the years, her stutter had improved, but it often reared its ugly head when Lizzie was around new people or was feeling anxious. It had taken her a long time to get over her belief that her stutter must have been a punishment for causing her mother's death. It was dear Sarah who'd helped Lizzie begin to heal from the tragedy.

"I think your stutter is connected with your suffering, poppet," Sarah had gently explained to eleven-year-old Lizzie. She'd wrapped her arms around Lizzie and held her close as Lizzie confided her shame and guilt. "You were just a baby, sweet girl, and the shock and tragedy of your mother's passing caused a deep and painful hurt in your heart. But your mother loved you so much, and her love is still with you." She'd laid her hand on Lizzie's heart. "Inside you." Sarah had become a second mother to Lizzie, who was forever thankful that her father had married Sarah when he did. Her stepmother had helped to heal their entire family.

The late duke had been very fond of Sarah as well, but Lizzie and her sisters had always known that their late mother, Penelope, had been the love of their father's life. Sarah had known this as well, but that didn't stop her from being a loyal wife to the duke and a wonderful stepmother to his daughters.

Lizzie wiped an errant tear from her cheek. "I'd better get back to work, or I'm liable to start blubbering full force," she said to Potsy, who nudged Lizzie's hand with his soft head. Potsy always understood her occasional melancholy and would sit quietly with her, offering his warmth. Thinking about her beautiful and kind mother and how she died always filled Lizzie with sadness. She sniffled and wiped another tear from her cheek.

Lizzie refilled the can to water the other fruit trees, plants, and flowers. It was a relaxing activity, and she slipped into a dreamlike state while doing it, and in this hazy state, her mind began to wander. She'd professed to everyone in her family that she was perfectly fine and happy just as she was, but secretly, in her heart, she dreamed of falling head over heels in love. What was more, she dreamed of having someone fall head over heels in love with her. If only she could meet a wonderful man who could see past her affliction and had the patience to wait for her to become comfortable enough that her stutter faded away.

Oh, how she yearned for her very own fairytale ending, just as her sisters had been blessed with. Of course, she wasn't jealous of her sisters. She was happy for their happiness. Lizzie's older sisters Agnes and Patience had married for love. Agnes had two sons and Patience had two girls. Agnes's husband Richard Bentwood was a member of the Whigs and a rising star in Parliament. Patience's husband, Lionel Arthur, was the scion of the Sinclair family, owners of paper mills in both England and Canada.

"There is nothing wrong to want happiness for oneself, is there, Potsy?" The dog trotted beside Lizzie as she refilled the watering can again. Lizzie thought about her reoccurring dream of a handsome man waking her up with a kiss and her infirmity vanishing without a trace. *Such is the stuff of dreams,* she reminded herself.

The sound of approaching male voices yanked her from her reverie, and her heart began to hammer in her chest. Frantically she looked around for a hiding place. Female voices would have not caused such palpitations, but to hear male voices and know she had no way of avoiding discovery and conversation filled her with panic. Feeling like a trapped animal, she whipped her head around as she frantically sought a place to hide. "Potsy, look at me, I'm a mess," she whispered. "Come, let's hide." She grabbed the dog and hid under the potting table, hoping that she could remain hidden and undetected.

The men entered the greenhouse, and she recognized the familiar baritone of the duke, which would have made her come out from her hiding place with some sort of excuse of perhaps looking for a bulb that had rolled under the table, but a second male voice made her stay put. *Hopefully they'll just take a quick look around and continue down the path to the lake.*

The door squeaked. "I say, Villiers, your description of the greenhouse doesn't begin to do it justice. Not only is it an engineering and architectural marvel, but the profusion of flowers and greenery is astonishing. And you say your cousin is a horticulturist?"

"Yes, everything in here is Elizabeth's doing. She truly has a gift for growing anything."

Lizzie could feel her face heat at the compliment, but she held still as the tip-tap of their shoes neared. They walked among the rows of plantings pausing but a few feet from where Lizzie was hiding with Potsy.

"I should like to meet this lady. I have never heard of any young, unmarried woman who spends her days in such productive activity. Most of the Society ladies I've met aspire to rise at ten, drink chocolate in their rooms, and then spend two hours deciding what to wear. The rest of their day is reserved for shopping, visiting friends, and drinking endless cups of tea." He chuckled.

"Yes, and as one of England's most eligible bachelors, you have your pick of all those productive young ladies of the *ton*," Phillip teased.

"Don't remind me. Not a day goes by that my mother doesn't mention it. I swear, if she weren't so easily shocked, she'd probably ask the famous Mrs. Dove-Lyon to concoct some matchmaking scheme. Come to think of it, I wonder if she may have contacted her already. Last time I was at the Den, Mrs. Dove-Lyon made a few innuendos about finding me a suitable bride. I'm sure she'll be after you soon—after all, you're a duke and a war hero."

"I'll not be going that route, I can assure you. Besides, I'm sure my eye patch will scare away even the most stalwart of debutantes."

The stranger chuckled, a deep, resonant laugh that surprisingly filled Lizzie with a tingling warmth. "On the contrary, my friend. I bet that eye patch of yours will have those young ladies swooning at your feet."

"Lord, I hope not," Phillip said.

Lizzie was having a hard time keeping Potsy still. He squirmed every time the duke spoke. And she feared she couldn't hold him back much longer.

"My, my, look at the size of these pineapples. They're extraordinary. Fresh fruit in the winter months costs an arm and a leg. And have you any idea what I spend on flower arrangements at Dartmouth House? I had no idea how damn much those flowers cost. Your cousin must save you a veritable fortune. You're a lucky man."

"I've never thought of it that way. It's Elizabeth's passion, but you're right; we are most fortunate indeed to have such bounty thanks to Lizzie's talents."

"Perhaps you and I can form an arrangement. My mother is enamored of white orchids, and I know you enjoy betting on the horses. Perhaps we might strike a deal, if you're so inclined?"

"The deal would have to be struck with Elizabeth. Everything in here is hers."

She wished Potsy would stop squirming. *Oh no! Too late!* Potsy was so mad with excitement that he escaped from her arms. The spaniel ran to the duke and plopped down on his rear as he'd been taught, wagging his tail back and forth at lightning speed.

The duke scanned the room as he knelt to the dog. "Potsy, old boy, what are you doing here alone? How did you manage to sneak in without Lizzie's knowledge? I hope you haven't been digging up her iris bulbs again."

Lizzie sneezed and covered her mouth in horror. *Drat! Drat! Drat!*

Two pairs of elegant black men's shoes appeared in front of the table, and in unison the owners of the shoes knelt. Two pairs of surprised eyes regarded her.

"Elizabeth? What are you doing under here?"

"C-c-c-cousin…" Her eyes brimmed with tears as she struggled to get the words out. She took the duke's proffered hand, and he helped her from beneath the table. The anxiety of the situation brought on her affliction in full force.

"I-I-I d-didn't expect to s-s-see a-a-anyone in h-here." She closed her eyes and struggled to gain control. Unable to continue, she knelt and picked Potsy up. "P-Potsy made off with some of m-my b-bulbs, and I w-w-was…"

"And you were retrieving them when we barged in," the duke said, kindly finishing her sentence.

She nodded, wanting to bite her tongue until it bled, such was her frustration.

Phillip turned to his friend. "Lucien, may I introduce my cousin, Lady Elizabeth Villiers. Elizabeth, this is my friend Lucien Radcliffe, Earl of Dartmouth, who heard about your greenhouse and the miracles within and asked to see inside." He proudly waved his hand around the greenhouse. "This is Elizabeth's creation, and we thank her wholeheartedly for the beauty she brings to our lives."

The earl smiled at her and reached for her hand. "It is my great pleasure to meet you, my lady. I am in awe of your horticultural talents."

Lizzie held out her hand and was mortified to see her nails encrusted with dirt, but it was too late to pull back. The earl, the most handsome man she'd ever seen, was tall, as tall as Phillip and just as broad of shoulder. When he bent to kiss her hand, a lock of his black, wavy hair fell over his forehead in a most beguiling way. But it was his blue eyes, which reminded her of an azure sky on a clear morning, that stole her breath. With his lips just inches from her hand he hesitated, his gaze settling on her filthy nails. "Perhaps we have caught you at an inopportune moment." He patted her hand instead of kissing it.

She pulled her hand back so suddenly that she stumbled backward, lost her balance, and landed rump first in a basin of water. "O-o-oh n-n-no!" Cold, mucky water had drenched her gown from hem to waist.

Potsy barked in excitement, scampered to the basin, and jumped right in, splashing about and licking Lizzie's face.

The two men both burst out laughing.

"Potsy, stop. It's not bath time!" Lizzie was mortified. Had she been alone she would have found humor in the situation, but certainly not now. Not when a handsome stranger had witnessed the mishap. She was once again the Dreadful Debutante.

Lucien and Phillip rushed to help her out of the round wooden tub, but they were still chuckling as Potsy kept splashing about.

"Phillip, p-p-please grab P-P-Potsy!" she sputtered.

Her cousin reached for the spaniel and held tight while Lucien reached out and tugged Lizzie out of the tub.

"I m-must g-go," Lizzie managed as her gaze skittered away from the earl. She dashed toward the door.

"Lizzie, wait!" Phillip shouted after her. "You're soaking wet."

She shook her head and broke into a run. Her only thought was to get away. She didn't dare look back. Knowing he was laughing only made things worse. Phillip laughed too, but he didn't count. He was like a brother to her. She could only imagine what the handsome earl was thinking. Memories of her dreadful debut four years ago came flooding back to her, and it was all she could do to keep the tears at bay. She ran and ran as fast as she could. But no matter how fast she ran, she could still hear the earl's laughter echoing in her head.

Chapter Two

London, England
January 30, 1816

Lucien Radcliffe watched as the cards were dealt for another round of baccarat. Mrs. Dove-Lyon stood by his elbow, her face set in stone, giving no indication of her thoughts as she watched the betting and the action play out. Lucien was betting with the house, and after losing the last round, he doubled down on his previous wager. The dealer revealed his winning hand. In most betting games, the house held a slight advantage, which was unquestionably true of baccarat. The three cards were nine—a winning hand for the house, and because he had bet with the house, it was also a winning hand for him.

"You are lucky today, my lord," Mrs. Dove-Lyon said.

Lucien nodded. "I am lucky in many ways, the least of which is gambling."

"You are still unmarried, my lord. Perhaps the time is ripe to remedy the situation, if I may be so bold."

Lucien might have taken offense, but since his return to London from Buckinghamshire, his unmarried state was often on his mind. However, he would not be one of the Black Widow's toffs who succumbed to her machinations or tricks to trap them into marrying one of her brokered arrangements. "I take no offense, madam. It is something I ponder from time to time." With the skill of a solicitor, he turned the tables on her. "You have been a widow for many years, yet I do not see a ring on your finger, and I wonder how a woman like yourself has managed to remain unattached?" He grinned as he awaited her reply.

Her charming laugh warmed him. "I am older and settled in my ways. And I need no man to complete me—or support me, for that matter." She looked around her establishment at the throng of guests. The tables were full, and the betting was fierce. "You're a very clever man, my lord," she said with a sly smile. "Perhaps you can assist me in my current dilemma. My birthday is in April, and every year I throw a party for myself, but though I have racked my brain to devise exciting means to celebrate, so far, no theme has inspired me. It must be unlike any other soirée. I wish it to be selective, with only certain friends and patrons in attendance. Do you have any suggestions?"

Lucien looked pensively at the cards in front of him. He was bored with his routine for the first time, and even the excitement of winning didn't ignite his interest. The altercation with Elizabeth still bothered him to no end. He could still see her peaches-and-cream complexion charmingly streaked with potting soil, which in no way detracted from her beauty, and he'd been nearly left speechless by those beautiful green eyes. He'd longed to tangle his fingers in her golden hair.

Yes, the *ton* was full of beautiful young women, but from the moment she'd jumped up from under that table, his heart had done a dozen somersaults. Her vibrant, golden beauty took his breath away. And, truth be told, he was in awe of her talent in creating such beautiful flowers and fruit trees. And then to see her so distressed after falling into the tub of water... He felt no better than the lowliest cad for not coming to her rescue. Instead of offering her comfort after her dunking, he'd laughed. By God, he'd *laughed*. Well, in all fairness, Phillip had laughed too. And they were laughing at the dog's antics. Unfortunately, Lizzie hadn't seen it that way and had run off. He'd started to go after her, but Phillip stopped him, saying Lizzie was the kind of woman who required solitude to regain her equilibrium.

When Lucien reached out to Phillip the next day to inquire after Lizzie, the duke had explained to him of her lifelong affliction, triggered by the traumatic experience of witnessing the death of her mother. Lucien was shocked by Phillip's revelation, and his regard for Lizzie had overflowed. That she could have the strength to create such beauty after such a deeply tragic loss left him in awe.

The next day Lucien had wanted to pay his respects to Lizzie in person, and to apologize for his lack of chivalry, but Phillip declined. "I think it would be better if you gave Lizzie some time. I promise to tell her of your visit," he'd said.

And so, Lucien had heeded his friend's advice and returned to London, but he felt like a heel for doing so. He was frustrated beyond belief. Few knew that he had once borne his own impediment, a condition that had nearly destroyed him. He had once been a stutterer, something his late father never understood and considered a defect. As a child, he suffered endless criticism, which made his stuttering worse.

It wasn't until he was almost seventeen that he stumbled on the solution. He'd joined the choir at Balliol College at Oxford University and discovered singing to be therapeutic. Lucien overcame his nightmare on his own, and was now an erudite speaker who could parry with the best of them. He could also carry a tune, and discovered he had a pleasing tenor voice. He enjoyed singing at holiday gatherings for family and friends alike.

"My lord, your mind seems to have floated away from our discussion," Mrs. Dove-Lyon teased, bringing him back from his wayward thoughts.

"My sincere apologies, but I think I have an idea that might be of interest," he said. "What say you to a masked ball? A celebration where dancing, music, exquisite food, and romance are in the offing. Regarding its exclusivity, you might create a golden invitation, that only a select group would receive. No one would know why they were chosen. As word got out, as it always does among the gossip-hungry *ton*, it will create quite a stir, and will undoubtedly become the most sought-after ticket in Town."

A glow of excitement lit Mrs. Dove-Lyon's face as she regarded him. "You do surprise me, my lord. What a clever idea, and naturally, you have guaranteed yourself an invitation."

"Glad to oblige," he said, inclining his head. "And an event I look forward to. Please let me know if I can be of assistance. I might have a few suggestions for guests that might provide additional value to the Lyon's Den. It has not escaped me that you have had great success in arranging some of the most successful matches in England in recent memory. Matches with many ladies whose reputations are, shall we say, slightly tarnished. I imagine it is a very lucrative business that pays you well."

"It is no secret that I sometimes play the role of Cupid for a price. Fortunately, the high and mighty tend to look the other way. Truthfully, putting together two people who can benefit each other has its allure and gives me great satisfaction. Of course, it goes without saying that the benefit to the Lyon's Den is my first concern, and the funds from this sideline are substantial. When I have compiled my list of guests, you and I shall have a conversation. I know I can trust in your confidentiality." Mrs. Dove-Lyon nodded and glided away, disappearing into the crowded gaming den.

Lucien couldn't help but grin. His conversation with the Black Widow of Whitehall had lifted his spirits, and his thoughts returned to the lovely Lady Elizabeth. That he, of all people, had been so insensitive to the beautiful young woman's plight made him sick to his stomach. It was not enough to say he was sorry. Sorry did nothing to repair the damage done. Those tears tumbling down her muddy cheeks had not only left streaks on her face but left their mark on his heart. He wondered what thoughts and dreams lay in the depths of her brilliant emerald-green eyes. He wanted to know everything about her.

He thought Elizabeth a remarkable woman and unlike any other among the aristocracy. Not only was she gifted with an exceptional talent, but the fact that she did the work herself, literally getting her hands dirty, was truly admirable. He regretted not kissing her hand that day, dirt or no dirt. *Damned idiot!* The blooms and fruits within her greenhouse were the most magnificent he'd ever seen. What was more, he knew firsthand that a speaking impediment did not reflect who a person was inside. He was certain that beneath that beautiful face and curvaceous form was a woman of unmatched intelligence and desirability. Of course, he couldn't help but notice her delectable curves, drenched as she'd been from her tumble in the basin. *If only I had been as clever as Potsy!* And now, the opportunity to know her better might be managed.

He cashed out his winnings and waved for his valet. Mrs. Dove-Lyon had opened the door, but now he must make certain that Elizabeth walked through.

LUCIEN AND HIS uncle, Charles Medford, Lucien's mother's brother, circled each other in the boxing ring, their shirtless torsos shining with sweat. The two men nimbly danced around each other with footwork honed from years of practice. Uncle Charles had years ago taken Lucien under his wing and introduced him to the sport of pugilism. Charles had been trained by none other than "Gentleman" John Johnson, who'd also trained Lord Byron, the Duke of York, the Duke of Hamilton, and the Prince of Wales.

"I sense something is troubling you, Lucien." Charles shifted from foot to foot and delivered a jab, making contact with Lucien's shoulder. Lucien should have blocked it, but his mind wasn't totally present, which wasn't a good thing when boxing with his uncle, who was built like the side of a barn, with legs like tree trunks, and fists like bricks. Charles was an avid sportsman who regularly frequented the Epee training facility next door, as did Lucien.

"Truth is, there's this woman."

"Aah," said his uncle. "The root cause of every man's confusion lies always with the fairer sex. And may I ask who this young woman is and why you are troubled about her?"

Lucien threw a punch, but only grazed his uncle's chin as the older man ducked his head just in time.

"Close but not close enough," Charles said with a chuckle.

"Her name is Elizabeth Villiers, and she is the youngest daughter of the Duke of Buckingham."

"I know of the family. The duke was a fine man, and I was sorry to hear of his passing. As I recall, there was a bit of a scandal when the duke remarried about a decade ago, the daughter of a friend. A very much younger woman, is she not?"

"That would be Sarah Farnsworth Villiers, and a more gracious or beautiful lady I have yet to meet. I detest the gossip mill that would smear the reputation of such an intelligent and elegant woman." Lucien had sensed from the first a tender rapport between Sarah and Phillip, perhaps even unknown to each other. He thought they would make a brilliant match. Both were two of the most honorable people he knew.

Lucien blew out a frustrated breath as he brought himself back to the boxing ring. The men had been circling and sparring, and their breathing was ragged. "Let us give it a rest. I need your advice in this matter," Lucien said to his uncle.

"Of course, son," Charles replied. "I will do anything in my power to help."

They sat on a bench and quenched their thirst from a jug of water. "Uncle, I cannot even fathom it, for I have never felt the like before, but from the first moment I set eyes on Elizabeth Villiers, I was deeply attracted to her. And while she is a beautiful young woman, it is not only physical attraction that I feel. How strange is this?"

"Ah, then you have experienced love at first sight."

"What?" Lucien arched a brow. "Preposterous."

"Then how else do you explain the fact that you are tied up in knots just thinking about her, and you scarcely said two words to her? Trust me, love at first sight exists. For it happened to me with your aunt Lydia. From the moment I saw her across a crowded ballroom, I could not get her out of my mind."

"Uncle, I'm afraid I made a mess of things. There is something I have not told you. Something that I fear has caused a terrible misunderstanding." Lucien told his uncle everything that had transpired in the greenhouse on the Villiers estate. "Both Phillip and I laughed when the dog Potsy jumped in and began splashing about. I fear, however, that Lady Elizabeth misinterpreted our reaction, and she ran out of there before either Phillip or I could assist her. And there is something more, something which I think is the main reason that Lady Elizabeth ran off in such a distressed state." He blew out a breath. "Elizabeth suffers from the same affliction of stammering that plagued me growing up, and I'm afraid my worst memories returned to me—and that could have been the reason why I was not thinking straight. That I did not rush to reassure that lovely young woman shames me."

"I understand, Lucien," Charles said, giving his shoulder a brief pat. "I remember the way it was for you as a boy, with your father's cold and cruel treatment of you. And my dear sister did her best, I know. But I remember how it was for you when you were in the grip of a bout of stammering. I also know how hard you have worked to overcome it. My God, son, it is something to be proud of."

"Thank you, Uncle. Your support has always meant a great deal to me and made all the difference in the world."

"Would that I could go back in time and give that louse the walloping he deserved."

Lucien couldn't help but agree with his uncle—his father had indeed been a louse, a philandering, abusive man who had made his mother's life miserable and his own a living hell. Lucien had felt a sense of relief at his father's passing, as well as a determination that he would not live his life the way his father had.

"But there is something else I wanted to tell you." Lucien filled Charles in on everything, including his suggestion to the Black Widow of Whitehall for her birthday celebration. "I feel it is an opportunity to make amends and hopefully enable a fresh start with Lizzie. She won't know who I am, as I will be masked and costumed."

"Aye, it is an excellent situation to make an inroad with Lady Elizabeth." His uncle nodded. "I know you are an honorable man, Lucien, but I must ask, what are your intentions toward this girl?"

"Didn't you just say what I am feeling is love at first sight?"

"Feelings and attraction are one thing, but she is a lady, not a courtesan."

"My intentions are noble, Uncle. I cannot get her out of my mind. I believe I'm in love with her."

"Then win her heart."

Chapter Three

April 1, 1816
London, England

Lizzie stared at the ornate embossed card on her dressing table. The mysterious invitation had been one of three delivered to Waverly Castle in January. One addressed to Sarah, one for the duke, and one for her. Each invitation had arrived in a gold envelope and was written on a sheet of vellum embossed with gold lettering.

You are cordially invited to
Le Bal Masqué Mystère
The Mystery Masked Ball
In celebration of Mrs. Bessie Dove-Lyon's birthday.
Attendees will arrive promptly on April 1st, 1816, at the hour of seven o'clock.
Prepared to be dazzled and bewitched,
On a night you shan't soon forget.
Dinner will be served at midnight.

Expect to be home by morning light.
Admittance shall be granted
To the bearer of this golden ticket.
RSVP to Lyon's Gate Manor,
More notably known as the Lyon's Den,
Cleveland Row, Westminster, London

Lizzie's first reaction had been an emphatic *no*. She had no desire to attend another ball that could end in disaster. Her last encounter with an eligible man had been more than disastrous, and she'd only herself to blame. She'd been mortified when both Phillip and the earl laughed, even though she knew deep down it was Potsy's antics that had caused their reaction. But rather than laugh and shrug it off as she should have done, she'd behaved like a child and run off.

Of course, she'd caught a cold and stayed abed for almost a week after that. And dear Phillip had been so kind to her, which only added to her guilt over her silly reaction. He had also told her of the earl's ardent apology and his desire to visit with her so that he could atone in person. But Lizzie had refused, so embarrassed was she about her own behavior, and she was worried she'd stammer and stumble so much that the earl wouldn't even be able to understand her. Despite her intense and immediate attraction to the handsome earl, she could not chance it.

And then the invitation arrived, and it was another opportunity to dance and smile and flirt at a ball, but she was afraid to go. Neither the duke nor Sarah would accept her refusal. They were determined to attend and would not go without her. She had pleaded to no end, but the duke put his foot down, and that was that. In the blink of an eye, they were in London at the duke's residence, and Lizzie and been pulled into a whirlwind of activity with seamstresses and fittings. Thank goodness Sarah had been by her side the entire time. She didn't think she would have gotten through the past few weeks otherwise.

Lizzie looked in the mirror as Sarah put the finishing touches on her hair. She crowned Lizzie's head with a green silk French hood embroidered with colorful faux gemstones. The headdress matched Lizzie's green silk gown, with its tight bodice and square neckline that displayed a jewel-encrusted braid across her bosom. She bit her lip in agitation and tried to take deep breaths to calm her nerves.

"Lizzie, relax and stop fidgeting. Try to exude the confidence of Anne Boleyn when she returned to the English court from France. She was a self-assured woman who captured the heart of a king."

"She also lost her head because of that same king," Lizzie countered.

"One thing I am certain of is that you will not lose your head tonight. Though maybe you should," Sarah said with a chuckle. "But as I doubt that will happen, you have nothing to worry about. Phillip and I will be there to keep watch over you. I want you to enjoy yourself, Lizzie. Smile, dance, and flirt. Once you don your mask, no one will know who you are. Imagine how liberating that will be."

"By liberating, do you mean I won't stumble over my words?"

"Oh, dear heart, when a man is truly interested in you, he will take the time to know you from the inside, where it counts. A good man worth his salt will see beyond your stammer and help you overcome your shyness. This is the kind of man I wish for you, my darling. I know you wish for it too. You deserve the same love and happiness as your sisters have."

Potsy yelped and jumped up on Lizzie's gown as if he seconded Sarah's reasoning.

"Potsy, get down. I would prefer not to wear your paw prints this evening." Lizzie giggled, scratching her impetuous spaniel's ears.

"See, even Potsy is in full agreement." Sarah smiled as she

tucked a stray golden curl from Lizzie's coiffure back in place.

Lizzie reached for Sarah's hand and held it in both of hers. "These past ten years you have been mother, sister, and confidante to me. A dearer and more devoted friend I could never have asked for."

"Oh, Lizzie, what a lovely thing to say. You are so dear to me." Sarah wrapped her arms around Lizzie and hugged her close. "Now, before we both start blubbering and ruin our costumes, let us finish here. I'm certain Phillip is champing at the bit to be off." Sarah walked to the bed and opened a gold box, taking out the ornate masks they were going to wear to the ball. She handed a green satin mask dotted with gemstones to Lizzie and donned an orange satin mask embroidered with red and white Tudor roses.

"It truly will be a magical night. Your mask only enhances your beauty. And remember, you can express yourself with your eyes and a smile—who needs words? You are a woman of mystery. Let them wonder about you. Phillip and I will be there, so you have nothing to fear."

Lizzie drew in a deep breath and gazed at herself in the mirror. She could scarcely believe who stared back at her. *Beautiful* was not a word she ever thought of herself. But tonight, she felt beautiful, and she truly did feel like a woman of mystery.

"Who knows whom you might meet? I've heard rumors that many of the *ton* did not receive invitations. They are desperate and have offered a tidy sum to anyone willing to sell their ticket. However, given the reputation of Mrs. Dove-Lyon, I expect every eligible bachelor in London will be there, along with many an eligible young lady." Sarah's brows rose, and her smile revealed deep dimples in her cheeks.

"Oh, fiddlesticks, no man will lose his heart to me even if you have made me look like a princess. You've outdone yourself, Sarah. How clever you are to have come up with the idea for these costumes. I doubt Elizabeth Regina ever looked as dazzling as you."

Lizzie studied Sarah's costume—orange silk modeled after the Rainbow Portrait of Queen Elizabeth. It had been a year since the death of Lizzie's father, and it was the first time Sarah wasn't wearing black. The dress Sarah had designed with the modiste was embroidered with wildflowers and studded with pearls. The low-cut bodice displayed a fetching glimpse of her cleavage. It was a daring costume, but Sarah was still young and vibrant and deserved a new life. She too would be given anonymity by wearing her jewel-encrusted mask. Lizzie wondered if Sarah would also like to meet an eligible man she might one day marry and have children with.

"And what of you, Sarah?" Lizzie asked softly. "Do you wish for love and happiness and children of your own?"

Sarah gazed in the mirror, and Lizzie could see she was pondering the question, perhaps considering how best to answer.

"Yes, I would like to remarry someday," Sarah said at last, "but certainly not in the near future."

"What kind of man would he be?"

Sarah sat on the bench at the foot of the bed and folded her hands in her lap. "I think thoughtful and considerate, like your father. A man who does not dismiss a woman's opinions or condescend to keep the peace."

"That does not sound very romantic."

"Are you asking if I desire passion, amorous embraces, and kisses that melt my heart and body?"

Lizzie could feel the blood rush to her cheeks. "I would never be so bold. Oh dear, it's not my place. I'm so sorry."

"Don't be silly. You're my friend. And to answer your question, yes, I want that too. I wish him to be handsome, passionate, madly in love with me, and unable to live a day without me or keep his hands off me." Sarah winked, making Lizzie giggle. "And now, I think we really should be going. We don't want to be late for the party, and we've kept the duke waiting long enough."

If I am honest, I wish the same as you, my dear Sarah. I will be twenty-four this year, and what do I have to show for it? No babies to hold in my arms. All I have worth nurturing are my flowers and fruit.

But if Lizzie married, she would have to leave Waverly Castle, Sarah and Phillip, and her greenhouse. Would she be able to manage in a new life? Would she be happy?

She brushed aside her worries. It seemed unlikely she'd ever have to deal with those concerns, in any case, so why worry about something that was never going to happen? But Sarah had a good point. Tonight, she should try to let go of her inhibitions—perhaps the mask would be the thing for her to have a truly enjoyable evening without the fear of stumbling or stammering.

Lizzie and Sarah descended the magnificent white marble stairs, their low-heeled slippers sinking into the plush red oriental runner. Phillip waited at the bottom looking up at them. He had refused to bother with frippery or a costume. But Sarah had coaxed him, and he agreed to a satin mask that covered half his face. And he had dressed up, and wore a royal-blue frock coat. A watch chain hung from his fob pocket hidden beneath his brocaded waistcoat, and an orange satin ascot tie added a splash of color against his high-collared shirt.

Lizzie whispered to Sarah. "His cravat matches your gown. Did you plan this together?"

"Of course not," Sarah whispered back, but Lizzie would have had to be blind not to notice the dazzling smile of pleasure on Sarah's face. Seeing the way they looked at each other, Lizzie could not help but think what a wonderful couple they would make.

LUCIEN DASHED DOWN the stairs, feeling confident and looking forward to seeing Elizabeth. He stopped to say goodnight to his uncle and family, who had retired after dinner to the library. He was staying at his uncle's townhouse while in London, as his own was being refurbished. His mother had opted to stay at the family estate in Devon for the duration.

His uncle Charles and nephew Carlton were playing chess, and Aunt Lydia was instructing their young daughter Victoria in needlepoint. It was as happy a family scene as he could imagine. Everyone looked up when he entered and exclaimed in excitement at his costume.

"Oh, Lucien," said his aunt, jumping up and fussing with the ruffles on his jabot, "your costume is marvelous." She kissed his cheek. "What a dashing pirate you make, don't you think so, Charles?" she said, turning to her husband. "I believe he looks so handsome, he will no doubt make every young lady swoon."

"I imagine the old ones will do more than swoon." Charles chuckled.

"I shall ignore that comment, Uncle," Lucien said with an arch of his brow before turning back to his aunt and kissing her hand. "But I thank you, Aunt Lydia, for your gracious compliment."

Eight-year-old Victoria interrupted, "Mama, why would Uncle Lucien make ladies swoon?"

"That's what ladies do," ten-year-old Carlton said with a roll of his eyes. "Don't you know, Vickie, they get lessons in how to swoon so they can catch a husband? And one day you'll be getting those lessons too!"

"Well, I refuse to swoon, and you can't make me either," Victoria said with a firm nod. "Instead, I shall walk up to a young man and say, 'Hello, my name is Victoria Medford; so lovely to meet you. If you play your cards right, perhaps I'll marry you!'"

Charles exchanged a meaningful look with his wife. "I will not be addressing this subject, Lydia. I believe this is far more in your purview."

Lydia wrapped her arm around Victoria. "Darling, if you do that, I shall applaud you."

"Don't worry, Father," Carlton said in an authoritative tone. "I'll be there to make sure Victoria ends up with the right bloke. If not, I'll punch his lights out."

Now it was Charles's turn to roll his eyes. "Heaven help me."

Lucien chuckled at the family's antics. "I would love to see that! But for now, I must be off." He donned his mask and bowed to everyone, and Victoria clapped her hands in delight.

His aunt, niece, and nephew bade him a good night, and Uncle Charles held his thumb up and said, "Good luck!"

Lucien was out the door when he heard young Carlton ask, "Is Uncle Lucien going to the gaming den's party? I've heard of the Black Widow of Whitehall, the one all of London talks about."

Lucien smiled as he got into the carriage Charles had loaned him for the night. His aunt and uncle certainly had their work cut out for them, but he doubted they would have it any other way.

Lucien sat back against the fine leather seat as he anticipated the evening ahead. He couldn't help but hope for the same happy life, and a loving wife to shepherd their clever children into becoming fine adults.

Perhaps tonight will be the night when hope turns into truth.

Chapter Four

April 1, 1816
London, England

Lizzie had never felt so daring and yet so at ease at the same time. Sarah had been right—the mask made all the difference. She looked about, taking in the throng of costumed guests whose laughter echoed throughout the high-ceilinged room. The golden light from the crystal chandeliers gave the surroundings a magical, sparkling glow.

A man with a donkey mask on his head introduced himself as Bottom. He led them into the main hall, which he explained was usually filled with tables and men gambling. "Upstairs overlooking this room is the ladies' gambling parlor, which you are welcome to attend in the future should you care to try your luck at the tables." He snapped his fingers, and a beautiful woman wearing a half mask appeared with a silver tray with champagne flutes. "May I introduce Oberon, one of our dealers."

"Are you all named for Master Shakespeare's characters?" asked Sarah.

Bottom grinned. "*A Midsummer Night's Dream* is Mrs. Dove-Lyon's favorite play."

Sarah turned to Phillip. "You didn't share anything about the Lyon's Den with us, Your Grace. Since I've surmised this is a place you have spent some time in, I cannot help but wonder why."

"I-I..." Before he could answer, a man dressed as the Sun King, Louis the XIV, approached, took Sarah's hand, and bowed to kiss it.

"May I have the great pleasure of dancing with you, Your Majesty?"

Phillip was quick to respond, "Ahem, I do not believe that is appropriate."

"Oh, fiddlesticks, there are no rules when wearing a costume," Sarah whispered to him. "It's only one dance, Phillip. I promise I won't vanish in a puff of smoke." She turned to the white-wigged king. "I'd be delighted."

"Enjoy your dance," Lizzie called out as the Sun Kind led Sarah through the throng to the dance floor. Her stepmother threw Lizzie and Phillip a smile over her shoulder.

The orchestra struck up a vibrant waltz, which sent everyone spinning at a dizzying pace.

Lizzie could see that Phillip was hot under the collar as he scanned the crowd looking for Sarah. Having seen the expression on his face when she and Sarah descended the stairs earlier, she was now sure that Phillip's feelings for Sarah were far greater than he'd let on. Now, with too many twirling couples, too much noise, and too many distractions, he seemed like a caged lion, ready to pounce on any overzealous gentleman who dared stand too close to Sarah, which was impossible not to do while waltzing.

"You look, Your Grace, like Little Bo-Peep. Have you lost someone?" The widow Mrs. Dove-Lyon glided up to them. "And who is this charming young woman?"

"Happy birthday, Bess. May I introduce you to my cousin Elizabeth Villiers." Barely glancing their way, Phillip continued to scan the room.

"My dear, welcome to the Lyon's Den."

"Thank you for inviting me," Lizzie said. "Although I have no idea why you did."

"I always take an interest in my clients' families. The duke is a particular favorite of mine, and I'm quite keen to see him wed."

"My dear Bess, please direct your good intentions to a more promising cause," Phillip said.

"Oh, look." The older woman nodded across the room. "Queen Elizabeth is pausing from her dance and refreshing herself."

Lizzie watched Phillip in amusement as his gaze flew in the direction the widow had indicated. There, surrounded by half a dozen men, stood Sarah fanning herself. "You will excuse me," Phillip muttered, then, turning back, added, "Dear Bess, would you mind keeping Elizabeth company while I see to Sarah's safety?" Not waiting for a reply, he strode across the room.

Lizzie suppressed a giggle. *The lion has just been let out of his cage, and woe to any man who gets in his way.*

"Lady Elizabeth, have you, by chance, come in search of a husband?" Mrs. Dove-Lyon asked.

"Me? Oh, goodness no. I'm a lost cause on that front."

"Trust me, my dear, you are anything but a lost cause." Mrs. Dove-Lyon's shrewd look brought a flush of heat to Lizzie's cheeks. "In fact, there is a handsome gentleman here this evening who holds you in high regard."

Lizzie glanced around the room as if she might find this mysterious man looking her way. "Well"—she fanned herself—"he has not made himself known, so perhaps you are mistaken."

"I am never mistaken when it comes to matters of the heart. Besides, my dear, the night is still young. I think you will be most pleasantly surprised at who your secret admirer is when he unmasks himself to you."

Lizzie pondered the widow's words, which seemed laced with more than one meaning. Still, her heart pounded in her chest at the very thought. Who in the world could this mysterious masked man be?

LUCIEN STOOD IN a corner sipping a glass of champagne. Not for a minute had he taken his eyes off Elizabeth. Her beauty was like a siren song that penetrated his heart, and her every movement held him captivated. But seeing her alone with Mrs. Dove-Lyon worried him. He could not fathom what they might be talking about. And he knew how wily the Black Widow of Whitehall was. He wouldn't put it past her to reveal his involvement in Elizabeth's receiving an invitation. Or worse, Mrs. Dove-Lyon could be planning a match between Lizzie and another member of the *ton* without his knowledge. Lucien must act, and quickly, to ensure he had a private moment to speak with Lizzie tonight, or everything might go up in a puff of smoke.

He wasn't given long to ruminate before Phillip arrived at his side looking like he wanted to throttle someone. "I don't understand what's gotten into Sarah. Dancing with Lord Marley, and now yet another oaf just whisked her onto the dance floor. They're like a pack of vultures. Now that she's out of mourning, they're all circling their prey."

Lucien shook his head at his friend. "For God's sake, man, cut in and ask her to dance, and put yourself out of your misery."

"Dance? You think I should ask her to dance?"

"It's the only way to keep the vultures at bay."

"Yes, of course! Capital idea, old man." Phillip thumped Lucien on the shoulder and strode away.

Lucien chuckled as he watched his friend disappear into the crowd. One day Phillip would realize how he truly felt about Sarah. Until then, he would continue to grumble and growl when other men paid her court.

Then again, was Lucien not doing the same when it came to Lizzie? He'd been staring at her from a distance all night and had yet to approach her. Lucien turned back to where he'd seen Elizabeth and Bess chatting. And his heart dropped. Bess was now standing with Admiral Snowden. *Damn! Where is Lizzie?*

Making his way over to the widow, he greeted the older man and then dropped a whisper in Bess's ear.

"Where did she go?"

"Where did who go?" The Black Widow's brows rose, and amusement tickled her lips into a knowing smile.

"You know exactly who I mean. Lady Elizabeth Villiers."

"Ah, yes, of course." The birthday celebrant tapped her fan on his shoulder. "I believe she went in search of the ladies' retiring room."

"Alone?" He bit back a curse. "Have you any idea how many rogues are about?"

"She is in no danger. I have guards everywhere keeping the peace, but I know you won't be satisfied until you have her in your sights."

Damned right! "If you'll excuse me, I shall leave you and Admiral Snowden to continue your conversation."

Turning on his heel, he made for the stairs. He didn't care that the place was crawling with Bess's burly guards. He could name at least ten men at the ball who would think nothing of cornering a young woman like Elizabeth and compromising her virtue.

Determination quickened his stride. *There is no way in hell I'll let anything happen to her.*

CHAPTER FIVE

"OH, DRAT!" Lizzie leaned against the upholstered chaise and wiped her teary eyes. What had started out as a delightful evening full of promise had turned into a debacle.

She had felt such exhilaration stepping outside the normal confines of her everyday life. She had even imagined herself with a reprieve from the speech impediment that had plagued her since childhood. Why, she'd spoken to the charming and droll Mrs. Dove-Lyon for nearly ten minutes and never stammered once! Not even when the notorious widow had divulged to Lizzie about a secret admirer. Imagine that! That someone could possess a secret admiration for her was truly a revelation. It was as if the heavens had delivered her a star to wish upon that could make her dreams come true. And then an older gentleman, Admiral Snowden, approached them and greeted both Mrs. Dove-Lyon and Lizzie with warmth. Lizzie had even managed to chat with the man a few minutes before she felt the need to excuse herself.

As she'd made her way out of the ballroom to seek the ladies' retiring room, she'd passed a group of giggling young ladies. She knew that kind of laughter all too well—cruel and laced with ridicule. The trio was giddily whispering loudly enough for Lizzie to hear, no doubt on purpose.

"*I tell you, it's her.*"

"*You mean the one everyone joked about five years ago at the queen's ball?*"

"*No, it was six.*"

"*Yes, I remember now.*"

"*The Villiers girl who stuttered and shamed herself in front of Prinny.*"

"*I can still see his face and the way he was stumped as to what to say. He hurried away from her as though a nest of hornets were after him.*"

"*Remember the gossip rags dubbed her the Dreadful Debutante.*"

"*Oh, how droll.*"

Her heart dropping to the floor, Lizzie had rushed past them and then come to a halt. She'd been running away from those harpies for years and denied herself the pleasure of attending balls and soirées. She'd denied herself the enjoyment of dressing up in a beautiful gown and dancing until dawn. Well, no more! She had nothing to be ashamed of. She was a good and kind person and had never done anyone wrong. She didn't deserve their ridicule. Hell, no one did.

I'm done with running away.

She'd taken a deep breath and straightened her shoulders. Turning back, she approached the trio with as much grace and dignity as she could muster.

"Yes, I am the D-D-Dreadful D-D-Debutante," she'd begun. "B-but let me tell you that I w-w-would n-n-never stoop s-s-so low as to m-m-make sport of another person's a-a-affliction, for it is the height of c-c-cruelty to do so." Lizzie took another deep breath. *You can do this!* "Y-y-you should be ashamed of your behavior." She felt stronger and more in control with each word she said. "A true lady would never cackle with such glee as you have done at the expense of another. Shame on you." And with that, she'd spun on her heel and made her way up the stairs with her head held high like a queen.

Oh, but she had been proud of herself! Her stammer had disappeared as she continued to speak. The trio of gossips had stared at her with mouths agape. But the effort had taken its toll on her anxiety, and she'd needed a quiet place to calm down and have a good cry. Mrs. Dove-Lyon had told her where the ladies' retiring room was, but with all that drama, Lizzie had forgotten which way to turn. She'd made her way down a long hallway until she finally found a door unlocked. Entering the room, she'd breathed a sigh of relief. The room was lovely and comfortably appointed, with a red velvet Empire recamier in front of a fireplace with a cheerful fire. The cozy oasis had drawn her inside with its beckoning warmth.

This room was indeed a good place to have a good cry. Weeping into her handkerchief, she didn't hear the door open and close behind her, and turned with a gasp of surprise. A man dressed as a pirate had entered and reached his hand out to her. Lizzie jumped up and began to move as far away from him as she could.

He raised his hands in a placating gesture. "Do not be afraid. I won't hurt you."

His voice was melodious, and she had a strange feeling that she'd heard it before, but she couldn't quite place it.

"I'm sorry if I frightened you, but I overheard those gossipmongers, and I saw what you did. And I am in awe. Truly in awe of your courage and your dignity, my lady. I followed you to make certain you were all right."

Lizzie nodded, a little in awe herself at his words. Who was this mysterious masked man? Her initial trepidation faded away and her instincts took over. Something about him put her at ease, made her feel safe. Nevertheless, she kept her distance as he took a few steps closer. He wore a white silk poet shirt untied at the neck, with ruffled sleeves tucked into tight black trousers that displayed muscled thighs. The deep V of his shirt revealed a few tufts of dark chest curls that played peekaboo as he moved around the recamier and sat. His disheveled hair was dark and wavy, and dark-lashed blue eyes met hers through the eyeholes in the mask. His eyes were beautiful and quite mesmerizing.

"I understand how u-upsetting it must have been for y-you. I-I..." He ceased speaking and took a deep breath, releasing it slowly.

Did he just stutter? Lizzie was certain she was hearing things. Slowly she walked back to the recamier and sat down next to him.

"I'm sorry they hurt you," he said in a raspy voice.

That voice sounded even more familiar now. Without thinking, she reached out and gently touched his cheek. "Thank you," she whispered, pleased that she didn't stammer. "You are most kind." She was captivated by the empathy in his eyes, and the sincerity of his gaze made her fingers tremble. She had never caressed a man's face or body, and felt a tingling heat flood her senses. The slight beard stubble on his clean-shaven face felt pleasantly prickly beneath her fingers.

Get a grip on yourself, you loony bird, or he'll think you're some sort of wanton.

"Forgive me. I forgot myself." She pulled her hand away and attempted to stand, but her knees buckled. Her heroic pirate came to the rescue once more and swept her up in his arms.

I'm in his arms. This gorgeous stranger picked me as though I were as light as a feather and is now holding me in his arms. And we are alone in this lovely, cozy, and comfortable room.

She gazed into his eyes and touched his cheek once more. She wondered what the rest of his skin might feel like if she caressed it. A yearning she had never felt before surged through her veins with the realization that she would probably never get another chance like this again. A chance to embrace the magic of the moment.

What was more, he was looking at her with an intensity that quite took her breath away.

"I must confess that my entire world shifted on its axis when I saw you arrive tonight," he said in that low, melodic voice that had fast become her favorite sound in the world. "I followed you up here because I was concerned for your safety, but the truth is I have been wanting to speak with you for what feels like an eternity. I-I... Blazes!" He shook his head as though frustrated. "I've never felt so tongue-tied."

Lizzy knew something about being tongue-tied and stumbling over your words. And then she did something unthinkable, brazen, so out of character that had she stopped to think about it, she would have certainly died on the spot before doing it. She cupped his face and kissed him. Not knowing what she was doing, she feared that her inexperience and rather halting kiss would make him pull away in distaste. But remarkably, the opposite happened.

The dashing stranger kissed her back! He sat back down with her still in his arms and, with a deliciously wicked tongue, schooled her in the ways of kissing. She responded in kind, loving his taste and the increasingly sensuous play of their tongues and lips.

The power of blood surging through her veins dizzied her. Her nipples pebbled and began to throb, and that was echoed by an even more deliciously intense vibration between her thighs. She wanted to know every part of him in the most carnal way imaginable. Her hands moved as if controlled by an outside force, traveling up and down his back, exploring his musculature. A most unladylike hunger ripped away Lizzie's inhibitions, transforming her into someone she didn't even know had been inside her—a woman who must give passion and take it, regardless of the consequences. A groan escaped him as she pressed kisses along his jaw line and down his neck. She took that as a positive signal that he was filled with the same passion she was.

She felt him gently lift the hem of her gown, and the slight trembling in his hand was an admission that he, too, was wading through uncharted waters. Yet he persevered, and she thanked the heavens he did. As his large hand caressed her thigh, she felt the heat of passion build inside her. Her breath caught as he neared the most intimate part of her and stopped. For the most prolonged moment, they stared at each other. It wasn't a standoff, more a consideration for what the other was feeling.

Lizzie was certain she would never experience anything like this again. Fortunately, she hadn't ruined the moment with words, especially the soul-crushing, stuttered words that might have made her feel awkward instead of wanton. And oh, she did love this new wanton feeling. If not for this wondrous man who set her heart racing with his kiss, she might have returned home, never experiencing this kind of passion. Sheltered and naïve though she was, she was all too aware that should they be discovered, her reputation would surely be ruined. Being alone in this room with a strange man—in fact, any man—had destroyed any prospects she might have had of marrying.

Don't be a ninny. There are no prospects, and there never will be. She had all but resigned herself to being a lifelong spinster anyway, so what did she have to lose?

Who would ever know if she and this magnificent man gave in to their passions? It could be their secret, and no one would be the wiser. He didn't know who she was, and she didn't know who he was. They might go through the rest of their lives never knowing each other's identity. What an arousing thought. No, this chance for love would not be stolen from her. Her curiosity was too great, the awakened passion within her too strong.

She'd seen enough of horses and other animals in the countryside to know what mating was all about. She didn't imagine a man and a woman to be much different except for the pleasure aspect, and that was the aspect she most yearned to experience. But she was not so forward to ask it of him, and so she waited and hoped until his azure eyes finally asked the unspoken question she'd been waiting for.

And she nodded and smiled her reply.

CHAPTER SIX

LUCIEN WAS WALKING a tightrope, balancing his overwhelming desire for Lizzie that pulsed through his body with his wish to behave respectfully to the woman he was falling in love with. She opened her arms to him, offering him what he dared not imagine. The trouble was, the only thinking part of his anatomy was not thinking at all.

The most desirable woman in the world, the woman who had taken over his waking and sleeping hours, had kissed him with such an innocent and open-hearted passion—and now, with a gentle nod, she'd told him she wanted more. But did she realize what that truly meant? He traced the silky-soft skin of her inner thigh as he gazed into her beautiful, drink-me-in green eyes. It was the most romantic moment of his life, an interlude he would cherish for the rest of his days.

Dare he go further? What difference would it make? He knew he wished to make her his forever. He knew she was as pure as the driven snow—yet she was everything he would ever need. This was the love he'd longed for. Elizabeth Villiers would be a wonderful mother; of that he had no doubt. And more importantly, she would be an incredible wife and partner. She would be his lasting happiness. And he would be hers, God willing. He would make it his life's work to make her happy.

She hesitatingly caressed his manhood, and he inhaled sharply. *My God*, if she could have this effect on him with the most delicate touch, imagine what it would feel like to be inside her. How could he possibly fight the chance to love her when his pulse pounded in his ears, his heart raced in his chest, and his cock throbbed beneath her hand?

She lay back on the recamier, tugging on his shirt, pulling him toward her. He leaned down and once more claimed those luscious lips. She kissed him with a passion that took his breath away. Ah, but she was a quick and clever learner. She guided his hands to the hem of her dress and sighed as the satiny material slid up her legs. All he could think about was this moment, his lips forever seared and imprinted with her kisses as she gave the greatest gift he'd ever been given. Forever he would want the woman whose body perfectly contoured to his, the woman unlike any other he'd ever known. The woman whose tender care made flowers bloom and plants grow and nurtured fruit that tasted sweeter than nectar. She would be his, and until she was, he would not rest.

Boldly she tugged at his trousers, tangling her hands with his as he freed himself from the confines of the fabric that could no longer contain his growing girth. He luxuriated in the touch of her stroking his skin. His head fell back, and his breath hissed through his teeth as her hesitant touch grew bolder and bolder still. *Slow down, man, or it will be over before it's even begun.* He wanted her to find her own pleasure before he joined with her—his fingers sought what the poets called "the instrument of love's music."

His loving manipulation made her hips rise and her breath come in short, sharp gasps. His tongue sought the sweetness of her mouth once more. One hand stroked her to cries of fulfillment as the other cradled her neck as she trembled beneath him. Pulling out his fingers, he licked each one and watched her moan and pant. Her eyes glowed with an inner light that made him yearn to plunge deep inside her.

Mounting her, he ran his cock over her clitoris to give her the ultimate pleasure between a man and a woman. Though he'd had more than his fair share of sexual encounters, none had been more than a night's entertainment for physical satisfaction. But this—this was something else, something entirely foreign to him. This was love, and love was not something to be trifled with.

He'd only partially penetrated her when he came up against her maidenhead. In his excitement, he'd completely forgotten she was a virgin. In truth, he'd never been with a virgin, and he was afraid to proceed, afraid to hurt her.

Her whispered words reassured him. "Please do not stop. I want nothing more than to feel you inside me."

It was enough; his need grew ever greater—he pushed into her, and her whimper became a moan of pleasure as the fullness of her chalice held tight to him. Clenching his jaw to stay in control, he pushed himself farther. Closing his eyes, he held on to the exquisite feeling of being completely inside her. Years ago, his uncle had told him that, in biblical terms, a woman's chalice was considered the sacred vessel protecting the masculine seed. But as he began to move within her, he lost all ability to think, and the only thing Lucien understood was the sound of Lizzie's breathy moans that filled his mouth as he kissed her.

Their music was rising and falling in a glissando that culminated in a crescendo and ended in an explosive chord and breathless finale. Lucien blissfully sank into her, filling her with his seed, exhaling full force. He lingered between heaven and earth in a place rarely reached by mortals. And the moment it was over, he wished it to begin again.

The sound of wood crackling in the hearth brought him back. He opened his eyes and found himself in awe of the creature that forever had changed him. Her eyes were closed, and the most satisfied smile curved her lips. Her legs were firmly wrapped around his waist while her fingers toyed with his hair. This openness and trust she showed humbled him. He kissed her, and those precious fingers cupped his face.

He blurted, "We will marry, of course, as soon as possible."

Gently she slid from beneath him and stood. "Thank you for the most incredible night of my life," she said in a husky whisper. "But I cannot marry you." She straightened her dress, shook out her skirt, and smoothed it until it hung neatly. "We are both wearing masks, and no one has discovered us. There is nothing to worry about." From a pocket in her skirt, she extracted a small gold mesh evening purse, pulled out a comb, and began untangling her golden curls.

"I beg your pardon?" he said, sitting up. He almost reached for his mask but caught himself. He wasn't dissuaded, but would revealing who he was make a difference?

She turned to him, her hand and comb hovering in midair. "You have given me the most wondrous memory that I shall cherish for the rest of my life, but there is no reason to alter our lives because of a moment of passion. I would rather hold the memory of what we shared in my heart for the rest of my days than ruin it with a rash decision. And I cannot allow any man to marry me out of obligation because of the dictates of Society."

"I see. Well, it seems as though you have a very clear idea of what you want." He rose and began putting himself back together, wondering what to say or do next, and then he caught a glimpse of her face in the mirror—and was pleased to see she appeared distraught, perhaps not as sure of her decision as she'd said.

Have patience, man—this might serve me well in the end. Let her think long and hard about what we shared and what she impulsively gave up.

He suppressed a smile as he saw how much she had indeed been affected by their lovemaking. She was still an innocent, and she could not hide her emotions. And those lovely green eyes told him more than words could say.

Chapter Seven

June 1, 1816
Buckinghamshire, England

"Potsy, the pansies are coming in beautifully, don't you think?" The dog yelped, sitting at her feet waiting for the attention he demanded. Absent-mindedly, Lizzie reached down and scratched behind his ears. "The blue and yellow will look lovely on the terrace."

Two months had passed since Mrs. Dove-Lyon's birthday ball, and all Lizzie could think about was the stranger who'd rescued her and transformed her. Her whole life, she'd felt herself a child, protected by her father and family. Having never been courted, Lizzie had remained "young and sheltered" in so many ways, but such was not the case anymore, and she reveled in it. Nor could she forget that, throughout their lovemaking and afterward, she hadn't stumbled or stammered once. Not once! The magic of their encounter had been like a soothing balm to her soul.

She recalled what had transpired after she left the pirate in that magical room. She'd returned to the ball and found the duke and

Sarah quite frantic with worry. She'd babbled some lame excuse of feeling dizzy from too much champagne and going to the retiring room to refresh herself. Sarah and Phillip were so happy to see her unharmed and merely indisposed that they never questioned her, and were only too happy to believe anything she told them.

She refused to allow herself any self-pity or regrets. She'd danced a few dances with several nice gentlemen who were all most attentive, but no one could touch the mysterious pirate. For the rest of the night, she'd secretly hoped to catch a glimpse of him, but it seemed as though he'd disappeared.

She'd wrestled with her thoughts time and again since that night, wishing she could have danced with the pirate instead of the other gentlemen. Wishing she had stayed in that room with him and not rushed out to find Sarah and Phillip. Wishing they could have made love again. After that first taste, she'd wanted more. So much more. Sometimes she gave in to her yearnings—reliving every sweet moment of her *brève affaire* with the handsome stranger.

Sighing, she picked a pineapple off a thick, leafy shrub. She held it to her nose and inhaled the delicious, ripe tropical fragrance. It pleased her that tonight's dessert would be a sublime, juicy fruit treat nurtured by her loving hands.

The door to the greenhouse opened, and the scent of summer rain filled the air. She turned, expecting to see Sarah or the duke urging her to join them for tea in the library. What she didn't expect to see was Lucien Radcliffe, the Earl of Dartmouth. The memory of his previous visit with Phillip made her cheeks heat with embarrassment. Well, she didn't care if her cheeks were as red as her heirloom tomatoes. She wasn't going anywhere, least of all scurrying under tables. She was done with that. Done with running away.

She recalled overhearing him exclaim about the pineapples and the profusion of flowers, and his wanting to make an arrangement with Phillip. Perhaps he wanted to inquire further about that. She regarded him, watching him approach, and couldn't help but admire how handsome he looked. His muscular frame filled out his frock coat, and the rain had dampened his hair, tumbling dark waves over his forehead.

"G-g-good day." She gave him a polite smile. *Drat! So much for being cool and in control.* Still, it was just a minor slip. "What brings you to Waverly Castle, my lord?"

"You."

"I beg your pardon?"

"It is you that has summoned me to Waverly Castle."

"You are surely mistaken. Why on earth would I summon you?"

"Perhaps I misspoke. My desire to see and speak with you summoned me here."

His dance of words was perplexing. "Well then, speak. What is it that has compelled you to leave London?"

He moved closer until he was nearly nose to nose with her. The old Elizabeth Villiers would have stumbled back. That was how she'd ended up in a bucket of muck at their last meeting. The new Elizabeth Villiers held her ground, retreating not an inch. His azure eyes examined her but revealed nothing. And she gasped as she beheld their unique color up close.

"Is there anything familiar about me?" he asked in a melodic voice.

"Whatever do you mean?" she replied, although her heart was beating in a staccato rhythm. "We have met before, though, as I recall, it was not pleasant."

"Oh, I daresay our last encounter was indeed pleasant."

He was speaking in riddles, and she dared not believe… "I still have not heard an answer to my question, my lord."

Lizzie was so engrossed by those blue eyes that she didn't notice he'd taken something out of his pocket. He raised the item over his face, and Lizzie's knees almost buckled. She gasped in shock as her whirling thoughts fell into place: Lucien was the pirate!

He grabbed her before she slid to the ground and pulled her firmly against him. "You may recall our liaison," he whispered in that unforgettable voice. "I certainly have not forgotten it. In fact, it is all I have thought about these last two months."

She felt lightheaded, giddy, and her ability to speak deserted her. How could this be? She wrestled with her thoughts and remembered him saying, *I followed you up here because I was concerned for your safety, but the truth is I have been wanting to speak with you for what feels like an eternity.*

Yes, their first meeting had been brief, and her mishap had taken center stage, but how could she not have recognized him at the ball? That masculine voice. And those eyes—my God, those azure eyes!

"Wh-when we made love, you knew who I was," she said in a hoarse whisper. "B-but why did you not tell me?"

"After our unfortunate meeting here in the greenhouse and my shameful behavior, you were all I could think about. You haunted my dreams and waking hours; all I wanted was to make amends. Mrs. Dove-Lyon sent you, the duke, and the dowager duchess the golden invitations at my suggestion."

"But why?"

"Because I was already in love with you, but, fool that I was, I didn't realize it until…"

"Why are you here?"

He took her chin between his thumb and finger. "To beg you to marry me and become my countess."

She pulled from his arms, needing some distance from his heady presence so that she could think. She began to walk through the rows of flowers and plants. Potsy, quiet as a lamb during Lucien's proposal, followed on her heels, whining. "Potsy, my darling, hush. I must think."

It dawned on her that, on some unconscious level, she must

have known the pirate was Lucien. His eyes and voice were so unique, how could she *not* have known? Besides which, if she hadn't felt a deep connection to him, how could she have behaved in such a wanton manner? She had allowed her instincts and feelings to guide her, and perhaps that was why she'd felt so comfortable in his presence, so safe, so cherished. Because he had communicated his feelings to her in his eyes, his kisses, his tender touch, and in his passion. Oh, that wondrous, sensual passion had quite overtaken her.

"I wish to announce the banns and marry as soon as possible. That is if you consent." Lucien, too, was close on her heels, following her as she wound through the rows of plants.

When she turned abruptly, he nearly bumped into her. "I'm with child," she blurted.

He froze in his tracks, but only for a heartbeat. "Oh, my darling." He took her hands and pulled her against him. "I am the luckiest man alive."

Tears filled her eyes. "Our first m-meeting was a disaster, and then our second m-meeting was heavenly. But you m-must understand, I-I have this t-terrible a-a-affliction. This s-s-stutter that rears its ugly head when I am anxious or n-n-nervous. B-but it's gotten so much better since you and I…since that night."

"Take a deep breath, my beauty, and let it out slowly," he said in a soft, tender voice.

She did and smiled. "You gave me the confidence that I needed. You helped me that night, and I only just realized how much."

"My darling, I must also confess that I had the same affliction and was able to overcome it. And if you remember, the night of the party, I did stumble a bit over my words. And that was because I was so overcome with emotion for you."

"You were overcome with emotion?" she asked softly.

"Yes. You see, it's because I am deeply in love with you, Lizzie.

Head over heels, in fact. I think from the moment you jumped up from beneath that table in the greenhouse, I was awestruck. You were so beautiful, so lovely. And knowing you'd created all of this with your two delicate hands..." He took both her hands in his and kissed her dirt-encrusted palms.

"M-my hands are dirty."

"I must confess, I do love a dirty-minded woman." He waggled his eyebrows and grinned.

Lizzie burst into laughter, and Potsy, never one to miss inclusion, barked.

Lucien got down on his knees and continued to hold her palms. "But I must tell you once more how much I admire you. That night when I witnessed you stand up to those gossipmongers who made sport of you, you were as regal as a queen."

Lizzie's eyes filled with tears.

"Elizabeth Villiers, will you marry me and make me the happiest of men?"

"Yes." She laughed through the tears now streaming down her cheeks. "I believe that's what people in love do?"

Standing up, he pulled her into his embrace and kissed her long and deeply. Potsy jumped up on his hind legs and barked. Between their pressed lips, she mumbled, "Calm down, Potsy. You're still my number one."

"I beg your pardon?" Lucien chuckled.

"Well, you're my number one man, and Potsy is my number one male...dog, that is."

He threw back his head and laughed.

"Lucien."

"I love the sound of my name on your lips, darling Lizzie."

"I love the sound of my name on yours." She wrapped her arms around his neck. "Will you promise to teach me how to overcome my stammer?"

"I promise," he said, leaning down for another kiss. "We'll have to practice morning, noon, and night."

"Oh, I promise to be a very good student. I'm a quick learner."

"Yes, I know."

Lizzie smiled and pulled down his head for another heart-stopping kiss.

The End

Additional Dragonblade books by Author Belle Ami

The Lost in Time Series
London Time (Book 1)
Paris Time (Book 2)
Tuscan Time (Book 3)

About Belle Ami

Belle Ami writes breathtaking international thrillers, compelling historical fiction, and riveting romantic suspense with a touch of sensual heat. A self-confessed news junkie, Belle loves to create cutting-edge stories, weaving world issues, espionage, fast-paced action, and of course, redemptive love. Belle's series and stand-alone novels include the following:

TIP OF THE SPEAR SERIES: A continuing, contemporary, international espionage, suspense-thriller series with romantic elements. TIP OF THE SPEAR includes the acclaimed *Escape*, *Vengeance*, *Ransom*, and *Exposed*.

OUT OF TIME SERIES: A continuing, time-travel, art-thriller series with romantic elements. OUT OF TIME INCLUDES includes the #1 Amazon bestsellers *The Girl Who Knew da Vinci* and *The Girl Who Loved Caravaggio*, and the new release, *The Girl Who Adored Rembrandt*.

THE BLUE COAT SAGA: A three-part serial, time-travel, suspense thriller with romantic elements set in the present-day and in World War II. THE BLUE COAT SAGA includes *The Rendezvous in Paris*, *The Lost Legacy of Time*, and *The Secret Book of Names*.

The Last Daughter is a compelling and heart-wrenching World War II historical fiction novel based on the life of Belle Ami's mother, Dina Frydman, and her incredible true story of surviving the Holocaust. The story begins at the dawn of World War II and follows the Nazi invasion and occupation of Poland, focusing on the Nazi's six-year reign of terror on the Jews of Poland, and the horrors of the death camps at Bergen-Belsen and Auschwitz, where more than six-million Jews along with other vulnerable innocents were slaughtered.

Belle is also the author of the romantic suspense series THE ONLY ONE, which includes *The One, The One & More,* and *One More Time is Not Enough.*

Recently, Belle was honored to be included in the RWA-LARA *Christmas Anthology Holiday Ever After,* featuring her short story, *The Christmas Encounter.*

A former Kathryn McBride scholar of Bryn Mawr College in Pennsylvania, Belle, is also thrilled to be a recipient of the RONE, RAVEN, Readers' Favorite Award, and the Book Excellence Award.

Belle's passions include hiking, boxing, skiing, cooking, travel, and of course, writing. She lives in Southern California with her husband, two children, a horse named Cindy Crawford, and her brilliant Chihuahua, Giorgio Armani.

Belle loves to hear from readers—
belle@belleamiauthor.com
Twitter: @BelleAmi5
Facebook: belleamiauthor
Instagram: belleamiauthor

TO TILT AT A LYON

by Abigail Bridges

CHAPTER ONE

Monday, 3 January 1814
Embleton House, London
Half-past noon

SIR GORDON RYDELL snarled. "No."

Phyllida, the recently widowed Duchess of Emberton—and his father's sister-in-law—fluffed her black silk skirts around her ankles as she shifted on the settee near the receiving room's fire and glared at him. "What a lovely expression. I cannot imagine any woman of the *ton* resisting such unrelenting charm." As if Gordon had not understood his aunt's sarcasm, she sniffed and gestured toward the invitation on the low table between them. "You might at least look at it."

Gordon's scowl deepened. "Unnecessary. I have no need or intention to attend a *mystère masque*, no matter who is hosting it or how unique the invitation." He crossed his arms and pressed deeper into the wingback chair. "How did she even know I was here anyway? I have been in London less than a week." He had, in truth, only come into the city to attend the ceremony during which he had received a baronetcy—and to discuss a business opportunity with his cousin Matthew, the new Duke of Emberton and Phyllida's oldest son. Gordon had not expected to be ambushed in the opulent sitting room by the duchess about this . . . nonsense . . . as they awaited the call for luncheon.

The second son of the family, Mark, who occupied the other end of the settee from his mother, leaned forward and scooped up the envelope and single piece of paper. "Mrs. Bessie Dove-Lyon knows everything about the *ton*, especially anyone likely to need her services."

"I do not need—"

"You are an ancient bachelor with a fortune, a shiny new title, and no wife. I would even wager that Mrs. Dove-Lyon knew you would receive the baronetcy on New Year's Day before you did." Mark wagged the invitation. "Thus . . . this. Which arrived yesterday, just before you did." Mark's grin held enough mischievousness that Gordon almost smiled.

Almost. "I am not ancient."

"Good King Richard did not live as long."

"In the twelfth century."

"Still. Two and forty is almost grave-bound." His cousin, who was close to Gordon in age, continued to smirk. "Especially where the young women of Society are concerned. So I have been repeatedly told. You already have silver in those golden curls of yours. And where you reside while in town is certainly no secret."

Truth. On all counts, unfortunately. Emberton House had been a second home for Gordon and his brother William since they were children. So much so that after their father died, they had sold their own town home, preferring to stay here whenever they came into the city. Despite the elegance of the furnishings and the wealth the Rydells possessed, the house was a place of refuge and comfort.

And he had aged, and not particularly well. He barely resembled the younger man who had left England to secure his father's fortune. The years had brought riches but also a plague of storms at sea, rough journeys through the American wilderness, and the stress of losses as well as successes. The lack of a wife, also true, bothered him less. His heart had long ago been given to only one woman, one who had been forbidden to him. Finding a woman who could take her place in his life—or heart—would be impossible.

Mark went on. "Your money, however, is ageless. Prepare to be a target of every marriage-minded miss in the *ton*."

"But I have no interest—"

Phyllida's tone turned indignant. "Have you completely forgotten how our Society works during your time in America? Barbarians, obviously. You have been made a baronet and have a substantial fortune due to your father's investments—"

"And mine, thank you."

"But that is not the only reason you left."

Gordon glared at Mark. "You will not mention that, if you do not mind."

Mark raised his hands in surrender as Phyllida went on. "But you are the second son of a second son. In the past, you would have been of no attraction for an eligible young lady—

Probably prompted by Mark's comment, Gordon's mind flashed to a particular young lady, his heart and soul, the one who had never been far from his mind, even after all the years abroad. *"You cannot marry her! You cannot marry at all until you have made something of yourself, have a position. And never her. She is beneath you, the daughter of a knight, a commoner. Impossible!"*

Phyllida's voice pierced through the blistering words of his father. "But you are a baronet now, and richer than Croesus, so your standing to draw the attention of a worthy wife—"

"I do not—"

"Do you plan to dishonor your family's name? Leave no legacy at all? Where do you plan to place that fortune when you die?"

Gordon stared at her. "When I die?"

"Do you even have a will?"

"Duchess—"

"It is always best," Mark interrupted, "not to argue with Mother. Listen, nod, and pretend to care." He held out the invitation.

Phyllida glared at her son. "You are an absolute rotter."

Gordon froze while reaching for the invitation, staring at his aunt. Mark's eyes gleamed with humor—and something more. Something faintly suspicious. "Do not concern yourself, Gordon. This is how we are together. She detests my lack of respect—"

"Because it is abhorrent and will carry you into scandal."

"But she is always polite when out in Society."

Taking the envelope, Gordon muttered, "I must have been gone longer than I realized."

"Ten years." The words snapped from Phyllida. "Since your father died."

"*Because* my father died." Mark cleared his throat, and Gordon shot him a withering glower, even as he continued speaking to his aunt. "His overseas investments would not tend to themselves. My brother took care of the properties here." Gordon refused to defend his actions any further—much less explain that more than his father's death had driven him from the country. He glanced down at the envelope, which featured only a lion stamp.

"And now William has died without an heir, and you are even richer. Do not make the same mistake." Phyllida clasped her hands in her lap. "You have no other brothers, and you do not want the wealth to pass to some distant, unknown cousin. The Rydells have certainly had their share of reprobate relatives."

"Many of whom show up at our back door come Christmas," muttered Mark.

"I could leave it to Mark. Not too distant in blood or location. And only mildly a reprobate." Gordon turned the paper over in his hand, peering closer. The "invitation" itself—a fine foolscap with gold flecks in the paper weave—held only a family crest bearing a holly sprig and the initials BDL. No details, no instructions.

"Bite your tongue, sir," Mark said. "I am still determined to avoid all responsibility in this family." A second son himself, Mark made a good show of indifference, but Gordon well knew how devoted he was to all the Emberton clan, especially his older brother Matthew.

"A son would be better."

Gordon's scowl returned.

Phyllida released an exasperated sign. "Why do the men in this family so resist marriage? It is your duty."

I would have married—

Mark leaned back against the settee, addressing Gordon. "I keep reminding her marriage is not the problem—it is all the protocol and irritating rules about courtship. Indulgent, overwrought balls and simpering conversations with pretentious waifs who have little more to say than a good horse."

Gordon looked at his cousin over the top of the invitation. "This is why you have taken up with an actress?"

"As I said, scandal."

Mark stilled. "I thought you had only been back a few days."

"I have been in London a few days. I have been in England two months. Even I hear things." He waved the invitation. "There is nothing here. How do you even know what it is for?"

His aunt glanced at her son, then answered. "Because that invitation—and Mrs. Bessie Dove-Lyon—are notorious. Everyone in the *ton* knows about it, and how rare the invitations are. Everyone wants one—it is the most sought-after event of the season. And perfect for seeking a mate without being a target. You can hide behind a mask and pretend to be some noble from the past or a peasant from the north."

"I suspect I would make an extremely poor peasant."

"Your arrogance would give it away." Mark's eyes held a playful challenge.

"You think I am arrogant?"

"We all are. Curse of the aristocracy. We cannot help thinking we are better than the folks who empty our chamber pots and grow our food."

"Mark, do not be disgusting." Phyllida peered at Gordon. "Does this mean you will go? The messenger said the invitation was solely for you. If you do not attend, I'm sure Mrs. Dove-Lyon will see it as a cut."

"This does not concern me. But"—he glanced from Mark to Phyllida—"I have to admit my curiosity has been stirred. Why would this woman invite me? Someone she does not know and who has been out of Society—out of the country, for that matter—for years. And if everyone is wearing a mask, how am I to know which woman to approach?"

The door of the room opened, and the Rydell butler entered. He nodded at the duchess. "Luncheon is served, Your Grace."

"At last." Mark stood as did Gordon, who offered his hand to his aunt, helping her to her feet. Mark stepped in behind them. "There are only two things you need to remember, Sir Gordon. One is, the Lyon does nothing without a financial motive."

"Sounds like my sort of woman."

Mark chuckled. "And since invitations are sent at her whim, everyone there has something to gain or lose before the masks come off when the clock strikes midnight."

"That makes finding a suitable match an impossible quest, as if I am Alonso Quijano about to snatch up a lance and set off from La Mancha on an adventure where there is none to be had."

Mark clapped Gordon on the shoulder. "Well, if you are going to see finding a wife as a quest to tilt at windmills, then I have the perfect costume in mind for you."

Monday, 3 January 1814
Tyburn Hall, London
Half-past two in the afternoon

MISS ELEANOR ASQUITH ran one finger over the exquisite white silk of the mask lying on her lap, enamored of its finely crafted beauty. White and silver beads outlined it, and black and white feathers sprang from every possible point along the top and sides. Across the face, a delicate, embroidered musical staff danced, starting on the left cheek, up over that eye and down across the nose, turning upward again under the right eye and disappearing into the feathers just above the right ear.

Luxurious. Elegant. And it could not possibly be hers.

Could it?

"Mother!"

Ella winced at the shout from Lady Charlotte Weston, the woman for whom Ella acted as a constant companion. Charlotte snatched the mask from Ella's lap and marched from the receiving room into the corridor, raising her voice even louder. "Mother! You must come see what Ella has received. There has been a horrible mistake, and you must right this immediately. Mother!"

In the blessed silence that followed, Ella pushed a raven lock of hair behind her ear—at least one of her black strands escaped her lace cap several times a day, no matter how hard she tried to keep them in place—and looked at the box on the low table in front of her. The package, which had been addressed personally to her and delivered by messenger, had arrived shortly after luncheon. She and

Charlotte had just settled in with their needlework projects in the Westons' receiving room, a warm albeit somewhat shabby room in light green and yellow, with soft pillows and a small fireplace emitting a heat that permeated the room. They did so every afternoon, dressed and coiffed, in case visitors came by, as if Charlotte were still a fresh, young debutante instead of an eight and twenty spinster attended by her equally eight and twenty paid companion and erstwhile chaperone.

Visitors never came by.

The past month, however, had provided a bit of relief from the daily routine, as the family had spent the Christmas holiday at their country home. As Charlotte took long rides and shopped the local village, Ella had been free to roam the Berkshire landscape, write, and sing her beloved folk ballads in remote corners of the house. No longer the heart and anchor of the family—that had been relocated to Mayfair, fueling the rumors that the country house would soon be sold—the massive home held myriad empty chambers that echoed blissfully as Ella's alto voice filled the spaces.

Yesterday had brought their return to the city, however, and the end of Ella's respite. Then, today, the mysterious box had arrived, startling Ella and infuriating Charlotte.

A white square lay in the bottom. As Charlotte strode down the corridor toward the conservatory, Ella picked up the envelope. The front bore only a lion stamp, and as she had with the mask, Ella traced the figure with a finger before opening the envelope, her mind filled with a dozen questions. From the inside she slid out a single piece of heavy foolscap, which sparkled in the light from the nearby window. The paper had gold threads woven into it, and Ella slowly rotated the page, loving the glimmer from the intricate markings. Like the envelope, the paper held only a stamp, this one a family crest with the initials BDL and an ornamentation of holly.

"What is that?" Charlotte re-entered the room.

Ella shook her head. "I am not sure."

"Let me see!" Her companion held out a hand as she dropped the mask back into the box.

Ella passed the envelope to her. As Charlotte examined it, a scowl knotting the muscles in her face, the whisper of soft silk announced the arrival of Margaret, Countess of Tyburn. The tall, slender lady, her hair a sweet brown laced with silver, closed the door, her words a quiet hiss. "Charlotte, do stop screaming. I have no interest in disturbing the neighbors. What is the problem today?"

Charlotte thrust the envelope toward her mother. "This. And that"—she pointed at the mask—"arrived this morning. Addressed to her"—now she pointed at Ella. "Obviously there is some mistake. Whatever it is, it should have come to me."

The countess examined the envelope and sliver of paper, growing quite still... and quite pale. "Amazing," she murmured, her fingers quivering. After a moment, she peered at the mask, then looked up at Ella. "My dear, do you have any idea what this is?"

Ella folded her hands in her lap and sat straighter. "None, your ladyship."

The countess handed her the envelope. "This is an Invocation Mystère, possibly one of the most sought-after invitations among the *ton*."

Charlotte crossed her arms. "So there *has* been a mistake. It should have come to me. I am a member of the aristocracy. Not her."

Ignoring her daughter, the countess picked up the box lid, which lay on the table a few inches from the box. She turned it over, reading Ella's name, which had been penned in precise calligraphy: Miss Eleanor Asquith, daughter of Sir James.

Ella swallowed. "What is a... an Invocation Mystère?"

The countess replaced the lid. "Each year, Mrs. Bessie Dove-Lyon—" At Charlotte's gasp, the countess nodded at her daughter—

"Yes, that Mrs. Dove-Lyon, proprietress of The Lyon's Den." She looked again at Ella. "The Lyon's Den is a notorious gambling establishment but is frequented by some of the most elite members of Society. Each year, she hosts a masque ball for her birthday on April first. It is the one event of the year that everyone ignores and everyone wants to attend. But invitations are rare. Even more unusual is the Invocation Mystére. Only a few are sent, and they are personally picked and addressed by Mrs. Dove-Lyon." She bent over to peer at the mask again. "Although they are not usually accompanied by a mask as well. Curious."

Ella's confusion ran deep, causing her stomach to tighten. "But why me? Charlotte is correct. She is aristocracy. I am not."

"I am afraid that is a question for Mrs. Dove-Lyon, although I suspect the inclusion of your father's name on the box may be a hint."

Ella's brows furrowed. "My father?"

The countess settled beside Ella on the settee. "Your father was a good friend of Colonel Sandstrom Lyons, Mrs. Dove-Lyon's husband. Sir James stayed by her side when the colonel died, helping her in many ways. She repaid him by helping him find his first wife—your mother—and his second."

Ella looked down at the invitation in her hand. "I—I had no idea."

"Most people did not. Your father was a very private man and both his wives respected that. So, apparently, did Mrs. Dove-Lyon."

"But you knew?"

The countess nodded. "Your father told me when we brought you on as Charlotte's companion."

"When . . . when he knew he was dying." Five years after, Ella still had trouble voicing the words.

A pause. "Yes." The countess touched her hand. "He wanted you well placed. But he told me that if things became . . . difficult . . .

to contact Mrs. Dove-Lyon."

Charlotte flounced down on an armchair near the fire. "Oh, rubbish. How difficult could being a companion become?"

The countess' shoulders stiffened, and she chewed her lower lip a moment, staring down at her lap. Ella waited, as she usually did when Charlotte's behavior frustrated her mother, an almost daily occurrence. The countess had infinite patience, although sometimes it took a bit of control to maintain it.

She also knew they all had differing ideas of what constituted "difficult." As usual, Charlotte only thought of herself, but Ella had seen the signs of other "difficulties" in the Tyburn household—the same ones she had noticed in her own home before her father had died in poverty. The disappearing furniture and artwork. The empty rooms. The lighter social calendar. Less expensive meals and frocks. Although little compensated for her service, Ella's position was non-essential to the household and would be at risk as times grew harder.

Still... the countess' last statement sent a surge of comforting warmth through her. "He wanted to make sure I was provided for."

The countess lifted her eyes and her expression softened. "Precisely."

Charlotte stood and reached for the mask again. "This is all nonsense. You should contact this woman right now and tell her she has made a mistake."

The countess blocked her daughter's hand and stood, glaring at her. "Charlotte, you will cease this right now. Sit down. Because I can assure you that Mrs. Bessie Dove-Lyon does not make this sort of mistake. The invitation came to Eleanor, and it will be Eleanor who attends that ball."

Charlotte remained standing, arms akimbo. "Ridiculous. She cannot go! I should. She does not even have the kind of gown suitable for such an event."

"Then we must remedy that."

"She does not have any money!"

The countess smiled, a slow and sly reaction, as she glanced at Ella. "Actually . . . she does."

Chapter Two

Friday, 1 April 1814
The Lyon's Den, Whitehall, London
Half-past nine in the evening

GORDON FELT LIKE an absolute fool. Throughout January and February, he had refused to attend to this absurd event, finally acquiescing mid-March under the relentless badgering of his aunt and cousin—and his own curiosity. Now he stood in the main gaming hall of the Lyon's Den, his back against the wall, as he watched the crowd grow and mingle. Dressed as a disheveled Spanish knight errant from two centuries earlier, Gordon felt as out of place as his character must have in the oppressive town society when he longed to be on the plains of La Mancha. No one else wore a breastplate, much less one that scraped against the plates draped over his shoulders. Not true armor, of course—it was all made out of some kind of molded tin—but even with the quilted tunic beneath it, it made him itch and felt as if it weighed at least two stone. Fortunately, despite Mark's growing insistence, Gordon had refused to carry a lance. Even he knew such a thing would be dimly viewed by the wolves of the Lyon's Den, that serious and inscrutable team that oversaw the security of the establishment.

He glanced again at the tall, well-built men who hovered near each entrance and in front of Mrs. Dove-Lyon's private office. He knew they were former soldiers who had honed their skills on the Peninsula and could easily bounce an unruly patron straight out the door. Most stood even taller than he did—his height of well over six feet did give him an advantage as he continued to survey the hall from beneath the curving metal brim of his morion, that open-faced helmet that was much hotter than he expected it to be. And he still had no answers. Although Gordon had been here many times prior to leaving for America, he had never once set eyes on Mrs. Dove-Lyon nor had any idea why he would be invited.

Tonight the hall had been transformed. Rather than the riotous and sparsely lit gaming facility of his memory, this room glowed, light showering the room from overhead chandeliers, freestanding candelabra, and wall sconces. The heavier gaming tables were dark and unattended, and the lighter ones had been removed. Beverage stations stood next to the walls, including one not far from Gordon's position, offering an impressive array of champagne, claret, port, madeira, ratafia, rum, ale, and that eternal presence at every ball—lemonade. In an alcove on the far wall, a small orchestra tuned and settled.

Men and women alike milled about, all masked, all costumed in garb ranging from peasant girls with simple masks to a domineering Queen Elizabeth, whose skirts threatened to clear a beverage table each time she wandered close. Jesters, of course, and more than a few lusty milkmaids. They all waited for the dancing to begin, glancing at the musicians and moving in clusters around the room like murmuring starlings. Some were showing off—flaunting extravagant costumes and flirting outrageously—while others seemed unsure what to do or say, how to play a part at a masque ball.

Hermits and monks clustered together—many of whom had already partaken of far too much wine and ale. Two lurid and exaggerated Napoleons staggered about, patting their rounded bellies and weaving among the occasional ghost, a Punch, and three sultans. Several ladies had indulged in Egyptian costumes, including one in a white sarsnet dress, and two who appeared to think Egyptian women wore very little above the waist. Cupid—a drunken and red-faced pudge who should never expose that much bulging flesh—wandered by and saluted Gordon with his bow, his arrow having been confiscated at the door.

Trying not to laugh, Gordon merely nodded, grateful for his own dark brown felt mask. No one would ever know who he was, and the thought that he would meet a woman to court in the midst of this cacophony—even if he wanted to—remained a ludicrous notion. He recognized no one and contemplated, yet one more time, fleeing for the door as soon as the stream of arrivals abated.

"Sir Gordon?"

Gordon blinked at the broad-shouldered wolf who stopped before him. "Yes?"

"Please follow me." The man turned and strode away.

His curiosity now spiking, Gordon stepped in behind him, a little surprised to find himself standing at the door of Mrs. Bessie Dove-Lyon's office. The wolf knocked once, then opened it and gestured for Gordon to enter. As Gordon stepped inside, the man closed the door, shutting out much of the revelry.

Mrs. Dove-Lyon—or at least Gordon assumed it was the lady in question, as he could not see beyond the veil covering most of her face—sat behind her desk, calmly pouring a cup of tea from a fine porcelain teapot. The office, elegant yet functional in its design, overflowed with vases of hothouse flowers in all colors and fragrances, an absolute riot of sight and scent. Prominent among the clusters were numerous bouquets of holly sprigs, reminiscent of the ones on the family crest of the invitation. A reminder that a particular celebration lay behind the festivities. Mrs. Dove-Lyon obviously had a plethora of admirers and well-wishers.

Gordon cleared his throat. "Mrs. Dove-Lyon. May I wish you a joyous birthday?"

Mrs. Dove-Lyon added sugar to her tea and stirred it. "Thank you, Sir Gordon. Please be seated." She tapped the spoon gently on the edge of the cup and set it aside.

Gordon eased down into one of the cabriolet armchairs in front of her desk, his armor plates scraping together as they shifted.

She sipped her tea, then closed both hands around the cup. "I thought you might come to see me before now. You have stayed in the city these past three months, even though you had planned to return to one of your brother's houses. In Kent, I believe. Are you that lacking in curiosity as to why you received one of my Invocations Mystére?"

"Forgive me if I seem ungrateful, Mrs. Dove-Lyon. I do not lack curiosity. Wondering why I received the invitation has indeed haunted me. To the point that I almost did not come. But over the last few years, I have discovered that patience is an equally effective strategy. In business, if you drive a potential client or business interest too hard or too fast, the potential for success can be crippled . . . or even collapse entirely."

A smile flicked over her lips, then vanished. "Indeed." She sipped her tea once more, then set the cup aside and folded her hands in front of her. "You were invited, Sir Gordon, because you owe this house a substantial debt. And I am calling it in."

Gordon stared at her, words failing, as he wracked his brain for any vowel involving the Lyon's Den. Yes, he had gambled here as a younger man, often, but he always paid any money owed at the end of the night. In fact, he had made sure that he had no outstanding debts when he left England after his father's death. Even if he had, his brother William would have cleared them had he known. "Madam, I'm sure you are mistak—"

"It is not a debt of currency. It is a debt of honor. Which you now have the opportunity to settle, if you have the courage." She reached for the tea again, apparently allowing him time to think.

Realization flared in his mind, and Gordon felt his stomach clench. *Oh dear God. Surely she did not mean—*

The cup returned to its saucer. "Ah. I see you remember. Good."

His throat tightened, and his words emerged like wheels on gravel. "I have never forgotten. But the man is dead. Surely she is mar—"

"Indeed. These five years hence. His death, however, does not abdicate your responsibility to his household. As Sir James had no male heirs—rendering his daughter quite vulnerable after his death, especially given what happened—he left the administration of his estate to me, specifically to my lawyers. With precise instructions regarding you."

"He despised me."

"Would not any father, given your behavior?"

"I would have—I meant to mar—" Gordon stopped and gave a low growl. "He forbade me from taking care of the situation. He banished me from his presence—and hers. Surely, she has—"

"Understandable, do you not think?"

Gordon almost exploded from his chair. "I would have married her! She means—meant—" He stopped, gripping the arms of the chair.

Unmoved by his anger, Mrs. Dove-Lyon shook her head. "The second son of a second son? With no future and apparently no honor?"

Understanding settled over Gordon, a cold shower of comprehension. "But now I have money."

"As he saw developing in the years following your own father's death. Thus his change of heart—and mind."

"Why did he not approach William? He would have taken action to set things aright."

"After you dishonored him as well as his daughter? After you were cast away in such a manner that your leaving to take care of your father's investments became the only option? Your brother refused to see him, based on the way you were treated."

Gordon recalled his last encounter with Sir James Asquith. The man had called him out, almost disemboweling him with a rapier when Gordon had refused to engage. The duel had ended with Sir James collapsing from exhaustion, declaring that honor would never be satisfied. "He did try to kill me."

Mrs. Dove-Lyon's mouth quirked. "You had ruined his daughter."

"But no one knew. Not about the duel. Not about what had happened between Miss Asquith and me. She would have been free to—"

"No ruination of her reputation, no. But there are other types of ruination, including that of the heart."

Gordon felt the words as a blow to his chest. "What are you saying?"

"You left after the duel. She refused all others. Adamantly. And has openly threatened to kill you upon your return. She blames you for her father's early death, even though you were long out of the country."

The words sank deep into his mind. "She has never taken a husband?"

"She refused all suitors. She is now a spinster hired out as a companion to one of the most disagreeable women in the *ton*. This is how she will end her days unless you develop as much honor in the next few hours as you have money."

Gordon leaned back in the chair, his breath stalling in his throat, his thoughts suddenly consumed by the idea of Eleanor—his sweet, raven-haired beauty—as a spinster shackled to a shrew. His gut churned, an image of her flashed through his mind, scalding him. She had lain beneath him, eager and compliant, consumed by her bliss, enchanted by his claiming of her, eyes wide with adoration. Her fingers had flitted over his skin and through his hair as if he were a precious artifact, barely to be touched. The first time of many they had lain together—their affair had lasted almost a year before her father discovered it.

"Will you accept my challenge?" The words held a dark undertone, part challenge, part warning.

Gordon swallowed. "Yes."

"Then go. You have until midnight to redeem yourself. She is on the floor in a mask as unique as she is. Recognize the mask, recognize the woman. You will need to woo and win her, and bring her here, to my office. If you do not do so before midnight, if you see her only after the masks come off, then you will have lost her forever. I will see to that, sir. I will also see that word is spread that you do not honor your debts—either of currency or honor. Do you believe me?"

He did. This woman could easily ruin him—or at least do a great deal of damage to his reputation. And she would. "I do."

She picked up the cup again. "Then go."

Gordon left, ignoring a strange and annoying feeling beginning to blossom in his chest. A most dangerous emotion.

Hope.

ELLA FLED TO the far wall of the Lyon's Den gaming hall as soon as she had pulled away from the crush of people entering through the narrow doors. There the musicians sat tucked away, tuning their instruments and flipping through pages of music. Musicians—her people. She felt safer there, more comfortable closer to an environment she knew well. She recognized a few of the players from past musicales she had attended with Charlotte. Ella had always been a favorite at such events, with her skills at the pianoforte, flute, and harp—and her voice—welcome even among those who performed for a livelihood.

If only she had been skilled enough—or brave enough—to attempt such a path. Few women did, of course, and those who did were not always well thought of. And she had already disappointed her father enough.

What would he think of her tonight?

Coming alone had created a battle with Charlotte, who had insisted she should accompany Ella as a chaperone. That thought had made Ella shudder and the countess laugh—which had surprised them both. But the countess had been a surprise through almost all the preparations for this night, starting with the announcement that Ella's father had left a small stipend for "special instances," squirreled away by the countess for the past five years. Money now used for a costume frock that matched the mask. An instructor had been hired to refresh Ella's long-dormant dancing and conversation skills. Ella had felt like a princess, her anticipation and eagerness for this ball driving Charlotte mad.

It was as if everyone in the household—from the lowest maid to the earl and countess themselves—knew this would be Ella's last chance to become something more than a paid companion to a cranky spinster.

And Ella had wanted this. Craved it. She had dreamed of the dances and elaborate costumes. Now, however, with her back flat against the wall, Ella felt as if she had stepped off a cliff into the ocean, adrift and lost in her black and white gown, festooned with enough beads to sink her to the bottom of that sea. Her high-waisted, black satin bodice topped a black satin slip covered with white lace drape. Black beads formed a spiral pattern throughout the lace and weighted the hem. A sash, embroidered with black, silver, and white beads anchored her waist, forming a broad bow in the back that trailed down the train. Her short, white, puffed sleeves were scalloped on the bottom edge and trimmed with black lace. She wore a pearl necklace, bracelets, and earrings. A white satin turban covered her hair, and black and white feathers sprang from the folds in the fabric. White kid slippers and gloves—along with that mask—completed the ensemble.

That mask. How she loved that mask!

Ella had practiced walking and dancing with it on so much the stiffened fabric had formed to her face. She had adjusted the feathers until they no longer tickled when she moved. But the thing she loved most about it was the music staff that graced its front. Curious, she had taken it to the pianoforte to play the notes, gasping when she realized they were not randomly drawn.

They were the twelve bars of "Robin Adair," a ballad of lost love. A ballad she had sung in fun as a girl, then relentlessly ten years ago—her own heart broken—until her father demanded she never sing it again. And she had not—at least not when he could hear her. She had finally stopped completely after his death. Although she could love and hate her father at the same time—he had been the reason her heart and life had been shattered—it seemed disrespectful at that point. After all, his heart, too, had been broken by what had happened.

And the man she had sung it about had disappeared, not only from her life but from England. A man she could never forgive.

Or forget.

Damn him.

But the discovery made Ella even more curious about how she had come to receive the mask. She had written to this odd woman, Mrs. Bessie Dove-Lyon, but had received no response. Perhaps, if she could confront the lady tonight, Ella might receive some answers.

She studied the crowd. The wild array before her reminded her more of a circus at Astley's than a Society ball. Parodies of royalty and knights of an earlier age gamboled about, and a corsair spun by her, leaping and bounding to some unheard saber dance. A harlequin waggled his bells at her, leering at her decolletage before skipping off to loop an arm around a half-clad servant girl, who giggled and gave him a playful slap.

Ella suspected she knew exactly what her father would think about all this. His dedication to the protocol and proprieties of a Society they barely graced the edge of had taught her a great deal—but had cost her even more.

Laughter burst from a group of men dressed like Huguenots, and a shabbily dressed Don Quixote emerged from a door directly opposite her. Unlike the rest of the crowd, who seemed to be having the time of their lives, the don appeared unsettled, his mouth downturned and his fists clenched at his side. He turned and slid into a crowd near a beverage table, looking at each face closely, murmuring to them. The women began to flirt, and the man's mood improved, even as his eyes continued to search the masked faces around him.

Why did he seem so familiar?

"My lady!"

Ella jerked, staring up at a bare-chested, domino-masked Pan.

"May I have this dance?" He held out a hand, wiggling his fingers at her. Small horns sprouted from his black curls, and his legs and hips were covered with goat skin, held together by a codpiece that appeared to have been stuffed with a gourd.

It was going to be a bizarre night.

Chapter Three

Friday, 1 April 1814
The Lyon's Den, Whitehall, London
Quarter-past eleven in the evening

IF GORDON DID not set foot in another ballroom for the next fifty years, it would be too soon. Fortunately, he would be long dead before that.

So he hoped.

After almost two hours of peering into dozens of masks as he danced more than ten rounds on the floor, his feet ached, his eyes burned, and the heat of his "armor" had left him marinating in his own sweat. The clock inched ever closer to midnight, and he still had seen nothing and no one who even faintly resembled his memory of Eleanor Asquith. None of the flirtatious women—and a few men—had that rare combination of a unique mask, luscious raven hair, full curves, and enchanting blue eyes. Nor that melodious alto that had so often sung to him folksongs from ages past.

A memory flicked behind his eyes then—a tree in the garden behind the home she had shared with her father. The soft grass beneath it, and his head in her lap as she plucked a nearby flower for him to sniff. Her voice lilting through a sweet ballad from the Scottish border—

"Tell ya fortune, luv?"

Gordon blinked, staring down at a woman who appeared to be wrapped in a dozen multicolored scarves . . . and little else. Her eyes behind a simple mask leered at him as she ran a finger across his breastplate, clutching his forearm with the other. "Ooh. Strong, handsome fella such as yourself shouldn't be over here next to the wall. Come out with Miss Isabella and let me tell ya future, 'cause I know it's going to be most"—she licked her lower lip—"satisfying."

Gordon's stomach churned, and he lurched to the side, pulling from her grasp. "Um, no. But thank you, my lady," he added hastily. She might appear to be a county fair soothsayer, but he had already discovered that many of the women dressed as milkmaids and doxies were, in truth, ladies of the *ton*. And perfectly willing to instruct him as such when he spurned their advances. He looked around, seeking an escape, any kind of escape, from the mass of people in the hall. Spotting the double doors leading to the facility's gardens, he strode in that direction, dodging a man bearing a tray of champagne, and dancers in the midst of a scotch reel. He pushed through the doors, grabbing a deep inhale of the cooler night air and pausing to get his bearings.

He stood on a narrow veranda edged by a low stone balustrade. Marble steps descended from each end and directly in front of him, all providing access to a dense garden of trees, shrubs, and flower-lined paths. The garden itself bordered Green Park at the rear, and the pavement leading to Lancaster House and Clarence House to the side and front. The park's adjacence gave the impression that the garden stretched much farther than it did, providing a bit of seclusion and peace.

Giggles sounded to his left, and a wandering couple vanished behind a hedge, which began to rustle furiously.

So much for the peacefulness.

Gordon took another deep breath and strolled to the steps in front of him, intending to wander onto the path. He stopped abruptly on the top tread. At the bottom, near a post anchoring the foot of the stairway, a woman stood, her fists clenched at her sides as she stared out into the night. Her entire body trembled, and she muttered to herself, creating a hissing sound that echoed off the stone.

His brows furrowed as he studied her. Gordon had seen her intermittently during the past two hours but had never been able to get close. Like him, she seemed to be on her own quest, moving from group to group, pausing then striding to yet another cluster of folks. Unlike the other ladies present—who had chosen either bright colors or the dullest of browns for their costumes—she had stood out because of the simple black and white design of her gown. Few frills, except for the feathers in her turban and those around the sides and top of her mask. From a distance, the mask appeared white, but now Gordon realized it had some kind of black spotted scheme on it.

He took a few steps down, annoyed at the scrapes and squeaks his own costume made.

She stilled and her muttering stopped.

He descended another step. "My lady, are you all right?"

She stiffened. "If you do not mind, sir, I came out here to be alone."

Two more down. "I did not mean to intrude, but you looked most distressed."

Her head snapped in his direction, her eyes narrowing. "What did you say?"

Another tread. "I only wished—" From this distance, he could see the spotted design was a musical staff. A somewhat familiar-looking one... His hand reached out toward her. "What a most unique mask. Do you know what song that is?"

The narrowed eyes flew wide. Deep blue eyes.

"Wherever did you find such a—"

She punched him.

Pain shot through Gordon's right jaw and exploded up into his head. A coppery taste flooded his mouth, and he staggered backward, his hand pressed against his lips. "What the devil—"

"You rotter! You demon bastard!" The woman bounced, shaking her left hand, then clutching it against her stomach with her right. "Bloody hell, that hurt!"

Gordon stared at her, realization seeping through him, spearing his heart. *No.* This could not... This woman could not be his Ella. Too thin, her face below the mask drawn and pale. His Ella had soft, round curves, the kind that could lure a man into the starkest temptation. Would never use such words. This woman looked... hard.

But those eyes.

He braced his jaw in one hand and swallowed, the metallic taste easing. "Are you... Eleanor?"

She stopped bouncing, glaring at him. "You did not recognize me?"

Gordon shook his head. "I... no... but your voice. Your eyes."

Those eyes glistened suddenly and her lips trembled. "You did not know me?"

A moment of panic gripped Gordon, tightening his chest. After all these years, she was here, his Ella was here, right in front of him, a miracle, and he could feel her slipping away. *What was the right answer?* He felt so close, yet she appeared as fragile as a bird, about to escape a net. *I was looking for a younger, plumper woman* did not seem to be the words to say in that moment. And the truth stung.

He lowered his hand and held it out to her. "Does it still hurt?"

Her voice cracked. "Yes. How the devil do men fight with their bare hands?"

Easing closer, his hand closed on her forearm. She jerked, but allowed him to pull her injured hand free, cupping it in his own. The softness of her glove against his skin eased some of his fear as he ran his fingers over hers. "Nothing seems broken."

Her entire body quivered. "It still hurts."

"I'm sure. It hurts when men do it as well. Eventually you get used to it."

"Men are stupid."

Gordon swallowed a laugh. "I will not argue that point."

Her eyes lowered as she watched him massage her hand. Tears dropped from her eyes, slipping beneath the mask. "Why did you leave?"

Gordon froze, fighting an abrupt surge of anger. *Why would she not—* "Your father did not tell you?"

Ella opened her mouth to speak, then merely shook her head. "He said you were a man without honor."

His breath caught. "I left a letter."

"There was none."

The spike of rage that shot through him felt as if it cracked Gordon's heart. "I wrote—"

She shook her head again, the tears flowing freely now. "I should have known. He wished me to hate you. But I could not. Any more than I could love an—" She stopped, chewing her lower lip.

Something Ella had always done when hurt or confused.

No more. He released her hand and slipped the mask from her face, pulling her toward him. "My darling, I am sorry. I tried—"

Stiff against him, she pushed against the breastplate. "You are wearing armor. And hot. I have no desire to be held by a stove." And a giggle broke through the tears—

And his frustration and anger. "Ella—"

The giggles multiplied. She moved away, putting her hand over her mouth in a weak attempt to stifle them. Then, in the middle, a gasp. "You left me! Ten years! Why are you here now?"

Enough. Gordon reached for her arm. "Come with me."

"Where?"

"To the woman who set all this in motion. Who can tell us why."

And, to his surprise, Ella came with him, giggles still coming in bursts and fits.

It was almost midnight.

***

THE MAELSTROM OF thoughts and emotions circling her head and heart threatened to drown Ella. Anger, frustration—and joy— swarmed through her, erupting in those damnable giggles. Her head spun and her feet stumbled as she allowed Gordon to pull her across the gambling floor of the Lyon's Den.

Her earlier frustration at not being able to locate Mrs. Dove-Lyon, no matter who she asked, no matter where she looked—no matter who had touched her—had sent her to the gardens to regain her composure. Only to have the demon from her past reappear out of the night. Her haunting angel, the specter from her deepest longing, her harshest nightmares. The man she hated. The man she loved. The only face she ever imagined when she touched herself at night, longing for the ways he had touched her so long ago. Yet she recognized his voice first, the sweet baritone that could woo with words and song—and had. Then she spotted the golden curls peeking from the edge of his helmet—the silky strands she had so often brushed and entangled with her fingers. The desire in his deep brown eyes when she had tugged on them.

And ten years of rage borne of love exploded.

Her hand still ached.

She knew, of course, about what had happened to him. One could not visit a modiste without hearing whispers about the Rydell brothers, those men who had chosen business investments over the more acceptable professions for an aristocratic gentleman, the insinuations that gentlemen who made their livelihood in that manner were somehow "less than." And one did not exist within the *ton*, even on its fringes, and not hear news that Sir Gordon Rydell had returned to London. News that had reignited all the longings she had thought buried beneath her grief. The cravings to feel his hands against her skin again. But Ella never thought she would ever see him, much less that he would behave as if the past decade had never happened.

As if he still adored her.

The man who tugged her across the floor, however, did not appear to be "less than" in any form or manner. Even draped in tin armor, Gordon Rydell appeared as fit as he had been ten years ago, his arms tightly muscled and—she glanced down—his thighs firm. Those thighs—

She tripped. As Ella plunged forward, Gordon dropped her mask and steadied her, his hand tight on her waist. As she regained her balance, she looked up at him. The concern in his eyes felt so familiar, as did the warmth of his hand, that her breath halted. As if the past decade had never slipped away from them, Ella leaned in, her gaze on the softness of his cupid-bow lips, the square line of his jaw. Images she had so often dreamed about, now real and before her.

"Are you all right?" His voice, raised over the clamor, seemed too loud, too harsh, and it broke through her momentary reverie.

She nodded. He released her waist and scooped up the mask as he led her again toward the wooden door.

The man guarding it knocked once, then opened it as they sailed inside. Behind a desk and surrounded by a tumult of flowers, a woman looked up from a ledger, her face concealed behind a veil.

"I found her," Gordon announced.

The woman glanced from him to Ella, then back. "So I see. She was not supposed to remove the mask before midnight."

"Oh." Gordon seemed to deflate a bit. "I took it off her."

"Why?"

"She was crying."

The woman stiffened and her head snapped toward Ella. "Did he hurt you?"

Ella licked her lips, trying to understand why they were here. "You are Mrs. Dove-Lyon?"

The woman nodded. "Did he hurt you?" she repeated.

"Why did you not answer my letters?"

The office went silent as they both stared at her. Ella straightened and cradled her bruised fist in her other hand. "I have been looking for you all evening. Why would you invoke my father's name to get me here, then not explain why?"

The woman studied her a moment. "If you knew this was a machination to get you to cross paths with Mr. Rydell again, would you have come?"

"No."

"Why not?"

"Because I have never forgiven him for leaving. For what that did to me . . . to my father. I—I never wanted to see him again, even though I could not—" Ella stopped, chewing her lower lip.

Gordon moaned, stepping away from her.

Mrs. Dove-Lyon's voice softened. "Even though . . ."

Ella gave a quick shake of her head. She would not say it.

"Even though . . . he has never loved another either?"

What? Ella felt as if all the air had been sucked from her lungs, and her hands went cold. She swallowed. "I—I—do not . . ."

Mrs. Dove-Lyon stood and came to her. She reached for Ella's hand, which caused her to wince. The woman looked down at her hand, then at Gordon. His jaw remained bright red, and a touch of blood lingered at the corner of his lips. "You hit him?"

Ella nodded.

"A damn fine left cross." Gordon wiped his mouth with the back of his hand.

Mrs. Dove-Lyon smiled. "Good for you." She motioned at the two armchairs in front of her desk. "Please sit." Ella did, and Mrs. Dove-Lyon eased down into the other one, as Gordon retreated behind a spray of roses. "Your father had been a fine friend to my husband, and later of mine. He watched your anguish, expecting you to resolve in your mind that Mr. Rydell would never be in your life again. But you did not. Instead, you settled into a spinster's mindset from the time you were twenty. Far too young, but nothing Sir James did would budge you. He made up his mind to do what he could, and he worked with my lawyers and me to secure your future. He thought he would have more time to find you a decent position, but he did not. Charlotte Weston may not be an ideal companion, but the countess is kind and looks out for you."

"She does indeed."

"And when your father realized Sir Gordon might eventually return, he put all this in motion—although neither of us thought it would be another five years before he set foot on English soil again."

Gordon growled. Mrs. Dove-Lyon ignored him. "Your father came to regret how everything ended."

"Why did he choose you?"

"Because wayward men, unmarriageable women, and unresolved relationships are the nature of my business. I am paid handsomely to make certain things happen between people."

Gordon cut his eyes at her. "Who paid you for this? Sir James?"

A fleeting smile crossed Mrs. Dove-Lyon's. "He asked me to set the actions in motion, but when I heard you planned to return to London, I reached out to someone with an equitable interest in seeing this matter resolved. Someone dedicated to seeing everyone in her family safely married and respectable. Someone with a great deal more money than Sir James ever had."

Gordon stepped closer. "Who?"

"Your aunt."

"I will kill her."

"No, you will not." Mrs. Dove-Lyon stood. "It is almost midnight. I must go." Ella rose as well, and Gordon moved from behind the flowers. "Sir Gordon's task tonight was to find you and bring you to this office. That was his choice." She picked up a key from her desk and offered it to Ella. "Now the choice is yours. This is to a room upstairs. The number is on the key. If you wish to see this evening play out to its conclusion, you have two choices. You can leave now. Alone, although I can see that you are escorted in safety. Or you can take the key, and—if Sir Gordon is willing—retreat with him to this room and see if you resolve any unanswered concerns from the past."

Ella looked from the key to Gordon—who seemed quite pale under his mask—to Mrs. Dove-Lyon's face. "In one night?"

The woman gave a single nod. "There are not as many unanswered questions as you might think."

Ella searched Gordon's face again. He appeared impassive, but his nostrils flared, and down at his sides, his fists clenched and reddened, one of them crushing her mask.

She reached for the key.

Chapter Four

Saturday, 2 April 1814
The Lyon's Den, Whitehall, London
Quarter-past midnight

Gordon was not quite sure what he would have done if Ella had not taken the key—the relief when she did felt like a warm wave flushing over him. She stared at it in her hand a moment, then looked up at him, her eyes wide, her brows arched, her mouth tense. He knew that expression, remembered it the first time he reached for the ribbons in her hair, the ties on the front of her bodice.

She was terrified . . . of him.

He approached her tentatively, holding out his elbow, as if to lead her to the dance floor. "Miss Asquith?"

With a slight nod, she closed one hand around the key and slipped the other through the crook of his arm.

With a brief smile, Mrs. Dove-Lyon moved to the door and opened it. "You are welcome to stay down here for the next festivities. Supper will be served—buffets in the dining rooms—just after midnight, after the hurrahs about my birthday have ended. Or you may ascend now. You will have all the privacy you need until morning."

Ella looked up at him, her voice a bare whisper. "Now?"

"Please."

She chewed her lower lip again as their hostess gestured toward the stairs. "Fourth floor. Far above the madness."

The clock in Mrs. Dove-Lyon's office began its midnight chimes as they left, and Gordon could hear the rousing cheers in celebration of her birthday as they climbed, the sounds fading as their steps carried them upward. Ella's grip on his arm grew ever tighter, but her eyes remained on the stairs in front of them. She glanced at the key again as they reached the top. "412."

It was the last door on the right, as far from the gambling floor of the facility as anyone could possibly go and remain in the building. Ella released his arm and inserted the key in the lock, her hands trembling as it turned. She pushed open the light wooden door and he held it as they entered. The room, small but polished clean, held a narrow wardrobe near a high window and an accent table and two chairs next to the fireplace. The space was dominated, however, by a heavy four-poster bed, draped in white cotton linens. Fat pillows lined up against the headboard, and a down-filled cover had been turned back.

Closing the door, Ella pushed the key back into the lock and turned it, securing their privacy. Yet she remained facing it.

"Ella?"

"Could you"—she turned—"could you please remove that"—she gestured at the armor. "It makes me feel as if I should search for a windmill to tilt at."

He smiled. "No windmills. Just me."

"I can barely look at you without snickering."

Gordon's eyebrows arched. "Do I look that ridiculous?"

"Yes."

The one declarative word set him to laughing as well. "Then help me with the ties." He slipped off his mask and helmet and placed them on the table next to her mask, then raised his arms.

Almost as if relieved to have some task to do, she crossed to him and began unlacing the coarse twine that held the breast and right shoulder plates in place. He let her, not attempting to aid her. "I am afraid I have . . . steeped . . . a bit in it."

"You always did." She pulled the right shoulder plate off and leaned it up against the wall near the table, then moved around his back and began working on the left shoulder plate.

Gordon stilled. "I . . . what?"

Her eyes remained focused on the knots. "You were always a walking furnace. Hot when no one else was. Damp at the most unfortunate times and places. You cannot be unaware of this."

He felt oddly chagrinned. "No, but my valet—"

"I am sure Mr. Waters does the best he can. But he has a lot to contend with." She flicked a glance at him. "Is it still Mr. Waters?"

She remembered. "It is."

Ella sniffed. "He always made sure you smelled like peppermint and wheatgrass. I do not know how, since most scents would have evaporated with your heat. He must have concocted some special form—

"Why are we talking about my scents?"

She set the second shoulder plate next to the first and began to work on the final ties of the breastplate. "You are the one who brought up the . . . steeping."

"But you remembered how I smelled?"

"It is how you smell now as well." She paused as the breastplate slipped free from his body and looked at him from beneath lowered lashes. "I remember everything about you."

Gordon thought his chest would burst. "Everything?"

Ella blinked, then moved to put the breastplate down. She returned to his side and reached up, threading her fingers through his hair. "Every moment." As she watched his face, she entangled the damp curls in her fist... and pulled. "Everything," she whispered, her lips close to his.

Desire shot through Gordon like a falcon strike, sudden and penetrating. Every muscle tightened and his loins tensed, his cock hardening. His breath caught, and his arms wound around her waist, pulling her against his body. She gasped as her eyes closed, the muscles in her face and neck turning soft and pliant as she tilted her head back. He sought her mouth with his, crushing his lips against hers as his tongue delved deep, searching, a man starving for the affection, the sensuous touch he had not felt in far too long.

Ella moaned, a deep haunting sound that echoed into his throat as she arched against him, her fingers now raking through his hair, down his neck, the tips digging into his shoulders. Gordon eased out of the kiss, nipping her lower lip with his teeth. "I have so long dreamed of this."

"I remember," she whispered, kissing the soft skin near his ear, "your touch. Every stroke. Undress me?"

Gordon slipped her from his arms even as his lips caressed her neck, trailing down to her collar bone. "Turn around."

She did, and he loosened the ribbon ties holding the back of her gown together as she unwrapped the turban on her head. Feathers and hair combs flicked free, ticking to the floor as the ebony strands cascaded in silken waves over her back. The satin frock fluttered to the floor, and he untied the stays beneath and pushed them down over her hips. He steadied her as she stepped out of both. Gazing at her, now clad in only her chemise, slippers, stockings, and pearls, Gordon could barely breathe. Ella was, indeed, much thinner than he remembered, but so arrestingly beautiful, so much more a woman than a girl, he knew he could stare at her for hours. His hands lingered, cupping her buttocks, and she gave a soft laugh.

"You always did like that view of me."

He slid his hands over her hips, pulling her against him, his fingers searching for the firm mound at the top of her thighs. "Always. And more."

With a sigh, she pressed against him, leaning her head back on his shoulder and snuggling her hips against the solid ridge of his erection. He sucked in air, closing his eyes against the sensation. Pressing through her chemise, his fingers found the sweet seam of her sex and pushed in, lifting her.

Her voice remained a quiet whisper—"Yes!"—as she reached up over her head with one hand and cupped his face. "I remember everything you did to me. Everything we did." She pulled away enough to turn and face him. "Why do you think I could not tolerate the thought of any other lover?" She pushed up on her toes to kiss him. "You are my heart." She paused, her eyes narrowing with desire. "I belong to only you."

Something in him cracked at that, and Gordon grabbed her, lifting her off the floor. "Ella!" He swung her around, carried her to the bed, and flung her down on the pillows. Her face lit with a happy brilliance as she bounced, then watched him strip the rest of his costume free, from the roughhewn trousers to the sash holding the quilted tunic and shirt in place. He yanked off his boots, and her smile widened as he stood next to the bed, erect and eager. Then he reached down and lifted one foot. He slid her shoe off and kissed her ankle. "Why do you think," he asked slowly, "I could not tolerate the thought of any other lover?" His kisses moved up her calf and thigh, pausing at the top of her stocking. "You are my heart. Only you." Another kiss, then he pulled the stocking from her leg.

With a sudden twist of his hands, Gordon tied one end of the stocking around her ankle, then he looped the other end around one of the bedposts, knotting it. "I remember too." His eyes focused on her face, he repeated the action with her other stocking, her other ankle, the other bedpost. "Only you belong to me. You and no other."

THE WORDS SANK into Ella, into her heart and mind like a soothing balm. They were the vows they had spoken to each other the night Gordon had claimed her, had shown her how intimacy between two people could be so much more than a man rutting on top for lineage and legacy.

She belonged only to him. Always and forever.

Gordon reached down and snagged the sash of his tunic from the floor. She gave him a slow smile as he wrapped one end around her wrists, affixing the other end to the headboard. "You remember?"

She nodded and eased her eyes closed, waiting... but not for long.

He began with the tips of his fingers, tracing them over every inch of her flesh, from her cheek, down her shoulder, then circling her hardening nipples with a light tease. With both hands in play, his fingers caressed her waist and hips, gliding over her belly and down between her thighs. Ella shivered, desire washing over her as he skipped lightly over her moistening folds, the pressure growing firmer as he followed the lines of her legs, down her calves, pausing briefly at her toes.

Then he lifted her foot and began the reverse journey, this time with his mouth. The gentlest of kisses intermingled with abrupt nips and licks. By the time his tongue drew a firm line across the swelling lips of her sex, digging in to find the tender and swollen bud there, Ella had begun to whimper. "Please!"

His laugh, a low vibration against her stomach, tickled as well as aroused, and Ella squirmed, pulling against her bonds.

"Not yet."

A groan of frustration escaped her, and Ella arched against him, her pure arousal fogging her mind and making her lightheaded. Her body craved him, needed him.

His hands joined his mouth as he cupped her breasts, firm grips that brought the hard peaks to his lips. He sucked, nibbled, and licked until Ella writhed and bucked beneath him so furiously he could barely keep his mouth on her. She called his name, begging him again.

He laughed again. "Tell me," he whispered. "Tell me what you want."

She opened her eyes, glaring at him. "You rotten bastard! Fuck me!"

"Again."

"Gordon! Damn you!"

His grin turned wicked, and he settled his hips between her legs, the hard length of him pressing tight between her folds. "Again."

Ella pushed her hips up, trying to open herself more. "Fuck me," she hissed. "Claim me."

The light in his eyes turned dark at that, and his smile faded as he braced on one arm, raised his hips, and reached down to smear her flooding moisture over both of them. Then he pushed his cock into her. Slowly. Firmly.

Completely.

His fullness sent a wave of pleasure through Ella, washing hot and beautiful over her as his thrusts carried her higher than she had ever been able to achieve alone. As her peak built, sending shudders through her body, she forced her eyes open to watch him—as he was watching her.

"My beauty!" His voice was a hiss as he increased both his speed and his roughness, pushing her higher. His eyes, wide and hungry, never left her face.

"Release me," she begged. "Now."

He knew what she was asking, as he always had. Shifting slightly, he reached up and yanked on the sash. Her hands shot free, and her pleasure crested as she grabbed him, digging her fingers into his back. It triggered his release as well, and he groaned, shuddering, as he emptied into her.

Their motions slowed, then stilled. Ella pulled a portion of the sheet up, wiping the sweat from his face. It had matted his hair and dripped in streams down his temples and cheeks. "The most unfortunate of times," she said, patting the cloth across his forehead.

Gordon eased out of her but did not roll away. "Why do you think," he asked softly, "I could never tolerate the thought of another lover?"

She smiled. "Because I am your heart."

He nodded. "And you always will be."

Saturday, 2 April 1814
The Lyon's Den, Whitehall, London
Dawn

GORDON WATCHED ELLA sleep. She lay with her back against him, her legs and arms curled up, almost like a child. Her raven hair flowed over her shoulders and breasts and brushed against his chest. The night had been long and filled with talk of their pasts as well as their mutual explorations of each other's flesh, cherishing and arousing each other in ways neither had experienced since their parting. Questions had been answered, and long-untended desires quenched. They were sore and exhausted, but a settled sense of contentment had settled over Gordon, such as he had never felt.

He would never leave her again, not until one of them died. He would have her as his wife, and as long as she had breath, he would love and protect her. God help anyone who stood in his way this time.

But his businessman's mind alerted at such thoughts, and Gordon knew they had a great deal to do. A wedding, reconciling the various households and inheritances that were still outstanding. Meetings with his lawyers and investors, who expected him to return to America within a few weeks. Would she go with him? Would she be up for such rugged travel? The thought of leaving her behind sent an icy spear of dread through him. He could not. Perhaps he could hire an agent, he did have responsibilities here now—

Ella stirred, releasing a long sigh. Behind the lids, her eyes danced but she did not waken as one hand slipped behind her, coming to rest on his thigh.

Thoughts of business vanished, vapors in the light of her touch. Sore. Exhausted. But he wanted her again.

Gordon kissed her temple and wrapped an arm around her, holding her against his chest. The details could wait. Instead, he simply reveled in the love, the adoration of this woman. And, for now, that would be enough.

The End

Additional Dragonblade books by Author Abigail Bridges

The Ashton Park Series
To Stop a Scoundrel (Book 1)
A Rogue Like You (Book 2)
Nothing But a Rake (Book 3)
The Duke I Came For (Book 4)
By the Rosemary Tree (Novella)

The Lyon's Den Series
Into the Lyon of Fire

About Abigail Bridges

Abigail Bridges wrote her first historical romance, titled *The Belle of the Ball*, when she was thirteen. It was, of course, horrid. But it firmly established her love of all things Regency, a mild obsession with Georgette Heyer, and a determination to become a writer. After a master's degree in English and years of being paid to write and edit other types of material, she has returned to her first love. She is busily binge-reading all her favorite authors, resuming her study of the history and culture of the Regency era, and plotting like a madwoman. She does all this in a small cottage near Birmingham, Alabama.

Twitter: @AbbyBridgesAuth
Instagram: @abigailbridgesauthor

The Lyon's Wager

by Jenna Jaxon

Chapter One

London
Late March 1814

"This just arrived for Lady Elizabeth, my lady."

Lady Elizabeth Moody, only daughter of the Earl of Caistor, raised her eyebrows and glanced at the envelope lying on the silver salver the butler presented to her mother for inspection. The missive did indeed bear her name, which was odd. No one ever wrote to her. She sipped her tea, pondering this unexpected development.

"I imagine it is from Lord Flackwell telling us when he will be arriving in London." Her mother plucked it from the tray. "Thank you, Harrison. That will be all."

The butler bowed and retreated, shutting the door to the drawing room behind him.

"I do hope his lordship will be joining us before the Season begins." Mamma turned the envelope over, running her finger over the red wax seal. "It will be quite the triumph to be seen dancing with your betrothed at your come out ball."

"Is that an *F* embossed there, Mamma?" Bess, as the family had always called her, rather thought it didn't. There were actually two letters intertwined in the sealing wax. She peered closer at it. Was that a *D* and an *L* there? Although she wracked her brain, Bess could come up with no one it might be. Of course, whomever it was from, would have to be more appealing than her intended.

"Of course, it must be an *F*, ninny. Who else would it be from if not from Lord Flackwell?" Mamma broke the seal without looking at it further. She pulled a sheet of odd, gold-flecked paper out of the envelope, glancing front to back, but there was no writing that Bess could see. There was, however, another seal.

"What is that mark, Mamma? It's faint, in the wax." This time the wax was blue, the seal more elaborate with three initials intertwined and an emblem. "May I, Mamma?" Gently, Bess took the paper from her mother's hands, a tingle of excitement seeming to jump from the paper to her fingers. Oh, something augured well for her at last. She studied the paper closely. There was the same *D* and *L* close together with an added *B* and…Bess peered at it harder. "It's holly, Mamma. A sprig of holly."

"And nothing more?" Her mother was getting perturbed. "Really, who plays these sorts of games?"

"What games, my dear?" Papa, followed closely by Lord Flackwell, entered the drawing room.

"Good afternoon, Lady Caistor, Lady Elizabeth." Lord Flackwell bowed politely, though disinterestedly.

"Oh, gracious, my lord." Her mother jumped at Lord Flackwell's voice, then smiled her widest. "We are pleased to see you so soon. You have arrived in London ahead of schedule. Aren't you pleased to see his lordship here so soon, Bess?"

Bess's surprise did not excite pleasure in her bosom—quite the opposite in fact—however she drew herself up, pulling on an acceptable social smile. "Good afternoon, my lord." She'd been instructed to make herself as pleasant as possible to Lord Flackwell, whom she was going to marry in June.

Of course, she'd been instructed all her life that a woman's duty was to marry as well as possible, and the Earl of Flackwell's title was both ancient and revered, his wealth more extensive than her father's. His lordship, a long-time widower, had no heir, and therefore was understandably eager to wed again. However, the earl himself, while he looked very distinguished, was closer to her father's age than to her own. It was not an uncommon occurrence in the aristocracy—her cousin Amanda had married a gentleman more than twice her age—still she'd hoped to be able to marry a younger man or at least one she'd chosen herself. Unfortunately, neither of those things had come to pass.

"Someone has sent Bess a letter with no writing on it. Only a seal of some sort." Mamma handed the letter to Papa, rubbing her fingers afterward as though they had been dirtied. "I cannot think it appropriate for anyone to do such a thing."

"Good grief." Papa stared at the letter, his eyes widening. "Do you know what this is, Margery?"

"Some sort of hoax I expect." Mamma seemed to dismiss the letter and stirred more sugar into her tea. "A young lord she met at your aunt's house party last month perhaps, looking for some kind of flirtation."

"Oh no, my dear." Papa's gaze left the letter and came to rest on Bess, his eyes wary. "This is a Golden Ticket. The most exclusive ticket in London. They only arrive once a year and only to a very select few. I've heard of them but have never seen one…until now."

Her mother laughed, a sharp sound that resembled breaking glass. "That is neither a ticket nor yet golden, my dear."

"It is an invitation, Margery." Papa continued staring at Bess until she wanted to squirm in her seat. Her father was acting as though *she'd* done something wrong. Which she hadn't, at least, not that she knew. "To Mrs. Dove-Lyon's birthday celebration."

"What?" Mamma jerked around so quickly, her tea flew out of the cup, landing on the ends of Papa's coat.

"What?" Lord Flackwell stepped forward, grabbing the letter out of Papa's hand.

Bess remained silent, although her heart sped up. She didn't have any idea who Mrs. Dove-Lyon was, or how the woman knew of her, but a strange feeling of excitement, of impending adventure raced through her. Here was something that could make her life special before it was taken over by the duties of an obedient wife.

Unfortunately, an obedient wife was the last thing she wanted to be. Especially with the earl. She'd hoped several other young gentlemen would ask for her hand, but they had not. And then there had been one who'd asked for her hand, the one she'd hoped with all her heart, from the moment they met, would offer for her, but he hadn't done so in time. Only no one would have been in time, she'd discovered. Bess clenched her jaw.

Her father had made a bargain with the devil to save his own soul. She sighed. What might have happened, had her father not been forced to agree to Flackwell's terms? If she'd been allowed to marry that handsome young gentleman, who'd of course been refused by her father.... How much would she now be looking forward *eagerly* to her wedding?

"Well, there's no question of Lady Elizabeth going to this…this lurid event." Lord Flackwell puffed out his chest, as though he was the most important man in the room. "She is my fiancée and I forbid it."

Bess's lips drew down into a tight pucker. She wasn't Lord Flackwell's wife yet, thank you very much. Until she was, Papa decided whether or not she could attend any events. "Papa, I should like to go to this party if it is such an exclusive invitation. Won't that reflect well on our family, if it becomes known that I have received an invitation and so many others have not?"

"I have said I forbid it, Lady Elizabeth." The wretched Flackwell had come to stand beside her, perhaps trying to intimidate her.

Bess gazed up at him, seething inside but studiedly calm on the outside. "I would like to have a word with my father, if you please, my lord."

"Caistor, I tell you I will not have it." Blustering about, Flackwell began to pace around the room. "God himself doesn't know what goes on at these Mystere Masques. You cannot be thinking to let your innocent daughter attend, can you?"

"Papa?" Bess gave her father a speaking look he should know well. She rose and inclined her head. "A word if you please?"

"What is it, Bess?" Although from his hesitant tone, he knew full well what she would say.

"I wish to go to this Mystere Masque." She glanced over her shoulder at Lord Flackwell. "You must tell his lordship that you have agreed to this, and there is no recourse—if there is to be a marriage at all."

"Bess," Papa hissed her name. "You have agreed to marry Lord Flackwell. The settlements have been signed."

"Settlements can be burned, Papa. Betrothals can be broken. You should never have agreed to this one." If Bess was going to get her way, she'd have to make the terms clear to her father. "I understand about your 'indiscretion' and that I am to pay the price for your thoughtlessness long before I was born. And I have agreed to be your sacrificial lamb and marry Lord Flackwell so he won't ruin the family. But I am the one who will have to live with your mistake for many years to come." She glared at her father. "If you do not wish me to renege on your agreement, then you will persuade him to give in with good grace and agree to my attending Mrs....Dove-Lyon's birthday party."

Papa frowned at her, but Bess took little notice. She concentrated on Papa's face as he struggled to come to terms with the fact his daughter had outmaneuvered him. Again. Bess stared into her father's eyes and refused to blink.

After a long moment, Papa grunted and turned away. "Very well. I will handle Flackwell. But you are to stay at the masque only two hours, from ten o'clock until midnight. At the stroke of midnight, I will be there to fetch you home."

"Agreed. Although I wish to arrive at nine. Nine until midnight. That is the bargain." Bess smiled pleasantly at Lord Flackwell over her father's shoulder. She was going to have to get used to many uncomfortable things after her marriage. Papa could endure Lord Flackwell's displeasure this once.

She had a lifetime of living to do in the span of three hours, and Bess intended to make every single moment of it count.

"Did you receive your invitation to Mrs. Dove-Lyon's birthday party, Akeley?" Charles, the newest Duke of Welwyn, cut into his thick, rare beefsteak, popped the piece into his mouth and chewed with gusto. He and his friend met for dinner at their club every Thursday to discuss the most tantalizing news of the week and the most recent *on-dits* of interest to the *ton*. "The soiree is in two days. If you haven't received it by now, perhaps you are no longer in the lady's good graces."

"It'll arrive," his friend growled, sawing his meat as though he was trying to butcher the cow all over again. "I've been a damned good customer at the Lyon's Den for years. Mrs. Dove-Lyon isn't about to forget me."

"Care to wager on that, Akeley?" Charles looked up from his

steak, a rakish tilt to his head. "A mere one hundred pounds that your invitation doesn't arrive before the birthday celebration begins."

"Christ, Welwyn. You'll wager on which way a crow will fly, won't you?" Akeley finally managed to separate a piece of steak and wolfed it down, scarcely chewing at all.

"Well, wild wagers have been known to happen in the Quartermain family, I grant you." Charles shrugged. "What can I say? It's in my blood. My father once wagered on which of his younger brothers could hold his breath longest without passing out."

"And did he win?"

"He did. Only because they both passed out at the same time and Father declared a victory because neither of them could prove or disprove who had passed out first." Chuckling, Charles sipped a rich, red Bordeaux, then sliced off another piece of steak with the precision of a military surgeon.

"By God, you do get it honest." Akeley shook his head and quaffed some wine. "Do you think Mrs. Dove-Lyon has taken offense to something I've said or done?"

"Are you feeling guilty?" Charles eyed his friend. They really didn't come straighter than Darius, Lord Akeley.

"Not particularly."

"Then take the bet and we'll see come April first."

"Oh, very well. Done."

"And..." Charles swirled his wine in the goblet, measuring his words, "I'll set you another wager, if you're game."

"When have I ever not been?" The long-suffering tone of Akeley's voice made Charles smile.

"I think you know that I have been looking to marry almost since the moment my father died last year." This was only the truth. His father's unexpected death had sobered Charles immensely. He'd not thought he'd have to shoulder the burdens of the dukedom so soon, and the most important duty of the heir, which his father had drilled into him from the day Charles had had his first shave, was to sire the next heir. Once that was done, and the succession secured, then he could take up his other duties—such as siring the spare in case disaster struck in the nursery.

Charles had taken these instructions in his stride but had been more engrossed in the preparations for his Grand Tour the last time his father had spoken to him about it. After he'd returned from his tour, he'd set out to fulfil his duty and had been intently looking for a wife. At that point, however, disaster had struck, when his father had tragically died of an inflammation of the lungs at the age of forty-five. Devastated, Charles had assumed control of the dukedom and sworn an oath to his father to marry within the year.

"Yes, I know you have been earnestly combing the marriage mart." Akeley nodded.

"I have been to every ball or soiree ever since I put aside my mourning for my father, looking for a young lady who will suit me and who will make an exceptional duchess." Charles cut another piece of steak, bit into it, and chewed thoughtfully.

His friend frowned. "I would have thought that even with the paucity of entertainments during the winter months, young ladies of good breeding would have abounded. Are you truly so particular?"

"Of course, I am, Akeley. Aren't you?" The cavalier question brought Charles's glare to bear on the man. "Would you sully your line with a lady who might falter when faced with a catastrophe during a social engagement? Who might not be able to run your households in an acceptable and efficient manner? Who might, God forbid, embarrass you with a lack of intelligence and wit when you are out in company?"

Akeley looked as though he wished to crawl under a rock. He set his knife and fork down and took up his goblet. "I hadn't thought of it like that, Welwyn. I thought you simply found a lady you respected, one who could converse with you without making you look stupid, and one who looked as though she could give you an heir." He shrugged. "I'd no idea you had to think about so many other things."

"Well, if you wish your earldom run efficiently and your reputation to remain stellar within the *ton*, then you'd best heed my words and follow my example." Charles resumed his dinner, adding a bit of potato to the meat.

"But you're not even married yet." Akeley's voice had taken on a decidedly whiny tone.

"I plan to be by April second." Charles washed his dinner down with a hearty draft of the wine.

"You plan to marry in three days?" The earl's eyes nearly popped out of his head. "To whom?"

Shrugging, Charles drained his glass of wine. "I've no idea."

Akeley took a moment to digest that before his mouth dropped open. "You don't know whom you're going to marry?"

"That is where the other wager comes in, you see." Charles leaned forward, his chin resting on his interlocked fingers. "I am willing to wager you five hundred pounds that I will meet a lady at Mrs. Dove-Lyon's birthday celebration and persuade her to marry me the day after the masquerade."

"You must be mad." Akeley stared at him as though he'd grown two heads.

"No, simply optimistic. Mrs. Dove-Lyon's soirees always draw the most alluring, intelligent, and passionate of ladies. If ever there was a hunting ground for duchesses, this will be it." Charles leaned back, envisioning the dim room, lit by hundreds of candles, ladies in fantastic costumes dancing with him in the most sensual way possible.

"So you do take something as base as passion into account on your hunt as well?" A slight smirk appeared on Akeley's face.

"Of course." Did the man have no sense at all? "There must be attraction between you, and a deep, abiding passion if you are very fortunate. Believe me, Darius, one kiss and you will know if the lady is the right one."

"And how do you expect to be able to kiss this young lady with all the world watching?"

Charles laughed and held the final piece of steak up before his mouth. "That is why Mrs. Dove-Lyon's establishment is the perfect place for this sort of hunt. With everyone else intent on fulfilling their own pleasures, they will scarcely take note of anyone else's indiscretions." He shook his head. "This is not Almack's, Akeley. This is the Lyon's Den, where the lions roar and the hunt for a sleek lioness is on. To the winner go the spoils." Charles put the steak in his mouth, his brows rising. "Are you in for another wager, then?"

His friend seemed stunned, and well might he be. It was a risky proposition on Charles's part. He had no idea if he could actually win this wager, although usually when a wager was involved, he was so determined to win, he did everything within his power to get his way.

"Damnation." Akeley tossed his napkin onto his half-eaten plate. "Yes, I'm in. Seems too good to be true, actually. A sure thing almost." He cut his gaze toward Charles. "Nothing shady going on, is there Welwyn? This is on the up and up? You don't have a lady you've already proposed to attending so you can make good on this wager?"

"Akeley! You cut me to the quick to question my motives so." Charles wasn't truly surprised at his friend's query. He himself would have inquired if such a wager presented itself out of the blue. "I assure you, I have no idea who will attend this party." He smiled widely. "I'm simply wagering that the perfect wife for me, will be."

Chapter Two

April 1

THE LIGHT OF a thousand candles lit up the main room of the Lyon's Den, as though it were noon instead of nine o'clock at night. Charles, dressed as Julius Caesar in warrior dress, complete with metal breastplate and a helmet that hid his features admirably well, gazed about the tightly packed room in search of feminine company. This room was usually given over to the gambling tables, but tonight all gambling was suspended in favor of the celebration at hand. Charles had been a patron of the Lyon's Den for years, his family's penchant for wagers making this place the perfect spot for him to indulge in the Quartermains' favorite vice.

Tonight's wager, however, would prove more important to him than any other he'd ever made. Charles had found that when he set himself a finite task—such as finding a wife tonight—he was more focused, and much more likely to accomplish his goal than if the parameters were vaguer. And it was high time he married. He couldn't continue to moon after a woman who was beyond his reach, much as he might wish to do so. Best begin his hunt.

To his right side was a cluster of masked ladies and gentlemen, all laughing and flirting. One lady, dressed as a dainty shepherdess, he recognized as Lady Joanna Longford by her height and the distinctive mole on her right cheek. He'd actually considered her for his duchess, however she'd recently become betrothed to one of the Knowlton brothers.

He didn't recognize the woman next to her, in the guise of Aphrodite, immediately. She wasn't so tall as Lady Joanna, with golden hair down her back, though that might be a wig. She looked about the room as she laughed with her friends, her gaze predatory gaze as she glanced from this guest to that. Charles hastily turned to his left before she could ensnare him. Something in the way she assessed the gentlemen around the room made him want to shiver—and flee her frankly ravening glances.

He focused instead on another group, this time solely of women, laughing and talking, and sending "come hither" looks at the gentlemen around them. Their invitations, however, did not possess the cold and calculated aura of Aphrodite's. These ladies were out for a good time. One of them could well be the woman he sought. With an affected air of grandeur, Charles strode toward them, acting the part of Julius Caesar as he envisioned it should be done. "Good evening, ladies. I bring you greetings from Rome."

"But of course you do, General." The nearest of the ladies smiled, that "come hither" look very apparent in the blue eyes that snapped with merriment. "One only need take a single look at such bulging...muscles to know you must be a warrior of some skill." She grasped Charles's bare arm and clung to him.

Well, he liked boldness in women above all. Charles smiled down at her.

"You are Julius Caesar, aren't you?" The lady, dressed as Diana, goddess of the hunt, had a very fetching, very revealing costume in the Grecian fashion—a flowy white gown with deep decolletage, plus a bow and quiver of arrows hung on her back. Her rich chestnut hair was piled up on her head in a mass of ringlets that threatened to come loose and cascade down her back at any moment.

Charles dearly loved to see a woman with her hair flowing over her shoulders. It gave rise to the image of her lying underneath him on his bed, her hair fanned out over his pillow as they... He shook the image out of his mind before it got him into difficulties. "I am in fact Julius Caesar. And you are Diana, I believe." He motioned to the quiver on her back. "The arrows give you away."

"As does your helmet and imposing bearing." She squeezed his arm and leaned her cheek upon it. There was a slight stirring in his groin. At least he could be aroused by the lady. A point in her favor, he supposed. "Shall we find a less crowded spot to...compare our hunting strategies, Diana?" He was employing one of his most successful strategies—getting his possible prey away from the herd to test her mettle and to see how strongly he reacted to her physically. A kiss, as he'd told Akeley, was a good indicator of how passionate a lady might be. And how easily she might be tempted to stray from the *ton*'s strict moral code. It was a two-edged sword, of course, but then, that was part of the game, wasn't it?

"A true huntsman would scarcely need to ask, Your Grace." The lady's dark eyes smiled from behind her golden mask. She'd guessed his identity. Pity he didn't have a clue about hers.

"But a gentleman must, Diana. This way, I believe, will afford us some privacy." He grasped her arm and led her down the long room to a quiet little nook he'd discovered here not long ago. He didn't expect it to be unoccupied, but at least it was out of the way of the hoard of masked revelers. "Here we are."

The little alcove, scarcely more than an oddly angled wall that created enough space for a couple to speak—or do other things— without being observed by others, was amazingly free of occupants.

Perhaps the clientele tonight cared less about propriety than he did. They had passed several couples kissing passionately without regard for the onlookers who laughed or made lewd suggestions about how they could better occupy their time.

Without a word of warning, Charles swung his Diana around until her quiver of arrows bumped the wall, then he sank his mouth onto hers. The helmet made this somewhat challenging, but the metal nosepiece was pliable enough that their lips were not impeded at all. To his delight, the lady did not protest such abrupt treatment, but warmed readily to his advances. She pressed back against him, then unexpectedly thrust her tongue into his mouth, surprising him greatly. He ran his hands down her body, scarcely covered at all in the sleek Grecian folds of her costume. Damn it, her generous curves should be exciting him more than this, but the night was scarcely begun. There was plenty of time—

"Is that champagne?"

The dulcet voice of a woman behind Charles broke through his thoughts. He raised his head.

"Thank you, that's lovely."

He knew that voice. Whipping his head around, he spied a slim lady in a long, dark-blue velvet gown, a circlet of gold in her long dark hair, a golden mask across her face sipping the champagne with avid pleasure.

Oh, my God. Charles froze, his heart beating in a frenzy of odd thumps and irregular rhythms, his cock surging forward, too eager to be controlled. How had *she* come to be here?

Slowly, he returned his attention back to his Diana and came to the realization the woman whose breasts he was still stroking was looking up at him with murder in her eyes. "I beg your pardon, Diana." He hastily removed his hands from her and bowed. "A ghost from my past has arisen."

"That's not all that's arisen, Your Grace." Her gaze strayed pointedly to his groin, where his erection, earlier a mere stirring, had now tented the skirt of his costume rather dramatically.

Had Charles not been so agitated by the appearance of the woman behind him, he might have been quite embarrassed by his more than obvious lust. As it was, all he felt was a great need to break with this lady so he could pursue the other. "I fear I must leave you, beautiful Diana. I have to lay this ghost to rest before I can make promises to another lady."

"I fear once you lay that ghost, Your Grace," she jerked her head toward the lady in blue, "you will have no desire to lay any other." She dipped him a hasty curtsy, then stalked away.

Charles sighed, but in relief. Then turned toward the lady who had consumed his agonized thoughts for months. For a moment, he let his eyes feast on her, the ebony hair flowing straight down her back, the slim figure accentuated by the simple cut of the medieval-esque gown she wore, the almost regal tilt of her chin as she gazed about. Her whole essence seemed to exude excitement at the prospect of the masquerade. He hoped to God he wouldn't quench that eagerness, but rather channel it toward him.

"Good evening, Lady Elizabeth."

She jumped and turned toward him immediately, the champagne sloshing over the lip of the glass she held. Behind her glittering Venetian mask, intricately decorated with paste jewels that made her blaze in the candlelight, her eyes widened in surprise, then glowed with what could only be abject pleasure. "Good evening, Your Grace."

He'd not expected her to remember him, much less recognize him. For one of the few times in his life, Charles was speechless. All he could do was stare into the beautiful face, yearning to hold her once again. The strains of the orchestra about to begin another dance broke the spell. If nothing else, he could hold her in his arms on the dance floor. "Would you do me the honor of this dance?"

Without hesitation she smiled and nodded. "I would be delighted to partner you, Your Grace."

Weak with desire for her, Charles offered his arm. "As we have met and danced before, my dear, I wondered if you would further honor me by calling me Charles?" It was a bold move, but an opportunity he could not forgo. "Would you, my lady?"

"With pleasure, Charles." She smiled so widely, the edges of her eyes crinkled. Setting the glass on the tray of a passing footman, she took his arm. "And you must call me Bess. It would make me very happy."

He led her onto the floor just as the orchestra struck up a waltz. He took her left hand and raised it in a graceful arc above them, then grasped her waist. She did likewise to him, her hand seeming to burn a path straight through to his flesh, a brand he could feel as though a hot iron had touched his side. "Your happiness is my sincerest wish, Bess."

And they began to dance.

TRY AS SHE might, Bess couldn't take her gaze off the duke. She had known him the moment he appeared before her, his height, the set of his shoulders, the crisp scent of his cologne had her recalling Lady Crosby's party in February when they'd met for the first time. She'd not even needed his pleasantly low voice to confirm that it was the Duke of Welwyn before her, decked out like the conqueror he was, at least to her.

The steps of the waltz came automatically—she'd insisted her dancing master teach her the steps so she could at least dance it with her husband if Mamma forbade it elsewise. Of course, that had been before she'd agreed to the betrothal to Lord Flackwell. Until this moment she'd believed she'd never dance the waltz with anyone, because she certainly wouldn't tolerate doing something so intimate with that gentleman. At least, not something she *could* say no to.

So now she could revel in the dance with a gentleman who hadn't been far from her thoughts since that night in February. She'd recalled that set of dances—it had been Mad Robin, Lord Fuddington, and a Scottish reel that had left her breathless for more than one reason—and her handsome partner many times in the past two months. And now she'd have another dance, the scandalous waltz no less, to remember in the years to come. It suddenly didn't seem fair that Papa could command her to marry a man she wouldn't choose to wed in a hundred years rather than the wonderful gentleman who now held her so tightly, her entire body heated from the close contact.

"I must admit I am surprised to see you here at the Lyon's Den, Bess." His sensual voice made her heart beat faster. "Are your parents here as well?"

"Oh, no." Thank goodness they were not. "A single ticket came two days ago, addressed to only me." If Bess could discover whoever had sent that invitation, she'd thank them in so many ways for giving her this last chance to be alone with the duke.

"You received an *Invocation Mystére*?" The astonishment in his voice told her this was quite an anomaly, much more so than she'd originally believed.

"If that's what they call that golden paper with a seal on it." They were twirling around the dance floor—not fast, but still, her head was spinning with the nearness of him.

"It is. And I would give a goodly sum to know why it was sent to you." He grinned down at her, making what she could see of his handsome face through that wretched helmet look utterly charming. "I'd also like to thank them profusely."

"So would I." She squeezed his hands. "Just because now, I've gotten to dance with you one more time before I'm married to Lord Flackwell." It made the pill of that marriage even more bitter, to have had this time with the duke. With Charles. But she wouldn't trade it for every single one of the crown jewels.

"Did your father tell you I'd offered for you?" The sharpness in his tone sent a shiver down her spine.

"Yes, he did." She'd been listening at the door outside Papa's study when she'd been told the duke had requested an audience with him. So Papa couldn't very well deny it when she confronted him with the question. "Only he told me he'd refused to break the arrangement with Lord Flackwell."

"Did he say why?" The edge in the duke's voice could have cut steel.

Oh, but Bess didn't want to talk about this. Not now, when she only had a few minutes left with Charles. She'd much rather speak about something else, something frivolous they could laugh about that she could then savor on the coldest days of the rest of her life. Still, he deserved to know. "Flackwell has a hold over my father. Not money, but a particular knowledge Flackwell has about Papa that he does not wish generally known. I am the price of his silence."

Charles uttered a low curse and shook his head. "If I had sufficient reason, I would challenge Flackwell to a duel and kill him rather than have you marry a man against your wishes." He peered down at her. "I merely assumed it was against your wishes, but you have not confessed that to me. If I am wrong, I will beg your pardon this instant."

Sighing for what could not be, Bess shook her head. "I am not being forced to marry him—Papa has not said in so many words he would disown me or cast me out of the house if I didn't marry him—but I agreed to it to keep Papa's secret safe. But that was before—"

Bess looked away from him. No need to make either of them more miserable.

"Before what, Bess?" The soft words wrenched her heart.

"Before I met you," she said, her voice little more than a whisper.

Suddenly, she was crushed against his chest, his powerful arms engulfing her, pressing her painfully against his metal armor. Then, as though he realized he might be hurting her, he released her, grabbed her hand, and led her from the dance floor. God knew she hadn't meant to cut their dance short, not if it was all she'd ever have of him. But the determined look on his face said he would not be gainsaid, and Bess was not inclined to argue with him.

They wove in and out around groups of people laughing and chatting, dodging couples kissing and doing things Bess wasn't even certain she understood. No wonder Charles had been amazed that she'd been invited to such a lewd and lascivious function. Now, she was as well.

At last, they fetched up near a doorway, although Bess truly had no idea where they were. They did seem to be out of the way of most people and far enough from the orchestra that the noise level had lowered to a dim roar. Charles moved them through the narrow doorway and suddenly they were all alone in semi-darkness.

Finally, Bess felt able to take a deep breath—then held it in amazement as Charles suddenly dropped to one knee, grasped her hands and said, "Lady Elizabeth Moody, will you do me the honor of becoming my wife?"

Chapter Three

"What are you doing, Charles," she hissed at him. Even though thrilled at the proposal, Bess's anger bubbled up. If her father could be persuaded to break the betrothal with Flackwell this would be the most perfect moment of her life. But it could never be, no matter how much she wished it.

"I am proposing to you." Charles continued to look up at her, his eyes behind the helmet glittering in the faint light. "May I have your answer, please?"

"Please get up. And stop teasing me." Tears pricked Bess's eyes. How much would she love to say yes to this man. She tried to pull her hands from his grasp, but he held her fast. "Are you trying to make me miserable?"

"On the contrary, my love. I am trying to make us both happy." He sighed and shook his head. "Let me ask this. If your father could be persuaded to allow it, would you marry me?"

Her heart gave a huge leap in her chest. "Yes, of course I would." Nothing would make Bess happier. "But he won't."

At last Charles rose, a smile on his lips. "We will see about that. Come with me."

He grasped her hand and led her out of the doorway, back into the loud and rowdy crowd. Again they wove through and around hoards of laughing, talking, drinking guests, until finally Charles shouted, "Akeley!" Then they surged forward so fast, Bess almost tripped on her long gown.

Abruptly, Charles stopped in front of a gentleman dressed rather wildly as an Eastern Pasha, as best as she could make out. He wore a huge red turban, dressed in myriad loose multi-colored robes and pants, and sported a black mask and a huge black mustache.

Charles leaned toward the man, speaking directly into his ear for several moments, until the man jerked back, his eyes wide. He shook his head vigorously, but Charles grasped his arm and stared the man down. "In twenty minutes, without fail. Look for the helmet." Charles glared at the gentleman until he nodded.

"Your wish, Sahib, is my command." The gentleman sighed, then shot a look at her and a grin spread over his face. "A hell of a way to win a wager."

"But necessary. I'll expect you."

The gentleman nodded and Charles grabbed her hand. "This way."

They went back the way they had come until they stood once again in the doorway. Charles led her through it and Bess could make out a narrow staircase. Servants' stairs most likely. She peered up the stairs that wound upward into the darkness. "Where do they lead?"

"To the third floor. Come, we must hurry."

"What are you doing?" Bess pulled her skirts up and they began to climb the steep polished wooden staircase.

"I know a sure way to make your father allow us to marry." He squeezed her hand but continued his punishing pace.

"Don't you think you should let me in on the plan?" Bess was starting to puff, her breath coming in gasps. The man must be fitter than she, if he could take all these steps at a run.

"When the time comes, my dear." They reached a landing with corridors leading left and right, closed doors lining either hallway.

Bess thought she could hear faint noises from the rooms, then a sharp laugh. "What are these rooms for?"

"Best not ask, my lady." Charles continued up the stairs to the next floor, his pace a bit slower thank goodness.

Bess was flagging badly by the time they reached the third floor. It, too, had corridors to the left and right as they had been one floor below. She gasped for breath as Charles looked one way, then the other.

"Let's try this one." He turned to the right and strode down the carpeted hallway, lit by a series of sconces that burned with a flickering light. He stopped at the first door, put his ear to it, then shook his head and moved on to the next. Charles repeated this puzzling action twice more before he listened at a door far down the corridor, then nodded and pushed it open.

The room was simply furnished with a large four-poster bed with no curtains or canopy. The cover looked to be of middling quality, in a simple design of dark blue flowers on a light blue background. Sconces on the walls along with the fireplace gave off sufficient light. A large mirror and rather lurid pictures of unclothed women in shocking poses adorned the walls, making Bess wish to leave immediately. "Charles, what is this place? Why are we here?"

He pulled the Roman helmet off his head, revealing his ruggedly handsome face and dark head. "Let me say simply it is a bedroom, Bess. The bedroom where we will anticipate our wedding night."

She stared up at him, stunned by that announcement. Shaking her head, she stepped back, putting some distance between them— not that she believed he would seize her and force himself upon her. Even their brief acquaintance had shown her the duke was a gentleman before anything else. "What are you talking about?"

"If you wish to break your betrothal to Lord Flackwell, this is the way to do it." He looked at her earnestly. "Once you are no longer a virgin, Flackwell will likely break it himself."

"And this is how you hoped to get my father to agree to our marriage?" She looked at him askance. "I thought you mean we might elope to Gretna Green."

"We could do that, if it wouldn't take a week's worth of travel over treacherous roads. Springtime floods are common, and I would not risk losing you in an accident." He reached out and lifted her mask, pulling it over her head and dropping it on the floor. "This way we can be married by this time tomorrow." He grazed her cheek with his finger, sending a shiver down her spine. "Do you not trust me, Bess?"

Gazing up into his face, alight with desire, she felt a sudden rush of heat throughout her body and a yearning low in her belly. She would never feel such a thing for Lord Flackwell if they lived as man and wife for fifty years. So if she didn't want her life to be a farce filled with loathing for her husband, she had best act now. "Yes, Charles." She breathed deeply. "Yes, I do. But what about my father? Flackwell will ruin him if I don't marry him." She hung her head. "I'd never forgive myself if that happened."

His eyes darkened with a combination of admiration and desire. "Let me take care of that. But come, we must act quickly." He strode back to the door, opened it, and set the helmet outside.

"Why did you do that?"

He was back at her side, taking her face in his large hands and bringing it close to his. "To warn others away who might wish to use this room."

"Are there others at the masquerade who would...do this same thing?" What a den of iniquity she'd stumbled into. Thank God Charles had found her before someone else had taken a fancy to her.

"Why do you think it took so long to find an unoccupied room?"

He smiled down at her, then his lips were on hers and all coherent thought vanished.

Although Bess had heard about kissing from some of the other young ladies of her acquaintance, it had never happened to her. However, if all men kissed like Charles, she was surprised there were any unmarried ladies at all. His lips pressed hers firmly, his tongue insistently pushing against the closed seam of her lips. When she relaxed them a trifle, he slid through easily, filling her mouth unexpectedly and sending a jolt of excitement down to her core.

He pulled her body against his, and she grunted as the hard metal breastplate dug into her. With a curse he broke the kiss long enough to fling the offending item off, bearing his naked chest to Bess and making her gasp. She'd never seen an unclothed man before, and sight of his taut muscles from chest to waist made her throb deep at her core. With a throaty groan she launched herself at him, grabbing him around the neck, wanting to feel his unfettered flesh against her.

Lifting her off her feet, Charles cupped her bottom, his hands on that intimate part of her making her feel oh so naughty. He carried her over to the bed and laid her on top of the covers, his lips moving down her neck, making her gasp at the riotous sensations running through her, all coming together at her core, which had begun to throb insistently with each touch of his lips.

"Oh, Charles," Bess moaned as his hands slipped down her legs, then slid back up, dragging the skirt of her gown with it so her legs were suddenly cold with the lack of cover. The chill brought her back to herself, to the realization of what they were about to do. That sobered her quickly and she pulled Charles's head up from where he was kissing the exposed flesh above her breasts. "Charles."

He blinked several times, trying to focus on her, almost as though he were drunk, although she highly doubted that. "What is it, love?" He seemed to come to himself and peered down at her.

"Are you all right? Did I hurt you?"

"No, but..." She trailed off. If she wanted to gain her freedom, and the husband of her choice, this was no time for modesty. Although Bess prided herself on being a no-nonsense sort of person, still it was embarrassing to have to ask this at such a moment. "You haven't hurt me yet, but you are about to do so, aren't you?"

His face softened as he stroked her cheek. "Yes, I am. I have to, sweetheart. It's simply the way of it, but it only hurts the first time." He seemed to study her closely, his hand cupping her face. "Do you know what I'm going to do? Other than hurt you?"

And here was more embarrassment. "No, I don't have any idea." She tried to keep the tremor out of her voice, but it was the not knowing that was making this so hard. "Mother said I didn't need to know about anything until my wedding day. And the less I knew, the better. But now, I don't think that's true."

Charles exhaled sharply. "I don't think so either. Please promise me that when our daughters marry, you will inform them well ahead of time as to the particulars?"

Bess smiled at that, some of her fear alleviated. He truly expected them to have a life together. A good life with children all around them. And what they were about to do was how those children were created. That much she did know. "I promise."

"Very well." He ran his hands down her chest, cupping her breasts and squeezing them, making them ache in a good way. "I now wish we had the luxury of more time and a more respectable place, but we must work with what is at hand. Here—" He pulled the sleeves of her gown down off her shoulders, exposing her corset. "What I'm going to do first is give you as much pleasure as I possibly can. Beginning with your beautiful breasts."

Before she could register that, he'd slipped his hands inside her corset and pulled her breasts right out, letting them sit atop the edge of the garment, bared to his lustful gaze. The hungry look in his eyes was enough to make Bess's breath come harder, make her core tighten.

He stroked them slowly, his fingers rough against her smooth skin, circling a finger around each nipple until they drew up into tight little points of their own accord. Both of her breasts seemed swollen and tight, a more pleasurable sensation than she would have thought. She arched her back, offering them up to Charles to do with what he wanted.

When he lowered his head and took one nipple into his mouth, she thought she would die. Never had she dreamed he would do such a thing, but as he licked and sucked her flesh, his tongue dancing all around her aroused nipples, Bess strained against him, wanting more of this sublime attention. Her body throbbed with the pleasure he gave her until she moaned and shifted underneath him.

"You like that, love?" Charles raised his head enough to look at her.

She nodded weakly, amazed at the things he was making her body experience.

"How about this?"

His hand was suddenly under her skirt, brushing the curls in a place no one but she and her maid had ever... Good lord! "What...what?"

"Shhh, it's all right. This won't hurt. It's another way a man gives pleasure to a woman." His soft, assured voice crooned as his fingers stroked her most intimate place. She expected her face to burst into flame at any second when he touched the little nub just above...

"Ohhh..." Bess writhed on the bed, her hips bucking as he continued to stroke and circle the nub, her core now throbbing incessantly. "Ohhh, Charles. What... what...Ahhh!" She shrieked as her body shattered, flying to pieces in a whirlwind that threatened to tear her apart. As she began to come back to herself, she stared up into Charles's very satisfied face.

"Did you enjoy your first rapture?"

"Rapture?" Panting, Bess didn't quite understand.

"From the look on your face just now, and the way you screamed, I have to believe I was able to bring you to what I call a state of rapture, the ultimate pleasure a man can give a woman." His smile widened. "Or a woman can give a man."

So now she was going to give him pleasure like that? She had no idea how to do that. "What do I have to do?"

"For this time, only bear with me, love." He opened her legs and pulled her toward him until her bottom was right at the edge of the bed. "What I'm going to do is put myself inside you."

"How do you do that?" This sounded so very odd. But this whole evening had been like a dream. And dreams didn't always make sense, did they?

"Good Lord." Charles hung his head for a moment, then raised it and stared into her eyes. "There is a part of me that is made to enter into the part of you just here." He brushed her intimate place with his finger and Bess gasped. "This is what's going to hurt, although I hope not for long. Then we can give each other that rapturous pleasure again. Do you understand, Bess?"

Bewildered, she shook her head, staring up at him. He looked so concerned, as though trying to make her comprehend through sheer dint of will. There was nothing to do but go forward. "No, not exactly. But I trust you, Charles." She nodded then laid her head back on the bed and covered his hand with hers. "Show me."

His expression softened, his eyes shining luminously in the candlelight. "God, I love you, Bess."

He *loved* her. If that was true, then nothing else mattered.

He bent and pressed a kiss on her lips, his heat searing her to the bone. His hands fumbled down below, something huge and hot bumped against her, then pressed itself into her opening. A white-hot pain made her cry out, as much by its unexpectedness as the actual hurt, then Charles leaned forward, covering her as a great fullness flowed into her. Bess panted against the pain, though it seemed to be subsiding quickly. The odd sensation inside her, however, remained.

"Oh, God." Charles groaned, pressing her down into the mattress. "Sweet Jesus."

"Is something wrong?" He sounded as though *he* was in pain, which couldn't be right.

"No, but you are so exquisitely tight, I may not last long enough to give you your pleasure." Sweat had popped out on his brow, and he was holding very still.

"Then do the best you can, love." She gazed into his face, wanting to ease his distress. "This is only the first time. There will be others."

"As assuredly as the sun rises, my love." Charles drew a deep breath and rocked forward, filling Bess even fuller, which she would not have believed.

The peculiar sensation no longer hurt, and as he leaned over her, part of him brushed the little nub, igniting a different kind of ache deep inside her. She moaned and raised her hips, chasing that fleeting touch, wanting more. He pulled out and she whimpered, but then immediately thrust back into her, again touching the nub, making her ache grow and spiral. It was wonderful and maddening at the same time. Bess strained toward Charles the next time he sank into her, now craving each touch.

He must have sensed that because he slid his hand between them and circled the little bud as he'd done earlier. This time, however, the motion acted like a bolt of lightning streaking straight to her core. She threw back her head and shrieked as she shattered around him, the sensation deeper than before, her whole body shuddering with the pleasurable waves.

Her cry must have affected Charles for he pumped into her frantically, then called her name as he strained into her, filling her with his heat. He slumped over her, panting. Charles dragged his head up to gaze lovingly into her eyes. "Are you all right? Did I hurt you terribly?"

Sweaty and drained, Bess smiled up at him. "I'm fine, you didn't—"

The door burst open and Bess screamed as the man dressed as the Pasha strode into the room. Pinned to the bed by Charles's big body, part of him still inside her, Bess had no way at all to shield herself from the man who came right up to the bed, peering at her and Charles before nodding.

"I take it I am to act as witness to my own loss of the wager, Welwyn?"

Charles nodded, then grinned. "I'll take your testimony as payment, therefore we are even." Then he sobered. "I am glad your invitation to this affair showed up, my friend. Your help is turning out to be invaluable. Now, leave us, Akeley. Speak of this to no one until I give you leave."

With a nod, the Pasha hurried out, closing the door.

Exploding with anger, Bess pushed Charles off her, then slid off the bed, pulling her skirts down as she landed on the floor. "What have you done, Charles? Who was that man? I am ruined and humiliated and it's all your fault. How...how could you?" Bess burst into tears.

His arms were around her in a moment and when she tried to fight him off, she might have saved her strength. He pulled her to him and dropped a kiss onto her head. "I am sorry my love, but it was necessary. A witness to your compromise will give your father no choice whatsoever but to break the betrothal. Without one, it is only our word that it had been done."

That did make sense. Her father was going to be loathe to give up his bargain with Lord Flackwell. A witness to her ruin would surely tip the balance in their favor. She sniffed and wiped her eyes, getting herself in hand. "You could have told me what you'd planned to have happen." Bess stepped back and smacked his arm. "At least then I wouldn't have been frightened out of my wits." She'd still have been embarrassed, though. "I will never be able to meet that gentleman…Lord Akeley…in public, Charles. Not when I know he's seen me"—she cast a glance at the rumpled covers and shuddered—"like that."

"But otherwise, you enjoyed yourself?" His gaze followed hers to the bed, a grin spreading over his face.

"Well, yes. I think you could tell I did." Her face heated, recalling how she'd cried out at the end. How could she not, when the pleasure was so intense she had to scream? Just thinking about it made her core throb once more. She raised an eyebrow at him. "You did as well, I recall."

"That was never in doubt, little one." He took her in his arms, the very touch of him making her need rise again. "I have been waiting for that moment since I met you. For a time, I didn't think it would ever happen, but I am so grateful that it did." His eyes darkened. "And that such moments will continue for the rest of our lives."

What a lovely thought. To have Charles and their pleasures to look forward to every day of her life. If she had anything to do with it, they might never get anything else done. Starting now. She slid her arms up around his neck, pressing herself to him until his manhood stirred against her. "Can that begin right now?" Swirling her hips against him, she gazed longingly into his face. "Please?"

CHAPTER FOUR

WITH A GROWL that came all the way from his groin, Charles grabbed her, pulling her gown up even as he pushed her against the wall with such force the blazing sconce jumped. "Sorry."

Her giggle said she was unharmed and even enjoying his rough tactics.

After he'd spent himself so thoroughly in their earlier encounter, he'd have doubted he could raise his cock again tonight—and certainly not so quickly. However, Bess's flirtatious look and breathy "Please" had hardened him to the bursting point instantly. He hoisted her up and with a single thrust, impaled her.

Her gasp and shudder almost ended him then and there. Peering into her face, her wide blue eyes dazed, her luscious lips curved into a sweet smile, he drew a deep breath and prayed once again for control. Slowly, he began to stroke into her, the tightness of her sheath gripping him continually, making him want to pound faster, to reach that sweet completion immediately. But then Bess wouldn't have her pleasures, and the thought of that, he could not abide. So he settled for a steady rhythm, in and out, all the while watching her face, waiting for that moment…

Her breathing deepened, her eyes closed, and her head rolled back as she cried out, "Yes, Charles, yes," just as her channel clenched around his member. He sped up, pumping wildly, his moans mixing with hers until he yelled, "Bess!" Then he spent himself, on and on, deep within her.

His legs weakening, he hurried them to the bed and laid them down, side by side, facing each other, his cock still buried in her, its true home forever more. As their breathing slowed, Bess opened her eyes, the dazed look now overlaid with one of pure satisfaction. Smiling, she cupped his cheek. "If I get that for saying 'please,' what do I get for a 'thank you'?"

FINALLY DRESSED—ALTHOUGH CHARLES had to admit their clothing would never be quite the same—with mask and helmet in place, he took Bess's hand and cautiously led her out of the bedchamber. Moans, groans, shrieks, and laughter emanated from the closed doors they passed as they hurried down the corridor to the servants' staircase. He glanced behind him, making sure Bess was all right. It was a miracle she could still walk after that romp, but she was easily keeping pace with him. God, what a woman!

They wound down the staircase to the main floor where Mrs. Dove-Lyon's celebration was still in full force. People were laughing, singing, drinking, dancing on and off the dance floor. Couples were taking advantage of the inebriated state of the guests around them, thinking they wouldn't be observed, and so letting their amorous natures prevail right out in the open. If he and Bess hadn't just participated in something akin to this spectacle, he'd insist Bess cover her eyes. Well, Mrs. Dove-Lyon did like to celebrate her birthday in style.

Heading for the front door, Charles kept a firm grasp on Bess's hand. He wasn't going to risk losing her in such a riotous crowd. A drunken lord, dressed in the garb of a medieval monk, staggered up to Charles, but he gave the gentleman a sharp push and the fellow went reeling off into a group of ladies dressed as muses, who screamed, then laughed and welcomed him. Charles pulled Bess to his side, surprised that she didn't seem frightened at all. She looked more curious about the surroundings and their fellow revelers than anything.

"This way, my dear." He steered her toward the establishment's front door, where the crowd had thinned, thank God. "Send for the Duke of Welwyn's carriage, please," he said to one of the retired soldiers standing guard at the door.

"Right away, Your Grace." The tall, bulky man nodded, then hustled outside.

"Why don't we wait outside, my dear? Perhaps some fresher air would do us good." He wanted her away from this den of iniquity before anyone accosted her. If that happened, he'd have to challenge them.

"I think that's a good idea, Charles. I am very tired. The air may revive me for the ride home." She sighed and leaned closer to him. "I wish I were going to your home."

"We will be going to *our* home before the earth has made another circuit around the sun." He hugged her to him. If he didn't think Caistor would send out a search party, he would take her to his home—and straight to his bed.

"Unhand my daughter at once you…you ruffian."

Bess jerked back, and Charles gave a low groan as Lord Caistor hurried over to them. Joy of joys, Lord Flackwell followed right behind him. Well, Charles supposed they would get everything settled here and now, rather than at a more civilized time and place.

"Lord Caistor, please allow me to identify myself." Charles drew the Roman helmet over his head and tucked it under his arm. "The Duke of Welwyn at your service, my lord." He nodded to Bess's father, then gave her erstwhile fiancé a withering look. "Lord Flackwell."

Lord Caistor grabbed Bess's arm and pulled her over beside him. "Come here, Elizabeth."

Charles subdued a growl, but just barely. "I will thank you, my lord, to refrain from abusing my fiancée."

Caistor looked at him as though he was mad. "What? Of whom are you speaking, Welwyn?"

"Your daughter has consented to be my wife tonight." Charles smiled at him broadly. "You may be the first to offer your congratulations."

"What the devil?" Flackwell bristled, bounding over to Charles as though he might plant him a facer. A farce that. Charles had at least three inches on the older man and probably a stone's more weight as well. "You can't be serious, Welwyn. Lady Elizabeth has been betrothed to me since January, as you well know."

Charles shrugged. "You are not yet married to the lady, Flackwell, and circumstances have changed, as has Lady Elizabeth's mind."

"Bess, stop this nonsense." Her father gave her a shake and Charles's hand clenched into a fist at his side. The man was treading on very thin ice. "Tell Welwyn that whatever game you elected to play in that…that gambling house, you are still betrothed to Lord Flackwell."

To Charles's great satisfaction, Bess shook off her father's hand and ran nimbly back to his side. "No, Papa. I am not." She looked up at Charles, a blush tinging her cheeks. "I cannot marry Lord Flackwell."

"And why the devil not?" Flackwell turned a snarling face toward Bess.

"Because she may, at this moment, be carrying the next Duke of Welwyn."

Biting back a grin as first Lord Caister then Lord Flackwell registered the import of his words, Charles put a protective arm around Bess. "Therefore, my lords, she can marry no one but me."

"Good God, Bess. What have you done?" Her father's face paled, the moonlight making him look like a wraith.

"She has consented to become the Duchess of Welwyn, my lord. And as my intended wife gains every ounce of protection my name affords. Which I will now also extend to you and all your family, my lord."

"Caister." Lord Flackwell turned to Bess's father, his face darkened in a monstrous frown. "If you value your reputation, Caistor, you will put a stop to this here and now."

Charles turned to gaze at Flackwell, thoughtfully. "Believe me, Flackwell, you do not wish to cross me in this. I understand that you are holding information regarding Lord Caistor that will severely affect his reputation in Society, should you divulge it."

"What of it?" Flackwell's stare was defiant.

"I only wish to make *you* aware that ever since I discovered to whom Lord Caistor had found it fit to betroth his daughter, I have conducted my own investigation into your personal history. As you may expect, I have found some rather unsavory ventures—nothing illegal, mind you, else I would have visited you ere this, demanding you withdraw your claim on the lady."

Flackwell's jaw trembled, with rage or fear, Charles wasn't sure. Still, he was enjoying this immensely.

"Now, however, I am declaring a full-scale inquiry into your business *and* personal dealings because anyone who will extort a gentleman in order to marry his daughter likely has something even more unpleasant in his own past he would not wish to come to light. And I promise you, I will not rest until I find that unpleasantness, Flackwell."

"By God, Welwyn you cannot simply take what is not yours because it suits you." Lord Flackwell, whose chest had been heaving for a good five minutes, stepped in front of Charles like a bantam cock spoiling for a fight.

"Actually, Flackwell, that is exactly what I have done." A smile puckered Charles's mouth.

"I will not have it, Welwyn." Flackwell bounced on his toes, his anger soaring. He stripped off one of his gloves and threw it on the ground. "I challenge you, sir."

Charles stared at the glove, then nodded his head. "I will gladly pick this up, Flackwell, if you are certain you wish the challenge to stand. But just so you know, I do have a reputation with a dueling pistol."

Flackwell blanched but raised his chin. "You have debauched my betrothed, Welwyn. I cannot withdraw."

"What is going on here, gentlemen?" Out of the darkness, the black-veiled figure of Mrs. Dove-Lyon emerged, her head shifting from one man to the other. "Do I need to call Theseus and Egeus to break up this unruly assembly?"

"Not at all, Mrs. Dove-Lyon." Charles bowed to the lady, wondering if she could perhaps act as a catalyst and disarm the situation before it went too far. "We are merely about to discuss a preference of weapons, ma'am. Lord Flackwell has challenged me regarding my choice of wife."

"Indeed?" The tilt of the lady's veiled head conveyed her immediate interest. "Why would he do that?"

"Because he has violated my fiancée, madam." Flackwell puffed out his chest.

"Your fiancée, Flackwell?" Mrs. Dove-Lyon's voice was sharp. "Do you perhaps instead mean your wife?"

"What?" Flackwell's face seemed to collapse in on itself. "W...what did you say?"

His heart in his throat, Charles glanced from Flackwell to Bess, then to her father. Both of them looked as stunned as he felt. "Excuse me, Mrs. Dove-Lyon, are you saying Lord Flackwell is already married to Lady Elizabeth?"

"Oh, no, Your Grace." A light chuckle emerged from beneath the veil. "I mean he is already married to another lady."

Charles's jaw dropped. How had his investigation not revealed this vital information?

"My wife died years ago, Mrs. Dove-Lyon." Flackwell had rallied, drawing himself up straight and addressing himself to the woman.

"You have put that tale about for ten years, my lord. That does not necessarily make it true. As I have reason to know, firsthand." Mrs. Dove-Lyon addressed herself to Charles. "The lady housed in Manchester, who Lord Flackwell insists is his sister, is actually his wife, Agnes, Lady Flackwell."

"H...how do you know this, ma'am?" Lord Caistor had stepped forward, a rapt expression on his face.

"She is a distant relation of my late husband, my lord." The woman turned back toward Flackwell, her voice harsh. "Ten years ago, Agnes bore a child who died at birth. The loss affected her so grievously, her mind was left unhinged. Her husband put it about that he was taking her to Bath to attempt a cure, but in actuality, he put her in a home in Manchester where she's remained ever since, while her husband told everyone she had died. Unbeknownst to him, I have kept in touch with the woman who attends to her needs." Mrs. Dove-Lyon turned to Charles. "As you say, Your Grace, family is everything, especially when one has so little of it left."

Completely amazed by this revelation, Charles leaned over to whisper in the lady's ear. "I will give you my vowels in the amount of your highest fee for bringing this information to light, ma'am. I am so truly grateful to you."

"Then I will add that amount to your finder's fee, Your Grace." The veil hid the lady's features, but there was a smile in Mrs. Dove-Lyon's voice.

"My fee?" Charles frowned at the black-clad figure.

"Yes, Your Grace. I did happen to hear earlier this year that you were rather taken with Lady Elizabeth there." She nodded toward Bess. "But she was, unfortunately, already betrothed. So, I made a little wager with myself. You are fond of wagers too, I understand."

Slowly, Charles nodded.

"Well, I wagered that if I sent Lady Elizabeth an *Invocation Mystere*, she would accept it, you would find her, and the result would be a match made in the Lyon's Den." The enigmatic figure cocked her head. "Did I not win my wager, Your Grace?"

Charles's jaw had slowly dropped as Mrs. Dove-Lyon spoke. Now all he could do was nod.

"Very well then, you will send me your fees first thing tomorrow. And I will give you all a good evening."

"One moment, ma'am." Charles had one more burning question for the proprietress of the Lyon's Den. "Had I not found Lady Elizabeth tonight, would you have prevented her marriage to Lord Flackwell?"

The shrouded figure shook with laughter. "I assure you, Your Grace, Lady Elizabeth is not the first young lady I have prevented Flackwell from marrying, although I assume she will be the last."

"In that you are correct, ma'am. Thank you." Charles bowed to her, then remembered. "And may I say, Happy Birthday, Mrs. Dove-Lyon."

She waved a hand in acknowledgment, then turned and stalked off toward the Lyon's Den. "Tomorrow morning, Your Grace," she called over her shoulder. "Without fail."

"Without fail, ma'am." Charles nodded to the retreating figure, then turned to Lord Flackwell, who stood alone in the street, looking bewildered. "So, Lord Flackwell, I believe we will now come to an accord."

The earl looked up at him, dazed. "An accord?"

"Yes. To the effect you will cease to threaten Lord Caistor with exposure as I am certain his past transgression is not one tenth as heinous as yours. In addition, you will not attempt another betrothal, else your true tale will become the next morning's most notorious *on-dit*. Are we in agreement, my lord?"

Flackwell gulped and nodded.

Charles turned to Bess and embraced her, hoisting her up so her feet dangled almost a foot off the ground. "Now you are truly mine." His lips found hers, the sweetness of the woman he would spend the rest of his life with filling him with a heady intoxication. He broke the kiss off long enough to look at Lord Caistor. "I assume you no longer have an objection to my offer for your daughter?"

"None whatsoever, Your Grace." The dazed looked on the man's face turned to concern. "When will you be married?"

Slowly Charles let Bess slide down him, every inch of her touching him, making him harder than the London Stone. "I'll pay a visit to the Archbishop tomorrow morning"—after dropping off the hefty fee to Mrs. Dove-Lyon, of course—"so I expect we will be married by tomorrow afternoon."

"Isn't that rather soon, Your Grace?" Lord Caistor looked rather ill.

Charles peered down into Bess's face, her smile making him wish once more he was taking her home with him tonight. "No. Not soon enough."

Epilogue

Somerset, England
January 1815

THE SNOWS OF January had covered the ground until the green grass was nothing but a memory. Somerset's weather had not, however, concerned the Duke or Duchess of Welwyn for some weeks now. There were much more important things to be concerned about than the wretched weather.

Bess and Charles had contented themselves very well with sitting in the nursery, watching their two-week old son burble and coo and wave his tiny hands around. "I think I saw a smile just then." Bess stroked the wispy strands of dark hair on the baby's head, and Charles marveled anew at the fact they had actually produced a son exactly nine months from the night they met at the Lyon's Den.

When little Charles, Lord Amberlyn, made his appearance during the first week of January, a rather inebriated Duke of Welwyn, had had a calendar fetched and counted up the days while Bess lay fast asleep after her brief but harrowing ordeal. Now, with the babe thriving and Bess on the way to regaining her full strength, Charles could turn his mind to the next most important thing.

"He looks like you about the eyes, my love." Charles's pride in his progeny had no bounds. "If he's half as handsome as you are beautiful, he will not be able to keep the girls from flirting with him even in his cradle."

"If he takes after his Papa, he will do more than just flirt with them." Bess glanced up at him, laughter in her eyes. "That is exactly how he came to be here."

"And I wager neither of us has a complaint about that, do we, sweetheart?" He leaned over and kissed Bess's lips, warm and inviting. The past four weeks without the comfort of their connubial bliss every night had been all but torture for Charles. But the midwife had insisted he stay away from his wife's bed for two weeks before the babe was born and for another four weeks after his birth. The result was Charles's temper had frayed to the point he could think of nothing save his wife's gorgeous body, her silky thighs, and how exquisite it would feel to bury his cock between them.

"None at all, my love." Bess took his hand and squeezed it as they gazed down at the miracle they'd created.

"Then perhaps you'd like another wager, just to keep things lively, now little Amberlyn is here." He nuzzled her neck, the scent of jasmine in her hair intoxicating as any cognac.

"What wager?" Bess turned her head, giving him even more access to her neck.

"I will wager you that if we go upstairs to our bedchamber this afternoon, Amberlyn will have a little brother or sister by All Hallows' Eve this year."

"But Mrs. Morgan said not to—"

"For another two weeks, yes, I know what she said." He sucked on the tender flesh of her neck. "That doesn't mean we have to obey her words to the absolute letter. It has been *two* weeks." Becoming truly desperate, Charles nipped her skin just barely enough to make

Bess squeal.

The baby sent up a squall of his own at the noise and Nanny rushed in, taking him up and soothing him down. She sent a stern look at both of them, then walked out of the room, bouncing the little heir in her arms.

Bess glanced at Charles, then giggled. "We were naughty and got caught."

He sent her a lustful look of his own. "I know somewhere we can go and be naughtier and *not* get caught." He grabbed her hand, pulled her to him for one more kiss that scorched their lips. "Let's go put a spare heir in our nursery." Sweeping her up in his arms, Charles laughed when she shrieked, then hurried out of the room.

He had a wager to win.

The End

Additional Dragonblade books by Author Jenna Jaxon

The Welwyn Marriage Wager Series
Until I'm Safe in Your Arms (Book 1)
The Baron's Halo (Book 2)

The Lyon's Den Series
Pride of Lyons

About Jenna Jaxon

Jenna Jaxon is a best-selling author of historical romance, writing in a variety of time periods because she believes that passion is timeless. She has been reading and writing historical romance since she was a teenager. A romantic herself, Jenna has always loved a dark side to the genre, a twist, suspense, a surprise. She tries to incorporate all these elements into her own stories.

She lives in Virginia with her family and a small menagerie of pets—including two vocal cats, one almost silent cat, two curious bunnies, and a Shar-pei mix named Frenchie.

Blog: www.jennajaxon.wordpress.com
Facebook: facebook.com/jenna.jaxon
Twitter: @Jenna_Jaxon
Instagram: passionistimeless
TikTok: @jennajaxon1

Crossing the Lyon

by Jude Knight

Lenore and Ursula Kingsmead receive golden tickets to the Masque Mystère with a note that promises them a change of fortune. They could certainly do with one.

Alroy and Alban Beaumont buy tickets so they can escort the two sisters. They will not leave the women they admire unprotected.

Then the four discover that Mrs. Dove-Lyon sent neither tickets nor a letter. Are the tickets a trap? Only a fool would cross the Black Widow of Whitehall. A fool, or a person blinded by hatred and a lust for revenge.

When the trap is sprung, who will be caught?

Chapter One

The Lyon's Den, London, December 1813

Bessie Dove-Lyon eyed her visitor, thankful for her veil. With her expression concealed, she did not have to pretend to be pleased to be reminded of a past she'd rather forget. Bessie had been known to revisit those memories for the sake of a friend.

Della Dawson had not ever been a friend.

She allowed none of that to show in her posture or her voice. "What brings you to visit me, Lady Karzel?" Della had married several years after the disaster of her first love affair and its consequences. She was now widowed and rich. Perhaps she wanted a second husband?

The thought no sooner crossed Bessie's mind than she dismissed it. No. Not Della. She was still carrying a torch for the man who had jilted her twenty-five years ago, even though all the players in that tragedy except Della were dead and gone. Her lover, her daughter by him, the lady he married instead of her.

"A simple thing, Mrs. Dove-Lyon. Your revels are in April. I want golden tickets sent to a pair of sisters. Gentlewomen who have fallen on hard times. I am willing to pay handsomely for them to have this chance."

A charitable act? Bessie thought it unlikely, but perhaps she was overly cynical. After all, people could change. "Just the ticket?" she asked. "Or would you have me find them matches?"

Della's smile was even more feline than Bessie remembered. "Just the tickets," she said. Back in the days when she and Bessie had the same profession and similar ambitions, that smile had heralded trouble for someone. Bessie would need to be cautious.

"I will need their names to go on the tickets," Bessie said.

The smile faltered. "Is that necessary?"

"The names on the tickets must match the list given to the doorman, or the holder of the ticket cannot enter," Bessie improvised. In truth, the tickets showed no names. She was simply determined to figure out what Della was plotting.

Della huffed. "Very well. Ursula Kingsmead and her sister Lenora. I shall make sure they are delivered, Bessie."

She and Della had not been on first-name terms for a quarter of a century. "Very well, Cadella. Two *Invocations Mystère*. They will be ready for you to collect tomorrow afternoon." She named a price—double that of the already expensive tickets sold to those with the funds. Della did not blink.

"Half down, and half on receipt," Bessie added.

"My bodyguard has the money. He will pay you in full before I leave." Della's lips stretched into another threatening smile. "I know I can trust the Black Widow of Whitehall to keep her word."

Bessie bared her own teeth behind the veil, lips curved, eyes wary. "You are sure your young ladies will not require my matchmaking services, Cadella?"

The smile turned gloating and the alarm bells in Bessie's head went into a cacophony. "Oh, no," Della said. "I have it all organized, Bessie dear."

A few minutes later, Titan returned to Bessie's office. "She paid?" Bessie asked.

Her chief guard nodded. "Yes. And she and her guard have left."

"Very well. Titan, I have another job for you. Find out everything you can about two sisters named Ursula and Lenora Kingsmead. I want to know who they are, what their circumstances are, and above all, why Lady Karzel might wish to do them a good turn. Or a bad one."

"Address?" Titan asked.

Bessie shook her head. "I have no further information. Except that they are gentlewomen living in poverty."

His impassive face did not change. He simply nodded again and left.

Bessie spoke to the empty room. "At least the names are not particularly common. Titan will do his best, and his best is considerable. I suspect Della means to use me in one of her unpleasant games. She will discover that I am not to be crossed."

Late February 1814

URSULA WAS EXCITED about today's trip. She had not seen her twin sister for more than two months. Since December, fog, snow, and ice had made travel dangerous, and the rare intermittent thaws were no better. They turned every road into a sea of mud, making a two-hour journey into an impossible odyssey. Even the post was often delayed, but precious when it did get through, always with at least one letter from Lenora, and often with several.

The weather had been so bitter that, by the end of January, the Thames was a sheet of ice between London Bridge and Blackfriars

Bridge. Or so it was reported in the newspapers that occasionally made their way to the Beaumont household, where Ursula had taken shelter from the deadly cold.

Nora's letters also talked about the terrible conditions. The fog, in particular, made the light poor, so that Nora and the other seamstresses had to strain their eyes by lamplight instead of relying on the light from the large windows in their London workshop. As a reward for doing exquisite work despite the conditions, Nora wrote, Madame Le Brun had declared a one-day holiday to attend the Frost Fair that had sprung up on the ice.

That had been weeks ago, and at last, Ursula was on her way to London to visit. She twirled in front of the scrap of mirror that was all she had. It showed only glimpses of the gown Nora had made for her, but Ursula was sure it must suit her, for Nora had impeccable taste.

Her skirts felt odd, as did the stays that cradled her breasts. Usually, the bindings she normally wore to maintain her disguise as a young man squashed them nearly out of existence. Ursula was glad to be in women's clothing for the day and to remember who she really was. Miss Ursula Kingsley, gentlewoman.

The knock on her door stopped her preening. "Ursa? Are you ready?"

"Coming, Ban!"

And there was the rest of the reason she wanted to look her best. Foolish of her. Alban Beaumont knew, none better, that Ursula was a gentlewoman no more. He had first met her as Ursa Kingsmead, the local gardener, and odd job man. Ursula and Lenora had changed their last name after their father had been disgraced and had committed suicide.

It was as Ursa Kingsmead that she rented the disused gate lodge on the Beaumont's estate in the Middlesex countryside. It was Ursa who had been driven by the cold to spend the winter with the

Beaumont brothers and their father.

No lady could have taken a room in a bachelor household, but Ursa Kingsmead could. The cook and the maid-of-all-work did not live in, and Ursa avoided them, for the male disguise would not stand up at close quarters day after day. And she needed to be Ursa to earn a living.

She had explained it to Ban once. "I had no skills that could earn me an income as a woman," she had said. "I couldn't sew like my sister, Lenora. No one was ever going to employ my father's daughter as a maid. Nor could I, without references and with my father's reputation, expect to win a position in the traditional roles for a gentlewoman, as a governess or a companion. But gardening was my mother's passion. I used to help her, and I carried on after she was gone, doing more and more of the work myself as my father let our servants go."

"And gardeners are men," Ban had acknowledged.

She had shrugged. "So, I became a man."

As a man, though, she could not act on her sizzling attraction to Ban Beaumont. *Neither can you as a woman*, she reminded herself, as she put on her coat, tied the bow of her bonnet, and took up her reticule. There. She was ready.

Her birth was as good as his. She had been educated in all the usual skills and manners of a lady. No more. Even if she was right about the glint of interest in his eye, he could have no respectable offer to make to a gardener and odd-job-woman. And he was too much of a gentleman to attempt a dalliance. He was no risk to her virtue, and she should be ashamed of the discontent that thought provoked.

Ban was waiting at the foot of the stairs to escort her out to the carriage, and his brother Alroy was on the box, though she knew Roy planned to join them inside the carriage once they picked up their driver from the inn.

"You look charming, Miss Kingsmead," he called down from the box.

"You do," Ban assured her as he handed her up into the coach and followed to take the backward-facing seat opposite it.

Ursula and Lenora had been only seventeen and still in the schoolroom when their father's house of cards toppled, his creditors swooped, and she and Lenora found themselves on the streets of London with only the possessions they could cram into a bag each. She had no experience with compliments from gentlemen. "Thank you," she said. *That should be appropriate.*

Ban was not as openly handsome as his brother Roy, though they were much alike in form and features. Roy had hair as bright as a flame, a ruddy complexion, and green-blue eyes that were unaccountably warm, even though they were the color of the deepest part of the bay where she had grown up. Ban had almost no color at all. His hair was white, his eyes a pale grey, and only the most subtle of pinks touched his complexion with evidence that his blood was as red as any other man's.

They were different in demeanor, too. Roy was outgoing, friendly, talkative, and frequently charming. Ban was altogether quieter—more inclined to listen than to speak. Though when he spoke, he had a quiet charm all his own, an intelligence and wry humor that she found far more appealing than Roy's more effusive ways.

"I am excited about seeing my sister." It was a trite remark, but she felt she had to say something.

"I am looking forward to meeting her," Ban said. "I want to see if you and she look alike."

Ursula shook her head. "Not very much at all. She is fair where I am dark. She is short and I am tall. We are as different as chalk and cheese, but until we were seventeen and had to seek work, we were always together. She is my dearest friend."

"As Roy is mine," Ban agreed.

The carriage stopped, and a moment later the door opened, and Roy joined them.

He took the seat next to Ban and immediately opened a conversation with his brother. Normally, Ursula would have been all too happy to join in, but her mind was too much on Nora and on guessing what was so urgent that Nora had begged Ursula to come to London as soon as she could.

Was it about the *Mystère Masque* for which they had received tickets? Nora had written about it, and was not at all sure they should go, for the yearly event had a reputation for debauchery on a grand scale. In later letters, she had changed her mind, for her employer said that the golden tickets were much coveted, and the note that was enclosed in the envelope promised an opportunity to change their fortunes.

The brothers were talking about why they were going to London. Mr. Beaumont Senior had lost almost all of the family's wealth, leaving just one run-down estate. The brothers had spent seven years rebuilding.

Roy was off to Tattersalls to meet the owner of a stallion he hoped to buy. He managed the tenant farms, helped to work the home farm, and was beginning a horse breeding program.

Ban handled their accounts and their investments and was also going to a meeting. The topic was investing in a sort of container that would revolutionize—Ban's words—food preservation.

"Does it taste any good?" Roy asked. "Will there be a market for it?"

"Military," Ban said. "The army will leap at it. Navy, too. Preserved food on a long march or a longer voyage? It will taste better than dried meat and beans, I should imagine."

"Good point. We should try some, Ban. If it is in the least edible, I say we invest."

Investment. Horse breeding. Farming. Ursula wished she could have done as well. To be fair, as men, they had opportunities she and Nora didn't. And Mr. Beaumont Senior had not died leaving rapacious creditors to pick over the bones he had left.

As destitute women, it had been all she and Nora could manage just to keep body and soul together while retaining their pride and their virtue. And they were virtuous, even if Ursula did dress as a man. Even if she did live in a house with three unmarried men and travel unchaperoned in a carriage with two of them.

At least Nora had a safe home in her employer's attic. The modiste valued Nora's skills, but her protectiveness toward Ursula's sister also suggested an affection to which the woman would never admit.

I do not need to worry about Nora. But still, Ursula worried.

CHAPTER TWO

Ban and Roy rehashed the same discussion they'd had half a dozen times already and finally allowed silence to descend. If you could call it "silence" when the hooves of their horses and others rang against paved surfaces in some places and rocks in others, harnesses jingled, wheels rumbled, birds raised a chorus from every tree, and passersby added voices to the serenade of the morning—songs, complaints, and friendly greetings.

The farther they penetrated into London, the more the noises of people and their vehicles dominated the sounds of nature.

Ban examined Miss Kingsmead in surreptitious glances. He felt almost shy of her today. He was accustomed to the Ursa he had first met—the remarkably youthful man in shabby, ill-fitting clothes who worked in gardens around the area and never seemed to mind when Ban couldn't think of anything to say. Even discovering that Ursa was actually a woman had not changed their budding friendship. Except to add an edge of inconvenient desire.

Today, she was a lady, though her dress and warm winter coat were plain and in a subdued shade of green. Even so, they were an excellent foil for her own vivid coloring, which reminded him of the folk tales his nurse used to tell him when he and Ban were little. There was, he remembered, a girl in that who had skin as white as milk, lips as red as a rose, and hair the color of the deepest night. Nurse had never mentioned the girl's eyes. Ursula's were the blue of periwinkles and fringed with dark lashes that often made him wonder how he had ever imagined her to be a man.

She normally wore her hair pulled sharply back, plaited, and wound around her head under her hat, all the better to carry on her masquerade. Today, she had dressed it more softly, though all he could see were soft waves around her face, for the bonnet she wore hid the rest.

She was a pretty girl even when she pretended to be a man. As a lady, she took his breath away. She was not as alarmingly thin as she had been when she first stumbled to their door, wet through, and shaking after returning home to find that the hut she called home had inexplicably burned to the ground.

She caught him watching and smiled. "Thank you for allowing me to share your carriage."

Ban didn't tell her that he and Roy had planned this trip purely to give her passage to London. "It is not a problem," he said.

"Will your father be able to cope on his own?" Ursula asked. She blushed and added, "It is just that I see him, occasionally, when I am working in your garden. He looks out the second window from the right on the upper floor, but I have never seen him anywhere else. I wondered if perhaps he could not walk."

"He can walk, but he seldom bothers to walk beyond the limits of his room," Ban admitted. "He uses that room, which is his study, and the one next to it, his bedchamber." Remembering her own dismal family history, he added, "To be honest, it is a help. He leaves Roy to manage the one estate we have left, and me to look after the investments."

Roy shuddered. "I don't like to remember the years he was out all night, and sometimes for days at a time, and would come home reeking of brandy, cheap perfume, and other things too disgusting to mention. We would always know he'd lost yet another one of the Beaumont properties or signed chits for yet more money than we could pay without selling off more of what remained to us."

For the past two years, Father had been absorbed in trying to interpret the Rosetta Stone, of which he had managed to acquire a tracing. He ignored anything and anyone that was not a glyph carved in a rock.

At least it was a relatively inexpensive obsession. Far better than the conviction that had lost them all their estates except this one, and almost everything else they owned as well. Father had been convinced he had a system for winning at cards. By the time Ban and Roy had found out about his losses, it was almost too late. "I have not yet perfected the system," Father had insisted. "I will win it all back."

It took weeks, and more losses they could ill afford, to persuade him to stop.

"At least you managed to save one estate," Ursula said. "And I believe the two of you are recovering what you have lost." She sighed. "Nora and I have barely been able to keep ourselves fed."

"Your father left you worse off than ours," Ban noted. "We had something we could work with. Also, I have to believe it is harder for women than it is for men."

Ursula gave an unamused bark. "It is, yes. For a start, women are paid far less than men for the same work, even if that work can be done by either a man or a woman."

They pulled up outside the modiste's. Before Ban could hand Ursula down, a woman in a dark blue coat and bonnet came out of the door and hurried toward them, a broad smile spreading across her face as Ursula appeared in the doorway.

"Nora," Ursula called, putting her hand in Ban's to descend to the paved area outside of the shop.

"Ursula," the other replied, and they fell into one another's arms.

Roy stepped down to stand beside Ban. "She's little, isn't she," he commented. "Doesn't look much like our Ursa."

Ursula had said they were very different, and it was true. The sister's hair was as white as Ban's and short was an understatement. She barely came up to Ursula's shoulder and Ban and Roy were taller still. "She has the same color eyes," Ban said to his brother. A rich blue just this side of purple. Ban could drown in Ursula's eyes, although oddly the same eyes on her sister did not have the same effect.

"Lovely eyes," Roy agreed. He gazed at Lenora. He looked as if he'd had a blow that had knocked him silly.

Ursula and Lenora broke apart and turned to the two men. Ursula beamed at them but spoke to her sister. "Nora, these are my friends, Mr. Alban Beaumont, and Mr. Alroy Beaumont. Ban and Roy, my sister, Miss Lenora Kingsmead."

The sister stepped forward, holding out her hand to Ban first, and then to Roy. "Mr. Beaumont," she said, and, "Mr. Beaumont." Ban shook her hand and Roy kissed it. She blushed at the kiss. "I must thank you. Ursula has told me of your many kindnesses."

"If we have been of service, we are glad," Roy assured her. "Your sister is our friend, and I hope you might regard us as friends, as well."

Lenora's blush deepened. "You may change your mind when I immediately ask you for a favor," she warned. "I want an escort for me and Ursula to a meeting this afternoon. If you can manage it. If you do not mind."

She put up a hand when Roy opened his mouth. "Please, hear me out. And know I will not blame you for refusing."

Ursula looked confused. "We have a meeting?" she asked.

"You told them about the tickets, did you not?" Lenora asked.

Ursula nodded.

"I am concerned," Lenora said. "Everything I have heard about the birthday celebration at the Lyon's Den tells me that maidens without protectors have no business there. However, the Black Widow of Whitehall made a point of sending us two of her golden tickets, a personal letter promising us good fortune if we came, and masks to wear. But Madame Le Brun, my employer, recognized the masks. They are… Let me just say they are not the masks for a maiden."

Ban understood her hesitations. Indeed, though he and Roy had not told Ursula this yet, they had sold some shares and paid the hefty fee for tickets of their own. If Ursula and Lenora insisted on going to the *Masque Mystère*, they would not be unescorted.

Lenora squared her shoulders and raised her chin. "I decided to ask Mrs. Dove-Lyon about her intentions. I wrote for an appointment and have been told to come to the Lyon's Den at two this afternoon. I know Ursula will come with me. Will you escort us?"

"Of course, we will," Roy said, without waiting for Ban's opinion. Since he agreed with his brother, he contented himself with nodding.

"Shall we pick you up here at twenty minutes to two?" Roy asked, and the ladies both agreed before disappearing through the door into the modiste's.

Ban asked for the carriage to be back by twenty-five minutes to two, and he and Roy set off to walk to their first appointments.

"I spoke for you," Roy said. "I'm sorry, but I couldn't let them go to that place alone. Especially Lenora. No offense to Ursula, but we know she can handle herself, though she shouldn't have to. But Lenora is such a tiny lady." He drew his brows together in a frown. "She reminds me of someone, but I can't bring whoever it is to mind."

"I have no problem," Ban said. "If you hadn't agreed for us both, I would have done so." He was not about to let Ursula walk into that sinners' palace without him at her side.

"Perhaps we will get to see the naughty masks," Roy said, hopefully.

"They are pretty," Ursula said. Lenora had laid the masks out on her bed. They were elaborate headdresses, made to fit over the entire head: delicate creations of gold wire and fabric, decorated with feathers, ribbons, and beads. She couldn't see anything upsetting about them.

Lenora touched the one on the left, which had the headpiece molded in the form of a helmet crowned with a wreath of roses, myrtle, and seashells. Doves and sparrows perched on the wreath, and the helm was a swan, its neck curving forward, and its body draped down the back of the helmet.

The part that covered the face also had roses, myrtle, seashells, and the tiny forms of flying birds etched into the cheeks and forehead, catching the light as Ursula lifted the helmet for a better look.

"That is what I thought," Nora said, "until Madame told me that it bears all the symbols that signify the wearer to be Aphrodite."

"The Greek goddess of love," Ursula stated. She still didn't see the problem.

"The Greek goddess of *physical* love," Nora said. "In the context of a debauch, I find that disturbing."

The other headpiece was also a helmet with a wreath of roses. The helm was a dolphin. The etching this time was on the helmet: lyres, roses, dolphins, and bows and arrows. The face covering was the likeness of a handsome young man. "This one came with wings and a bow and arrow," Nora told Ursula. "Madame says it is Cupid, the Greek god of lust."

"The men—at least the upper-class men—will know what those symbols mean, won't they? They learn that sort of thing at school, or at least at university."

Nora nodded. "Dressed in those masks and with costumes to suit, we would be advertising ourselves as strumpets," she said. "Madame agrees. She says it is unlike the owner of the Lyon's Den to attempt such a thing. Apparently, Mrs. Dove-Lyon is known as a fair employer and protective of her staff. Also, although she makes money brokering marriages, no one has ever been left worse off by trusting her choice, or so Madame says." Nora shrugged.

Ursula protested. "Nora, she runs a gambling den. Most likely one our father frequented. She makes people destitute and throws families out in the streets."

But Nora shook her head. "She does not force people to gamble more than they can afford, Ursula. Father made the choices that led to his ruin, and ours. In any case, I mean for us merely to ask for information. What does she mean by sending us such masks? What sort of future is she offering us?"

Ursula waved toward the items on the bed. "I should think those make it obvious that she intends to change our fortunes for the worse, Nora."

"Madame says it is not like her. We will ask, and then we can decide what to do." Nora was adamant. She usually allowed Ursula to take the lead, but when she had made up her mind to something, Ursula had found it easier to go along. Especially now. Nora was not going to change her mind, and Ursula was not going to leave Nora to go to a gambling den on her own.

At least they would have support. Ursula was very glad Nora had asked Ban and Ray to come with them. With two such fit and capable gentlemen, what could go wrong?

Chapter Three

Ban and Roy had to run the last part of the way to the modiste's and even so, the Kingsmead sisters were standing by the carriage, looking anxiously up and down the road. Ursula saw them and attracted Nora's attention, and they spoke to the driver and climbed into the vehicle.

Roy arrived a few paces ahead of Ban and leapt aboard. Ban stopped to put up the steps and waved to the driver before hauling himself up. The carriage moved off while he was still shutting the door.

"We must apologize for being late and disheveled," Roy was saying. "An elderly lady got her foot stuck in a grate partway across a corner and we stopped to help her before she was run over by a carriage. She was such a tiny person that she might well have been trampled."

Ban had waved traffic to one side or the other, while Roy had knelt in the mud tugging at the heel. All the time the old lady had berated them for being so slow. "Roy managed to get her free, but he tugged the heel right off her shoe. She was very cross about it." He was straightening his jacket and his cravat and using his hands to smooth his hair.

"It was one of those high-heeled boots they used to wear last century," Roy commented. He was also tidying himself up. "We've come across her before. Quite a bad-tempered lady."

"In autumn, her carriage came off the road just beyond our estate, and was sitting on an axle, with one wheel spinning in the ditch," Ban explained. "We gathered some of the tenants and lifted it back onto the road. Her ladyship stood there, haranguing everyone about how slow we were being."

Roy laughed. "She did not say 'thank you' last time, either. I'm glad you thought of suggesting I used my handkerchief to kneel on, Ban. I'd hate to turn up with dirty knees to an interview with the Black Widow of Whitehall."

"Why is she called that?" Ursula inquired.

They speculated about that for the remaining minutes of the journey. It had nothing to do with spiders, they decided when Roy suggested it, tongue-in-cheek. Ban wondered if it might be because of her habit of dressing in full mourning even all these years after the death of her husband.

The doorman at the Lyon's Den initially refused to allow Roy and Ban to enter with the two ladies. Ursula and Lenora insisted they could not attend the meeting without their escorts. The doorman asked them to wait, shut the door in their faces, and came back a short while later with another man, this one even taller and broader than the first.

"I am known as Titan," the man said. "And you are the Misses Kingsmead. I understand you are insisting on bringing these two men to your meeting with Mrs. Dove-Lyon."

"That is correct," Lenora said firmly. "I mean no disrespect to your employer, but I also have no reason to trust her. I do trust Mr. Alroy and Mr. Alban Beaumont."

Titan's eyes widened. He raised an eyebrow as he subjected Ban and Roy to a leisurely scan. Ban returned the assessment. The man was well-named—the titans of Ancient Greek mythology had been giants and gods. Titan was well over average size and looked as if he had been carved from stone. From the way the man held himself, Ban would not be at all surprised to discover that he had been a soldier.

"Very well," Titan said abruptly. "Please follow me."

Soon they were being ushered through to a small office. Titan invited them to take a seat. "Mrs. Dove-Lyon will be with you shortly." In fact, a woman entered the room only a minute or so after he had left it. She was dressed all in black and wore the full veil of a widow in deep mourning. "I am Mrs. Dove-Lyon," she announced. She faced Lenora for a long moment. "And you are Miss Lenora Kingsmead, who wrote to me." She turned her head. "And this is your sister, Miss Ursula Kingsmead."

Ban and his brother came under consideration next. "You are the brothers Beaumont. From your appearance," she said to Ban, "I would guess you are Alban since the name means 'white'." With her attention on Roy, she added, "And you must be Alroy."

"Since the name means 'red'," Roy drawled.

"Precisely. Very well, Miss Kingsmead. You asked for this meeting. How may I help you?"

Lenora lifted her head proudly. Her tone when she spoke was stiff with challenge. "My sister and I wished to ask your intentions, Mrs. Dove-Lyon. Madame Le Brun, the modiste for whom I work, says you are a fair woman, you have a name for treating your employees well, and you do what you can to protect the weak. You sent us tickets to your birthday masquerade, with a letter promising to change our fortunes if we attended. Three days ago, you sent us masks to wear."

"No," said Mrs. Dove-Lyon. "I did not."

The response caught Lenora as she prepared to speak again and left her with her mouth open in surprise.

Ursula spoke before Lenora had recovered herself. "Which part of that do you deny?" she demanded.

"All of it," responded Mrs. Dove-Lyon. "I provided the *Evocations Mystère* to an old acquaintance, on her request. I concede that I knew they were intended for you and your sister, but that has been my only involvement. Do you have the letter and the masks with you? I should like to see what has been done in my name."

Ban was inclined to believe the lady. Her voice vibrated with repressed anger. Lenora and Ursula exchanged a wordless glance. Perhaps they came to the same conclusion, for Lenora took an envelope from her reticule and handed it to the widow, and Ursula asked for the hat box that Roy had carried inside at her direction and placed it on the desk.

Mrs. Dove-Lyon removed a sheet of paper from the envelope, perused it, then put it down. She took the lid off the hat box and removed two wrapped items. She unwrapped them and placed them side by side on the desk before her.

"I have not had a classical education," Lenora told her, "but I have been informed that such masks and the costumes appropriate to them would attract...attention of a kind my sister and I do not wish to encourage."

Ban should think so! He *had* had a classical education and immediately recognized the symbolism of the masks. Venus and Cupid, as the Romans called them. Or Aphrodite and Eros, in the Greek Pantheon. The masks were an invitation to rape.

Mrs. Dove-Lyon understood, too. Even though her face was hidden by the veil, Ban could sense her outrage, feel it pouring off her. "This was not my work, Miss Kingsmead, Miss Ursula. I was promised that the person in question intended to do you a good turn. This—" her gesture toward the desk encompassed both masks and the letter—"This is unacceptable."

"Who is this person?" Lenora demanded.

Her question was met by a considering silence. "No," the widow said, after a long moment. "I am not prepared to disclose my acquaintance's identity at this moment." She held up a hand when all four of them opened their mouths to respond. Such was the lady's presence that they all stayed silent.

"In due time. You have my word," she said. She folded her hands on the desk. "Leave the masks with me. I shall provide replacements so that you can come to the party without any fear."

"You expect us to attend when you say some mysterious person seeks to do us such harm?" Ursula demanded, starting out of her chair in outrage.

Lenora put her hand on her sister's arm.

"If the letter is not from you, what purpose is there in us coming?" she asked. "And how can we be sure we will be safe?"

"I believe your escorts can answer the second question." A thread of laughter laced Mrs. Dove-Lyon's words.

The sisters turned to look at Ban and Roy. Roy raised his eyebrows at Ban. Fair enough. It had been Ban's idea. "When you first told us about the golden tickets, Ursula," he admitted, "Roy and I were concerned. We've never been to the *Masque Mystère*, but we've heard things about it that concerned us, and we didn't want you to go without any protection. So, we bought tickets. We are going to the masquerade."

Ursula had been so excited about the promise in the letter, but neither he nor Roy felt comfortable talking to her about the kinds of debauchery she might witness at the event. "If you have changed your mind, we will not go either."

"Why did you not tell me it was not a suitable evening for me and Lenora?" Ursula asked him.

"Because," Mrs. Dove-Lyon said, her voice dryer than ever, "like most gentlemen, he did not want to discuss indelicate subjects with a gentlewoman. The entire species is inflicted with the belief that we are tender plants who will wither away if exposed to mention of the naughtier behaviors that such gentlemen enjoy in private. With, I might add, people who are as female as us."

That was it in a nutshell, but Roy said, "We had intended to tell you both this afternoon." Which was also true.

Ursula faced Mrs. Dove-Lyon. "And the first question? Why should we attend?"

Mrs. Dove-Lyon picked up the letter that had come with the golden tickets. "Someone made promises in my name. I mean to see them come true, Miss Kingsmead. A change in fortunes. Furthermore, I suspect that the person responsible is not in possession of all the facts. I intend to give you the opportunity to meet at the masque. The choice, of course, is yours. I am not able to promise you will see nothing to offend you but I can promise you will see and experience nothing to harm you."

Ursula and Lenora exchanged a glance and Lenora spoke for them both. "We will have to discuss this matter. Thank you for seeing us today, Mrs. Dove-Lyon. We appreciate your honesty."

She stood, and Lenora followed her example. Ban and Roy hastened to get to their feet. "We will let you know what we decide," Lenora said and led the way out through the door.

Chapter Four

Ursula was still not entirely sure that going to the *Masque Mystère* was a good idea, but she had to admit she loved how she looked in her costume. Even more, she loved the look in Ban's eyes when he saw her.

He looked rather wonderful himself, and so, for that matter, did Roy and Lenora. They stood in Madame Le Brun's workshop, admiring one another.

"Put your masks on," Madame begged. "We all want to see them."

A chorus of agreement murmured from Nora's fellow dressmakers, all of whom had helped to make the costumes.

Four of them rushed to collect the boxes and brought them to the partygoers. Mrs. Dove-Lyon had outdone herself, sending two complimentary sets of masks to the modiste's.

Nora's transformation was magical, from the delicately wrought crown to the dainty dancing slippers. The headpiece used green as a base color but glittered in silver, gold, and crystals in delicate flowers and leaves, painted on the face covering, but formed of wire and mesh as the headpiece reached up into a crown whose every second carefully crafted peak bent over the green velvet cap to meet in the middle.

From beneath the headpiece, her fair hair hung loose, streaming down over her shoulders.

The gown had been made from the same green and was heavily embroidered with flowers and leaves to echo those on the headpiece. Crystals and sequins on the gauze of the overdress caught the light as she moved.

More sequins glittered on the wings of gauze that depended from her shoulder blades, cleverly supported by a harness under her gown.

Roy had likewise been transformed. His face was completely covered by the face of a golden stag, the horns of the stag rising above the crown that circled his head. In the mask and the green and gold robes he wore, he looked regal, almost godlike. His wings were green and veined in gold.

"The fairy king and queen," Madame Le Brun said. "Magnificent."

Roy offered Nora his hand with a bow. "My queen," he said.

She placed her hand in his and he escorted her away from the mirrors so Ursula and Ban could take their places.

Ursula put her headpiece on, the sight of herself in the mirror disappearing for a moment as the mask descended. There she was, in a mask that fitted like an overlong hat, covering her face to just above the lips.

A circlet held the whole thing firmly on her head. The gilded mask descended from the front, and strings of gold discs fell to her shoulders around the rest of the circlet. The front end of a golden cobra rose from the center of her forehead, curving gracefully to its head with garnets for eyes and a silver tongue.

The mask was shaped to her face, the almond-shaped eyeholes outlined in black with black eyebrows arching above.

Cleopatra. Pharaoh of Egypt. The costume matched the long, linen skirt with a colorful girdle that clasped in the front and the broad collar necklace made of bright paste gems. She also wore multicolored bracelets and anklets, and a pair of laced sandals.

Ban, in the costume of the Roman Mark Anthony, made Ursula's mouth water. The mask that covered all but his mouth and the chin was gilded to match Ursula's, as was his helmet and the breastplate of his armor. Were those molded curves really how his naked torso would appear? His short red tunic left his legs all but bare (and what splendid legs they were), and the cloak that hung from his shoulders was also red.

"Magnificent," repeated Madame. "My children, you are ready. Have a happy evening. Mr. Beaumont and Mr. Beaumont, take care of my dear Lenora and her sister."

Ban and Roy had once more hired a carriage, and after they were settled in it, Ban said, "Mrs. Dove-Lyon told us the same thing. We are sticking to you like glue, ladies, for the whole evening."

"Did she tell you what she had planned?" Ursula asked.

The men shook their heads. "Only what she had already said," Roy commented.

It was a short drive, but many people were making it, and they had to wait several minutes in a queue of carriages before their own reached the main entrance to the Lyon's Den, where they joined a masked throng, all in costume, all full of high spirits.

Some had been partaking of the more earthly kind of spirits, too, for Ursula caught a whiff of brandy when a man lurched up to her and reached toward her bare arm. "I'd like me a piece of—" he began, but stopped with a yelp when Ban grabbed his hand and twisted it.

"The lady is with me."

The oaf retreated, muttering, into the crowd. Ursula was grateful to Ban and Roy who used their strength and their scowls to hold their place and to keep her and Nora from being jostled as the line slowly moved forward.

Soon, it was their turn to show their tickets at the door and to pass through into the main hall of the place, where the new arrivals spread out across the room or drifted away into other rooms or up the stairs.

The Lyon's Den was breathtaking. Everywhere Ursula looked, candles glowed, their flames reflected in dozens of mirrors, with glitters dancing from the jewels and costumes of the assembled guests.

Ban captured a couple of glasses of wine from a passing servant and handed one to Ursula. Roy was doing the same for Nora. They stood near the entrance, sipping their drinks and watching the other guests.

And what a spectacular sight they were! Ursula could see gods and goddesses, witches, wizards, demons, beasts—both actual and fabulous—fairy folk and ghosts, characters from history, literature, and legend, and more.

Many of the costumes, particularly of the women, were far more revealing than Ursula had envisaged when they'd discussed Aphrodite and Eros. Ursula had never seen so many limbs through sheer fabrics or even bare. And that was not the only skin on display.

She was sure that her eyes bulged when a harem dancer floated by, in wide-legged trousers of some almost transparent material, waist bared, and with a swath of fabric around her breasts that barely covered her nipples. She was followed by a bare-chested genie in hot pursuit, for what purpose Ursula had no reason to guess, as several other couples, early as the evening was, did not wait to retreat to the rooms upstairs or to one of the many curtained alcoves before kissing and pawing at one another.

"Shall we walk?" Nora suggested. Roy offered his arm, and the pair of them set off around the edge of the floor. "Stay close," Ban warned, as he returned their empty glasses to a servant. Ursula needed no encouragement, clinging to his arm as the one sane place in a universe turned suddenly to chaos.

Not everyone was intent on lascivious behavior. Though the main room was given over to dancing, the gambling tables in the side rooms were already crowded, as were the tables set up for punch and other drinks.

An orchestra played, and people were waltzing. "Shall we?" said Ban. Roy and Nora were already gliding around the floor, intent on one another.

She nodded, and Ban took her into his arms. "One benefit of a masquerade," he murmured, "is that there are no rules about how many times we can dance together."

Ursula was not sure whether or not to be glad of it. Perhaps it was the atmosphere or the forward behavior she had witnessed, or the glass of wine she had consumed, but his touch made her feel heated in places she didn't usually think about, and she found herself wishing he would hold her closer.

Perhaps he wished it, too. Or so his eyes, glittering through the mask, suggested.

"Shall we walk?" she suggested, after the second dance, and he readily agreed. She scolded herself for being disappointed. Roy and Nora, too, had abandoned the dance floor. Ursula and Ban joined them.

Nora leaned close to speak into Ursula's ear. "There's my mask. The Eros one. By the third pillar talking to the man dressed as a cavalier."

"Or one just like it," Ursula agreed. As they watched, the cavalier tried to drag the Eros to the stairs that led to the private rooms, and the Eros did something—Ursula could not see what—that left her free of the man's grasping hands, and the man flat on his back on the floor. The Eros sauntered away while two of Mrs. Dove-Lyon's men hauled the man toward the front entrance.

As they passed Ursula, she could hear him protesting, "But the woman is a whore. Lady Karzel told me…"

Ursula and Nora stilled at the mention of that name.

"I know a Lady Karzel," said Roy.

Ban nodded. "Short lady. Bad-tempered. Keeps needing to be rescued from awkward situations."

"We know her, too," Ursula admitted grimly, and Nora nodded.

"Mostly by name and reputation," Ursula added. "We have not actually met her."

"I wager she sent the masks and the letter," Nora said. Ursula agreed. It all made sense, now.

"Lady Karzel?" Ban asked. "But why would she want to hurt you if you haven't met her?"

"We have no idea," Ursula admitted. "But we do know she played a part in driving our father to suicide, for he wrote about her in the letter he left. We believe she was the one who told lies to the villagers in our town so we could not stay there. We know she tried to threaten Madame Le Brun into turning Nora out into the streets."

"If it is Lady Karzel that Mrs. Dove-Lyon intends us to meet, I am not sure I wish to," Nora said, clinging to Roy as if he was her one anchor in an uncertain world.

"I want to," Ursula insisted. "I want to tell her exactly what I think of her."

"And you will." Mrs. Dove-Lyon materialized beside them. "Now that Lady Karzel has shown her hand, it is time to find out what she intended, and to resolve it for once and for all."

She beckoned, and they followed her past a curtain and through a door, then up a flight of stairs. At the top, a door opened onto a dark room, the only light coming from a pane of glass in the wall—a window that looked into a brightly lit room.

"You will be able to see and hear everything that happens in the next room," she told them. "A row of grates under the window lets sound travel clearly. Those on the other side of the window will not be able to see you as long as there is no light in this room. They will be able to hear you, however. Be very quiet."

"You said we would meet her," Ursula objected.

"You will," Mrs. Dove-Lyon promised. "Let me question her first. I believe the answers you are looking for will come more easily if she doesn't know you are listening. Sit, please, and do not make a sound. I will send for you, shortly."

She left them, shutting the door into the passage.

"I'm taking my mask off," Roy announced, and followed words with action, putting the stag's head on a table near the door. Ban was quick to follow suit, and Ursula and Nora followed. Ursula had been better off than the others, since her headpiece was largely open over her hair, but the face mask had become sticky and uncomfortable in the heat from the crowds. The others, whose heads were covered, must have felt it even more.

They resumed their seats on the chairs provided, and none too soon, for the door to the other room opened and Mrs. Dove-Lyon entered the room, followed by another veiled widow. The guard Titan brought up the rear, but stayed in the passage, closing the door at a nod from Mrs. Dove-Lyon.

"I am not pleased, Lady Karzel," Mrs. Dove-Lyon said, as she lifted back her veil, disclosing the face of an older lady who was, nonetheless, still a very attractive woman. The lines of her face hinted at strength and determination.

The other woman followed her example. "What is that to me?" she replied. "Your feelings are your own business, Mrs. Dove-Lyon." She looked older than the gambling den owner. Her face showed signs of a hard life in heavy lines that spoke of sorrow and anger.

The gambling den owner's voice was unyielding. "I think you will find otherwise. At our last meeting, you implied that the young ladies for whom you wanted the tickets would benefit from attending my party. Furthermore, in the letter you wrote, you signed my name to a promise of a change in fortunes. That makes what happened tonight very much my business, Lady Karzel."

Lady Karzel sat forward in her chair. Her voice lifted in excitement. "What happened tonight?" she demanded.

"Two women were attacked," Mrs. Dove-Lyon stated.

"What did you expect?" Lady Karzel taunted, her grin fighting to escape. "Women in provocative outfits, men looking for an easy lay, plenty to drink. Why blame me?"

"Because the men each attacked the two women wearing the masks you sent to Lenora Kingsmead. And both of them, when they were stopped, claimed you had told them the women were harlots provided by me to accommodate anyone who cared to have them."

Lady Karzel shrugged. The grin was now full-blown. "Men will blame anyone rather than take responsibility for their actions. You, of all people, should know that, Mrs. Dove-Lyon."

Mrs. Dove-Lyon's voice turned coaxing. "Why, Della? Why this campaign to destroy the two Kingsmead girls?"

"You know why." Lady Karzel glared at Mrs. Dove-Lyon. Her voice rose as she said, "You are no fool. You were there when Kingsley ruined me, then abandoned me for that woman. Hah!" There was no amusement in her laugh. "So. She was a lady. He could have made me a lady, but he didn't. Karzel did. He should have married me." The next words were shriller. "He took my daughter and then abandoned her, too."

Abruptly, she calmed. "I set out to make him and his wife both pay, but she escaped me. He did, too, in the end. His daughters can change their names to hide their father's disgrace, but they have not fooled me. I hope they were properly ruined."

She gave a gleeful giggle. "I did promise them a change in fortunes. I hope they suffered. I hope Kingsley is able to see them from

Hell, to see what he has done to them."

"Kingsley abandoned them, too," Mrs. Dove-Lyon pointed out. "First for the tables and later by dying. They have been building a life without him. He did nothing to cause tonight's trouble. You did it. You set a plot in motion to destroy two innocents."

"Not so innocent," Lady Karzel snapped back. "One of them lives with three men, and the other is a seamstress. No one can live on the wages of a seamstress. She must be bartering her favors. I haven't been able to find out who with, but it isn't important now. Not now that she is ruined." The gleeful note in her voice gave way to pleading. "You understand, Bessie. After what Kingsley did, I had to cut his family down and destroy it, root and branch."

The pieces of her family history that Ursula knew settled into a new and alarming pattern. Nora must have realized, too. She reached out for Ursula's hand. Her sister's face was white in the light that filtered through the window, her eyes staring.

Mrs. Dove-Lyon said, "Ah, Della. You have no idea what you have done. Or, at least, tried to do. "She turned to the mirror. "Will you come through now, please?"

Lady Karzel leapt to her feet. "Who is there? Who is watching us?"

Ursula stopped by the table to pick up her mask and put it on, and the others followed her lead. As they moved into the passage, Lady Karzel's declaration that she was leaving became less bold.

The passage was filled with large men. They faced one another, tension radiating between them. Ban moved up beside Ursula, and Roy hovered protectively over Lenora.

"Let them through," Titan commanded. The chief guard was standing with his back to the door to the next room.

"Our mistress…" said one of the other men.

"Is in no danger," Titan assured him. He opened the door, and Lady Karzel had almost reached it when Ursula walked inside, forcing her backward.

Once all four of them were within, Titan closed the door again, this time with himself on the inside, standing in front of the door, seemingly relaxed. Lady Karzel retreated to her chair, as sounds of a scuffle came through from the hall.

"What are you up to, Bessie," she screeched. "Who are these people?"

Mrs. Dove-Lyon ignored her. "Please be seated, ladies. Gentlemen, please remove your masks."

Roy and Alban obeyed, disclosing their faces to Lady Karzel. Ursula thought that they looked like warrior angels, each sternly beautiful.

Lady Karzel frowned in bewilderment. "The Messrs. Beaumont?" Her frown deepened to the anger that seemed to be the lady's dominant emotion. She rounded on Mrs. Dove-Lyon. "I recognize these two. Always following me around and insisting on poking their noses into my business. Are they working for you, Bessie?"

"We have not been following you," Roy protested.

"We have come across you in difficulties, and have done what we could to assist," Ban added, calmly. "If we had known you were plotting against our friends, we might have left you to sink in the mud or be run over in the street."

Lady Karzel picked up on his reference to Ursula and Lenora. "Your friends? You are *friends* with Kingsley's daughters?" She turned to look at the two sisters. "You! But Bessie said…"

Mrs. Dove-Lyon shrugged. "I said men attacked the women wearing the masks you sent. They did. Those wearing the masks were two of my ladies, and well able to defend themselves, which they did until the men I set to guard them took your two accomplices into custody."

The other widow appeared to shrink in her chair, hunching as if in pain. "No ruination?"

Ursula, not waiting for any suggestion from Mrs. Dove-Lyon, removed her mask. She glared at the enemy who had intended them such harm. "From what I overheard, our father ruined you, Lady Karzel. And you thought to treat me and my sister as he treated you. Even though he is dead and will never know. Even though neither of us has ever harmed you. Even though you have suffered the same thing and should have sympathy for a woman in that extreme." She shook her head, slowly. "I can forgive you for your anger. I cannot forgive you for hurting my sister."

Lady Karzel snorted her contempt. "Foolish chit. I had no success in hurting your sister. Madame Le Brun refused to believe I had the power to break her business if she kept Lenora on as a seamstress. And the Frenchwoman was right. The girl never went out without friends around her, so an abduction would not work. No one cared about the stories I told about her, or they didn't believe me."

"You had more success with my sister, did you not?" Nora's voice was hoarse, and Roy put a hand on her shoulder to offer his support. "You lost her several customers for her gardening work? You had the shack in which she lived burned to the ground?"

Ursula's eyes widened as her shoulders jerked back. *The fire had been deliberate?*

Lady Karzel sneered. "I admit nothing." The sneer turned to flaming anger. "She should have died in the cold, but you—" she pointed an accusing finger at Ban and then at Roy—"You took her in. You found her work and a place to live. Do you think I should have been grateful when you pulled my coach from the mud or collected the parcels I dropped? When you were standing in the way of my righteous anger?"

"Ah," said Nora, with a calm that Ursula could only envy. "But was your anger righteous? Our father married our mother instead of you. She died unhappy after he had betrayed her, again and again. He frittered away all he owned and shot himself. Done. You have your revenge. Why should you want to destroy me and my sister?"

"Because it is not enough!" The words were hurled at Nora in a shriek. Lady Karzel curled in on herself in her chair, and her voice changed to a lament. "He took my daughter. He promised to look after her until I sent for her, and when I did, he said she had died. He and that bitch, his wife—they killed my baby."

Ursula stared at Nora. *So, it is all true. But Mother said...* She examined Lady Karzel, trying to see what the woman must have looked like when she was young. Ban was doing the same. Even without what Ursula knew, he must be wondering.

"You were gone for some time?" Nora asked, mildly.

Lady Karzel made an impatient gesture. "What does it matter? Do you not think I have wondered if coming back earlier would have made a difference? Two years. What is two years? They should have been able to protect my baby for two years." Tears glittered in her eyes, and she dabbed at them furiously. Ursula had the sudden thought that the woman felt betrayed by her own grief.

Nora continued her questioning in that same mild but inexorable tone. "Why two years? You loved your baby." There was a slight inflection that made that almost a question. "Why leave her for so long, and with a man who had already shown he could not be trusted?"

Ursula was not the only one to see the strain that tightened Nora's into a fist and stiffened the muscles of her jaw, so her last few words showed her distress. Roy put a comforting hand on her shoulder.

Lady Karzel said nothing for a long moment. Ursula began to think she would deny Nora an answer. Then, in a quiet voice that had all five of them leaning closer, she said, "The money Kingsley had given me was running out. I had to find another protector or do something drastic. I took the last of my savings and went away, to where I could, perhaps, catch a husband who did not know of my ruination."

She looked up at Nora, pleading as if Nora's judgment mattered to her. Which it would, perhaps, when she knew all. "I thought to go as a widow with a baby but feared it would reduce my options. Besides, I had little enough money for myself and a maid, let alone my little pet and her nurse." She sighed, and the tears ran freely down her face. "I thought Lady Kingsley would take my side. We had been friends once, and she had given birth not long after me."

Mrs. Dove-Lyon was now watching Nora with what looked like amused fondness. *She must have guessed,* Ursula realized.

Nora nodded slowly. "I see, but two years?"

"It took that long for Karzel to agree to let me have my child," Lady Karzel explained, the tears drying up as if they had never been, and her voice hardening. "He would not let me travel to England but sent a courier and a nanny to bring my little Cordelia home to me. But all I got was a letter."

Reaching up to undo the fastenings on her mask, Nora said, "And all this grief and anger because of my father. I am sorry for your losses, Lady Karzel, but my death was not one of them." And she revealed her face.

Lady Karzel stiffened. "No!"

"Yes." Nora reached out sideways, and Ursula understood what she needed. They had always understood one another, as far back as her memory reached, and each had always been there to support the other. She moved to her sister's side and linked hands with her.

"Our mother told us at least part of the story years ago, as she lay on her deathbed. We had always known she had not given birth to me, but when I shared my fear that Father would throw me out once she died, she told me I was Father's daughter, though not hers."

Ursula took up the story since Nora became too choked with emotion to continue. "She said he had lied to the ton for more than fourteen years, passing my sister off as his legitimate child. If ever he tried to disown Nora or send her away, we could threaten to tell everyone what we knew."

"Mother told us you never came back for me, Lady Karzel," Nora said, her voice recovered. "She said Father told her you had died. She said she loved me at first for the sake of her friend, and then for my own sake."

"Mother was never your enemy, and Father did her as much harm as he did you, if not more," Ursula scolded. "You have not been fair."

Lady Karzel sat slumped in her chair, her mouth open, looking bewildered. She turned her eyes to Mrs. Dove-Lyon. "You knew this?" Then, with rising indignation, "Why did you not tell me?"

Mrs. Dove-Lyon shrugged. "I guessed when I saw your daughter, Della. Which was only two weeks ago, by the way. But look at her. If not for her eyes, which she has from Kingsley, she could be you, twenty or more years ago."

"Roy and I knew you reminded me of someone," Ban added to Nora, "but we couldn't call to mind whom."

Roy addressed Lady Karzel, his voice hard. "I trust you intend to call off your persecution, madam."

She nodded. All the words seemed to have drained out of her. Mrs. Dove-Lyon cast her a compassionate look. "Della, you need time to absorb this. Come. One of my people will take you somewhere you can lie down until you feel able to leave."

She opened the door and spoke to someone in the hall, and they waited until a woman, neatly dressed in a modestly cut gown, came in and took Lady Karzel gently by the arm. "This way, my lady. We shall soon have you feeling better."

"So, there you have it," said Mrs. Dove-Lyon to those who remained. "I must return to my guests. Tell Titan your plans, and he will conduct you back to the party or to your carriage, as you wish."

Before they could chorus their thanks, she sailed out through the door.

Epilogue

"With the evil enchantress defeated forever," Ban read to the assembled children, "the bear transformed into a beautiful princess. And the mouse transformed into a beautiful princess. Fairyland faded away and all was well with the world. Then Prince White married Princess Bear while Prince Red married Princess Mouse."

"But what happened to the evil enchantress?" asked Ban's seven-year-old daughter.

In the four years since he had published the story that he'd written to amuse his daughter Elizabeth, and Roy's daughter Bella, Ban had never been asked that question. He turned to look at Grandmama Della, who was sitting quietly in the corner of the nursery cuddling Roy's baby, little Cordelia. Ban's Matthew, who was the same age, was nearby, asleep in his cradle.

"The Lion bit off her head," declared Thomas, Ban's five-year-old son, from his throne on his mother's knee.

The elderly lady shook her head, and perhaps she thought he was asking her to answer the question, for she said, "The evil enchantress was mostly composed of hatred and spite, and those were washed away and dissolved into nothing by the courage and kindness of the princesses and princes, and the good magic of the Lion. But one tiny part of the enchantress's heart remained, for it was composed of love, and love does not dissolve or wash away."

She dropped a gentle kiss on the head of the sleeping baby. "Princess Mouse, who had kindness enough and love enough for a dozen princesses blew on that tiny piece of heart, and it flared into light like the smallest of fires, but the other princesses and the princes helped, and the fire grew, until the enchantress had a real heart, and it was no longer wicked, and she was no longer an enchantress."

Tears stood in Ursula's eyes and Lenora's as they put an arm around one another where they sat side by side, their five-year-old sons on their knees. Twins for Lenora and Roy, and Thomas for Ursula and Ban.

The transformation had started, at least for Ban and his family, the day Mrs. Dove-Lyon had sent for them, and they found Lady Karzel in her company, both of them with brand new copies of the child's tale that Ban had written, and Lenora had illustrated. When they asked for autographs, Ban began to believe that Lady Karzel was truly sorry for her sins against her daughter and her daughter's half-sister, and Lenora's soft heart had done the rest.

Grandmother Della seemed to have finished, so Ban took his cue to give the story its new ending and send all of these children off to bed. "The woman who had once been an enchantress came to live with the princes and their princesses, and all of their children, and became their grandmother and a much-loved part of their family, and they all lived happily ever after."

The End

Additional Dragonblade books by Author Jude Knight

A Twist Upon a Regency Tale, The Series
Lady Beast's Bridegroom (Book 1)
One Perfect Dance (Book 2)
Snowy and the Seven Doves (Book 3)

The Lyon's Den Series
The Talons of a Lyon

About Jude Knight

Have you ever wanted something so much you were afraid to even try? That was Jude ten years ago.

For as long as she can remember, she's wanted to be a novelist. She even started dozens of stories, over the years.

But life kept getting in the way. A seriously ill child who required years of therapy; a rising mortgage that led to a full-time job; six children, her own chronic illness... the writing took a back seat.

As the years passed, the fear grew. If she didn't put her stories out there in the market, she wouldn't risk making a fool of herself. She could keep the dream alive if she never put it to the test.

Then her mother died. That great lady had waited her whole life to read a novel of Jude's, and now it would never happen.

So Jude faced her fear and changed it—told everyone she knew she was writing a novel. Now she'd make a fool of herself for certain if she didn't finish.

Her first book came out to excellent reviews in December 2014, and the rest is history. Many books, lots of positive reviews, and a few awards later, she feels foolish for not starting earlier.

Jude write historical fiction with a large helping of romance, a splash of Regency, and a twist of suspense. She then tries to figure out how to slot the story into a genre category. She's mad keen on history, enjoys what happens to people in the crucible of a passionate relationship, and loves to use a good mystery and some real danger as mechanisms to torture her characters.

Dip your toe into her world with one of her lunch-time reads collections or a novella, or dive into a novel. And let her know what you think.

Website and blog:
judeknightauthor.com

Subscribe to newsletter:
judeknightauthor.com/newsletter

Bookshop:
judeknight.selz.com

Facebook:
facebook.com/JudeKnightAuthor

Twitter:
twitter.com/JudeKnightBooks

Pinterest:
nz.pinterest.com/jknight1033

Bookbub:
bookbub.com/profile/jude-knight

Books + Main Bites:
bookandmainbites.com/JudeKnightAuthor

Amazon author page:
amazon.com/Jude-Knight/e/B00RG3SG7I

Goodreads:
goodreads.com/author/show/8603586.Jude_Knight

LinkedIn:
linkedin.com/in/jude-knight-465557166

Mistaken for a Lyon

by Rachel Ann Smith

CHAPTER ONE

THE CANDLE ON the corner of Charlotte Grandstone's desk flickered as she raised the coveted invitation to the infamous Lyon's Den masquerade ball to eye level and studied the embossed image—the letters BDL along with a holly sprig. A lump formed in her throat as she set the parchment with golden flecks interwoven back down upon the wood surface. The shimmering flickers of yellow reminded her of the man whose eyes beheld the same allure. The man who evoked both ire and longing within her every time they met, and yet Elijah Etwell, the Earl of Camden, was also her nemesis. Every mission she had vied for had been assigned by the Head of the Foreign Office to Camden instead. The gentleman may be four years her senior, however, her skills as an agent were at the very least equivalent—if not superior—to his. Secretly collecting information on the activities of others and obtaining plans of the country's enemies was in her blood. Her parents had been devoted to protecting both the king and England so much that they had lost their lives at sea. Her brother was a high-ranking senior agent who had completed several missions, and yet the Head of the Foreign Office continued to deny Charlotte permission to travel abroad to conduct a mission of her own. Desperate to emerge from her brother's shadow, she was determined to be the first female field agent to officially lead her own team. Over the years she'd not once had one of her peers blatantly refuse to work alongside her, yet there had been more than one instance where she'd encountered mild resistance from some of her counterparts, which had only spurred her to work harder—to prove her skill and worth to the agency.

She stood, pushed back her chair, and bent to blow out the candle. With her cheeks filled with a puff of air, she paused and spied a shooting star streaking through the night sky. Charlotte straightened to make a wish, the same wish she had made on her birthday—to be assigned to a solo mission across the channel.

Charlotte picked up the golden ticket to this Season's Mystère Masque ball and held it up to the window. Moonlight shone through, illuminating the parchment, and a surge of excitement rolled through her. This was her opportunity to prove to the Head of the Foreign Office how valuable she was to the agency. She fully intended to expose the traitorous agent amongst them, who was colluding with the French. Obtaining the rare invitation was Charlotte's first obstacle, but thankfully her fellow members of the Wicked Ladies Salon had assisted her in obtaining a private meeting with Lady Amelia, the daughter of the Duke of Essex.

Her lips curved into a smile as she recalled Lady Amelia's delight in partaking in Charlotte's scheme to trade places for an evening. It was known by one and all that Lady Amelia had a propensity for causing scandal, which meant she was invited to all the wickedly exciting social engagements, and of course had no reservations in handing over her invitation to Charlotte. She slipped the golden ticket back into the nondescript envelope it came in and tucked it into her desk drawer before blowing out the candle. It was time for her to retire for the day.

There were a number of tasks remaining to be completed tomorrow to ensure her success. She was prepared and ready to oust the traitor that had placed both her brother, Thomas Grandstone, the Duke of Avondale, and her sister-in-law, Isadora's life in jeopardy. The Head of the Foreign Office may have believed her judgment was far too clouded to objectively execute the mission, but she knew there was no other agent more invested in ensuring the double agent was brought to justice.

Quietly, she padded over to her bed and pulled back the bed covers, but froze at the unusual, light rap of knuckles upon her door. She reached for the rather large and heavy candlestick she kept by her bedside as the door swung open.

An unmistakable chuckle that belonged to the one and only cad, Camden, preceded the code word, "Gooseberry."

Gah! Why was her archenemy at her door in the middle of the night?

Charlotte slid down to her knees and hid behind her bed. She peered over the top of her mattress. Camden closed the door to her chambers, then tiptoed to the center of the room. "Charlotte, please reveal yourself."

In only her night shift, Charlotte grabbed the corner of the bed cover and raised it to her chest, then slowly rose to her feet. "Lord Camden, pray explain what it is you wish to discuss that could not wait 'til morn."

The golden shards in the man's eyes brightened, reminding her of that time the lion at the Royal Menagerie had stared back at her, unyielding and fearless. Like then, Charlotte remained unearthly still, waiting for a response, daring not to move out of fear she might provoke a reaction that she might not recover from.

Camden took two steps closer and placed his hands behind his back before sinking into a deep bow. "Please accept my apologies if I scared you. That was not my intention."

"Scared! I'm not scared of you." The fib rolled off her tongue, but her overzealous tone undermined her words, even to her own ears. She gripped the bed covers even tighter to her.

The action drew the attention of Camden, who turned around, placing his back toward her. "I've come to discuss your plans for tomorrow eve."

"I haven't an inkling as to what you are referring." Charlotte tugged on the bed cover in order to take a step closer to her midnight visitor, but failed to dislodge the material, forcing her to remain where she was. Charlotte's blood began to boil at her inability to move about, placing her at a disadvantage. She wanted to confront Camden, to show him he did not intimidate her like he did others.

"You were ordered not to involve yourself into my investigation, yet merely an hour ago, I received word you have managed to secure one of the exclusive invitations to Mystère Masque." Camden raked his fingers through his hair and squeezed the back of his neck.

Hmm...the man standing in the middle of her chamber was rattled, unlike the agent who normally treated her with indifference. This was a chance for her to test out where Camden's loyalty fell—to the Head of the Foreign Office, or to her brother and his wife.

She stuck out her chin and replied, "I've not disobeyed any direct orders. The Head of the Foreign Office never said I was precluded from conducting my own inquiries."

"Argh!" Camden turned back around and began to pace about her room. "Why must you be as hardheaded as your brother?"

"I'm nothing like Tom."

"I'd argue that you are exactly like Tom, merely easier on the eyes."

Charlotte eyed Camden suspiciously. The man was known for utilizing flattery as a means to sway his opponent or gain their cooperation. She wasn't going to allow Camden to derail her plans.

She was going to unmask the traitor amongst their department before he could.

Camden probably suspected she had identified the man responsible for the attempted kidnapping of Tom and Isadora. It was the only logical explanation for his unexpected visit, yet when she studied Camden's body language—that radiated both frustration and concern—she sensed there was more to his visit than dealing with his current assignment for the Foreign Office.

Chapter Two

What in the blazes had possessed him to sneak into his best friend's sister's chambers in the middle of the night? Elijah Etwell, the Earl of Camden, stopped pacing and faced the lady who drove him to distraction. Charlotte Grandstone was the reason he had joined the Foreign Office, and why he had volunteered for assignments abroad again and again over the years—all to avoid temptation. Temptation that mounted instantly every time he laid eyes upon her. He clasped his hands behind his back and took a step forward, daring to test his self-restraint. In typical Charlotte fashion she stared directly back at him, her gaze challenging him. He wasn't about to lose to Charlotte, not this time. Especially not since she was the sole reason for his latest faux pas. Challenging Lady Minerva Malberry to a game of chess for her hand had been both an order and a personal quandary. One that had resulted in him having to face the fact that he was indeed in love with Charlotte, and that his loyalty would always remain to one woman: the one daring to stand before him in just her night shift, with no intentions of backing down from him.

"Flattery shall not gain you an advantage." Charlotte's ultra calm tone meant only one thing: she was hiding something from him, something extremely important.

"I was merely stating a fact. You are certainly more pleasing to gaze upon than your brother, who only scowls." His hands fisted behind him as his words rang in his own ears—he was acting like the besotted fool that he was. This was what he'd attempted to avoid all these years, confessing his true feelings for his best friend's sister.

"Tom rarely frowns, except for when he must deal with..." Charlotte stalled as he approached.

Mere inches between them, Elijah loomed over the woman he wished to kiss until her heart raced like his. "Don't stop on my account. Pray, continue."

She poked him once in the chest and glared up at him. "Heed my warning, Camden, nothing good can come of you visiting me like this in the midst of a mission. What is it you wish to accomplish?"

He'd come to warn her not to attend Mystère Masque tomorrow eve. If his sources were right, then the traitor he sought, Lord Blagden, would be in attendance. Blagden, a charming young gentleman of Scottish descent, was a fairly new recruit with three years of service. Although there were rumors that Blagden had indeed provided the Frogs with key information, Elijah had yet to discover evidence that supported such accusations. Based on the little time he'd spent with Blagden, he didn't believe the allegations against the man.

Elijah noted the steel glint in Charlotte's gaze. She was an excellent agent, recognized as one of the best by all at the Foreign Office, but Charlotte was also known for taking risks. Falsely accusing a fellow agent could result in dire consequences, and he suspected Charlotte was acting in haste. He needed Charlotte to hear him out without bias, but the chit remained determined to win the staring contest that he had inadvertently started.

The probability of him persuading her to alter her plans was slim, which meant he was left with only one option: to seek her cooperation. A deep sigh escaped him. "I wish to collaborate with you."

"Collaborate?" Charlotte cocked her head to the side and narrowed her gaze.

"Yes, like partnership." His answer garnered a dark scowl from Charlotte so similar to that of her brother's that he hastily added, "I'm asking if you would be interested in working together, to obtain the physical evidence needed to prove who the real traitor is amongst our peers."

Charlotte crossed her arms over her chest, securing the bed covers in place in front of her. "How surprising."

Silence descended upon them and the minx merely waited as he contemplated her response.

What was surprising—that he suggested they work together, or that he'd yet to obtain evidence? "Should I presume that you are in agreement, that we might work in harmony tomorrow eve?"

"You should." The devilish smirk Charlotte donned had him wishing he'd chosen his words more carefully.

With naught but hedonistic thoughts left, he bowed, and said, "Then I shall take my leave." Hand poised on the doorknob, he turned around and asked, "What color gown will you be donning for the ball?"

"I've yet to decide upon a gown; however, my domino shall be of ivory silk and gold with pearls." Her mischievous smile sent a shiver down Elijah's back.

He was no dunderhead. He understood Charlotte like no other, and she was quite blatantly telling him she had no intentions of working as a team. Her plans were privy to her and her alone, but she'd not disobey an order and interfere in his scheme. He needed to return to his lodgings and gain a good night's rest, for tomorrow he'd have to hunt down the evidence he sought before Charlotte got herself embroiled in the matter. It wouldn't be the first time he'd ensured her safety in secret, and he was certain it wouldn't be the last.

Chapter Three

Hands clasped tightly in her lap, Charlotte smiled at the gentlemen callers that filled the Avondale parlor. Not one of them had the sense to know when they had overstayed their welcome, and none of them captured Charlotte's attention or made her heart flutter like Camden. With her brother abroad, Aunt Cornelia once again was acting as chaperone. Charlotte sent a pleading gaze over at her aunt to act, however the dear woman didn't possess a mean bone in her body, which meant the chances of her aunt declaring visiting hours over and sending the men on their merry way were extremely slim.

Anxious to begin her preparation for the masquerade ball, Charlotte counted down the minutes until she couldn't remain seated any longer. Cheeks aching from smiling all morning, she was ready to be rid of the men littered about the room who were happily chatting amongst themselves.

Charlotte stood and said, "I must bid you all a good day." Ignoring the rules of etiquette, she marched out of the room and up to her chambers. It wasn't good form to leave poor Aunt Cornelia to deal with the men who supposedly were attempting to gain

Charlotte's interest, but there was naught she could do since her heart remained beholden to Camden.

She had been but twelve when she realized that her feelings for her brother's best friend were more than sibling affection. Drawn to Camden's charming laissez-faire demeanor, which was in stark contrast to her brother's no-nonsense attitude, she began to fantasize of a future with the man, until she discovered that Camden was the one responsible for her extended training, and had stolen mission after solo mission from her. Camden knew of her desire to become a high-ranking agent within the Foreign Office as her parents had been, yet he'd prevented her from achieving her goal. Even if she were in love with the man, she wasn't about to forgive him for all the years he'd delayed her progress.

She strode directly over to her desk and retrieved the golden ticket from the drawer. Tonight's ball was the opportunity she'd been waiting for to prove to the Head of the Foreign Office she was ready to embark on a solo mission abroad. Cornering and apprehending the traitorous agent would be no easy feat for Charlotte, especially since Mr. Mitchell was twice her size, and the man was a seasoned agent with more than a decade's worth of experience.

Seated at her desk for the hundredth time that day, she mentally reviewed her plans for the evening that required both perfect timing, and a healthy dose of fortune in order for her to accomplish her mission. Charlotte had set her plans into motion months ago, starting with the rumor that Lord Blagden was suspected to be the traitor. She of course did so with Lord Blagden's cooperation, who was just as eager to catch the true culprit as she. Her scheme hinged upon Mr. Mitchell's fondness for taking credit for actions he in fact hadn't taken, and his tendency to be blinded by rage when others were recognized for results Mr. Mitchell believed he was responsible for. The challenge Charlotte faced was to determine how best to goad Mr. Mitchell into admitting he was in fact the traitor. Lord

Blagden had pledged to appear at the masquerade ball and perform his part in distracting Camden, except Charlotte feared Camden would immediately become suspicious of the green agent's movements.

Charlotte returned her focus back to the invitation still in her hand. Guests were selected exclusively by Mrs. Dove-Lyon to join her in celebrating the date of her birth. No one knew for certain how many years the old dame had been on this earth. The only thing Charlotte knew for certain was that the woman defied the aging process, appearing younger rather than older each year. She mentally pictured the venue for the ball. The three-story building known to all as the Lyon's Den was situated in Whitehall, and housed stores on the first level, but tonight's activities would all take place on the second floor, where she would not only have to monitor the comings and goings on the main gambling arena, but also the other nine rooms that would be filled with masked revelers. Her goal: to steer and entrap Mr. Mitchell in Mrs. Dove-Lyon's private room, which her host had graciously agreed to lend her for the evening.

She jumped to her feet at a scratch at her door. "Enter."

"Charlotte dear, a messenger delivered this." Aunt Cornelia handed her a missive. Rather than turning and leaving, her aunt eyed Charlotte's desk and asked, "Penning a letter to your brother?"

With a practiced flick of the wrist, she unfurled the parchment and brought it up to eye level to read the one-word message *Sparrow*, penned in a bold, masculine script.

Recognizing Lord Blagden's penmanship, Charlotte rolled her eyes and released a sigh at the unnecessary confirmation of the man's attendance and preparedness. Had she not trained him well enough to weigh the advantages and disadvantages of sending such correspondence? The dangers of a message being intercepted and interpreted incorrectly amidst their investigation were great, and had dire consequences—they could be found guilty of treason and hanged.

She crumpled the note in her fist and met her aunt's gaze directly. "I think tonight is the night we have been waiting for all Season, Aunt Cornelia."

Eyes wide with recognition and understanding, her aunt raced to the door and muttered, "I shall go fetch the gown."

Alone once again in her chambers, Charlotte sank down upon the edge of her bed. For the first time since her brother left for his wedding trip, she wished Tom was available for consultation. Tonight would be the culmination of all her years of training. Failure was not an option—she had to succeed in obtaining a confession from Mr. Mitchell. Surprisingly, Camden with his golden bespeckled eyes came to mind. She flopped backward and stared up at the canopy of her bed. Aside from Tom, Camden too was renowned within the Foreign Office for his skill in identifying weaknesses within stratagems. Camden's words from his late-night visit came back to haunt her—a collaboration with the man was out of the question. He would be a distraction, not an ally, sweeping her off her feet to waltz about the dance floor and leaving her breathless. She flung an arm over her eyes to stop the fantasies distracting her from her preparations. Moments later she released a sigh of frustration and forced herself to sit back up. If she succeeded in avoiding Camden at Mrs. Dove-Lyon's masquerade ball in the gown she planned to don, she might be able to complete the mission without issue. However, if the man interfered, not only would her activities for the Foreign Office be placed in jeopardy, but also all her fantasies that she had secretly held dear to her heart. For in all her dreams, Camden fell madly in love with her upon sight in the gown she had fashioned and stored in her closet for the past three years. It would be a bruising crush to her confidence if Camden were to see her in the gown and proceed to ignore her like he did at every other ball they had attended in the past. She planted her feet on the floor and stood. The gown was specifically designed to tempt a man—no not any man, specifically Camden—but if she were to wear it in order to obtain Mr. Mitchell's confession and succeed, it would be worth the risk. The risk of never seeing the golden flecks in Camden's eyes twinkle like stars.

Chapter Four

WHERE WAS THE damn woman? Elijah scanned the gaming hall once again, hands balled into fists at his side. A good foot taller than most, he rarely had an issue locating Charlotte in a crowd. He'd been certain that he would be able to identify her immediately even if she were to don a domino, yet an hour after his arrival, he remained clueless as to her whereabouts.

Elijah turned to face Blagden, who nervously stood next to him. "What is the matter with you this eve?" Elijah pointedly lowered his gaze to the man's hands. Blagden had his fingers interlaced, and his thumbs tapped anxiously.

Blagden instantly shifted slightly away from Elijah and crossed his arms over his chest. "You would be nervous too, if your peers glared at you with accusing eyes."

From a young age, Elijah had garnered unwanted attention from those around him. He remembered how his palms would become sweaty, his stomach ached, and the burning feeling in his throat when he realized all eyes were trained on him. Uncomfortable and self-conscious, he would retreat and hide in his rooms. It was

Charlotte, who had snuck into Eaton during their first year to visit Tom, that had taught him how to ignore the looks from both gentlemen and women alike. He repeated the advice she had given him many years ago. "They know nothing of you or your character. Simply ignore them." Elijah noted Blagden's dubious frown and added, "Without evidence, it's highly unlikely you shall hang."

Blagden countered, "So you say, but your tone lacks conviction."

Offended by the young pup's lack of confidence in him, Elijah straightened, and decided to exert his authority as the most senior ranking agent present. "Go find Lady C and have her report to me posthaste."

Rather than rushing to do Elijah's bidding, Blagden continued to mill about, feigning troubles maneuvering through the crowd. The young agent's behavior was highly unusual, as if Blagden was intentionally not letting Elijah out of sight for some reason.

To test his theory, Elijah bent at the knees and blended in with the crowd when Blagden's attention was momentarily caught by a young lady dressed in a glimmering sapphire blue gown and silk turquoise domino. For a moment, Elijah questioned whether or not the woman who had waylaid Blagden was Charlotte, but upon second glance, the lady was too tall. Blagden suddenly rolled to his toes and systematically searched the room. Elijah remained low to avoid detection and to evaluate Blagden's next move. The boy's eyes skimmed over the crowd once more, and Elijah recognized the panic in the man's stance as Blagden twisted about and tried again to locate his target. Except who was his target, Elijah or Charlotte?

Elijah waited to see what the young agent would do next. Blagden surprised Elijah by retracing his steps, which meant only one thing: Blagden was not attempting to locate Charlotte as Elijah had ordered.

Beyond curious, Elijah weaved his way through the crowd,

intentionally capturing Blagden's attention while leading the man on a merry chase toward the gentleman's smoking room, where he fully intended to interrogate the agent and discover his purpose. Was Blagden really a double agent?

As Elijah made his way, he avoided the sultry glances of more than a few wealthy ladies on the hunt for a husband. Mrs. Dove-Lyon's reputation for matchmaking was impressive, but his heart already belonged to one elusive, highly captivating, extraordinarily intelligent woman—Charlotte Grandstone.

With Blagden close behind him, Elijah made a final push toward the double doors that marked his destination. A glint of gold and ivory silk from the corner of his eye caught Elijah's attention. Before he had even spun around, he knew it was Charlotte, except the lady entering Mrs. Dove-Lyon's private parlor looked nothing like his best friend's little sister. The ivory gown hugged the woman's hourglass figure to perfection, leaving nothing to the imagination. Heat rolled through him, settling in his loins. How in the devil had Charlotte's aunt allowed her to leave home in that gown?

Long, purposeful strides had him arrive in time to jam his hand into the small space between the door casing and the solid wood door. With a little pressure, he swung the door open and came face-to-face with a startled Charlotte.

BLAST BLAGDEN FOR failing to distract Camden long enough for her to slip inside. A half second longer and she would have succeeded in her mission. Instead, the man of her fantasies was standing directly in front of her, with his eyes ablaze, highlighting the golden flecks that mesmerized her. She blinked twice. His intense gaze didn't falter; instead, it remained focused and held a meaning she was at a loss to determine. Short of breath and confused, she swallowed hard and waited for her senses to return. She was an expert at reading the man and his thoughts, yet she couldn't decide if it was unadulterated anger or desire that had Camden glaring down at her.

She pressed the back of her hands to her cheeks, which were warm to the touch. Remembering that they were not alone, and that Mr. Mitchell was but a few feet away, she sank into a curtsy and greeted, "A good eve to you, Lord Camden."

Camden took a step forward, eyes still trained on her.

Slightly dazed, she took a step backward, retreating rather than holding her ground as she normally would have. Blast the man! Anger at her cowardly behavior replaced the panic flowing through her veins. The audacity of the man. She wanted to stomp her foot and send him packing, but the unladylike behavior would only garner Mr. Mitchell's suspicion. Instead, she forced her brow to relax and straightened.

Without a backward glance, Camden marched into the room and joined Mr. Mitchell by the fireplace. Both men stood shoulder-to-shoulder with their rigid backs to her, clearly intending not to include her in their discussion.

Ugh. Of course, it would be Camden of all people who would ruin her entire scheme for the evening. She raised her foot, intending to join her fellow agents and interject, however before she could even plant her first step forward, their mumblings ceased and they simultaneously turned to face her. Mr. Mitchell's charming features revealed nothing of his thoughts, while Camden's jaw was clenched tight, and his lips had thinned into a straight line.

Her gaze flickered between the two. "The three of us should not remain here long."

"I couldn't agree more." Camden gritted out, then added, "Mr. Mitchell, my thanks for your report. Let us meet on the morrow to discuss next steps."

Mr. Mitchell nodded, stepped forward, and bent at the waist to whisper in her ear. "My apologies, and best of luck to you, Lady C."

What in the blazes was going on?

The click of the door latch falling into place spurred Charlotte into action. She took a step forward, cocked her head to the right, and said, "Explain."

Once again, she found herself the target of Camden's hard glare. Her heart began to race with alarm. She was in danger. Real danger. All doubts of the cause for the shards of gold in his eyes to flicker were abolished—they were set aflame by desire. Heart melting desire that left her knees buckling. It wasn't but a moment later that she found herself supported by Camden's sinewy arm, wrapped securely around her waist.

Jaw relaxed, Camden finally answered, "Mr. Mitchell has been assisting me in my investigations, much like how Blagden has been aiding you."

"That means we have both failed." The reality of the truth that they had both devised the same tactic to lure the traitor out of hiding sank in. Suddenly weary, she thoughtlessly rested her forehead against Camden's chest. The loud thump of his heart was unmistakably accelerated.

She pressed her hand to the hard muscled wall, and he covered her hand with his and asked, "Shall we agree to stop wasting time and resources, and work together?"

"You can attest Mr. Mitchell is not a traitor?"

Camden released her, took a step back, and placed both hands behind his back. "Yes, much like you can vouch for Blagden."

A shiver of disappointment rolled through her. Without Camden's warmth, her skin pebbled, and the agony of failure shook her to her core. Months of inquiries and research were wasted. Meekly, she peered up at Camden. "I'm prohibited from interfering, remember?"

"You were ordered not to involve yourself in my investigation, but our leader never said I could not invite you to partner with me." Camden extended a finger and placed it under her chin, forcing her to meet his gaze directly. "Let's capture the traitor together."

A tenderness she'd never been privy to before shone in both his gaze and in his tone. "Are you certain you wish for us to combine resources, share stratagems, and be in each other's company for longer than a few minutes?"

"I hate failure as much as you. However, tonight I realized that along with failure comes opportunity."

What nonsense was Camden muttering? She repeated, "Opportunity?"

"Aye. A chance to correct my failings. To atone for my past stupidity. To…"

She rolled up onto her tiptoes and pressed the back of her hand to his forehead, ceasing his reply and dislodging his finger from her chin. Camden was making no sense, and until tonight he had always kept her at a good arm's length away at all times. Warmth seeped through the material of her gloves, but he wasn't fevered.

Charlotte removed her hand from his forehead and planted her hands on her hips. "I don't understand."

He looked to the ceiling and inhaled deeply, then held his breath for the count of three, and as he slowly expelled the air in his lungs he said, "I'm trying to tell you I'm no longer willing to stay away from you. I think I'm in love with you—have been for years."

She gasped and took four steps back. "You're confused. It's the dress that has your mind muddled."

His eyes raked over her from head to toe, then back up to meet her gaze. Brows knitted, he shrugged out of his jacket and stepped forward to drape the garment over her shoulders. "Charlotte Grandstone, I can assure you, I am of sound body and mind, and I promise you shall not regret agreeing to be my partner."

Stunned beyond words, Charlotte remained rooted to the spot as he leaned down and pressed his lips to hers. Her first kiss. She pinched her wrist through the material of her gloves to ensure she wasn't dreaming. Camden's hand stroked the back of her neck, and she raised both of her hands and planted them on his chest. Her fingers curled, to grip the material of his waistcoat. She should have pushed the brazen man away, yet she found herself holding on to him to steady herself as she raised up onto her toes and kissed Camden back. She might not have succeeded in revealing the identity of the traitor threatening the lives of her fellow foreign office agents, however, she had discovered the truth of Camden's feelings for her. How she would assist Camden in his investigation would have to wait, for all her thoughts scattered as the man's lips made their way across her cheek, down her neck, and along her collar bone. This was why it was forbidden for ladies to be left alone with a gentleman. The wicked, wicked, explosive jolts that shot through her each time he nibbled his way over her skin were captivating and addictive. She didn't want him to stop. She wanted more.

Chapter Five

Elijah inhaled, and his blood pumped harder and faster through his veins. He should cease and resist the temptation to kiss Charlotte once more. If Tom were to find out he'd taken advantage of Charlotte, he'd be facing one of England's best marksmen at dawn. Except Charlotte's soft skin was like a soothing balm on his lips, and he couldn't bear the thought of placing the socially acceptable distance between them.

His will to honor the boundaries of his friendship with Tom disintegrated. Giving into his decade-long fantasies, he placed a string of kisses along her jawline and whispered, "Tell me to stop."

"S-s-t-t-o..." Charlotte inhaled as he brushed the tip of his tongue along the curve of her ear. When she turned her face to him, their gazes locked, and she ordered, "Don't stop."

Beautiful, molten brown eyes that held no fear stared back at him. Years of desire to wrap her up in his arms and confess his true feelings bubbled to the surface. "Are you certain? For if you do not stop me now, there will be no turning back."

"I shan't regret my decision." Charlotte tugged on his waistcoat and he yielded, pressing his mouth to hers.

Fingers wound tight around her waist, Elijah basked in the delight of a willing Charlotte holding him close. The lady he'd convinced himself unworthy of was kissing him back with an enthusiasm that was beguiling, leaving him without the ability to think. He applied gentle pressure with his tongue, urging her to open for him, and when she did, he did not hesitate to sample her sweet mouth.

Having enjoyed the company of women in the past, Elijah had yet to ever really take part in the intimate act of kissing. Glad he'd refrained, Elijah lifted Charlotte by the waist and strode over to the settee and sank down, settling Charlotte on his lap.

The brazen minx wrapped her arms around his neck. "What are we to do next?"

Next?

He glanced down, and his eyes rested upon the tops of her full bosoms. They were in Mrs. Dove-Lyon's private room. The likelihood of being interrupted if he acted upon his desire to divest her of her gown and take his time to bring her to a climax with his fingers was unlikely... no, that was a lie, the odds were not in his favor. His cock twitched in his breeches, reminding him he should keep his thoughts in check. Charlotte was an innocent. He needed to regain control over both himself and the situation. Elijah cleared his throat, and like a dullard, answered, "I haven't the faintest idea."

Charlotte's brows came together as she frowned, and said, "If Mr. Mitchell isn't the traitor among us, and neither is Lord Blagden, who could it be?"

Here he sat uncomfortable, with his loins on fire, and the blasted woman wanted to discuss other matters. It shouldn't have come as a surprise. Charlotte had always prioritized Foreign Office affairs over everything and everyone, even her only living relative, Tom.

Hands at the ready on her waist to reposition her next to him, he forced a smile and replied, "Based on the intel I've managed to accumulate over the months, it could be one of two candidates, which is why I proposed for us to collaborate in order for us to capture the traitor before harm befalls one of our peers."

When he tightened his hold to shift her, Charlotte surprised him by winding her arms about him tighter and pressing her cheek to his. "Hmm..." The purr of her voice had him holding onto her instead of setting her aside.

Charlotte rested her chin on his shoulder and continued on to say, "Should I assume then that you came this eve with the intent to persuade me to partner with you, not to capture the traitor?"

"I'll admit you had me convinced for a moment that Blagden might in fact be the traitor, but the lack of evidence was a glaring obstacle, and prevented me from seriously pursuing Blagden."

She snapped backward to face him. "And do you have proof to link either of the two individuals you currently have under suspicion?" Sharing information critical to a mission was something he rarely did unless it was with his superiors. However, if he were to marry Charlotte, which was a reasonable assumption after what had transpired between them, he would have to become accustomed to sharing details of his activities with his wife. A warmth spread through him at the thought of having Charlotte for a wife. She possessed an inner strength that put his self-control to shame, and was by far the more intelligent one between the two of them. Charlotte was everything he didn't deserve. He didn't even attempt to mask the pride in his voice as he shared, "I might, with the aid of a master in linguistics or graphology."

"Ahh...then it is fortunate for you that your partner possesses both of those skills."

He chuckled at the cheeky grin Charlotte gave him, right before she leaned in once more and kissed him with a confidence that made him fall even more in love with her.

Chapter Six

ARMS FULLY STRETCHED above her head, Charlotte arched her back and smiled. It was going to be a great day. She was to meet Camden in Hyde Park to discuss the details of his scheme to oust the traitor and complete the mission that had kept him on home soil. On one hand, Charlotte unfurled her fingers and counted—it had been three months since his return from the Continent, the longest he'd spent in England since he'd attended university. She hugged her pillow to her chest and closed her eyes, recalling the amazing evening she had spent in Camden's arms. The warmth and protection she felt in Camden's presence was unlike that of the brotherly security Tom provided her. Having always had a fondness for Camden, yet at the same time having to deal with his prickly nature, Charlotte had pinched the man's arm black and blue to ensure Camden was in fact real and not merely a figment of her imagination.

A scratch at the door had Charlotte sitting upright. "Enter."

Her maid walked in and rushed over to the side of the bed. "My lady, Lord Camden is below awaiting you."

Hell and damnation, had she misjudged how long she had been

abed? "What time is it?"

"Barely a minute past eleven." Her maid raced over to the changing chamber and emerged with a pale blue day dress in one hand, and another in light pink in the other hand. "Which one?"

Charlotte rarely placed any thought into what color or style of gown to don for the day, but today she wanted Camden's golden flecks to glimmer like they had last eve.

Her maid looked at her anxiously, awaiting an answer.

Charlotte noted the slightly lower décolleté on the dress on the right and proceeded to point to it. "I believe I shall wear the blue one today."

She walked over to the porcelain basin and splashed cold water on her face in the hopes of awakening her groggy mind. Charlotte was the first to admit she wasn't a morning person, but the prospect of spending the day with Camden had her feeling rather energetic.

In minutes, her maid had her changed and her hair arranged in a simple high bun with curled wisps falling at her temples. She briefly glanced at her image in the looking glass as she proceeded to exit her room. There was no remarkable change in her appearance, yet she felt like a whole new person on the inside after experiencing Camden's hypnotic kisses.

With a bounce in her step, she descended the stairs and entered the morning room only to find Aunt Cornelia facing Camden with her aunt's arms stubbornly crossed over her chest, and her lips which were normally curved into a sweet smile were thinned into a tight, straight line.

Aunt Cornelia jutted her chin half a hair higher in the air and said, "In Tom's absence, I demand that you declare your intentions and—"

With his palms pressed tightly together in front of him, Camden implored, "My lady, I understand your concern, and I promise you that I fully intend..." Camden's response ceased as she came to stand next to them.

Charlotte pointedly glanced at Camden first, then turned to face her aunt. "Intentions? There is no need for such discussions. Lord Camden and I are simply working together on an assignment."

"Bah!" Aunt Cornelia reached out and placed her hands on Charlotte's shoulders firmly, but with her aunt's intrinsic, caring touch. "You, my girl, have always acted wiser far beyond your youthful years. I shall trust you will proceed with caution."

"Of course, Aunt Cornelia. You can trust me."

"Aye, it's not a matter of whether or not I trust you, it's a matter of whether I can trust the likes of him." Her aunt's gaze slid over to Camden, who straightened to his full height.

The urge to laugh at how her sweet loving aunt had, with a single gaze, brought Camden to heel had Charlotte wrapping her arms about her aunt's waist and stepping forward to embrace the woman who was like a mother to her.

Chin resting upon her aunt's shoulder, Charlotte said, "I promise to proceed with caution."

Aunt Cornelia squeezed her tight, then took a step back and released her. "If you agree to leave the door ajar, I shall grant you the privacy you wish."

Simultaneously, both Camden and Charlotte responded, "Agreed."

With a nod in Camden's direction, Aunt Cornelia regally walked out of the room, but not before positioning the door to her liking and stating, "I shall have the staff bring you both some tea."

DRESSED IN BLUE, his favorite color, Charlotte was as tempting and alluring as she was last night in the figure-hugging ivory silk gown that had changed his entire perspective of his best friend's little sister. Charlotte no longer trailed behind Tom studying his every move; instead, she blazed her own path through crowds, and she'd proven that her skills as an agent—trapping the senior agent Mr. Mitchell—were exemplary.

Elijah's gaze flickered to the door, half expecting Charlotte's aunt to reappear, however when the meddling woman didn't appear, he bridged the space between him and Charlotte. "Did you sleep well?"

Charlotte smiled and then whirled away from him before he could capture her in his arms like he wanted to. She waltzed toward the window and answered, "I did."

That was a relief, for he hadn't slept a wink. Instead, he had laid abed practicing various versions of the conversation he needed to have with Tom upon Charlotte's brother's return, each scenario heightening his level of anxiety, and all resulting in him meeting Tom at dawn in some dewy field.

The swish of material drew his attention back to Charlotte, who stood next to the window with her arms spread wide and the edge of the curtains in each hand. Sun rays filtered into the room and illuminated her form. She looked like an angel.

"Did you bring with you the items you need me to review?" Charlotte turned and walked—no, glided—toward him.

He reached into his jacket to retrieve the parchment that he had managed to intercept upon delivery to a known enemy messenger. It was the only clue Elijah had been able to amass during his investigation that had spanned over several months—much longer than he'd expected. The note pinched tightly between his fingers. He tentatively held it out for Charlotte. "There is little content to analyze, however, hopefully it is enough for you to identify the agent responsible for the disruption of multiple assignments."

She took the note from him and walked back to the crystal-clear glass planes that faced the gardens, and lifted the parchment up to the sunlight to read its contents. Charlotte's elegant profile stole his breath. She was beautiful even with her brows knitted together in concentration. "Do you recognize the handwriting by chance?"

Charlotte didn't acknowledge his question, and turned the parchment over to examine it from the back rather than the front. Damnation, why had he not thought of that? Viewing the handwritten script as a mirror image could sometimes help identify line stroke patterns, unevenness between letters, or word spacing—and a multitude of other idiosyncrasies that would be unique to the individual who penned the note.

Curious, Elijah strode across the room and came to a halt directly behind Charlotte, and looked over her shoulder. Hell and damnation, he indeed had the evidence needed. "I recognize the penmanship, do you?"

"No. Except there is one agent I know of who would encode a note with the word Ozymandias, and that is Lord Norcross."

Charlotte was right, Norcross was often known to quote popular literature. Eyes glittering with awareness, she glanced up at him over her shoulder for a moment before returning her attention back to the parchment in her hand. She turned it over once more to the front, then turned it upside down. "I can't detect any other hidden messages, can you?"

He shook his head. "Norcross was last sighted traveling north to Scotland."

"My brother shared with me that Norcross spent many months investigating some rather unsavory characters while abroad, and is suspected to have succumbed to a number of vices."

He had heard the same. He peered down at Charlotte, who appeared lost in her own thoughts. Elijah seized the opportunity to take a moment to think. Norcross was rumored to have contracted an unseemly disease, which could be the reason behind his altered behavior. Norcross was no new recruit, and until six months ago the Foreign Office had never encountered an agent sharing confidential information with the enemy.

Charlotte turned to face him, brows still knitted into a frown, and folded the note in half before presenting it to him. He smiled as he took the parchment from Charlotte and tucked it safely back into his coat pocket. A bolt of happiness hit him when Charlotte returned his smile and reached for his hand.

Leading him over to the settee, she asked, "Shall we sit and formulate a plan?"

He unbuttoned his coat and settled himself on the plush, velvet covered piece of furniture that had his mind racing with scandalous ideas. Elijah cleared the lump that had formed in his throat. "Would you care to share your ideas first?"

"I say we track down the man and apprehend him."

Her eyes shone with excitement, and there was naught for him to do but to agree. "I shall make the necessary arrangements for us to leave posthaste."

"I can't believe we are in accord without debate." Charlotte shifted to capture his gaze. "You are not one to normally agree with me so hastily."

"I doubt you would agree to remain behind, am I right?" He curved the left corner of his mouth up into a lopsided smile, then continued to add, "And since we already settled upon working together, I see no point in wasting time or my breath hashing out various scenarios, when ultimately I know you will only insist on accompanying me regardless of the consequences." And there were serious consequences for the two of them if others discovered that they were traveling together. Marrying a fellow agent might not be wise, but he'd suppressed his love for Charlotte far too long. Following his heart that thudded hard against his chest, Elijah rose to take his leave and begin the necessary preparations.

He was stalled when Charlotte reached out for his gloved hand and placed it against her cheek. "I'm no ninny. I'm fully prepared to accept any and all consequences of my actions."

Was that Charlotte's way of admitting she was prepared to spend the rest of her life with him? The endless list of reasons why he should not pursue Charlotte raced through his mind, forcing him to free his hand from her touch. Except he failed to take his gaze off Charlotte's upturned face, and the words "I sincerely hope so" tumbled out. Considering in a few short hours they were to embark upon a critical mission which required their focus, it simply wasn't the appropriate time to pour out his deepest desires for the future. Before he could utter more insensible words, Elijah marched out of the morning room, past Charlotte's aunt who was sitting upon a bench in the foyer, and out the front door. He needed to sort through not only his desperate plans to make Charlotte his wife, but also the slew of emotions he'd never dared to allow to surface before, but were causing havoc with his breathing and heart rate.

Chapter Seven

Hasty arrangements meant traveling with the barest of essentials, which Elijah was accustomed to. However, he was worried for his travel companion, who hadn't even so much as sighed nine hours into their journey.

Charlotte turned her sweet face to him and smiled. "If we continue on at this pace, we should be able to intercept Norcross by nightfall."

He had thought the same, but the dark circles forming under Charlotte's eyes had him questioning whether to push on or to resume their chase on the morrow. "Or, if we rest at the next coaching inn and set out early, we should still be able to catch the man before he enters Scotland."

For the first time on the entire journey since they had set out before dawn, Charlotte scowled at him. "If you were traveling alone, would you stop?"

"No," he admitted.

"Then…why would you risk missing the opportunity to apprehend Norcross sooner rather than later?"

His normal tactic of sparring with Charlotte until she became flustered and annoyed with him—in order to trick her into leaving a room or his company to avoid the temptation of hauling the woman into his arms—would fail, as they were trapped within his traveling coach. He crossed his arms over his chest as a means of preventing him from drawing her closer and huffed, "You look exhausted."

"Have I uttered a single complaint?" Charlotte tilted her head slightly and exposed the side of her neck that his lips were tempted to kiss.

He swallowed hard and restrained himself from acting upon his desires. With a shake of the head, he answered, "No."

Charlotte's eyebrows snapped together. "Then have I burdened you or slowed our progress in some manner I'm unaware of?"

Again, he had to answer in the negative. "No." Considering his mounting desires, it would be far safer for Charlotte if they were to continue on. With a sigh, he added, "You are right, we should continue on and seize the opportunity to reach the coaching inn. Norcross will most likely choose to retire in for the eve."

Her facial muscles relaxed once more, and she repositioned herself to rest back against the seat. Eyes closed, she finally exhaled deeply and said, "I wish for us to be completely honest with one another. If we are not, I firmly believe we shall fail to complete the mission successfully. If you need something of me, I respectfully request you to be direct and simply inform me of what it is that needs to be done."

She was speaking to him with the respect of a junior agent addressing a senior, not as a lady in love with the gentlemen she was traveling alone with. Her professional manner evoked admiration for her ability to remain focused on the mission at hand—focus he sorely lacked. Unable to resist, he shifted closer to her and slipped his arm behind her neck, causing her head to rest against his shoulder. "Rest. That is what I need you to do for now."

Exhausted and travel weary, Charlotte complied with Camden's order without argument and relaxed against his warm body. She wanted to prove that she wouldn't be a burden to him and that he could trust and rely on her as a partner. Which shouldn't have been a huge feat; after all, she was seasoned agent, a valuable asset to the Foreign Office. While she had no question as to her abilities to see to it that they caught Norcross, she couldn't help but guard her true feelings for Camden. Years of unrequited interest from Camden had conditioned her to be cautious.

She nestled her check against his warm wool coat, and mumbled, "Please wake me when we are within a mile or so of arriving at the inn."

"As you wish."

The even rise and fall of Camden's chest set Charlotte at ease, however, rather than letting sleep claim her, she took the opportunity to untangle the knot of emotions that had her heart and stomach aching. For years, she'd fantasized about capturing the attention of Camden, and while there were multiple occasions where she hadn't laid eyes on the man for several months at a time, her heart had never been tempted by another. She'd fallen in love with a man who was fearless, who volunteered for every dangerous mission possible. Wasn't it the adventure and danger she sought? Wrapped up safe and protected in Camden's arm, Charlotte questioned what it was that lured her to Camden. Had she subconsciously known he'd provide her with a sense of security that she'd not experienced before, nor realized how desperately she needed?

Camden's steady heartbeat was calming. Over the years she had both loved and hated the man next to her, both with a passion she could not deny. Camden evoked feelings within her that were never easy to ignore, and always lingered far longer than she wished. It had been a risk agreeing to accompany Camden, but the overwhelming desire to never leave the man's side had Charlotte wrapping her arm about his waist and pressing her body closer to his. She had sealed her fate when she agreed to partner with Camden, and she wasn't about to change her mind now.

The coach pitched to one side, forcing Charlotte to open her eyes and tighten her hold about Camden's waist.

The coach driver yelled, "Whoa!" and the coach shuddered to a stop.

Camden leaned to the side to peer out of the window. "Bloody hell." He turned back to face Charlotte. "There is another vehicle blocking the road. I'll go to investigate, but first I want you to promise me you will stay put."

With a nod, she said, "I promise."

Camden jumped out of the coach and marched out of sight. She was about to stick her head out the window when a large hand covered her mouth and nose with a handkerchief that was slightly sweetly scented. Unable to scream for help, she grasped her wrist, cocked her elbow and prepared to dislodge her attacker with an elbow to the ribs. Before she could make contact, a heaviness descended upon her. Unable to move, darkness claimed her.

Chapter Eight

Stripped down to his lawn shirt, Elijah rolled his sleeves up to his elbows. With the last streaks of daylight about to disappear, they would be forced to travel in the dark for miles—slowing their progress if he and his men could not remove the abandoned coach blocking the road. After scouting the area, it appeared the traveling party had continued on by horseback, leaving the vehicle with a broken wheel in the middle of the road. Fists balled at his side from the thoughtless and dangerous act of leaving the disabled coach without shifting it to the side of the road, Elijah stepped up to join his men. It wasn't the first time he and his team had worked to move an obstacle from their path. Elijah rarely had to issue detailed orders anymore to his team, whom he'd been closely working alongside with for near on two years.

He planted his hands against the worn, lacquered, black surface and called out, "On the count of three. One. Two. Three."

The coach barely shifted, and they encountered far more resistance than Elijah had expected. Brows furrowed, he took a step back, and a cold chill ran down his back. He turned around, half expecting to see Charlotte marching toward him, but there was no sign of the woman who never listened to his instructions. He broke into a run and rushed back to his travel coach. Charlotte would have had her head poking out of the window at the very least. Alarm bells rang in his head, and he forced his legs to move faster. With each footstep closer to his target his heart began to thud harder against his ribs. He'd failed his best friend and placed Charlotte in danger. He wanted his intuition to be wrong, and prayed he would reach the coach and the woman he loved would be patiently waiting for him with a smile. The odds were not in his favor.

He needed her. ...He needed Charlotte safe, and in his arms once more.

Lungs burning, he lunged forward and ripped the door open.

The coach was empty.

He fell to his knees. Charlotte was gone.

Both his fists slammed against the coach—damn, damn, damn!

The thunder of footsteps came to a halt behind him. Elijah rose to his feet and turned to face his men. Elijah scanned each man's features and stance carefully, searching for a sign that would reveal which of them had betrayed him. Except all the men standing before him were as shocked and angered as he was.

His driver stepped up and entered the coach, then exited through the other side. "Guvnor, come quick."

Elijah rounded the coach. "What is it?"

The driver pointed to the ground where a white handkerchief lay. "It must be laced with a substance to subdue Lady C. There are no other indications of resistance, and Lady C is not one to go willingly, nor is she careless enough not to leave any clues for us."

"Search the area." Elijah knelt down, leaned forward closer to the discarded material, and sniffed. His driver had been correct—the handkerchief reeked of chloroform. The potent chemical wasn't a substance easily obtained by most; however, it was more than accessible for an agent.

Elijah kneaded the back of his neck. How in the hell had Norcross been alerted?

Two distinct sets of footprints caught Elijah's attention. He followed the tracks around the coach and back to the road, but then the tracks disappeared, marred by his own and that of the others. Norcross was no novice agent, and had anticipated Elijah's rash reaction. The devil had used one of the oldest masking techniques known to agents to his advantage, but Elijah was also an experienced agent. Ignoring the rage mounting within, Elijah leaned back against the coach and inhaled deeply. If he were Norcross, he wouldn't have risked employing another to carry out the kidnapping of Charlotte. Knowing time was limited, combined with carrying the dead weight of a woman, the traitor couldn't have gone far. He narrowed his gaze and scanned the area, looking for a hideaway. There was a thick patch of woods slightly to the right that could be a possibility, but there were no signs of the grass being trampled in that direction.

His driver approached and said, "We found two sets of tracks, my lord."

Elijah followed his driver back to the spot where the men had found the deep boot impressions: one set leading to the left, and the other to the right. "Norcross was prepared, he brought a decoy along." Flanked by his driver and a footman, Elijah paced out five feet and then stopped. "The bastard has Lady C, yet neither of these tracks do not appear deep enough."

His companions knelt, studied the tracks closely, and nodded.

"Do you suspect these are the boot prints of decoys?" the footman asked.

Elijah wasn't certain. His fear for Charlotte's safety and guilt at having not protected her were playing havoc with his normally straightforward reasoning. "Possibly." He looked back over his shoulder, his gaze drawn back to the wooded area he'd spied earlier.

There were no obvious signs that Norcross had headed toward the woods, yet Elijah couldn't shake off the feeling that was where the double-crossing agent was hiding.

Abducting a fellow agent was a daring feat, even for Norcross. There was no longer any doubt in Elijah's mind that Norcross was the traitor he'd been ordered to track down and apprehend at all costs. Dusk was quickly setting upon them, and he needed to make a decision. Not leaving anything to chance, he sent his driver to follow one set of tracks and his footman to follow the other, while he pursued his hunch.

As he approached the edge of the woods, a peculiar tension settled in the center of his chest. He had to remind himself that if Charlotte were to regain consciousness, she was more than capable of defending herself. However, if she remained debilitated, she was entirely at Norcross's mercy. He needed to locate Charlotte, and quickly. Elijah lengthened his stride while taking care to tread as silently as possible. With the sun setting, the dense woods were devoid of light. Elijah took a moment to allow his eyes to adjust before forging forward. He should devise a plan, or at the very least stop to analyze his surroundings, but against all logic and his training, Elijah placed his faith in the unexplainable, intangible pull that drew him deeper into the forest.

HANDS BOUND BEHIND her back, Charlotte kept her eyes closed as her senses slowly returned. Blast. Blast. Blast. Being taken hostage meant she had let her guard down. She had failed. Every Foreign Office agent was well aware that while on a mission one should never allow distractions, and yet the lure of Camden's arms had led her focus to be diverted. Inhaling slowly so as not to give away the fact that she had regained consciousness, Charlotte struggled to suppress the gagging sensation that stuck her as the putrid scent in the air made her stomach riot. Where had Norcross taken her?

The undeniable mix of blood and decaying meat made it challenging for her to remain unmoving.

"While you are an excellent performer, my lady, you may cease with the act." Norcross's normally smooth, elegant voice was laced with undeniable sarcasm.

Her eyes fluttered open, adjusting to the dim light. The sole candle that flickered in the corner was barely bright enough to cast Norcross's shadow over her. With his back turned to her, Charlotte tugged at her bindings that were tight and low over her wrist, as they should be. However, Norcross had made the mistake of leaving her feet unbound, and she was free to breathe through her mouth. "What do you gain by kidnapping me?"

"Proof that female agents are a detriment and a hindrance to the agency." Norcross's foolish reply had Charlotte inhaling sharply, causing her to gasp despite the fact that Charlotte was fully aware that Norcross wasn't the only male agent who held the chauvinistic belief. Shock rocked through her at the man's logic.

Norcross's meaty hands were fisted at his side, and his breathing was erratic. She continued to study him closely. Agents were trained to remain calm and in control at all times, but Norcross was exhibiting signs of desperation, which was favorable for Charlotte. Along with desperation came mistakes. She would simply bide her time and gather as much information from her foe as she could until an opportunity to escape arose. If she remained nonthreatening, nonconfrontational, and adopted a meek, submissive demeanor that met Norcross's expectations, she might garner herself enough time to develop a well-thought-out escape; the only uncertain variable was Camden's arrival. The muscles in her shoulders tensed, slowing the blood flow to her hands. She was certain Camden would find her—he was the agency's most skilled tracker—but when he would arrive was the question. Her greatest fear of placing the man she cared for most in danger was no longer a possibility, but a reality. Heart racing, she counted to fifty to calm her nerves and regain control over her mind. Disarming Norcross was her first task.

Hands still fisted but now planted at his waist, Norcross began to pace the length of the room along the far wall and mutter under his breath.

Charlotte was unable to decipher all of the man's rantings that were not all uttered in English, which was not surprising since all agents sent abroad were expected to be fluent in at least French and German. When Norcross began ranting in Italian and Russian, two of the lesser-known languages amongst her fellow peers, Charlotte was grateful her brother had insisted she be tutored in as many languages as possible until she was permitted to cross the channel. As a result, she was able to translate the man's ramblings—*One night. I shall endure one night and set out at first light.*

Egad, Norcross planned to leave her. Brows furrowed, she attempted to decipher the logic in her captor's plan. There was none. Patiently, she studied Norcross, who had spent the majority of his service abroad. The longer she was able to study the man's rantings and movements, the more certain she became that the man was plagued by moments of confusion, which caused him to behave peculiarly. Intermittently, Norcross would appear to forget her presence, and spoke as if he were conversing with another. Tendrils of fear rolled down Charlotte's spine, for a foe who acted without clear reasoning was the most dangerous. She needed to find a way to loosen her bindings and escape, however, the room was devoid of furnishings. The candlelight was quickly dwindling. Fear of being alone in the dark with Norcross had her tugging and twisting the ropes at her wrist, but to no avail.

Norcross must have heard the rustling of her gown, for the man turned to face her. "It's been hours and Camden has yet to appear. It would seem that I have indeed outsmarted the Foreign Office's master tracker."

If she placated the man, it might gain her more information on her whereabouts. "It seems as if you have managed to evade Camden. A feat many on the Continent have attempted and failed."

"Exactly. The Head of the Foreign Office should have chosen another more worthy to try and capture me." Norcross turned and stalked to the window.

Her kidnapper was a fool, for there was no one better than Camden at tracking down his enemies. With no way to escape from her bindings, and with Norcross showing no signs of retiring any time soon, she leaned her head back against the wood wall and rested. She needed to conserve her energy for when Camden found her. There wasn't a doubt he'd come, it was merely a matter of time.

Chapter Nine

With long, measured strides, Elijah retraced his steps back to the coach. His heart raced with fear, warring against his self-control to take his time to formulate a plan to safely rescue Charlotte. The image of Charlotte, wide-eyed yet silent, hastened his pace. He had successfully located the tiny wooden shack and managed to peer through the slats to confirm Charlotte's presence. The woman appeared unharmed and in the same state of shock, as it was apparent that Norcross's ramblings were illogical and muddled, the exact opposite of what you would expect of a seasoned agent.

He shouldn't have left her, but Norcross was one of the Foreign Office's best fighters. The traitor's hand-to-hand combat skills were second to none. Having calculated the odds of him freeing Charlotte on his own without either of them coming to harm, he backed away from the woman he cared about the most with a heavy heart. The most logical scheme was for him to return with his men and overpower Norcross, yet even with the three of them, the probability of no one suffering an injury was slim.

Moonbeams reflected off the lacquered walls of his traveling coach. Thankfully both his driver and footman had returned and were atop, scouting the area. As soon as they spotted him, they scrambled down and stood at the ready.

Elijah ran his hand through his hair, then stopped to address his men. "Lady C's being held captive in a small structure, about a mile in."

Well trained, both men continued to wait in silence for their orders. Elijah wanted to race back and simply overtake the traitor, but that would be foolish. "Since we do not know Norcross's true purpose, we must proceed with caution. His actions to date have been erratic and illogical, contrary to our training, which means predicting his next move will be rather difficult, and in turn makes him extremely dangerous. Our main priority is to ensure Lady C's safety."

His driver nodded and said, "Right. Is it safe to assume you shall be attempting to lure Norcross out into the open?"

"Yes, there's no room for all of us inside." He looked to his driver and added, "I believe Lady C's legs are unbound. While I bait Norcross to confront me, I'll need you to sneak in and escort Lady C to safety." Elijah turned to his footman and said, "Wait for my sign, then join the fray."

Plans formulated, his men fell into line behind him and Elijah set off in a jog. He would need his strength and wits to battle Norcross. No use tiring himself out before even reaching Charlotte.

THE LAST FLICKERS of light from the candle disappeared, and along with it went Charlotte's hope for Camden's assistance. Norcross's behavior continued to volley between agitated pacing combined with incoherent mumblings, and moments of calm, where he sat and methodically planned his next moves. It was during those glimpses of Norcross as a seasoned senior agent that Charlotte's anxiety elevated, for Norcross was renowned within the Foreign Office for his ability to smuggle people in and out of the Continent. Her captor was correct in his assessment that too much time had passed, and it was most likely that Camden had followed Norcross's decoys toward the border. Except she was struggling to believe Camden would have been so easily fooled.

Norcross peered out the window and up at the night sky. "A few more hours and I'll be free. With Camden defeated, there is no one I cannot outmaneuver. I shall roam as I please. No more orders. No more missions. Freedom."

Unable to empathize with Norcross's contentions with the agency, Charlotte gnawed on her lower lip. The Head of the Foreign Office was a fair and generous leader, only ever asking agents to serve by choice.

Charlotte couldn't hold her tongue any longer. "Why wait 'til morn to enjoy your newfound freedom?"

Norcross whirled around and stalked toward her; two more strides and he'd be in front of her. Mid-step, he froze at the crack of a branch outside.

They both looked toward the door.

"Norcross!"

Charlotte released the breath trapped in her chest at Camden's voice. Praise the Saints, he had found her. However, before she could even inhale once more, Norcross's thick hands wrapped about her shoulders and hauled her up to her feet. He half dragged her to the door and flung the flimsy barrier open, and pushed her out into the darkness. Legs numb from being seated for hours, Charlotte stumbled forward. Holding herself in check, she ignored her instinct to run to Camden. Instead, she regained her balance and shifted to her left to place as much distance as possible between her and

Norcross, forcing her captor to make a choice—attempt to recapture her, or defend himself against Camden.

She stalled at the sound of booted footsteps behind her. Had Norcross's accomplices returned?

Moonlight glinted off the surface of Norcross's knife as he retrieved it from his boot, and Charlotte's attention was once again trained on her kidnapper. She dropped to her knees, not to pray, but to increase the difficulty for the man behind her to recapture her.

"Norcross, surrender and no one shall be harmed." Camden stepped out of the thick woods with his own knife in hand.

She needed to flee, but she couldn't drag her gaze away from the two men about to battle before her. A warm hand wrapped around her wrist, and she glanced over her shoulder. Relief washed over her at the sight of Camden's driver busily working at the knot of her bindings.

The coachman glanced up at her briefly. "I'll have you free in a moment."

"Don't mind me, go help disarm Norcross."

"I have my orders, my lady, and they are to see to your escape." The driver continued to work on loosening the rope, and added, "His lordship will have my head if you are not free by the time he is done with Norcross."

Charlotte's lips curved into a slight smile at the man's confidence in Camden. She glanced back at the two men circling each other. Camden twirled his knife twice around his thumb, and his footman stepped out of the shadows.

Norcross's gaze flickered between Camden and the footman. He was clearly weighing his odds of success. "It will take more than the two of you to take me down."

The arrogant claim had Charlotte rising to her feet, and the driver cursed behind her. "My lady, please stay still!"

As soon as the rope fell away from her skin, Charlotte retrieved her own blade from her boot. Treading carefully, she approached the men and stood next to Camden, who was patiently waiting for Norcross to make the first move, which was the best tactic. However, after hours of listening to the man's incomprehensible ramblings about the Foreign Office, his displeasure at having to take orders from someone he believed to be inferior to him in every way, Charlotte's patience had been exhausted. From years of practice, she knew she could launch her dagger at her mark with supreme accuracy within ten feet. The evil gleam in Norcross's eyes had her momentarily stalling to calculate the man's arm span. If her calculations were correct, she could risk getting as close as fifteen feet without placing herself in too much danger. However, at that distance, she wouldn't be able to lodge the dagger deep enough into Norcross's shoulder to disarm him—but she could wound him enough to push the scales in Camden's favor. Not allowing her nerves to get the better of her, she raised her arm, and with a flick of her wrist released her blade.

The silence was broken by Norcross's outcry: "Bloody hell!" Charlotte's dagger lodged into the back of Norcross's hand, and moonlight shimmered off her kidnapper's knife as it fell to the ground.

A whoosh of air brushed against her cheek as Camden rushed forward before Norcross could dislodge her dagger from his injured hand. The coachman drew her back out of the way just as Camden launched himself toward Norcross. Grunts and groans filled the air as the two men fought for the upper hand.

It was challenging to distinguish who was who in the dark. The flicker of silver captured Charlotte's attention. She gasped, and closed her eyes just as one man pinned the other and raised his arm to strike the man on the ground.

Shaken, she wanted to cover her ears with her hands; instead, she hummed loudly to block out the moans and curses of the men.

She gripped the material of her skirts tight in her hands and held in the whimpers of fear. When all was silent, she slowly opened her eyes.

With a split lip and bruised cheek, Camden stood before her and asked, "Are you all right?" He cupped her face and studied her with concern-filled eyes.

She couldn't help but smile up at the handsomely disheveled man who never failed to make her heart race. With a nod, she collapsed into Camden's arms, devoid of energy. She was safe. He was alive, and that was all that mattered.

Epilogue

Laying abed in his country estate with his naked wife, Elijah wound his arms tighter about his wife's waist and shifted until her back was pressed tightly up against his chest. "We set sail in a week."

"Are you nervous?" Charlotte rolled over to face him.

She was as beautiful in the candlelight in the evenings as she was when the first streaks of daylight appeared in morn. He could no longer imagine going to bed alone, or not waking up to her precious features. He placed a kiss upon her nose and answered. "A little."

She leaned back a little to gaze directly into his eyes. "What has you worried?"

"I haven't been abroad in some months, and I fear I may have grown accustomed to the luxury of home." He ran the back of his fingers along her jawline and stopped at her chin to place his thumb over her plump pink bottom lip, then tilted her chin up. He wanted to kiss her and be done discussing their upcoming mission, but Charlotte was not one to be easily swayed. "Lady Amelia will not be easy to locate."

His wife placed a chaste kiss upon his thumb before answering,

"I agree. However, you have me. I, too, am a daughter of a duke, and can provide you with a perspective that will ensure we locate her before she comes to any harm."

"If we knew why the chit fled England in the first place, we would at least have an idea of where to begin our search." Elijah's jaw clenched in frustration at the lack of information he had been provided by the Head of the Foreign Office.

"Oh…I know exactly where Lady Amelia has fled to."

"Where? And how in heaven's name…" He rolled his wife onto her back and loomed over her. "Why have you not already shared this information with me?" His brain stopped functioning as Charlotte wrapped her arms around his neck and brought his mouth down to hers.

Before their lips touched, she said, "Kiss me first, then I shall tell you all I know."

He inched lower until he was a hair's breadth away from her, shook his head, and smiled. "Informants are paid after they deliver details…not before."

A giggle escaped Charlotte before she sighed and said, "I recently discovered—meaning I just received word late this evening—that Lady Amelia booked passage upon the Quarter Moon to Spain."

Before he could even begin to formulate reasons as to why the Duke of Essex's daughter might have ventured to Spain, Charlotte raised her lips to his and kissed him with a passion he would never cease to desire. All thoughts of their upcoming mission were pushed aside as he gazed down at his wife of three months and said, "I love you."

Charlotte pushed at his chest and he toppled over until they had switched positions. "And I love you…dearly." Normally, his need to control every situation would have him rolling her back over, except today Charlotte had him locked solidly between her thighs, and he couldn't budge. His wife leaned forward, placing one hand next to his head. The tips of her nipples pressed against his chest, and with her other hand she trailed a finger along the bridge of his nose. "Will you grant me permission to set the pace this eve if I share with you why Lady Amelia has run away?"

"Hmm." His cock hardened and twitched against her bare bottom. It hadn't been more than an hour since he had last spilled his seed inside of her, and he couldn't wait to do it again. Curious as to what his wife had in mind, Elijah placed his hands behind his head and said, "Share what you know of Lady Amelia's journey later, my love. I vowed to grant you all you wished on our wedding day, and I'm a man of my word."

Charlotte rose up to her knees and scooted back until she was poised over his cock, which stood at attention. With her gaze locked on him, she replied, "And I vowed to bring you joy for the rest of our days." She slipped her right hand between her legs and guided the tip of his manhood over her slit, coating it with the slick beads of pre-cum. "I, too, am a woman of her word."

If he had known relinquishing control over to his wife would result in such heights of desire, he would have done so weeks ago. Gaze focused on the woman who vowed to spend the rest of her days with him, Elijah expelled the breath he'd been holding as Charlotte slowly sank down upon him. Without reservations or doubt, he was eager to face the future with the only woman who knew him better than himself. He couldn't imagine his life without Charlotte, and he was determined to fulfill his promise to love and honor her until his very last breath.

The End

Want to discover if Camden and Charlotte succeed in locating Lady Amelia on the Continent?
Lady Amelia's story – Falling for a Lyon will be available in 2024.

Additional Dragonblade books by Author Rachel Ann Smith

Ladies of Risk Series
An Earl Unmasked (Book 1)
The Duke of Aces (Book 2)
King Takes Queen (Book 3)
A Yuletide Wedding (Novella)

About Rachel Ann Smith

Rachel Ann Smith writes steamy historical romances with a twist. Her debut series, Agents of the Home Office, features female protagonists that defy convention.

When Rachel isn't writing, she loves to read and spend time with the family. She is frequently found with her Kindle by the pool during the summer, on the side-lines of the soccer field in the spring and fall or curled up on the couch during the winter months.

She currently lives in Colorado with her extremely understanding husband and their two very supportive children.

Visit Rachel's website for updates on cover reveals and new releases – www.rachelannsmith.com.

You can also stay up to date with Rachel following her on social media.

Facebook: rachelannsmit11
BookBub: bookbub.com/authors/rachel-ann-smith
Amazon: amazon.com/Rachel-Ann-Smith/e/B07THSRH6B
Twitter: @rachelannsmit11
Instagram: instagram.com/rachelannsmithauthor
Goodreads: goodreads.com/author/show/19301975.Rachel_Ann_Smith

The Lyon's Last Chance

by Aurrora St. James

Chapter One

If one were looking for a wife, a masquerade ball where every woman's face was covered and a gambling den were perhaps not the best places to look, but Owen Granville chanced them anyway. He'd hoped to have a few more years before casting his anchor into the marriage pond, which he'd quite happily avoided until now. However, the death of his father last month had altered nearly every aspect of Owen's life, not the least of which was the need for a wife.

He snagged a champagne flute off the tray of a passing waiter and sipped the sweet wine as he wandered the edge of the main gambling floor. The smell of smoke and heavy spirits mixed with the boisterous laughter of the men and women casting smoldering looks of decadent promise at each other from behind a mask of anonymity. Owen was no stranger to the Lyon's Den and its many vices, of which he'd imbibed more times than he could count. It still came as a surprise to receive a golden invitation to Mrs. Dove-Lyon's *Mystère Masque*. The *ton* shunned the night of gambling and carnal delights while secretly coveting them. Unlike many of his peers, he never gave a whit about the golden *Invocation Mystère*, and as he pushed his way through the edge of the crowd, he wondered if the invite hadn't come because of his untimely change in circumstances. As the new Baron Granville, Owen was now a man of both title and wealth.

The invitation to the *Mystère Masque* came at the perfect moment. He'd heard quite a bit of talk regarding Mrs. Dove-Lyon's matchmaking, often to the unsuspecting gentlemen partaking in her establishment. Whether the gentlemen were willing to make the matches or coerced into them was a subject of debate, but such things didn't signify tonight. Owen intended to seek the woman out to inquire of his own matchmaking. He needed a wife quickly, and any suitable young woman would do. His stomach clenched uncomfortably at the thought, and he set his half-empty glass of champagne on a nearby table.

The delicate face of a dark-haired beauty brushed his mind. Owen frowned and banished her visage. He couldn't have the woman he wanted, and thinking of her only made his chest ache. He'd made a promise to his best friend, George Twisden, about it a decade ago. Then, as now, he meant to keep that promise. Just as he meant to keep the one he'd given his father on the man's deathbed—he'd stop gambling and living recklessly, and he'd marry and have an heir to keep the title from passing to his cousin Richard.

As if conjured by his thoughts, an unmistakable braying laugh broke over the sounds of music and revelry. Owen spotted Richard's unmistakable form amidst a crowd of gentlemen. The man looked remarkably like their grandfather, with his thick brown hair, narrow face, and dark brown eyes, currently concealed by a simple white domino mask. He carried a bit of weight around his middle, but dressed well and had impeccable manners that hid a fierce temper from polite society.

What the bloody devil was he doing here, anyway? Owen couldn't fathom why Richard Granville gained entry to the exclusive party any more than he had. What games did Mrs. Dove-Lyon play here? Because as sure as he stood here wearing a domino mask, he knew the woman must be scheming something. She was too intelligent to do otherwise. Inviting the two of them could be for no other reason.

Owen turned away from his cousin and wandered toward the gardens. He'd yet to see their enigmatic patroness welcoming her guests. Had she retired to her private chambers, or did she too wish for a breath of fresh air away from the stifling press of bodies?

The moment he stepped through the open door into the moonlit gardens, a body bumped into him and he heard a soft, feminine "oof." Owen gently gripped the woman's arms to steady her and looked down—way down—into eyes so familiar that his breath caught in surprise.

The lamplight shone down on luxurious, dark brown hair fashioned in ringlets and tied with golden ribbons that matched the mask covering half of her face, which had a fan of short peacock feathers to one side. He didn't need to see behind it to know the soft curve of her cheek or the dark sweep of lashes over the brightest blue eyes he'd ever seen. As small and delicate as she was, she fit perfectly in his arms, and Owen couldn't help his instinctive reaction to pull her closer. He slid his hand down one arm to encircle her waist and anchor her to him.

Call it destiny, luck, or whatever else came to mind—Owen had come to the masquerade in search of a wife and found the woman of his dreams. God help him, because George would kill him, but right at that moment, he couldn't summon the will to care. Grace Twisden was in his arms again, and if he had any say in the matter, she would stay there.

"Gracie," he whispered, savoring her nickname on his lips. A name he'd forbidden himself from speaking for far too many years. She looked ravishing in her deep blue gown embroidered with green and gold peacock feathers, accentuating the curve of her hips and delightful bosom.

She stiffened in his arms and took a half step back, her eyes wide behind her mask. Then she slapped him.

Chapter Two

When Grace Twisden made the agreement with Mrs. Dove-Lyon to find her a suitable husband, she hadn't considered that one of the prospects would be the last man that she wanted to marry in all of London. The one who'd humiliated her, broken her young heart, and then never spoken to her again. The man she sometimes still dreamed about in the dark of night. Mrs. Dove-Lyon had either excellent luck or a terrible sense of humor, and Grace wasn't sure which she preferred.

She curled her gloved fingers into her palm, ignoring the sting of the slap she'd delivered to Lord Granville, and averted her gaze from his fine form. Grace had taken a turn through the gardens, looking for the two men that Mrs. Dove-Lyon had indicated were her chosen suitors, whom she would know by their unique masks. How Mrs. Dove-Lyon was aware of what masks the men would wear this evening was a mystery that Grace hadn't given much thought to, but as she snuck another glance at the man before her, she wondered.

Owen wore a black silk coat that fit his broad shoulders and strong arms, and matching trousers that fit his muscular legs to perfection. His shirt and cravat were black, as was his waistcoat, which provided the only color on his clothes in the form of embroidered gold leaves, similar to those painted on his white half mask. But it was his blue-gray eyes and a smile that never failed to warm her insides that gave away his identity, along with the husky way he spoke her name.

A shiver slid down her spine, which she blamed entirely on the open door in which they stood, where the heat of the ball mingled with the cold air of an early April night.

Owen rubbed at his jaw where she'd struck him, and chuckled. "I've missed that spirit."

She resisted the urge to scoff at his statement. Owen couldn't miss any part of her because he didn't give a whit about her and never had.

Grace crossed her arms over her waist and glared at the floor. Mrs. Dove-Lyon had generously given her the option of choosing between two suitors. Grace's plan this evening was to find the gentlemen in question and spend time with each, then inform the woman which man she had chosen. From there, they would decide how best to snare the gentleman into marriage. It all seemed terribly sly, but the mysterious club owner assured her that this was the best way to find a husband in a limited time.

She supposed that she could thank Owen for speeding the process along. Grace had no intention of marrying him, therefore she chose the other gentleman. She had yet to locate the second man, but at this moment, that mattered little. She was growing desperate. If she didn't marry soon, her father would find a way to keep her at his side permanently, and she'd never be free. Never have a husband and family of her own. Her father had already ruined two of her matches. At first, she thought it had been accidental, a result of too much drink. But the second incident proved that he'd known what the results of his actions would be and took them regardless. He had no intention of letting her go, now or in the future, and she feared what his deteriorating mind might conjure next.

"What are you doing here, Gracie?" Owen asked. "A woman like you shouldn't be here."

Like her? Stupid and naïve? She raised her chin to look down her nose at him. The effect was ruined because he towered above her. He may be a couple inches shorter than her brother, George, and much wider with his thick muscles, but he was nearly a foot taller than Grace. "Not that it is any of your concern, but I'm here to find a husband."

She saw his eyes narrow behind his mask as he scanned the crowd around them, lingering on the unattended gentlemen. "Why in heaven's name would you resort to finding a husband in a gaming den?"

"Because Father never allowed me to have a coming out Season when I came of age, and George still believes that I should be in a short dress even though I am firmly entrenched on the shelf. If I am to have the husband and family that I want, then it falls to me to make my own match."

Owen stepped closer, his brow furrowed. "You're four years younger than I am. You should have had your Season long ago."

She wasn't at all surprised that he hadn't noticed. George didn't pay her any mind, and Owen hadn't spoken to her since their youth. "Father didn't want men of questionable intent anywhere near me and promised to find me a suitable gentleman. However, he's done nothing to find a suitor, and intentionally drove away the men I courted." Grace bit her lip, wishing she hadn't mentioned that.

Owen muttered a curse. "I'm sorry, Gracie. I—"

She took a step back to put space between them. "It is not your concern. I would ask you not to share this meeting with my brother, but I cannot trust your honor. Instead, I shall take my leave." Grace gave him a slight nod and turned back toward the garden.

His hand shot out and wrapped around her upper arm, holding her fast. She could feel the warmth of his skin through his leather glove and the heat of his body as he stepped up behind her. "You can trust me, Gracie," he murmured.

His warm breath brushed her ear, sending a delicious shiver through her body. It took great effort not to lean back into his warm, strong embrace. "No," she whispered. "I can't." Why did he have to smell so divine? Like leather and musk? Warmth bloomed low in her belly, and she was acutely aware of the brush of his chest to her back through the thin silk of her gown. "I want a husband who will keep his promises. Someone to care for me and any children we have. Not one who will run off with my brother at a moment's notice to fill his belly with ale, line his pockets at the tables, and bounce a ladybird on his knee."

She tried to pull out of his grasp, but he held firm and spun her to face him. "Marry *me*, Gracie. I will take care of you better than any man in all of England. And should we have children, I would consider myself a blessed man."

His words cut at her insides. She'd longed to hear them years before when he'd kissed her and promised to meet her the following day. That he spoke them now prodded at the wounds he'd left in her heart. If only he wanted her the way she once wanted him, but she knew he didn't, and shook her head. "You're too much like George and my father. Drinking and gambling in places like this until you forget you have others who depend upon you. Regardless, Mrs. Dove-Lyon has chosen another suitor for me, and I intend to marry him."

"Who?" Owen's voice rumbled with a deep growl.

She tried to pull away once more, but he tightened his grip until she was pressed to his chest with only her hands between them. "I will know him when I see him. Now, if you'll excuse—"

"Tell me what the other man looks like."

"No."

He gave her a gentle shake. "I'm trying to protect you. Do you even know his name?"

She shook her head. "As long as he is agreeable and can show more than a brief, *false* interest in me, he will do. Mrs. Dove-Lyon has already chosen him, and I understand she does research on each gentleman."

Owen snorted.

Grace shoved at his chest until he relented and released her. She stared at him, her heart thumping against her breast. "You confuse me. Once, you made me believe that you cared for me, only to humiliate me. Now, you offer to marry me and promise your protection when you haven't spoken to me in years? Is this another trick? Some elaborate bet meant to make a fool of me again?" It shamed her that her throat felt thick with emotion. She shouldn't allow him to affect her after all this time.

"Is that what you believe, Grace? That my intent is only to make a mockery of you?"

She nodded, afraid that her voice would tremble if she spoke.

Owen tilted her chin up until she looked into his eyes. He traced the curve of her lower lip with his thumb. "You don't know how often I've dreamed of these lips," he murmured.

Her heart clenched. Oh heavens, he was close. The desires of her youth warred with her good sense. She should push him away. Or... or laugh at him for his silly attempt at a seduction he wouldn't pursue. She should not be leaning toward him, wondering if his kiss would be different now that she was older.

He cupped her face with tender hands and searched her gaze. When she didn't pull away, he lowered his head and kissed her.

Grace swayed toward him as his lips moved over hers. This was different from before. The kiss in her youth was a sweet press of his mouth. Now, Owen captured her mouth with an intensity she hadn't expected. He urged her lips open and swept his tongue against hers. She moaned at the decadent taste of him, like champagne and the musk of his skin.

Long moments later, Owen broke the kiss, and his quick breaths fanned over her wet lips. "Marry me, Gracie."

His words broke through the haze of her desire like cold water. He appeared earnest, though she couldn't read the expression behind his mask. Grace wanted to trust his intentions, but she couldn't. He broke her heart once; she wouldn't let him do it again.

Instead, she would find the other gentleman that Mrs. Dove-Lyon chose and learn more about him before she married him.

Grace cleared her throat and blinked away the moisture that misted her eyes. "I'm sorry, my lord. I cannot marry you."

Chapter Three

Owen stared down at Grace, with those smoky blue-gray eyes glittering behind his mask in an expression she couldn't read. His fingers flexed on her upper arms, then he released her and took a step back.

A chill washed over Grace, and she shivered, already missing the warmth of his body. It was foolish, and it frustrated her that he could stir her emotions that quickly.

"How will you know the other man?" he asked.

She adjusted her mask a little, avoiding his piercing look. She shouldn't tell him. After all, there was nothing more to say between them.

"Grace."

She swallowed. "He will be wearing a white domino mask and a tricorn hat with a red feather."

Owen let out a rough sound that sounded like a curse. He took her arm and guided her onto the main gambling floor. Strains of music floated in the air, barely distinguishable from the raucous laughter of the costumed men and women around her.

"Owen, stop."

His lips flattened into a hard, unforgiving line, and he marched through the crowd, nudging people out of his way with ease.

"Owen!"

He glanced down at her but didn't stop.

"What are you about?" she demanded.

He suddenly drew her up beside him.

Grace realized that he stood taut, as if every muscle in his fine form froze in place. Before she could ask more, a braying laugh broke through the din. She turned toward the noise. A man in a white mask with a tricorn hat and red feather stood among a group of costumed gentlemen.

"That's him!" Grace moved to see him better. "That's—"

Owen drew her back to his side. "That's Richard Granville, my cousin."

Grace turned to him in surprise. "What? Richard?" She'd met him a time or two when he joined George and Owen on some boyhood adventure.

"Yes, and I will not allow you to marry him. I'll go to your brother and father before you become his wife."

She gasped and pulled her arm from his grip. "You will do no such thing. It is *my* choice whom I wed, and neither you nor my father will make that decision for me. I'll flee to Gretna Green if I must."

"Not with him," he bit out.

"Whyever not?"

"Because beneath the veneer of civility is a hard man like his father, and I won't see you hurt."

Grace looked back at the man. "Are you certain that is your cousin? He's wearing a mask. It could be anyone."

"I'd know that laugh anywhere."

It *was* distinctive. "Mrs. Dove-Lyon assured me that she investigates the gentlemen to make sure they are suitable before she matches them with a woman." However, if what Owen said was true, did the woman know that the two men she'd chosen for Grace were cousins?

"His manners are impeccable in unknown company, therefore it would be difficult for her to have known about his darker side. But you must trust me in this."

Before Grace could reply, she saw Mrs. Dove-Lyon approach the man in question. She always wore a veil, concealing her features in such a way that no one knew what she looked like or even how old she was. She said something to Richard Granville, drawing his attention.

He looked at the woman, then looked around the room. The moment he saw Grace, their gazes locked and a slow smile spread over his face. He gave her a slight nod.

Uncertain of what to do, she dipped her head in acknowledgment.

He must have been encouraged, because he said something to Mrs. Dove-Lyon and smiled. Their patroness then disappeared back into the crowd.

Owen swore. "He's coming this direction with intent. Was he aware that you meant to speak with him tonight?"

"I don't know." She only knew what they looked like in order to find them and learn a little about them before making a decision.

Owen muttered something she couldn't hear with the noise of the music and people surrounding them.

"I gave up on you once, Grace. I'm not going to do it again," he said. Then he started toward Richard.

What? Grace went after him and grasped his arm, pulling him back around. "What do you mean? You didn't give me up. You made a bet, you won, and then you left."

A corner of his mouth turned up, but the smile didn't reach his eyes. "Yes, I did." He extracted his arm from her grasp and turned away again.

Grace frowned at his retreating form. No, he wasn't going to leave without an explanation. He owed her that much and more. She stomped after him and pushed her way in front of him, putting her hands on his chest to stop him. For a moment, the hard muscles she felt beneath his waistcoat distracted her.

"Grace," he said, sounding weary.

"Tell me what you meant, Owen. Or am I not worth your time?"

He bowed his head and breathed out a heavy sigh. "Grace, you are always worth my time. You always will be."

She gripped the lapels of his coat and gave him a shake. "You say this now, but that is not how you felt the last time you returned home with George. You made a wager with your friends that you could kiss me. A wager that you won when you gave me my first kiss. I foolishly thought you cared for me, and instead I learned that you couldn't resist a bet. Even when it meant hurting the sister of your friend. Don't pretend that I mean something to you now."

Owen trailed his fingers down the backs of her arms and cupped her elbows in his warm palms. "George found out about the kiss—and the bet—and he was furious. He gave me a choice. If I never spoke to you again, he would stay my friend. Otherwise, I would lose his friendship, and I already knew I'd lost you after you learned of the wager. George was all I had. I couldn't lose him, no matter the cost. And it cost me *everything*, Grace." He traced his thumb over her lower lip. "I didn't need the bet to kiss you. I wanted to, and no kiss has ever been the same. If there is any chance of winning your hand, I'm going to take it because I love you, Grace. I always have."

Owen cupped her cheek and claimed her lips in a kiss that stole her breath. Then he released her and started toward Richard again.

Grace pressed her gloved fingers to her lips. It was hardly more than a brief press of his lips, yet it was as powerful as the other kisses he'd given her. Her heart pounded and her body heated, but her thoughts swirled in a dizzying circle. Owen Granville loved her? She could hardly conceive that what he said was true, even after he told her about his conversation with George. Had her brother demanded that Owen not speak to her? Quite likely, given George's short temper. But did Owen truly care for her? Could the love she once held for him be rekindled if they married? One glimpse into her heart told her it could, because she'd never stopped loving Owen, even after he'd embarrassed her with the bet. She'd hated herself for the weakness ever since. But what if he'd experienced the same?

She stared in the direction that he'd gone, conflicted in her feelings. Perhaps it was time to have another conversation with Mrs. Dove-Lyon.

Chapter Four

Owen stalked across the floor toward his cousin. Strains of string music filled the room while masked men and women danced and laughed. Some sought the deeper shadows, taking full advantage of the anonymity of wearing a costume and mask. One couple brushed past him, the woman's laugh breathless with anticipation as the gentleman with her urged her out of the crowds toward the garden, his hand low on her hip.

It reminded Owen of the way his friend Gabriel touched his wife Lily, and the sultry looks he gave her when he thought no one watched.

I want that with Grace.

Now that he'd seen her again, held her in his arms, he didn't want anyone else. He never had, and he'd been a fool to believe that any woman would do as his wife. But if he claimed her, he would lose his best friend forever. The decision gutted him. George had been his friend and confidant from his first year at Eton, when he helped free Owen from an abusive prefect. The prefect was an older student who had lorded his superior position above the younger students, treating them as personal servants. It was a respected pastime at the school, and no one spoke of the darker side of the tradition. Owen was fortunate to have George and other friends who opposed the treatment and stopped the prefect and those like him from continuing the abuse.

George showed him a home and family far different from his own, and they'd been inseparable ever since. Could he really give up that friendship for Grace?

Owen swallowed over the lump that settled in his throat and realized he could. He would do anything for Grace. He'd been wrong to accept the ultimatum George issued after he learned about the wager. At the time, he didn't think he could do without their friendship. Now, he had a chance to explore what he and Gracie might have had so long ago. He refused to pass that up. Not even for his best friend. His heart hurt with the thought, but he moved forward with determination. Gracie was his. She'd surrendered to his kiss, telling him without words that she still wanted him, and even though she had some misgivings, she was destined to be with him. Fate had brought them back together, and Owen would do whatever he must to hold on to her.

Ahead, he spotted his cousin in his simple white half mask and the tricorn hat with the red feather. He wore a costume of a black cloak and tailcoat over a brilliant red waistcoat, breeches, and boots like a highwayman's.

Owen stepped into his path. "I didn't know you frequented the gaming hells, Richard."

"Unlike you, I don't have the quid to spare on such frivolities. Instead, I must watch as you run through the family fortune in your excesses." Richard's eyes glittered with malice.

Owen scowled. They'd never been close, but Richard's insults caught him off guard. "Is that why you've sought out Mrs. Dove-Lyon? You want a rich wife to carry you into your dotage? Perhaps one with a family title?"

"Why shouldn't I? After all, your father barely gave my family enough of an income to survive. We've struggled for years. The poor relations to the mighty Granvilles, who even after a couple centuries never managed to land more than a barony. Do you know what it's like for a man to have to choose between medicine for his ailing mother and the special food she needs to stay healthy? No, of course you don't."

Owen didn't, because his mother's ailment was in her mind. She'd terrorized her husband and son for years before her death. "Your father was lucky to claim a single farthing. He attempted to murder my father for the barony before I was born."

Richard adjusted his hat, watching something over Owen's shoulder. "More's the pity that he didn't succeed, or it would be you scrounging for a wife instead of me."

Owen clenched his fists and attempted to rein in his anger. The men and a few women nearby cast curious glances at them. "Mrs. Dove-Lyon agreed to find you a match."

"Indeed. If you will excuse me, I was on my way to meet the lady when you stopped me." Richard pushed past Owen, who snagged his arm to hold him in place.

"She's not for you."

Richard laughed. "That is the lady's decision to make, not yours. Now kindly remove your hand or I will remove it for you."

Owen tightened his grip. "The lady deserves better than a man who takes a heavy hand to a woman. I'll see to it that she doesn't choose you."

Richard smiled, and a calculating gleam entered his eyes behind the mask. "She means something to you."

Damn. "Whether she does or not is of no concern to you."

"Who is she, Granville?"

Owen remained silent.

His cousin plucked his hand off his arm. "Then I shall find out for myself."

"Grace Twisden," Owen muttered. He gripped the back of his neck, feeling the muscles tighten and a headache threaten to emerge at his temples.

Richard rocked on his heels, a sudden smile teasing his lips. "Ah. It all becomes clear. Isn't it odd how a silly childhood bet could bring us full circle?"

"I should never have taken your dare to kiss her."

The man shrugged. "You did, and now she will be mine. Unless... What are you willing to do to call me off, Granville?"

Owen gripped Richard's cape in a tight fist and pulled him close. "You should be more concerned with what I will do if you do not go back to Mrs. Dove-Lyon and tell her you want a different woman."

Richard didn't look the least bit intimidated. "Increase the allowance paid to my family to fifty thousand pounds per year and I'll have no need of a wife."

Owen laughed at the man's audacity. He was not an earl like his friends Gabriel Hawthorne and Christian Huntington, and he didn't have anywhere near their yearly income, but his grandfather had invested well. Aside from the quid he regularly lost at the gaming dens, the family fortune was secure—but not so lucrative that he could pay his cousin an exorbitant allowance. "I'll give you ten thousand pounds *once*."

Richard snorted. "That won't see us through a year. Move aside, Granville. Grace Twisden is the daughter of a viscount, and I expect she will come with a rather tidy dowry once we wed."

"What happens when she displeases you? The first time she refuses to share your bed? Will you raise your hand to her the way you did your sister?"

"My father used a strong hand with my mother, my sister, and me. It taught us discipline and respect. My sister forgot that I deserved the same respect as the man of the house when my father died."

That reminder necessitated a doctor's call. Owen knew the fear that grew in your soul from such abuse. He'd lived it, and he'd be damned if Richard ever raised a hand to Grace. Worse, George would kill him for letting the man anywhere near his sister.

"I'll pay you twenty thousand pounds."

"Per year."

Owen shook his head. "Once."

"Forty thousand," Richard countered.

"Twenty-five thousand and not a crown more. That will give you time to seek a new bride through Mrs. Dove-Lyon."

Richard stared him down. "You're a man who enjoys a bit of sport, gambling away the family fortunes as you have."

Owen started to protest, but his cousin's next words stopped him.

"I'll wager you for her."

"She's not a prize to be won," Owen ground out.

"Isn't she? More to the point, isn't the opportunity to marry her the prize? If you win, I will forget my suit and return to our patroness in search of a different bride. However, if I win, you will not interfere in my pursuit of the lady."

"No."

"Then we have nothing further to discuss. Move aside."

"No," Owen growled.

Richard leaned close, his warm breath brushing Owen's cheek. "Then what is it to be, cousin? Accept the wager or stop interfering with the agreement that I made with Mrs. Dove-Lyon?"

His veiled threat said he'd have Owen removed if necessary. From what little Owen knew of their patroness, she did not care to have her business decisions meddled with. He caught sight of one of her wolves patrolling the outer edge of the ball. The man limped, but looked more than capable of tossing Owen out on his ear.

Owen considered his cousin. He'd sworn an oath to his dying father and to George that he would stop his reckless gambling. He'd break that promise if he accepted this mad scheme. But what choice did he have? He had to keep Gracie out of the hands of a man known to be harsh with women. Even if she persisted in her refusal to marry him, he couldn't let her wed Richard.

As he considered the wager, his heart picked up and began to pound in his chest, and his palms grew damp. The thrill of the bet, of calculating odds and deciding how much money he could risk for maximum returns, surged through his veins, making him feel alive. It took a great amount of effort to defuse the excitement. Down that path lay darkness. After he quit gambling, he'd gone through a period of intense need to be back in the hells with a drink in his hand and money on the table. Only the need to prove that he wasn't weak to his father and George kept him away. He refused to succumb to that need again. But this was Grace.

Owen's gut churned as he made the decision. One more bet and then he would truly stop.

Knowing he risked his friendship, broke his promises, and would once more face the lure of high risks that had a hard grip on his soul, he asked, "What's the game?"

Richard chuckled. "I knew you couldn't resist. Meet me in the garden right before midnight. Let's see who can go the farthest balancing three full wine glasses on top of one another without dropping them."

The absurdity of the wager wasn't uncommon. This hell was known for its more unusual bets, such as betting a man could ride backward for a certain distance or who could shoot the most wine glasses out of another's hand without missing. As bets went, this favored neither opponent. "I accept."

"Until midnight." Richard gave a slight bow and walked away.

Owen watched him stroll across the floor and enter the gentlemen's smoking room. What were the odds that Richard would carry the glasses farther? He did a quick calculation and decided that Richard could not win. Owen was more agile than his cousin, and any other outcome could force Grace into an unhappy marriage, which he wouldn't allow. But as he went to find her, a bit of worry seeped into his soul.

Chapter Five

Grace stood at the edge of the ball, fanning herself with her peacock feather fan, and glowered at the couples dancing a country reel. Mrs. Dove-Lyon had offered no advice to help her decide between the two gentlemen she'd been matched with. She'd stated only that any woman who took it upon themselves to find a husband instead of allowing their father to make a match should also be able to determine which of two gentlemen would suit her.

To think that yesterday Grace had looked forward to the evening and to whatever man her matchmaker might choose. She snapped her fan closed. Owen's revelation that he'd wanted to kiss her even without the bet surprised her. Her first kiss had come from him. It had been sweet and gentle, and all that she'd hoped for. He'd brushed his thumb over her lip, just as he had tonight, and promised to meet her the following day. Only he'd never shown up. She'd learned about his bet soon after, and it had crushed her.

Grace hadn't stopped caring for him, even when she hated herself for it. She'd warred with the feelings in her heart for years, trying to cover them with hopes for a husband who would care for her in return. One who would keep his promises, which neither Owen nor her father seemed capable of.

As for his cousin Richard, she barely remembered him. Her family had visited with his only a time or two, and her only memories were how uncomfortable she felt in the presence of his father. The man had been fearfully stern. Richard had been a rather quiet young man, at odds with George's boisterous personality. In the years following, she couldn't recall ever seeing Richard's name in the scandal sheets—unlike Owen, who made regular appearances, usually in an incident involving her brother.

Grace fanned herself again as her temper rose. George's exploits and her father's unwillingness to find her a husband were the reasons she was here tonight. Her father's need to keep her at his side bordered on madness. He'd had relations with her last suitor's mother to scandalize the man into breaking off their relationship. There seemed to be no escape until she learned of Mrs. Dove-Lyon. Grace thought she'd find a respectable man to marry. Instead, she had to choose between a man she hardly knew and one she cared for but couldn't trust to keep his word.

"You must be either extremely warm or terribly agitated," a deep, throaty voice said from beside her.

Grace looked up in surprise to see a gentleman standing next to her. He wore a domino mask that was half white on one side and half black on the other. His clothing was dark, making his almost silver-white hair and pale gray eyes stand out. "Pardon me. I didn't realize you were there," she said.

A corner of his mouth quirked. "You did seem lost to your thoughts. I fear your fan might not survive the night."

She blushed and closed the fan a little more gently. "I thank you for your consideration of the matter." The man was several inches taller than George and towered over her smaller frame. His eyes gleamed with a bit of mischief, but she didn't feel threatened by his presence.

"I beg your pardon for saying so, but a beautiful woman should not frown on a night full of frivolity like this one. She should dance, enjoy a walk in the moonlit garden, and whisper endearments to the one she cares for."

She met the stranger's gaze, expecting to see desire there.

He winked at her, but otherwise didn't show a bit of interest.

Grace considered his words and felt her conflicted feelings resurface. "What if—" What if the one she cared for wasn't the man that she needed? What if she chose incorrectly between Owen and Richard?

"The heart sees deeper into the souls of men than the mind. Trust what it tells you."

Grace's heart had wanted Owen the moment she saw him again. Despite her misgivings, being near him again brought back the desires of her youth, when she'd dreamed of marrying him. Could she trust that her heart saw his true nature?

The stranger took her gloved hand and raised it to his lips. "Men with a reason to change will do so," he said. "Trust your heart." Then he gave her a short bow and walked away.

It was the oddest conversation Grace had ever had, and yet it helped her make the choice she hadn't been able to earlier. If what the man said was true, her heart had already decided. She knew Owen, and his explanation earlier showed her that he'd never meant to harm her. If he'd met her as they agreed, they might even now be wed. The thought of a home and children with Owen made her heart flutter and her breath quicken with a certainty that felt right.

She found Owen a short time later close to where she'd first met him near the garden door. The moment he spotted her, he reached for her. She went into his arms without hesitation.

"Gracie," he whispered.

The way Owen held her made her feel treasured. She knew then that she'd made the right decision. As the stranger said, her heart had known the way. "Owen, I must beg your pardon for earlier. I was angry with you because of the bet. I didn't know that George made you stay away. If he hadn't, would you have come?"

He raised her mask, cupped her cheek, and pressed a kiss to forehead. "Yes. I wanted to be there, Gracie. I hated having to choose between the two people I loved. I should have chosen you then."

She shook her head. "No. George—"

Owen pressed a soft kiss to her lips. "I am choosing you now, Grace. Even if I lose my friendship with George, I want you to be mine."

She prayed it wouldn't come to that. It would hurt terribly to be the one that came between them a second time. "Ask me again," she said.

He stared at her for a moment, then took her hand and led her into the garden.

Grace followed in surprise. She'd hoped he would ask her to marry him. Instead, he led her down a path into the shadows. "Owen?"

He turned once they were far from the other guests and pulled her back into his arms.

Her heart sped up and a rush of warmth settled in her core. He was so handsome with the moonlight highlighting his dark hair and wide shoulders. She wanted to kiss him.

"I want only the moon to be witness," he said as he removed his gloves. Then he took her hand and held it over his heart. "Grace Twisden, would you do me the honor of becoming my wife?"

Tears pricked her eyes and clogged her throat. "Yes," she whispered. It wasn't her first proposal, and yet her heart threatened to burst with happiness.

Owen laughed and lifted her into his arms, spinning in a circle. Then he set her on her feet and pressed a kiss to her lips. What started out sweet turned sensual, and she felt her mask slip off and clatter to the ground.

Grace wrapped her arms around his neck, pressing closer. Her nipples pebbled and brushed against his chest, causing a delicious sensation when the fabric of her chemise rubbed against them.

He moaned and broke the kiss. "I've dreamed of kissing you in the moonlight like this. When we wed, I want to spend hours making you gasp in pleasure."

Grace shivered in anticipation. She didn't know much about what happened between a man and a woman in the marriage bed. It wasn't as if she could ask her father. However, she'd overheard George talking to his friends, and those conversations had been quite scandalous.

Reaching up, she removed his mask and dropped it next to hers, then pressed closer and lifted her mouth for another kiss.

Owen responded eagerly. He instructed her movements with his, guiding her mouth open and exploring with his tongue against hers. Each brush felt positively wicked, and she wanted more.

They kissed for long moments. Owen stroked his hands down her back and over the curves of her hips and encouraged her to do the same. He broke the kiss only to trail his hot mouth to the edge of her jaw and down her throat.

Grace gasped at the new sensations, melting against him.

Owen murmured his praise and held her tighter. "My beautiful Grace," he whispered against her skin. He pressed another quick kiss to her lips and then guided her back to a bench along the garden wall and pulled her into his lap. "Let me show you a little of what I dreamed," he murmured. Then he slid his hand beneath her skirt to her calf and met her gaze.

The heat of his hand on her bare skin in such an intimate place sent a thrill through her, teasing her with the promise of the forbidden. That he waited for her approval warmed her heart even more. Grace nodded and leaned in to kiss his jaw. She felt his rumble of pleasure beneath her lips and smiled.

He skimmed his fingers up the outside of her thigh slowly, as if he savored the touch, and then trailed them over the top and back toward her knee. "Has anyone touched you like this?" he asked. He kept his gaze on the movement of his hand beneath her skirt.

Was he concerned what her response might be? After all, she had come to Mrs. Dove-Lyon in search of a husband, and many women with poor reputations sought her out for whatever match they could get. "No. Only you."

The corner of his mouth tipped up and he smoothed his hand up her other thigh. His fingers dipped into the space between her legs and pressed against her mound.

She gasped. Heat raced to the spot where he touched, and she instinctively clenched her thighs closed.

"Open for me," he whispered against her temple.

Grace clung to him and did as he asked.

Owen stroked his fingers through her folds, making her shiver. He watched her as he explored, changing his touch until her breath came in soft pants.

She trembled all over from the delicious sensations, feeling her body spiral higher. She pressed her face into the side of his throat and wrapped her arms around his neck. "Owen."

He pressed his thumb against her, and she stiffened.

Grace felt like she no longer controlled her own body. She clung to him as he circled his thumb around her nub, over and over.

"Owen, I—" She didn't know what she meant to say, or how to make the feeling stop. It was too much.

"Yes, my darling. Let it overcome you," he murmured.

She didn't know how to do that, and opened her mouth to say so, but her body knew the way. She tensed, and then a rush of relief followed by intense pleasure washed through her. Grace sagged in his arms, still trembling as he slowly stroked her.

She lifted her head to look at him, feeling a sense of wonder.

Owen smiled. Then he captured her lips in a slow, deep kiss. "I'll never want another," he said.

His promise settled in her heart, soothing her fears. Owen was hers, and he was everything she wanted.

CHAPTER SIX

Owen held Grace for long moments after, savoring the weight of her on his lap and in his arms. Her thigh pressed against his hard cock in a delicious torture that he would gladly bear until he could have her in his bed. If he couldn't get her father's approval and a special license, he'd simply whisk her away to Gretna Green. Perhaps he should bundle her into a carriage now. They could leave tonight.

The thought sent a thrill of excitement through him, and that feeling gave him pause. It was what he often felt when gambling a large sum or wagering something reckless. If he was to be worthy of Grace, he couldn't be the kind of man who gave in to irresponsibility whenever it suited him. She wanted a man who kept his promises. If he took the wager with his cousin, he'd be breaking a promise to his father and George. Owen sighed, knowing he had to call off the bet. Maybe he could reason with the man.

"What troubles you?" Grace asked. She rested with her head in the crook of his neck and shoulder, her eyes heavy.

"My cousin. Richard needs an affluent wife and is unwilling to give up his opportunity to meet with you."

"But Mrs. Dove-Lyon gave me the chance to choose whom I wanted to marry."

"Even so, he is desperate."

"Why?" Grace sat up and looked at him.

"I'm afraid my father and his did not get on well, and as a result, my father was not inclined to give them much. I am ashamed to admit that I didn't know their financial circumstances were so poor. Now that I am baron, it is up to me to do what I can to aid them, but Richard holds a great deal of animosity toward me. He challenged me to a wager." Owen glanced away. "I shouldn't have accepted. I acted rashly."

She kissed his cheek. The soft brush of her lips touched his heart.

"Perhaps I can call off the bet. It may cost me financially, but it is the right thing to do." Owen helped her stand and then rose from the bench. The moon was higher in the sky, and his pocket watch said that it neared midnight.

He guided her back along the path, their little interlude of intimacy tucked away in his heart. If all went well this eve, he would have many more with Grace. For now, he needed to resolve things with Richard. He spotted the man ahead at the entrance to the gardens.

"Granville," Owen said, and strode to meet him. He sensed Grace lingering behind at the edge of the shadows where the lamplight didn't quite reach.

Richard raised his mask and flipped the edge of his cape over one shoulder. He waved to the waiter who trailed behind him with a tray of champagne glasses. "I knew you wouldn't disappoint, cousin."

Owen shook his head. "I've reconsidered. Let us find another way to settle this."

"Afraid you will lose and I will have a chance with the girl after all?" Richard raked his gaze over Owen and made a noise that said he found him lacking. "Where is the man who refuses to back down from a challenge? When we were young, I could wager you anything and you would accept."

"A man changes as time passes. Have you not also changed? Grown harder, angrier with your lot in life?"

"What would you know of my lot?" Richard snarled, his voice rising. "Have you seen my mother outside of a ballroom or dinner party? Did you notice that her gowns age as quickly as she does because I cannot pay to replace them?"

Owen felt his cheeks heat. "Then let us come to an agreement like men."

Richard stiffened. "Do you imply that my wager is not an honorable agreement that any gentleman might make?"

Several people now surrounded them, having wandered toward the raised voices, the music of the ball a backdrop to their whispers.

"Certainly not. It is an accepted pastime that I have thoroughly enjoyed. However, this disagreement is between us. The lady should have no involvement." Owen kept his voice low to avoid any more of a dramatic display.

"The lady is at the heart of this," Richard retorted. "You deny me the right to meet with her, to give you suitable challenge for her hand, and then refuse my wager for that opportunity? You are less honorable than your father."

Owen gritted his teeth. To paint a black mark on his father, so recently passed, made his blood rush with fury. "Call upon me tomorrow. I will draw up—"

Richard pressed close, bumping the toes of his boots against Owen's. "No. If you back out of this wager, I will consider your claim on the woman forfeit. You will show yourself as dishonorable." He gestured to the growing crowd around them.

Damn the man. Owen clenched his fists and took a deep breath, seeking calm. If he accepted the wager, his honor would not be at stake with the people surrounding them, but Grace would not look upon him with favor. Nor would George. He must make his cousin accept a different type of settlement.

"Be reasonable, man."

"Reasonable?" Richard all but shouted.

Owen felt a gentle touch on his back a moment before Grace appeared at his side. "Stop. Please," she said.

Richard's lips parted in surprise. He snapped his mouth shut and stood straighter, pulling at his waistcoat. "Lady Grace," he said with a short bow. "I admit that this evening has not been as expected. It has been some time since we knew one another, but it is my hope that we might become acquainted once again."

The man's cheeks turned ruddy as he spoke, and he raised a hand to smooth over his hair, only to have his fingers tangle in his mask.

"You are most kind," Grace said. She looked at Owen and then back to Richard. "However, it is no use. My heart lies with Lord Granville. I have been besotted with him since our youth."

Richard's mouth twisted in an ugly scowl. "We had an agreement with Mrs. Dove-Lyon."

"My agreement was that she would allow me to choose between two men. I have made my choice."

"How can you want him when he made a fool of you? I wagered that he couldn't kiss you that summer. He laughed and told me to gather my money. Did you know? You are nothing to him. He didn't care for you then, and he doesn't care for you now. He is only doing this to provoke *me*."

Grace visibly swallowed, and Owen saw a slight tremor run through her. Yet she raised her chin a notch and said, "That may have been true of the past. Not today. Lord Granville is an honorable man."

"The wager stands," Richard proclaimed.

This refusal to back down, to listen to reason, appeared to be fueled by a lifetime of pain and anger at Owen and his family. He had to try once more. "My father did your family an injustice. Now that he is gone and I bear the title, allow me to make recompense."

Some of the bluster went out of Richard, so Owen pressed on.

"Allow me to help care for your mother and sister and let Mrs. Dove-Lyon find you a wife you can appreciate, instead of one who may one day hold anger in her heart toward you because you pressed an unwanted suit."

Richard's gaze flicked to Grace and then back. "Why should I trust you, Granville? What have you ever done to foster trust in me?"

The barb hit its mark. Owen had been too wild this last decade to care for anyone other than himself and his few close friends. "We are cousins," he said. "I promised my father on his deathbed that I would curtail my reckless ways. I swore to take care of the barony and all within. That includes you and your family."

Richard studied him for long moments. After a time, he gave a single nod. "I accept this as your vow before witnesses that you will be true to your word. But know this—if you do not make a satisfactory recompense, then I will take it as a personal offense and demand satisfaction."

Owen had no desire to duel the man. "Until tomorrow."

Richard lowered his mask back into place, took one of the champagne glasses from the waiter who'd remained, looking as intrigued as the guests around them, and returned to the ball. Within minutes, the remaining people dispersed.

Owen pulled Grace into his arms and slanted his mouth over hers. He kissed her long and deep, then rested his forehead against hers. Their breaths mingled.

"No one can doubt your honor now," she said.

"There is still one who might."

"George."

He cupped her cheek and raised her face to stare into her vivid blue eyes. "There may yet be a duel in my future."

"You're his dearest friend. Surely you don't think him capable of—"

"Because he is my dearest friend, I *know* he is capable of calling me out," Owen replied.

Grace slid her arms around his waist and laid her head on his chest. "Then we shall make him and my father understand."

Standing across the field from Richard suddenly seemed the better option. His breath fanned over her hair when he sighed. "The hour grows late. Shall I escort you home? I will call upon your brother tomorrow and then make arrangements with your father."

She adjusted her mask back down with his assistance. When his own mask was back in place, he offered his arm. Grace accepted, resting her gloved hand there, and they returned to the ball. Most of the guests were filing out of the room toward the dining rooms, where a midnight supper was served. A few still danced, and as they entered, the musicians began the strains of a new song.

"Might I have a dance, Lady Grace? It would be a shame to attend the *Mystère Masque* without a single dance with the most beautiful woman in attendance."

Grace smiled and nodded.

He led her to the dance floor and gathered her into his arms for a waltz. How appropriate that their patroness would include a dance still deemed scandalous in some circles of the *ton*.

"I admit that I've never danced the waltz," Grace said. "The parties Father allows me to attend have only country dances."

Owen drew her closer and dipped his head. His lips grazed her ear as he said, "I am honored to be your first."

When their gazes met, he saw the sparkle of excitement and anticipation. As the music swelled around them, he committed the moment to memory. Grace Twisden was in his arms, and he had no intention of letting her go.

CHAPTER SEVEN

WALTZING WITH OWEN was exhilarating. They spun around the room, dancing between candlelight and shadows, eyes locked as if they were the only two at the ball. Being held this close during a dance would be uncomfortable were Grace with any other partner. With Owen, she wanted to be closer. He never took his eyes off her, and in their blue-gray depths, she saw a promise for the future that made her stomach flutter and her heart pound.

What she'd said to Richard was true. Owen was honorable. George had told her about many of their escapades, and in them Owen was usually the one to hold her brother accountable. Owen had changed since their youth, but when Grace looked in his eyes, she saw the man beneath. He'd taken his vow to his father and her brother seriously. He meant to uphold his promises, to them, and to her.

When the dance drew to its conclusion, Owen wrapped his arm around her waist and whisked her into the shadows. He pinned her to the wall, glanced about, and then kissed her soundly. Grace melted into him, giving herself over to the slow glide of his hot tongue and the flutter of excitement in her belly. Heat pooled between her legs where he'd touched her in the garden, and her breasts felt full and sensitive.

Owen broke the kiss and groaned. "We must marry quickly, my darling. I'll have a devil of a time keeping my hands off you until then."

Grace laughed and pressed another kiss to his lips. "Then I do hope you speak to my father and brother soon."

Owen nodded.

Grace could see the lines of worry at the corners of his mouth. "You're worried about George?" she asked.

"I am. But I meant what I said, Grace. I gave you up once for him. I won't do so again."

She ran her hand through his thick brown hair, wishing she could remove her glove and feel the strands. "I won't lose you either, Owen. Even if we run for Gretna Green."

"Then we're in accord." Owen dropped one last kiss on her lips and tucked her hand in the crook of his arm. "Let me take you home."

They collected her cloak and his greatcoat, and once he made certain that she was bundled up for the cool spring night, he guided her out of the Lyon's Den.

The streetlamps cast circles of light in the foggy air, giving the night a mysterious quality. At a distance, she could hear the rumble of carriages as they took weary men and women home from their late parties and balls.

Owen called for his carriage, then wrapped his arm around her waist and held her to his side.

"Are you warm enough?" he asked.

Grace laid her head on his shoulder and stifled a yawn. "I am when I am in your arms."

The sounds of an approaching carriage echoed through the fog, and it surprised her that the footmen had come to collect them that fast. The dark form of it took shape in the dense fog, and the horses halted a short distance away.

Owen pressed a kiss to her head and helped her remove her mask. He tucked hers and his own into a large pocket of his wool greatcoat. "Tomorrow, I should like to—"

"Ho there! Gran, is that you? What the devil are you doing here?" George called as he climbed out of the carriage.

Grace froze. A part of her desperately wished she was still wearing her mask so her brother didn't recognize her. She shrank a little more into Owen's side.

He tightened his arm around her and murmured, "You're mine, Grace. Now and always." Then to George he said, "I received the golden *Invocation Mystère* from Mrs. Dove-Lyon. I couldn't rightly pass up an opportunity to attend the infamous *Mystère Masque*."

Her brother chuckled, though she noted it lacked his normal humor. "No, I expect not. It's fortunate that I've never been invited."

He was close enough to see now as the fog parted around his legs. George was tall and lanky like their father, with light brown hair and brown eyes. He smiled often and loved to tease, with a natural charm that made women enamored of him. A trait he used to his advantage as often as possible. She loved his good humor, but her brother was also quick to anger. Grace tensed, waiting for his recognition and the fury that was sure to follow.

"What brings you, then?" Owen asked carefully.

"My father sent word that Grace wasn't in her bed, and he was worried. I rushed over, and after dragging all of the staff out of their beds, we discovered that she also had received an… But it appears you know that." He bit out the last words, his gaze narrowed on her. Then he transferred the glare to Owen.

He squeezed her waist once more. Grace was grateful that he hadn't removed his arm when confronted with his best friend's anger. It settled her fears as no words could.

"Was it your plan to meet her here, Granville? Did she sneak out of her bed for you?"

Grace gasped at the venom in her brother's words. "George!"

Owen met George's gaze. "Certainly not. As you well know, she also received an invitation. No one knows who the invitations go to except Mrs. Dove-Lyon."

"Then it is coincidence that I should find you together with your arm around her?"

"George, stop this at once," she said. "I am a woman grown. I am capable of making my own decisions."

He glared back at her. "You are here without a chaperone. Your reputation could be ruined for this."

"It won't be," Owen said. "I have asked Grace to marry me."

Even in the near dark of the street, Grace could see her brother's cheeks flush. He turned to Owen and shoved him back a step. "You bloody bastard. You swore to me you would leave her alone." He raised his fist, fury written in every line of his body.

Grace lunged for her brother, grabbing hold of his arm, while Owen raised his hands in a placating gesture.

"George," she snapped. "He's your friend."

"No, he isn't," George snarled. Then he frowned at her. "I thought you had better sense, Grace. Do you really want to marry a man that ignores his oath when it's convenient to do so? A man who made a fool of you for a bit of quid?"

She stood to her full height, her head barely reaching his shoulder. "He's only breaking his vow to you because he loves me, you oaf! He wouldn't have made a fool of me if you hadn't demanded he not see or talk to me. He agreed out of friendship for you."

George scoffed.

"Damn you, Twisden," Owen said. "I would never take advantage of your sister, and I resent the insinuation. You know me better than anyone."

George turned a gaze colder than any she'd ever seen on the man he called his dearest friend. "It seems I do not."

"I want to marry Owen. You know that I've cared for him since we were young." Her voice cracked and her throat felt thick. Her eyes pricked with tears. "Please, George. Won't it be wonderful to have Owen as part of our family?"

"I thought so at one time, but no longer," her brother muttered. "If you marry him, Grace, I will have lost both a friend and a sister tonight. Think about it." Then he spun and stomped back to his carriage.

Owen wiped his thumb over her cheek, smoothing away the tears that spilled down them. "Don't cry, darling. I will try to make him understand." He looked over his shoulder. "Stay with her, Zeph?"

"Of course," a smoky male voice said from behind them.

Grace turned to see that another man had exited the club at some point during their exchange. Pale silver-white hair dusted his shoulders, and eyes so light they were almost silver peered out from behind a mask that was half white on one side, and half black on the other. It was her mysterious stranger from the ball.

He came to stand beside her and winked.

Owen pressed a kiss to her temple. "I'll talk to him. Stay with Lord Lael. He'll protect you while I am gone, because it is not safe here at night. You can trust him, Grace. He's been a good friend since our time at Eton."

She nodded and took a small step toward the man, noting just how thick the fog had grown. "Make him understand," she whispered.

Owen cupped her cheek and then disappeared after her brother.

Grace looked up at the man beside her. He was taller even than George, making her feel tiny in comparison.

He reached for her gloved hand and brought it to his lips as he had at the ball. "I am Lord Lael, but please call me Zeph."

Oh. She'd heard his name often throughout the years but never met him. George kept most of his friends away from her after the betting incident with Owen. "Then you may call me Grace," she replied.

He bowed his head in acknowledgment, and a smile teased one corner of his lips. "Tell me, Grace. Did you trust your heart?"

She smiled. "I did. Now I need my family to understand."

"Whether they do is of no consequence. The human life span is short, is it not? Take whatever happiness and love you can, and treasure it."

Grace saw some emotion pass through his gaze, but it was gone too fast for her to identify. He spoke oddly, but if he hadn't found her at the ball, would she still be caught between her heart and her head? She put her hand on his arm and leaned up to press a kiss to his cheek below his mask. "Thank you, Zeph, for helping me and being Owen's friend."

"Perhaps not George's after tonight." He smirked and put his hand on her back, gesturing toward the door to the Lyon's Den. "Shall we wait inside where it is warmer?"

Grace allowed him to guide her back inside. She sensed that Zeph wasn't too concerned about George's temper. He must know her brother well indeed. Then her thoughts returned to Owen, and she sent up a prayer that he could get through to George and retain their friendship. Owen was intent on marrying her, but she worried that if he lost his friendship with George, it could leave a scar on their future that might never heal. What if he came to resent her in time?

Grace wrapped her arms around her waist and waited.

Chapter Eight

"Blast it all, George, stop for a moment," Owen growled as he raced after his friend. "You bloody, stubborn ox."

Twisden spun around when he reached the carriage and swung his fist.

Owen blocked the move and shoved him back against the conveyance. George threw two more punches, one catching Owen in the shoulder. George was taller, but Owen had more muscle. They'd sparred often throughout the years, though mostly when drunk. He grabbed George's fist on the next swing, slid his hand to the man's wrist, and whipped his arm down and back, forcing George to spin and be shoved against the carriage.

"Now are you willing to listen?"

"No," George said, struggling to break the hold.

Owen pressed his weight into his friend's back, pinning him. "I love your sister."

"You're not capable of love. You make promises you don't keep and you use people for sport. Your mother was right about you," George snarled.

The words flayed Owen's heart like a sharp knife, reopening old wounds and slicing hundreds of new ones. Owen swallowed over the rock that lodged in his throat. Then he let the man go.

George panted against the carriage. He shook out his arm and slowly turned around. "I'm sorry," he said. "I didn't mean—"

"You're right."

"No, Owen. I'm not. She was a cruel woman who used every opportunity to whip you and your father with her words as well as the lash."

"I lost count of how often she said that I was weak. Useless to others and shouldn't have been born. My father tried to tell me otherwise, but he was more the victim of her anger even than me. When I arrived at Eton, I thought I was free until I was assigned the prefect. That's when I realized that my mother spoke the truth. I *am* weak."

"No—"

Owen slashed through the air, cutting off his friend's words. "I am. I was weak not to stand up to her and protect my father. Weak to let the prefect cane me—and to allow you to dictate what I knew to be wrong with Grace."

"What do you mean, with Grace?" George leaned back against the coach wall and studied him. "You accepted a bet, Gran. Against my *sister*."

"I accepted it because Richard had goaded me for hours. I had no issue taking his quid for something I'd wanted to do for months. The time we spent at your house during those years gave me more joy than any I'd ever known. A big part of that was Grace. The way she followed along whether we wanted her to or not. Full of happiness and life, questioning us on a thousand things that we didn't know the answers to and made up anyway. Her spirit shines bright. How can a man not love her? I was smitten from the start. I watched her grow into a beauty, and the months we were back at Eton, she filled my dreams. I very much wanted to kiss her before the bet. Even without it, I doubt I'd have waited much longer."

"Why didn't you tell me?" George asked.

Owen cleared his throat, trying to rid the rasp of emotion from his words. "I didn't know how to tell you what my feelings were when I didn't understand them myself. Her kiss changed everything. I knew I fancied her before then. I didn't know that I loved her until that kiss. Before I could sort myself out, you learned of both the kiss and the bet."

"Richard gloated," George muttered.

Owen should have known his cousin would crow about the wager. Richard had lost money to Owen, but he'd also put Owen in an uncomfortable position with George and knew it well. "You made me choose between two people I loved," he said.

George thumped a fist against the carriage. "Damn it all."

"Grace was too young still, and I thought my feelings would pass in time. I expected that she would find a man to marry during her first Season and be happy. I couldn't lose you, George. You were all I had when I first arrived at Eton. You showed me what family, what *life*, was supposed to be like. I knew that I was too weak to take on the prefects at Eton alone. I needed you, even though you never needed me. How could I have done anything other than make the promise you demanded?"

"Owen," George whispered. "You're strong. You've always been the stronger of us."

"I stayed away from Grace, as I promised. After our kiss, we were to meet the next day at the stream. I didn't go, and I never spoke to her again. She accused me tonight of only caring about the bet, not about her. We hurt her, you and me." Owen gripped the back of his neck and stared at the cloudy night sky. "I lost myself in drink and wagers whenever I couldn't banish her from my mind. No kiss could compare to hers, no matter how many women I tried."

"That's why you wouldn't stop gambling," George said.

"Not until you made me give you another promise."

George scrubbed his hands over his face. "And tonight?"

"I didn't know Gracie would be there. I found her quite by accident. She'd made arrangements with Bessie Dove-Lyon to match her with a husband."

George stood up straighter. "She *what?*"

"She said your father didn't give her a coming out. He discouraged her matches, and she hinted that one gentleman broke off what was near to an engagement because of him. She wants a family of her own and didn't believe she could have that without contacting Bessie Dove-Lyon."

George swore, then looked pensive. "How did I not notice that she didn't have a proper Season?"

"Why did you think she hadn't married?"

"I thought she preferred to stay at home with our father. Though now that I consider the matter, I see that he is far more eager to have her at his side than she is. Poor Gracie. We've done her a disservice." George opened the door of the carriage. "I will talk to him tomorrow, and together, we will find her a suitable husband."

Owen's heart sank. He'd hoped that by telling George what was in his heart, his friend would see how much he wanted her. That he meant to take care of her and make her happy. Yet it was clear that George still considered him weak, and therefore not a suitable match.

I love her, George.

You're my closest friend. Why can't you see that I would give her everything simply to see her smile?

No one will care for her as I do.

The words clogged his throat, so he remained silent.

George climbed into the carriage and leaned out the open door. "Will you ask Zeph to take her home? I'll see you at the townhouse later."

He'd begun to shut the door when Owen finally forced some words out. "No. I will open the family townhouse after Grace is home safely."

George paused and leaned back out. They stared at one another.

Owen felt as if he couldn't breathe as pain lashed his heart. But Grace was worth the suffering. She always had been. He'd just been too weak to fight it then. Now, he'd give up a hundred friends for her, starting with George. "Goodbye, Twisden. I wish you well."

Owen turned and walked away. He stuffed the anguish in his heart down as deep as it would go and went to find Grace. Only she could soothe his heart.

Chapter Nine

The carriage door slammed moments later and bootsteps thundered. Suddenly George was in front of him, stopping him with a hand on his shoulder.

Owen didn't trust himself to speak, afraid he'd break down and beg George not to sever their friendship.

His friend balled his hand into a fist and punched him in the same shoulder. "You would have done it. You'd have walked away."

"I would. I am."

"You love her that much?" George demanded.

Owen nodded. He'd said what was in his heart. Now he waited to see why George had stopped this.

"And she loves you?"

"I believe she does. I asked her to marry me, and she agreed. Mrs. Dove-Lyon gave her a second choice for a match, but Grace chose me."

"Who was…" George shook his head. "I don't want to know. Swear to me you'll make her happy, Granville. I know it's unfair to force you into another promise, and I bloody don't care. Swear it."

Owen's lips twitched. "I swear that I will make her happy. I will love her as no other man could. She's going to become my wife, George."

"My father might not give his blessing."

"You haven't either," Owen pointed out. "It doesn't matter. Even if I have to wed her in secret, I will. She's mine. I won't let her go again."

George huffed out an annoyed breath. "And you think *I'm* the stubborn ox."

Owen chuckled.

George gripped his shoulder and gave it a light squeeze. "I won't apologize for punching you, but you have my blessing."

Owen's eyes stung, and he blinked back a sudden flood of moisture. "And our friendship?"

"You're wrong about one thing, Gran. I do need you. No one else keeps me out of trouble."

Owen moved past him and opened the door to the Lyon's Den. "No one is fool enough to want that responsibility."

George laughed and entered behind him.

They found Grace pacing beside Zeph as he told her a silly story. She laughed at the appropriate times, but Owen could see the worry in her eyes. The moment she spotted them, she ran straight into his arms.

Owen pulled her to his chest and held her close. He pressed a kiss to her temple, feeling her tremble, and rubbed a soothing hand up and down her back.

"What happened?" she asked.

"He gave his blessing."

Grace looked up in surprise, then twisted around to see her brother. "Truly?"

George nodded. "Though I daresay I will spend a great deal more time in the scandal pages if Owen is home with you. Who will keep me out of trouble?"

"You could try keeping yourself out of trouble, brother," Grace replied.

"Nonsense. Why would I do that?"

Zeph placed a hand on George's shoulder. "I shall take up the gauntlet," he said. "It's what friends do."

George laughed. "This is indeed an improvement. I cannot corrupt a man who is more likely to corrupt me further."

The corner of Zeph's mouth turned up in a small smile. "One never knows what adventures lie ahead." He placed his top hat on his head and tipped it, then left the club without another word.

George looked at Owen and Grace, who was still in his arms. "I too shall take my leave. I'm trusting you to get her home safely and with her reputation largely intact, Gran."

"You have my word," Owen said. This was a promise that would be easy to keep. Grace was too precious to him.

George kissed her cheek and murmured something, then took his leave.

Owen held Grace for several long minutes, savoring the knowledge that she was where she was supposed to be.

She stood up on her tiptoes and gave him a soft kiss. Then she yawned.

He chuckled. "Come, my darling. Let me take you home." He wrapped an arm around her and guided her back outside, where his carriage finally awaited.

Owen guided her into the warm interior and, as soon as the door was closed, settled her on his lap.

Grace laid her head in the crook of his neck.

"I'll arrange for the special license tomorrow," he said.

"What of my father?"

"George will speak to him tomorrow also. Regardless, I have waited years for you, Grace. My patience wears thin. I want to marry you as soon as we are able."

"I never dreamed I'd hear those words from you," she whispered.

"I never thought I'd have the chance to say them." He cupped her cheek and raised her eyes to his in the dim interior of the carriage. "I love you, Grace Twisden. I have since the first day we met, and I will until my last breath on earth. You are my last chance at happiness."

She sucked in a breath, then kissed him. "I love you too, Owen. Let's take that chance together."

Owen kissed her, sealing their promise. He'd taken one last gamble, putting his relationships on the mark, but in the end, he'd won Grace, and she was worth more than all the quid in the world.

The End

Additional Dragonblade books by Author Aurrora St. James

Taken by Destiny Series
The Earl's Timely Wallflower (Book 1)
Tempting the Reclusive Earl (Book 2)

About Aurrora St. James

Aurrora St. James has been writing romance since she was a teen. Fortunately for the world, those stories will never see the light of day. Now, she loves writing sexy, paranormal romances featuring tough and sometimes dark heroes, women who find their inner strength, and a touch of humor added in for spice. In particular, she enjoys writing both Medieval and Regency romances that whisk readers into the beautiful landscapes of history, where love can overcome anything.

When she's not writing, you'll find her reading, drinking coffee, making her own journals, or watching old B, C, and D-movies. She lives in the Florida jungle with her husband, a slightly crazy dog, and a cat that thinks he's a brontosaurus.

Social Media:
Website: www.aurrorastjames.com
Facebook: facebook.com/AurroraStJamesAuthor
Instagram: instagram.com/aurrorastjames
Pinterest: pinterest.com/ladyaurrora
Bookbub: bookbub.com/authors/aurrora-st-james
Amazon: amazon.com/Aurrora-St.-James/e/B00E46VJD8
Goodreads: goodreads.com/AurroraStJames

Made in United States
Troutdale, OR
11/29/2023